Praise for the Zoe Chambers Mystery Series

BRIDGES BURNED (#3)

"I'm a huge fan of Dashofy's Zoe Chambers series and I loved *Burned Bridges*. The action starts off with a bang and never lets up. Zoe's on the case, and she's a heroine you'll root for through the mystery's twists and turns—strong and bold, but vulnerable and relatable. I adore her, and you will, too."

– Lisa Scottoline,
New York Times Bestselling Author of *Betrayed*

"So polished, so intriguing, and so darn good."

– Donnell Ann Bell,
Bestselling Author of *Buried Agendas*

"Dashofy has done it again. *Bridges Burned* opens with a home erupting in flames. The explosion inflames simmering animosities and ignites a smoldering love that has been held in check too long. A thoroughly engaging read that will take you away."

– Deborah Coonts,
Author of *Lucky Catch*

LOST LEGACY (#2)

"A vivid country setting, characters so real you'd know them if they walked through your door, and a long-buried secret that bursts from its grave to wreak havoc in a small community—*Lost Legacy* has it all."

– Sandra Parshall,
Author of the Agatha Award-Winning Rachel Goddard Mysteries

"A big-time talent spins a wonderful small-town mystery! Annette Dashofy skillfully weaves secrets from the past into a surprising, engaging, and entertaining page turner."

– Hank Phillippi Ryan,
Mary Higgins Clark, Agatha and Anthony Award-Winning Author

CIRCLE OF INFLUENCE (#1)

"An easy, intriguing read, partially because the townfolks' lives are so scandalously intertwined, but also because author Dashofy has taken pains to create a palette of unforgettable characters."

– *Mystery Scene Magazine*

"Dashofy takes small town politics and long simmering feuds, adds colorful characters, and brings it to a boil in a welcome new series."

– Hallie Ephron,
Author of *There Was an Old Woman*

"The texture of small town Pennsylvania comes alive in Annette Dashofy's debut mystery. Discerning mystery readers will appreciate Dashofy's expert details and gripping storytelling. Zoe Chambers is an authentic character who will entertain us for a long time."

– Nancy Martin,
Author of the Blackbird Sister Mysteries

"New York has McBain, Boston has Parker, now Vance Township, PA ("pop. 5000. Please Drive Carefully.") has Annette Dashofy, and her rural world is just as vivid and compelling as their city noir."

– John Lawton,
Author of the Inspector Troy Series

"An excellent debut, totally fun to read. Annette Dashofy has created a charmer of a protagonist in Zoe Chambers. She's smart, she's sexy, she's vulnerably romantic, and she's one hell of a paramedic on the job. It's great to look forward to books two and three."

– Kathleen George,
Edgar-Nominated Author of the Richard Christie Series

"A terrific first mystery, with just the right blend of action, emotion and edge. I couldn't put it down. The characters are well drawn and believable...It's all great news for readers. I can't wait to meet Zoe and Pete again in Vance Township, Monongahela County, PA."

– Mary Jane Maffini,
Author of *The Dead Don't Get Out Much*

BRIDGES BURNED

**Books in the Zoe Chambers Mystery Series
by Annette Dashofy**

CIRCLE OF INFLUENCE (#1)
LOST LEGACY (#2)
BRIDGES BURNED (#3)

BRIDGES BURNED

A ZOE CHAMBERS MYSTERY

ANNETTE DASHOFY

HENERY PRESS

BRIDGES BURNED
A Zoe Chambers Mystery
Part of the Henery Press Mystery Collection

First Edition
Trade paperback edition | April 2015

Henery Press
www.henerypress.com

This is a work of fiction. Any references to historical events, real people, or real locales are used fictitiously. Other names, characters, places, and incidents are the product of the author's imagination, and any resemblance to actual events or locales or persons, living or dead, is entirely coincidental.

ISBN-13: 978-1-941962-39-8

Printed in the United States of America

To my mom, with love.

ACKNOWLEDGMENTS

I want to thank the incredible group at Henery Press: my editorial team of Kendel Lynn, Anna Davis, Rachel Jackson, and Erin George; Art Molinares, who answers all my business and publicity questions; and graphic designer Stephanie Chontos. And a huge thank you to Fayette Terlouw for creating this fabulous cover art.

I strayed into some foreign territory while writing *Bridges Burned*. Thanks to Kathie Rumbaugh for answering my banking questions, to Tiffany Nolan for answering my insurance questions, and to David Dean for helping with my police procedure questions. I'm beyond grateful to Joe Collins, Wes Harris and the rest of the gang at Crimescenewriters, without whom this story could not have been told (at least not by me) and to Chris Herndon for all the gory photos of dead bodies. Also I owe a huge debt of thanks to Lee Lofland and the instructors at the Writers Police Academy who helped me add a layer of authenticity to the story.

And a special shout-out to my Sister in Crime, Diana Stavroulakis, who keeps watch over my writing for any legal slip-ups.

Any mistakes in any of those areas are solely mine.

Thanks to my ever-vigilant critique group, Jeff Boarts, Judy Schneider, and Tamara Girardi who deserve much more acknowledgement than I can possibly give them here. You guys are the best.

And thanks to Anne Slates and Mary Sutton for being my sharp-eyed proofreaders, because I cannot see my own typos to save my life.

I can't express enough gratitude for the support and guidance of my fellow Pennwriters and Sisters in Crime. You are my friends, my co-workers, my teachers, and my publicity team...and so much more. Thank you.

Finally, to Ray, who is still waiting for the movie to come out, thanks for having my back even when you had your doubts. I love you.

ONE

The intense heat and drought of late July must have set everyone's nerves on edge. Chief Pete Adams had no other explanation for the spate of domestic dispute calls his Vance Township Police Department had received as of late. At least "domestic dispute" meant something different in rural Monongahela County than it had when he worked with Pittsburgh's Bureau of Police. Too often he'd walked into situations wondering if he'd end up taking a bullet. This week he'd dealt with two unarmed marital screaming matches, two farmers brandishing a shovel and pitchfork and quarreling over a wayward bull, and a frantic family terrified by their son who was off his meds and smashing lawn furniture.

Not a semi-automatic in sight. Pete loved it.

Until he wheeled into Jack Naeser's driveway to find the paunchy, red-faced sixty-year-old waving a revving chainsaw and bellowing like that wayward bull. The object of Naeser's tirade appeared to be Ryan Mancinelli, a good twenty years Naeser's junior and every bit as livid as the older of the two. Mancinelli was Naeser's next door neighbor—and son-in-law.

A row of hedges, exquisitely sculpted with a precision which clearly did not come from Naeser's chainsaw, stood between the two men. A young woman on Mancinelli's front porch clutched a handful of tissues to her face. An older woman holding a broom like a baseball bat stood halfway between Naeser's house and the chainsaw wielding man himself.

Mother and daughter.

Pete was acquainted with the family because the Naesers' other daughter was his police secretary. As he climbed out of his department

SUV, he offered a silent prayer that he wouldn't have to shoot the stubborn old fool today. "Mr. Naeser."

Jack Naeser continued to spew profanities at his son-in-law. "You won't listen to good sense. I'll cut the whole goddamned row to the ground!"

"Over my dead body, old man." Mancinelli's arms, dark from long hours working construction in the summer sun, were knotted and tight.

If Mancinelli decided to slug his father-in-law, the older gent would most likely not get up unassisted.

"Whoa, whoa, whoa." Pete strode toward them, hands raised, nonthreatening, yet commanding. He hoped. "Let's all cool off a moment. The air conditioning's out at the station, so neither of you would enjoy sitting in my holding cell."

For the first time since Pete had arrived, Naeser acknowledged his presence by swinging toward him. The chainsaw came around too.

Pete stepped back and brought one hand down to his sidearm. Not releasing it. Yet. But ready. "How about shutting that thing down before someone gets hurt?"

"The only thing I plan to hurt are these goddamned hedges." Nevertheless, Naeser cut the motor and the contraption fell silent.

"That's better." Pete reached out and took the saw. "Now tell me what seems to be the problem."

Both Naeser and Mancinelli started telling their stories at once. Mrs. Naeser and her broom stomped over, adding her version. A weepy Ashley Mancinelli joined the group, all talking over each other.

Pete brought his middle finger and thumb to his lips and cut loose with one of his patented ear-piercing whistles. The two couples shut up.

"Now, one at a time," Pete said.

Naeser opened his mouth, but Pete held up one finger which he then pointed at Naeser's wife.

She sputtered for a moment as if she didn't know how to speak without the other noise drowning out her words. "These two—two jackasses are fighting about the hedges."

"I got that much, ma'am. *Why* are they fighting about the hedges?"

She nodded toward her husband. "He can't see to pull out of the driveway because the hedges are too tall. We asked Ryan to trim them down some, but he won't."

"They'd look hideous," the younger man snapped.

Naeser planted his fists against his hips. "You'd rather I pull out in front of a semi and get killed?"

Mancinelli shrugged.

Swearing, Naeser stepped toward the hedge and his son-in-law. His wife grabbed him from behind. "Stop it, you pig-headed fool."

Pete rubbed his forehead where sweat beaded and a dull ache threatened. "Mancinelli, if these hedges are a visual impediment to Mr. and Mrs. Naeser's view of the road, they'll need to be cut back."

Mancinelli folded his wiry arms across his chest and tipped his head toward his own driveway. "I have no problem seeing."

"Because you drive a big ass pickup truck, you son of a bitch," Naeser shouted. "I drive a Hyundai."

Mancinelli's eyes narrowed. "They're *my* hedges on *my* property. You touch them, old man, and I'll kill you."

Pete blew out a heavy breath. Why did people always threaten homicide in his presence?

"I'd like to see you try," Naeser countered.

Both women jumped back into the fray, daughter wailing, mother shaking her broom and threatening to knock sense into the two idiots. Maybe a few hours in an un-air-conditioned holding cell might be the best choice after all. In the midst of the melee, Pete's police radio crackled.

His secretary's voice sounded unnerved, but he couldn't make out Nancy's words above the shouting match. Had she somehow gotten wind of his "visit" with her family?

"All right." Still holding the chainsaw, Pete stepped between Naeser and the hedge. "Mr. Naeser, I'm placing you under arrest."

"What?" The man's shocked question was echoed by his wife and son-in-law.

Pete displayed the saw.

"Assault with a deadly weapon. You'll have to come down to the station with me." He swung around to Mancinelli. "I'll need you down there, too, to swear out a complaint."

"Oh." The younger man appeared to give the prospect of an afternoon in the police station serious thought. "Well. I don't know. I don't really want to see Jack arrested."

Mrs. Naeser gave her husband a nudge with the broom. "For heaven's sake, you danged fool. Apologize. We're all family." To Pete she asked, "If he apologizes and Ryan doesn't want to press charges, do you still have to arrest Jack?"

Nancy's frantic voice sizzled over Pete's radio again.

He hefted the chainsaw. "If Mr. Naeser promises not to threaten either his son-in-law or the hedges with this thing."

Naeser had deflated, but his displeasure was clear. "But I can't see traffic coming when I try to pull out."

Pete turned to Mancinelli. "He has a good point. The way I see it, you have two choices. Completely remove the first six feet of the hedges...or trim them, so your wife's father can see over them."

Mancinelli's jaw tightened.

Pete stepped around the hedge to Mancinelli's side and lowered his voice. "Come on, man. Admit it. You'd feel pretty lousy if your beautiful wife's dad was seriously injured or worse because of your own stubborn pride."

Mancinelli's shoulders slumped. "All right. I'll trim them. But only the first six feet. The rest stay high. I don't want that nebby old man poking his nose in my business."

Two minutes later, after relinquishing the chainsaw into the custody of Mrs. Naeser, Pete slid behind his SUV's steering wheel and keyed his mic. "Vance Base, this is thirty. What's going on, Nancy?"

A moment passed before static burst from the speaker. "Chief, I've been trying to raise you. There have been multiple reports of the smell of natural gas at Scenic Hilltop Estates. The gas company's been notified, and the fire department is en route."

In his rearview mirror, he watched the shouting match between Naeser and Mancinelli start up again. Mrs. Naeser, however, was carrying the deadly weapon and her broom to the garage and out of temptation's way. "Roger that," Pete said into his mic. "I'm on my way over there right now."

* * *

"*Ter-ROT.*" Zoe Chambers barked out the trot command in two syllables. The dark chestnut two-year-old colt circling her twenty feet away at the other end of the lunge line continued his lanky extended walk. She flipped the long whip in the direction of the horse's hind legs and repeated the command.

This time he broke into the faster gait, but tossed his head in expression of his displeasure.

"Pretty cool."

The unfamiliar voice from across the large indoor arena distracted Zoe for a moment, something she couldn't afford with this colt. He'd already bucked her off twice when she'd tried to ride him, forcing her to revert to basic ground work. She couldn't allow the idea of a hundred-and-thirty-pound female being no match for a thousand-pound equine to further ingrain itself in his head.

She gave a hard snap to the lunge line while taking a big step to the left, as though cutting off the horse's forward movement. At the same time she called out, "*Whoa.*"

The colt skidded to a stop and turned to face Zoe with a snort.

"Good boy," she cooed.

The stranger who had interrupted her training session applauded. The sound echoed under the arena's rafters, and the skittish colt leapt sideways.

The man clearly knew zilch about horses. Zoe muttered under her breath as she reeled in the long flat nylon lead, drawing the colt to her in the process. With one hand on his halter, she patted his neck and then led him toward their visitor. "Can I help you?"

The man stood silhouetted by the sun shining through the big open door. Zoe couldn't see his face, and didn't recognize his voice or his stance. He ambled toward her. Once he was fully in the shade, she got her first good look at him. Tall and built like an overstuffed box, he wore dark-rimmed glasses and a short-sleeved plaid shirt partially tucked into his khaki trousers. She guessed him to be fortyish, but his dimpled smile made him look much younger. Cute. In a nerdy kind of way.

But definitely not very bright where horses were concerned.

He extended his hand. "Name's Dave Evans. I'm looking for Mr. or Mrs. Kroll."

Zoe wiped her dusty palm on her jeans before shaking his hand. "They're not home right now." Mr. Kroll was still in rehab, recovering from a gunshot wound and head injury he'd incurred a month ago. His wife spent most of each day at his side. None of which Zoe was willing to share with a stranger. "I'm Zoe Chambers. I manage the farm for them."

Evans pointed at the horse. "That's pretty impressive, how you handled him out there. You can actually control him with only a long rope? And he keeps going around in circles?"

On a good day. "That's right."

He gave a nod of appreciation and echoed his earlier comment. "Pretty cool."

"Is there something I can help you with?"

Evans fumbled in the pocket of his rumpled khakis and pulled out a small leather folder. "Mr. and Mrs. Kroll... Any idea when they'll be home?"

"Sorry. No."

He extricated a business card and held it out to her. "Perhaps you could give this to them when they return?"

She studied the card. *David Evans. Evans Land Development. Baltimore, Maryland.*

"I've managed to acquire several farms in the area. We're putting in upscale homes. Providing work for local construction laborers. Growing the local economy."

Zoe handed the card back. "I don't believe the Krolls would be interested."

Evans shook his head. "Please. Give it to them anyway. I hear Mrs. Kroll's been ill recently. And Mr. Kroll was seriously hurt. Am I correct?"

"Not entirely." Zoe patted the colt's neck. "Mrs. Kroll's 'illness' isn't recent. In fact, she's been in remission for a year. And Mr. Kroll is recovering nicely. No one here is ready to sell out."

"Keep the card all the same. You never know. I've already purchased several of your neighbors' properties. And I pay top dollar. The Krolls won't find a better deal anywhere."

Zoe shoved the card into her jeans pocket where she expected she'd forget about it until she did her laundry. "I'll give it to them, but don't hold your breath."

"That's all I can ask." He bumped his glasses up on his nose. "Except for one more thing. I don't suppose you're free for dinner tomorrow night, are you?"

The unexpected proposal took her by surprise. "No. I'm not."

He gave her a shy smile. "My loss. But you have my card if you change your mind."

As Dave Evans turned away, a boom that sounded like a cannon rattled the barn windows. The ground beneath Zoe's feet bucked. The colt reared, dragging the lunge line through Zoe's fingers, searing her hand. Stall doors clanked against their hinges.

"What on earth?" Evans clung to the big barn door's frame.

Zoe dug in her heels to keep the colt from dragging her. "Whoa, boy," she called, keeping her voice firm, but low.

From outside, a rumble continued in the distance, like thunder. But it didn't fade away, and the sky was cloudless.

Zoe reached the colt and grabbed his halter. Clucking to the spooked animal she guided him to an empty stall, unclipped the lunge line, and swooshed him inside. After latching the door, she jogged across the arena.

Dave Evans stood outside, staring slack-jawed into the distance. Zoe looked in the direction he was staring and gasped.

Flames leapt above the trees on the hillside nearly a mile away. A thick plume of smoke rose from the inferno. The roar reminded Zoe of the farmhouse's oil furnace when it lit, only louder.

"Good God," Evans whispered.

She glanced at the barn. The colt was secured in a stall with hay and water. The gates were latched. The feed room closed. "If you'll excuse me," she told Evans, "I have to go."

She'd taken only a step when he caught her arm. "You aren't going over there, are you?"

Zoe jerked free. "I have to. I'm a paramedic." As she raced down the farm lane toward the house and her truck, she prayed her medical skills would be needed more than those of her other occupation. Deputy coroner.

TWO

Pete had just turned from Route 15 onto the road leading to the new housing development when one of the homes at the top of the hill exploded, rocking the ground beneath his SUV. What the hell? He jammed the accelerator to the floor.

He'd never been in a war, but imagined the scene must be what a battlefield would look like. One house in the development was leveled. Splintered two-by-fours were scattered across the lot like toothpicks. Smaller bits of debris, swirling on the super-heated air currents, continued to rain down over the equivalent of a city block. Flames and smoke licked the blue sky. The vinyl siding on the two houses closest to the explosion dripped down the exterior walls like candle wax. People—the neighbors, Pete assumed—stumbled around the wreckage. Screams and sobs punctuated the deafening roar of the fire.

A Vance Township fire engine was parked two houses away from the conflagration. Volunteers in full turnout gear heaved folded loops of hoses onto their shoulders and dragged them toward the flames. One of the men fumbled through a side compartment, yanking out a large wrench.

Pete pulled up behind the engine and jumped out.

His radio crackled. "Chief? Chief Adams? Are you there?" So much for proper radio procedure.

He paused and keyed the mic clipped to his shoulder. "I'm here, base."

"Thank God," Nancy breathed. "There's been a report of an explosion."

He watched as the fire crew connected a line to hydrant. "I'm aware of that. In fact, I'm looking at it. Get on the horn and order all the men in. County and State, too. Make sure the gas company is on their way." He noticed one of the firefighters sitting on the ground next to the truck as a second man taped a bandage to a bloody gouge on the first one's head. "And confirm EMS is responding."

"Copy that. Base out."

Pete strode to the two firefighters. "Give me a report."

"We responded to a call of natural gas odors," the uninjured man said. "It was pretty strong. We'd started canvassing the houses when..." He hoisted a thumb toward the burning rubble. "Boom."

The second fireman touched his head and winced. "Thank the good Lord we parked here. If we'd pulled up a little farther..."

"Injuries?" Pete nodded at the man on the ground. "Besides you, I mean."

"Unknown. No one has come to us, but our guys haven't had time to check on the neighbors."

"How about the house?" Pete dreaded the answer to his next question. "Anyone inside?"

"We don't know." The standing firefighter reached down and helped his buddy to his feet. "But we have more manpower on the way."

Pete clapped him on the shoulder. "So do I."

Sirens wailed from somewhere down in the valley. Or else his ears were ringing. Hard to tell. The deafening roar of the gas-fed flames sounded like a jet engine. One of the firefighters barked out an order and the man controlling the nozzle cranked it open. The hiss of pressurized water added to the commotion.

Pete headed toward a group of bystanders and searched for a familiar face. Scenic Hilltop Estates with its trendy homes had attracted an influx of new township residents, mostly city folks moving to the country. Or a romanticized version of it. More than once, he'd had one of these newcomers march into the station to complain about the smell of the nearby farm. Never mind the farm had been there for generations.

It was one of those complainants he recognized now and approached. "Mr. Tierney, isn't it?"

"Yes." Glassy-eyed, the man tugged at the collar of his polo shirt. "Stephen Tierney." His voice was as thin and reedy as the man himself.

"Can you tell me if there was anyone at home over there?"

Tierney looked around at the other bystanders then at the fire. "Over there? No. The place was vacant. They—the former owners—defaulted. The bank evicted them a month ago. The house was supposed to go up for sheriff's sale pretty soon." He ran shaking fingers through his short-cropped hair.

Pete dug his notebook and pen from his pocket. "Do you know the family's name?"

"Farabee. Holt and Lillian. And their daughter. Good people. Hated to see them go. Although, now..." Tierney shook his head, and for a moment, Pete thought the man was about to burst into tears.

Movement on the road below drew Pete's attention. An older model brown Chevy pickup with an emergency light in the front window sped toward them, lurching to a stop behind his SUV. Farther down, a pair of fire trucks turned onto the road leading up to Scenic Hilltop Estates, air horns blasting. A police cruiser—one of his—and a Monongahela County ambulance followed. But Pete's focus stayed with the willowy blonde who jumped from the cab of the Chevy. Zoe reached behind the truck's seat and heaved out a canvas duffle before slamming the door and trudging up the hill toward him.

"Mr. Tierney, do you mind sticking around? I want to ask you a few questions, but I have to talk to someone first."

Tierney continued to pull at his collar, never taking his gaze from the fire. "Yeah. Sure."

Pete stepped away from the crowd as Zoe approached. For a moment, and only a moment, he pushed the horrible fire out of mind to admire the woman making her way toward him in dusty jeans and a nicely snug dark blue t-shirt. In theory, they were "dating." Had been for the last month. In reality, both were too busy or distracted to do the whole social thing. They encountered each other at calls like this. They played poker with the gang almost every Saturday evening. And they occasionally met for dinner at one of the local bar and grills, same as they'd done when they'd been "just friends." As much as they tried for something more, so far work and life had gotten in their way.

Her gaze danced between him and the scene beyond.

"Hey," she said loud enough so her voice carried over the rumble. "What do we have?"

"The house was vacant."

She blew out a breath. "Thank God."

Pete watched over her shoulder as more emergency vehicles climbed the hill, red and blue lights flashing. "I'm going to set up a staging area by my vehicle. Why don't you make a pass around the perimeter to see if any of the neighbors were hurt by flying debris? Don't get too close."

She wiped a sleeve across her forehead. "Not to worry. It's hot enough today without fighting a fire."

And yet, there were the local volunteers in heavy bunker gear doing just that.

"I'll send more manpower out to you as soon as they check in. For now, call me if you need immediate backup."

She snapped a playful salute at him. "Aye aye, *Capitan.*"

"*Capitan* my ass," he called after her. "It's *Chief Capitan* to you."

Zoe fluttered a dismissive hand over her shoulder as she hiked away.

Pete chuckled and headed downhill toward his SUV. The additional fire crews were lugging gear from compartments on their trucks. Pete spotted the fire chief and waved. Bruce Yancy held up one finger in a be-there-in-a-minute signal. Pete pointed toward his SUV. *Over there.* Yancy nodded again.

Minutes later, Pete stood in front of his vehicle, coordinating his troops. His two full-time officers, Kevin Piacenza and Seth Metzger, grabbed rolls of yellow crime scene tape and started up the hill to rope off a perimeter. On the radio, Nancy reported county was on its way, ETA five minutes. Pennsylvania State Police were only a minute behind. The gas company couldn't give them a solid time of arrival, but had a man en route.

Yancy snorted. "Better be more than one man."

"Are we gonna have to wait for West Penn Gas to shut off the line to the house or can your guys do it?"

"We'll get it." Yancy motioned at the firefighter holding a wrench and standing next to the lead man on the team closest to the inferno. "Just have to knock the flames down enough so he can get to the meter without being fricasseed."

"Chief!" someone yelled.

Both Pete and Yancy turned. Kevin Piacenza loped toward them. From the frantic expression on the young officer's face, Pete knew this wasn't going to be good.

Breathing hard, Kevin skidded to a stop in front of them. "One of the neighbors on the other side of the fire just told me he thinks the family was still living there."

Before Pete could process the news, a frantic shout went up from somewhere nearby. He looked around. A man charged past him, headed straight toward the remains of the house, bellowing, "No!"

Pete launched after him. The crazed fool was racing full tilt toward the flames, wailing like a damned banshee. "Stop!" Pete called, knowing full well he was wasting his breath.

The roar and the heat grew more intense. The man hit and burst through the strand of yellow tape as if it were a finish line in a marathon. Pete pounded after him, ignoring a jolt of pain from his recently healed broken foot. He gained ground, but not enough. No way was he going to catch the guy before he'd run into the blaze. The idiot showed no signs of slowing.

Pete caught a blur from the corner of his eye—a streak crossing from his right. The streak slammed into the man, tackling him, driving him into the rubble and the mud. Pete dove on top of them.

Zoe came up sputtering and spitting, her face smeared with muck. The man she'd pile-driven into the ground pushed up to kneel. Pete jerked him to his feet. "What do you think you're doing?"

The man, tall and all lean muscle in a black t-shirt and jeans now oozing with mud, stared horror-stricken at the flames. "My wife," he moaned. "My wife was in there."

The news that a victim may have been inside the obliterated house dropped a pall over what had previously been little more than a chance for the volunteer fire department to play. There wasn't enough left of the structure to make a rescue attempt. Even though the gas had been shut down, the fire was burning too hot and the scene was too dangerous to start a search-and-recovery mission.

The firefighters had turned a stream of water on Zoe, leaving her soaked to the core, but at least she didn't feel like a mud wrestler any longer. Three ambulance crews were busy with patients, neighbors who had suffered cuts and scrapes from flying debris or broken glass from their own windows. Zoe, one elbow bleeding from a nasty gash, balanced on the rear bumper of Medic Two and ripped into a packet of sterile pads with her teeth. She'd patched up more lacerations and abrasions in her years as a paramedic than she could count. Bandaging her own wounds one-handed was a little trickier. She pressed the 4x4s onto the cut. Blood seeped through, but at least it would help hold the bandage in place while she finished dressing the injury.

As she reached for the roll of stretch gauze, someone extended a hand over her shoulder, beating her to it.

Pete came around in front of her. "Need help?" He had a large bundle tucked under one arm.

"Since when have you become a medic?"

He gave her a crooked smile. "And you've never ventured into *my* line of work."

"Point taken. Any word on the guy's wife?"

"Seth and Kevin went door to door, and I questioned the bystanders. No one's seen her. But there are remains of a minivan in what used to be the garage."

"Doesn't sound good."

Pete tossed the bundle onto the ambulance floor. It unfolded enough for Zoe to recognize it as a jumpsuit. "I thought you might want to change into something dry."

She glanced down at her sodden and clingy t-shirt, grateful she'd put on a navy one instead of white. "Thanks."

He peeled the bloody sterile pad away from the cut and made a face. "This might need stitches. Give me another bandage."

Zoe shoved a handful at him and leaned back, allowing him to finish the job she'd haphazardly started.

"That was a damned foolish stunt you pulled out there."

She studied his face. His scowl was too forced. He might be upset with her, but she read concern there, too. And something else. Maybe...admiration. She smiled.

"What's so funny?"

"Someone had to stop the guy from becoming a French fry. With your gimpy foot, you weren't gonna catch him."

Pete lifted his gaze from her arm to her eyes. She waited for him to respond with a wisecrack. Instead he lifted a hand and brushed a damp strand of hair from her forehead. "I appreciate the help." He went back to the patch job on her elbow. "Just don't do it again."

"No problem." She winced. Besides the gash, she had a strong feeling she'd have a few bruises following her tackle. "Hitting that guy was like ramming an oak tree trunk. Have you questioned him yet?"

Pete pressed the end of the self-sticking bandage onto itself. "No. I left him with some of your coworkers to get cleaned up and calmed down. I'm headed over there now."

"Do you think there's any chance the guy's wife *wasn't* really inside?" She squinted at the burning heap, barely recognizable as a structure.

"Can't think of any other reason for a man to want to be a French fry."

She cringed at having her own insensitive words tossed back at her. "Sorry."

The corner of Pete's mouth twitched. "The curse of anyone on the front lines. A sick sense of humor." He motioned toward the jumpsuit on the ambulance floor. "The coroner hasn't arrived yet, so you might want to be there when I question Frenchy. Get changed out of those wet clothes. I'll wait."

Inside the ambulance's patient compartment, Zoe made quick work of stripping from her soaked barn clothes and stepped into the Vance Township Police Department's jumpsuit. One size fits all. Provided the wearer was over six-foot and weighed at least two hundred pounds. Zoe rolled up the sleeves and cuffed the bottom of the legs. There wasn't much she could do about the rest of the extra fabric.

She opened Medic Two's rear door to find more fire equipment had arrived from the neighboring borough of Phillipsburg and Mt. Prospect Township. A white Ford extended cab pickup with a West Penn Gas emblem on the door rumbled up the hill, picking its way through the emergency vehicles.

Zoe found Pete next to his SUV, coordinating efforts with the state troopers and county officers. He spotted her and waved her closer. The other men moved off to handle their assignments.

"Let's go," Pete said to her.

The man Zoe had intercepted had also received a fire hose shower. They found him wrapped in a blanket and shivering on the jump seat inside Medic Three flanked by two paramedics who were checking him over and patching up a scrape on his jaw.

One of the medics completed his assessment and climbed out. He jabbed Zoe with his elbow. "Nice tackle there, Chambers. Next time we play football, you're on my team."

Zoe made a face. "Very funny, Barry. How is he?"

"Physically, the guy's in good shape. Vitals are slightly elevated, but considering..." Barry Dickson shrugged. "Emotionally, he's a wreck."

Zoe thanked her coworker, and he ambled off.

Pete leaned into the ambulance. "Sir? Mind if I ask you a few questions?"

The second paramedic pressed a final piece of tape onto the bandage and excused himself.

The man turned toward Pete and Zoe. Devoid of the mud, torment plastered his suntanned face. Zoe guessed he was about her age, although at the moment anguish piled on at least a dozen years.

"Has anyone seen my wife?" His husky voice carried a hint of a southern upbringing. "Maybe she got out."

Pete put a foot on the back bumper and used his knee as a desk for his notebook. "What's your wife's name?"

"Lill." The man choked. "Lillian Farabee."

Pete looked up. "Farabee? Are you Holt Farabee?"

The man's eyes widened. "Yes. Did you locate her? Is she okay?"

Pete shook his head. "I don't know. I'm sorry. I was under the impression you and your family had been evicted."

Zoe shot a look at Pete. "Evicted?"

He nodded in her direction.

Holt Farabee steeled his shoulders, but his eyes didn't reflect the bravado. "Who told you that?"

"One of your neighbors. I asked him if anyone was in the house, and he told me the place was vacant."

Farabee deflated. He twisted the gold band on his left ring finger. "I guess it's no use trying to hide it anymore. Yeah. The bank seized our house. But I kept a key."

"No one changed the locks?" Zoe asked

Farabee gave her a puzzled scowl. "No." He dragged the word out until it sounded like a question rather than an answer.

Pete jotted a note. "How long ago did you move out?"

"About three weeks, I guess."

"And when did you move back in?"

"A few days later."

Zoe climbed in beside him, taking the seat vacated by Barry Dickson.

Farabee stared at his wedding band. "We had no place else to go. No family around here. We couldn't afford to keep living out of a motel."

Fire Chief Yancy bustled past and did a double take when he spotted Pete. "There you are. Just wanted you to know we have the fire contained. It'll still be a while before we get it completely out and can get in there to recover the remains, though."

Zoe stifled a groan. Yancy wasn't known for his tact.

"Thanks, Yance," Pete said through a tight jaw.

Yancy waved, oblivious to the fact the husband of the remains in question was sitting there. "No problem."

As the fire chief strode away, Holt Farabee let out a strangled groan and doubled over, burying his face in his hands. "Oh dear Lord. I've killed my wife."

THREE

Pete checked his notes while he waited for Holt Farabee to regain his composure. Zoe had draped an arm over the man's shoulders and was patting him in the uncomfortable manner of one trying to soothe a complete stranger.

Farabee scrubbed his face with the back of one arm and tried to lean back in the ambulance's bench seat, but whacked his head on the overhead storage bins. He muttered a curse then said, "I'm sorry."

Pete wasn't sure if he was apologizing for swearing, for making Pete wait to continue his questions, or for killing his wife. "Sir, do you want to clarify your last statement?"

Farabee rubbed the knot on the back of his head. "What?"

"You said you killed your wife."

He froze. "Oh. No, I didn't mean it like that. I meant it's my fault. I mean..."

Pete thought Farabee was about to double over again, but he drew a deep breath and met Pete's gaze.

"I mean," Farabee said, obviously choosing his words with great care, "she's dead because I moved her back into the house. We weren't legally supposed to be here. But I wanted to fight the eviction order." He paused, twirling his wedding ring on his finger. "I told her they'd take the house over my cold, dead body. Mine. Not hers."

"I understand you have a daughter."

Farabee nodded. "Maddie. Madison." He slouched down in the jump seat, apparently having learned his lesson about the storage bin, and let his head drop back against the wall. "Dear God. How am I gonna tell Maddie about her mom?"

"Where is Maddie now?"

A troubled scowl crossed Farabee's face as he stared at nothing in particular.

Pete had a feeling there was a lot more happening behind the man's eyes than he was letting on. "Mr. Farabee?"

He blinked. "Yes?"

"Your daughter? Where is she?" Pete hoped the girl hadn't been with the mother.

"She's with a friend from school. I dropped her off earlier."

Zoe, who'd been listening to the interview in silence, shifted in her seat to face Farabee. "Why did you take her to visit her friend today?"

Pete contained a smile. Zoe was thinking the same thing as he was.

"What do you mean?" Farabee asked.

"Is this a regular play date? Why today?"

He seemed clueless. "Lill had a job interview in Brunswick. I had a call about giving an estimate on an addition." His jaw tightened, and again Pete had a strong sense the man was holding back. A lot.

"An addition?" Zoe prodded.

A flash of anger in his eyes quickly faded. "I'm a carpenter. Unemployed carpenter. Someone phoned about having me put a new addition on their house. I thought this might be the job to bail us out of this mess. But when I got to the address he'd given me, there was nothing there. I tried calling the guy back. Figured I'd gotten the address wrong. But there was no answer. No answering machine. Nothing."

If Farabee was attempting to create an alibi for himself, he sucked at it. "Do you have the guy's name and number?" Pete asked.

Farabee shifted in his seat and reached into his pocket. "The name was Smith." He pulled out a phone and tapped the screen once, then twice. He turned it over in his hand and pressed a button. With a loud sigh, he said, "I guess it's not waterproof. I've got everything written down in my car if you need it."

"I do."

Farabee studied his lifeless phone. "I need to go pick up Maddie. I don't want her finding out about her mom from someone else."

"I'll have one of my men take you." Farabee was in no condition to be behind a wheel. Pete noted the name of the family who was babysitting the daughter before directing Seth to escort Farabee and retrieve the information on "Smith."

As Seth and Farabee drove away in one of the Vance Township cruisers, Zoe hopped down from the patient compartment and stood at Pete's side. "I think I've been hanging around you too much," she said.

Startled, Pete shot her a questioning glance. "Why?"

She motioned after the departing Holt Farabee. "Because here we have a man in obvious agony over a horrible tragedy, and all I can wonder is why he's already so sure his wife's dead when her body hasn't been recovered yet."

"You're starting to think like a cop."

Zoe gave an exaggerated sigh. "Oh, crap. Just shoot me now."

Pete had a few more questions for Stephen Tierney. Key among them—how could he have missed the fact that the evicted Farabee family had moved back in? But Tierney was no longer part of the looky-loo crowd. Pete made his way to the house Tierney owned, hidden behind an eight foot tall wooden slat privacy fence.

Behind the fence was a fashionably oversized, cookie-cutter two story house, faced in brick and swathed in beige vinyl siding, same as the other four remaining homes. The lawn was pristine green turf bordered with expertly groomed landscaping. Of course, no one outside the fence could see it.

Tierney answered the door before Pete had a chance to ring the doorbell. "How soon before all those fire trucks are gone? They're blocking the road, and I have someplace I have to go."

"And where might that be?"

Tierney eyed Pete as if this were a trick question. After a moment's deliberation, he apparently decided it was safe to answer. "The airport. I have to fly to Chicago on business."

Pete thought back to their previous encounters and recalled Tierney worked for one of the conglomerates headquartered in Brunswick. "What kind of business?" Pete tried to keep his voice light, conversational.

The man continued to study Pete. "I've told you before I work at Monongahela National Bank."

Ah. Yes. That was the one. "What time do you have to leave? I can probably help direct you out."

Tierney relaxed. "Forty-five minutes. No later."

Pete nodded amiably. "Not a problem. In the meantime, I have a few more questions for you."

Tierney leaned against his doorjamb and crossed his arms, making it clear Pete would not be invited inside for coffee. "Make it quick. I have to finish packing."

Pete thumbed through his notebook, but kept his gaze on Tierney. "You told me your neighbors had been evicted."

"Right."

"And they'd moved out a month ago."

"More or less. Yeah."

"Have you noticed any activity over there since they left?"

"Activity?"

Pete held the man's gaze and waited.

"What kind of activity?"

Pete shrugged. "Cars coming and going. Lights. Anything."

Tierney pushed away from the doorjamb. "Are you saying...someone was staying over there?"

"Are *you* saying you didn't know?"

"Of course I didn't know." He slipped a finger into his collar. "Who?"

"Didn't you see Holt Farabee running toward the fire a little while ago?"

"No. I came back here right after I spoke to you earlier." Tierney loosened his collar from his throat. "You mean Holt was staying over there even after being thrown out?"

Tierney's surprise seemed genuine enough. But something about the man was setting off Pete's bullshit meter. "Not just Holt."

"Lillian? And the little girl?"

Pete waited and watched.

"But, you said Holt came in after the fire. So he's okay. And Lillian and their daughter weren't home, right?"

"You expect me to believe you haven't noticed anything suspicious? You haven't seen lights over there? You haven't seen their car in the driveway?"

"No. I haven't."

Pete took one huge stride closer to Tierney, who was several inches shorter, and glared down at him. "They're only a hundred or so yards away from here. How could you not notice anything?"

Tierney held his ground and pointed toward the Farabee house. "Look." When Pete didn't turn, Tierney said again, "Look."

This time, Pete obliged. Not only did the eight foot tall fence keep nosy neighbors from seeing Tierney's exquisite landscaping, it completely blocked the view of the other houses in the development. Pete made a slow pivot, taking in the entire periphery. Not a hint of the farm bordering the property was evident. In fact, Tierney's lot could have sat smack in the middle of the city, or on the moon for that matter, for all Pete could tell from inside the fence.

"No," Tierney said. "I did not notice any activity. Now tell me...Lillian and their daughter. They weren't home, right?"

Pete studied the man. "The daughter is at a friend's house."

Tierney appeared to shrink. "And Lillian?"

"She seems to be missing."

"Oh my God." Tierney reached out to steady himself against the doorjamb. Tears gleamed in the man's eyes, and for the first time today, Pete believed Tierney's reaction was sincere.

Zoe hiked to the highest point of Scenic Hilltop Estates, her feet squishing in her still-wet boots. The lot on the peak of the hill remained vacant and overgrown. She sat down in the weeds, plucking a piece of over-ripe timothy grass, browned from the drought and summer heat, and combed the furry seed head.

At the edge of the next lot, a sign proudly proclaiming the housing development's name tilted as though a car had run into it. *Scenic Hilltop Estates.* What a joke. Paved roads looped around the empty pasture. Already, bits of green poked up through cracks in the asphalt. Mounds of reddish-orange clay indicated where additional houses should be, but brown, sun-dried weeds sprouted from the dirt spoke of aborted efforts. Scenic Hilltop Estates had boasted all of six completed homes. Five now. Of those remaining, three had shattered windows and two suffered melted siding from the heat of the fire.

Not so scenic.

Zoe stuck the stalk of timothy between her teeth and chewed on it, releasing a flavor that matched the smell of freshly mown hay. Bees buzzed nearby. A hot breeze whispered through the grass. Idyllic—except for the still-smoldering heap of rubble which had been the Farabee house.

Firefighters continued to pour water on it while several men wearing uniforms from the gas company stood nearby, waiting to sift through the debris.

Was Lillian Farabee in there? Zoe shuddered.

She spotted a familiar figure with a familiar gait striding away from a house with a high privacy fence. The kind with the slats so close together, no one could see in. Or out. Why bother living in "Scenic" Hilltop Estates if the only scene you wanted was a wall of wood?

As she watched, Pete stopped on the road, looked around, and headed up the hill toward her.

"What are you doing up here?" Pete asked. "Loafing on the job?"

"I'm not *on* the job. Everyone who needed medical attention has been treated. Until someone locates a body, there's nothing else for me to do. I'm off duty today anyhow. So I'm just taking in the view." She gazed across the valley to the next hillside. "If it weren't for the trees, you could see my place from here."

"Did you see the explosion from over there?"

"I felt it." Zoe told him about working on the colt in the indoor arena when the blast occurred. She didn't mention her visitor. "Did you get any answers from the neighbor down there in the fort?"

Pete scowled and turned to look down the hill. "Oh. The fort. Yeah. That guy's an odd one. He's from Pittsburgh. Moved out here to live in the country, or so he says. But he's filed at least five complaints against Leroy Moore."

Now it was Zoe's turn to scowl. "Leroy?" The quiet, unassuming farmer who owned the bulk of the property between the housing development and the Kroll farm. "What kind of complaints could anyone have against him?"

Pete huffed a short laugh. "The cattle stink. The manure stinks. Moore's running his tractor too early in the morning or too late at night or too close to the property line. Take your pick."

She eyed Pete incredulously. "Are you serious? It's a *farm*. And it's been a farm forever. Did the guy not happen to notice it before he bought his property?"

Pete shrugged. "I've asked Tierney the same thing. He never gives me much of an answer." Pete's expression soured. "Didn't give me much of one now either. He's the one who'd told me the Farabees had moved out and the house was empty. I asked him why he never noticed they'd moved back in."

"And?"

"He said he doesn't see the neighbors coming and going because of his fence."

"But still...There are—were—six lousy houses. How can he not notice someone living in one of them?"

"Good question. His reaction to hearing Lillian Farabee is missing and may have been home at the time seemed genuine enough. In fact, he took the news rather hard for someone who didn't even know she'd been living a hundred yards or so from his front door."

"Really?" Zoe pondered a few scenarios. Scenic Hilltop Estates, meet Peyton Place. "What do you make of that?"

"I'm not making anything of either Mr. Tierney's poor neighborhood watch skills or his concern for Lillian Farabee. Yet. Believe me, I'm not letting any of it drop."

Zoe didn't doubt it.

"Speaking of not letting it drop..." Pete struck what Zoe thought of as his stance—right hand resting on his sidearm, left hand on his hip. "How about dinner Friday night?"

She winced. "This is my weekend on duty." The three Monongahela County EMS nightshift crews worked every third Friday night through Monday morning, which made building a social life difficult.

"So you're going to miss the poker game this week, too?"

"Unfortunately." Zoe noticed some increased activity at the explosion site. At the same time, another familiar figure moved away from the investigators and headed up the hill toward them. "Here comes Wayne."

Pete glanced over his shoulder. "All right. I know it's short notice, but how about tomorrow night?"

"Tomorrow? Thursday?" She ran a quick check of her mental calendar. But it never seemed to be the previous commitments that got in their way. "Okay. I'm pretty sure I'm free."

County Police Detective Wayne Baronick's footsteps grew closer.

"Good. I'll pick you up at six," Pete said.

Before Zoe could reply, Baronick cut loose a piercing whistle. "Are you two having a picnic or do you want to know what I've come up with so far?"

Pete offered a hand to help Zoe up. "You may be off duty, but apparently I'm not."

Baronick waited at the Scenic Hilltop Estates sign for them. Zoe took another long look at the bold lettering.

Pete's cell phone rang, and he dug it from his pocket.

Baronick sidled over to Zoe. "You know," the detective said, waggling his eyebrows suggestively, "if you ever get tired of hanging out with that old buzzard, I'd be more than happy to show you the town."

"I already know the town." She skimmed through the information about available lots and settled on the bottom two lines.

Dave Evans
Land Developer

The guy from the barn.

Pete put his phone away without answering it and glared at the detective. "What have you got?"

"I tracked down the name of the lending institution holding the mortgage on the..." Baronick motioned toward the debris field. "On what used to be the Farabee house."

"And?"

"MNB."

Zoe was about to excuse herself from the drudgery of cop talk, but Pete swearing loudly stopped her cold. "What?" she and Baronick asked in unison.

Pete looked like a wolf scenting blood. "Monongahela National Bank. And guess who happens to work for them."

FOUR

Pete had Bruce Yancy move one of the fire engines to clear a path for Stephen Tierney. But at the entrance to Scenic Hilltop Estates, Pete directed the fort dweller to stop his white Lexus and motioned for him to lower his window. A blast of frigid air conditioning smacked Pete in the face as he braced a forearm against the driver's door.

"What is it now?" Tierney fingered the built-in computer screen in his car's dashboard, not bothering to meet Pete's gaze. "I'm running late."

"You mentioned working for Monongahela National Bank. What's your job there?"

"I'm an Investment Group Manager. Why?"

"Just filling in some blanks. Did you happen to know your bank holds the mortgage on the Farabee property?" Couldn't really call it a house anymore.

"Of course I know." Tierney tapped the screen one more time and gave a self-satisfied nod, apparently pleased with his settings. "MNB holds the mortgage on everyone's properties up here. Mine included."

"Thanks." Pete stepped back and waved Tierney on. As Pete watched the Lexus cruise down the hill toward Route 15, he wondered what the hell an "Investment Group Manager" did to be able to afford a car like that. He added the question to his notebook. Along with a reminder to verify MNB's involvement with the other homeowners on the hill.

For the moment, the Phillipsburg and Mt. Prospect Township VFDs were packing their gear, leaving only Vance Township's fire department to put out hotspots and help the gas company guys poke through the debris. The county fire investigator had arrived to oversee the investigation. One lone news truck remained and other than the stunned neighbors, most of the onlookers had drifted away. Pete left Kevin to work the scene alongside Baronick with the order, "Call me if they find anything."

By the time Pete returned to the station, his shift had technically ended. However, with the reports he had yet to write, he'd be lucky to get home by dark.

Nancy looked up when he shuffled through the front door. "Are you all right?" She had that worried mother-hen look on her face, and Pete wondered if she'd learned it from Sylvia Bassi, his former long-time secretary.

"I'm fine. Why wouldn't I be?"

Nancy pointed at her computer. "I was watching some of the pictures of the explosion online. It sounded pretty awful."

"It was pretty awful." He didn't mention it would be a lot worse if and when they located a body. "Why don't you go on home?"

Her fingers curled into soft fists, hovered over the keyboard, with the look of someone hesitant to ask a question.

"What is it?" he prompted.

She relaxed her hands, letting them settle in her lap. "You were at my folks' place earlier."

"I was."

"Is everything okay?"

He didn't think it necessary to point out he rarely got called to someone's house when everything was okay.

"Your father and brother-in-law had a little disagreement over hedges."

She lowered her head with a sigh. "Those two. Dad and Ryan used to get along. I'm not sure what changed between them, but it's tearing Ashley apart."

"I gather whatever *it* is, it's more than just the hedges."

"I wish I knew." Nancy straightened. "Anyhow, I can stick around a while longer if you need me."

"Go. Have supper with your husband and kids."

She gave him a tired nod. "You have a couple of messages on your desk." Grabbing her purse from the bottom drawer in the file cabinet, she ducked out the door.

Pete shuffled down the hall to his office. A full, fresh pot of coffee sat on the stand in the corner. He poured a cup and flopped into his worn office chair. Taking a sip of the hot brew, he put on his reading glasses and picked up the stack of pink message notes. Most of them had to do with township business. Budgets. Too much overtime. He crumpled those and tossed them in the trash can. One, though, caught his attention. *Call Chuck Delano.*

Pete dug his cell phone from his pocket and skimmed a finger over the screen. *Missed Call. Chuck Delano. New voicemail.*

He'd been surprised to see the name from his past flash on the screen while he'd been standing on the hill with Zoe and Baronick. He hadn't seen or talked to Chuck since Pete left the Pittsburgh Bureau of Police to take the position of Chief for Vance Township. He and Chuck had taught at the Training Academy together. They'd worked out of Zone One together. They'd responded to the call of shots fired together. A drug deal gone bad left one kid dead in the street. Chuck had taken a bullet in the leg. And Pete had returned fire, stopping the threat and ending the life of the shooter. Only later did Pete learn the man wielding the gun was a mere boy of fifteen.

Pete shook off the memory and keyed up the message.

"Hey, Petey," said the familiar gruff voice. "Are you sick of arresting cows and sheep yet? Call me, buddy boy. I've got a job offer you can't refuse."

Zoe parked her twenty-plus year old Chevy pickup in her usual spot behind the farmhouse and sorted the mail she'd collected from the box at the bottom of the lane into two piles—hers and the Krolls'. Bills. Advertisements. More bills. Credit card applications. More bills. Lately, her landlords' mail had been heavier than usual and mostly bills from the hospital, doctors, and rehab.

She slid down from the driver's seat and stood a moment, surveying the sloping hillside down to the house. The usually immaculately groomed farmyard was sorely in need of mowing. With Mr. Kroll out of commission, maintaining the lawn and the fields was yet another task that fell to her. With only so many hours in the day, she'd let the job slip low on the priority list. Even worse, the fields across the farm lane were waist-high in the delicate white blooms of Queen Anne's Lace.

Zoe definitely needed to find the time to fire up the tractor before Mr. Kroll came home. Otherwise he'd take one look at his farmland and have a stroke.

She picked her way down the well-worn path to the back porch. Only total strangers used the front door. The enclosed porch spanned almost the entire rear of the circa 1850s house. The windows were flung open to catch traces of a late afternoon breeze.

Zoe crossed the porch to the door on the far left and knocked. Minutes passed. Mrs. Kroll must not be home yet. Zoe was about to set their bundle of mail on the bench next to the door, when it swung open revealing a pale, haggard older woman.

A weary smile crossed Mrs. Kroll's face. "Zoe dear. I'm so glad you're home. Come in. Please."

"I just wanted to drop off your mail. I know you're tired—"

Mrs. Kroll stepped back and motioned to Zoe. Tired or not, the woman wanted Zoe to come inside.

"Alexander was in a hurry today," Mrs. Kroll said, referring to her son. "He dropped me off and left. I didn't realize there was a problem until after he'd gone."

"Problem?" Zoe held out the mail to her.

"Yes." Mrs. Kroll took the bundle, giving it a pained glance. "Thank you, dear."

"What kind of problem?"

Zoe's landlady turned and headed through the small kitchen into the anything-but-small dining room with Zoe trailing. Mrs. Kroll flipped a switch on the wall, but nothing happened. "Our electric is out."

"Did you call the power company?"

Mrs. Kroll tossed the bundle of mail onto the table. "No. I called Mrs. Hardy down the road to see if she had already reported it, but they have power. Apparently we're the only ones who don't." The woman's voice had climbed into the shrill panic range.

Zoe looked around. Sunshine poured through the large nine-over-nine paned windows, so lights weren't needed yet. "Did you check the rest of the house? Maybe it's just a breaker."

"Everything is out." Mrs. Kroll flung her arms as if indicating the entire world. "Upstairs and down. I can only assume your half is out, too. I didn't know what to do."

"Okay, let me check my place first." Zoe turned to backtrack out through the kitchen to the porch.

Mrs. Kroll caught her arm. "Go this way. It's shorter."

The older woman led Zoe into the center hall and to a door located under the main staircase.

Zoe loved this old house. Technically, it didn't boast any secret passageways—at least none hidden behind bookcases or accessed by revolving panels—but the door under the stairs came close. Courtesy of worn hinges, it dragged and scraped against the floor when opened. To the left, steps dropped away into the black abyss of the basement. Zoe fumbled for the chain to the light fixture and found it. But a quick tug confirmed Mrs. Kroll's diagnosis. No electric. Straight ahead was another door. Zoe gingerly picked her way through the dark passage and walked face first into a spider web. She swiped at it, muttering and hoping the thing had been uninhabited. Shoving the other door open, she stepped into her combination living room, dining nook.

Until that moment, it had never occurred to her neither of those doors had a lock. Not that she ever worried about Mr. or Mrs. Kroll "breaking" into her half of the house. They owned the place and had keys.

Her two orange tabby cats, Merlin and Jade, scampered into the room at the sound of her footsteps. Both meowed a greeting which obviously translated to "feed me."

"In a minute," she told them.

A further check confirmed the entire house was without power.

"Well?" Mrs. Kroll called through the passageway.

"Nothing," Zoe called back.

"What should we do?" The poor woman sounded on the verge of tears. "I miss having Marvin here. He always takes care of these things."

"I'll check the breaker box. Give me a minute." Zoe headed through the swinging door into her kitchen, an addition to the original structure. It boasted white painted cabinets, original to the add-on, a massive walk-in pantry, and a vintage Hoosier cabinet. In the Hoosier's drawer, she found what she needed. A flashlight. She clicked the switch. Good. At least the batteries weren't dead. She retraced her steps to the passageway. And the wooden plank stairs to the pitch black cellar.

"Be careful, dear," Mrs. Kroll said.

The first time Zoe had gone down to the basement, she'd thought about what a great setting it would make for a Halloween party. Mammoth fieldstone foundation, roughhewn beams overhead, uneven dirt floor, and dusty cobwebs everywhere. Minimal decorations would be needed. But with only a flashlight to guide her, she decided it would be an even better setting for a horror flick. *Don't go down to the basement.* She snorted a laugh at her fears. Suck it up, you coward.

Using the beam from the flashlight, Zoe picked her way along the planks, which had been laid on top of the uneven earthen floor. On one side, shelves built into the wall held home-canned peaches and green beans from Mr. Kroll's orchard and Mrs. Kroll's garden. From the layer of dust coating the jars, Zoe assumed the canning had been done many years ago, perhaps prior to her landlady's leukemia battle. A room opened to the left.

Zoe didn't have to look. She knew it was the root cellar with a bin of potatoes. She continued through the dark into a large, open space and flashed the light on the oil furnace, silently hibernating during the hot, muggy summer months.

Her destination was a second room, next to the root cellar. She had no idea what it had been used for originally, but it now housed two oil tanks, a water heater, and the electrical box. Light streamed between the shutter-like slats protecting a small window high in the foundation, making this space a little less ominous. A single bare bulb fixture with a string attached hung in the center of the room. She yanked the string once. Nothing.

Zoe opened the metal door on the breaker box and studied the array of black switches inside. None appeared to have been tripped. She fingered the one larger breaker at the top. The main. She thumbed it all the way to the right, off, then flipped it back to the left.

The bulb overhead came on. Mrs. Kroll's whoop of joy floated down from upstairs. With a smile, Zoe shut the box, clicked off the light, and retraced her path to the stairs, now brightly lit.

Mrs. Kroll greeted her like a warrior returning from the crusades. "Zoe, dear, you're wonderful. Thank you so much. I don't know what I'd have done without you."

Zoe waved her off. "No problem."

"You have no idea how much I appreciate your help." Mrs. Kroll covered her face with her hands and choked out a sob.

The landlady's sudden tears threw Zoe off guard. She caught the woman by her bony shoulders. "Are you all right?"

"No," she wailed.

Zoe guided her into the dining room and eased her into a chair. "Can I get you something? A glass of water? Tea?"

Mrs. Kroll fished a tissue from her pocket and pressed it to her nose. "Thank you, no. I'm okay. It's just been a rough day."

Zoe's mind flashed back to the explosion and fire—and the missing wife and mother. It hadn't been a great day for quite a few people. She sunk into the chair next to Mrs. Kroll. "Is there anything I can do?"

The woman sighed. "No. I don't know. I miss having Marvin around. And the doctor says he's not responding to treatment as quickly as they'd hoped."

This was news to Zoe, and her face must have registered it.

"He'll be fine." Mrs. Kroll reached over and patted Zoe's hand. "It's just taking longer than expected. More time in rehab. Our insurance coverage is only picking up part of the charges. And they're threatening to stop paying altogether. They say he's only allowed so many days in a skilled nursing facility. Plus there was all the time he spent in the hospital. You wouldn't believe how much those bills are."

Zoe could only imagine.

"I don't know where we're going to find the money." Mrs. Kroll folded her skinny arms on the table and rested her head on them.

Zoe stared across the room and out the window at the green fields and the hillside covered in black specks she knew to be Angus cattle in the distance, the bucolic tranquility a stark contrast to the anguish radiating from poor, frail Mrs. Kroll.

Music erupted from Zoe's pocket. She dug out her phone, and a piece of paper came with it, fluttering to the floor. Franklin Marshall's name lit the screen. The coroner. "Hey, Franklin. What's up?"

"I'm heading out your way. The state fire investigator just called. They found a body at the explosion site."

A body. Lillian Farabee. Zoe squeezed her eyes shut, which failed to block the mental image. "Do you need me to meet you there?"

"No, I think I can handle it." There was a vague note of sarcasm in his voice. "However, I do want you to assist with the autopsy first thing in the morning."

Crap. Zoe's mind spun through her library of stored excuses. She wasn't on duty. She didn't have to give any riding lessons. She didn't have to take the cats to the vet. She had no dog to eat her homework.

Franklin Marshall must have heard the hesitation in her voice. "We had a deal. You haven't paid up yet."

She was well aware of the "deal" she'd made with him a month ago when she was desperate to gain fast access to some old records. He'd "promoted" her in order to give her the credentials she needed. In return, she'd agreed to assist him on six autopsies, a chore she made every effort to avoid. The sight of dead bodies didn't bother her. The smell, on the other hand...

"Zoe?"

"What time?"

"Eight o'clock. Sharp."

She sighed. "I'll be there."

Franklin muttered something as Zoe hung up, but the paper on the floor caught her eye.

Mrs. Kroll had lifted her head. "Something wrong?"

Zoe didn't feel up to explaining. "I have to go to work early tomorrow." She bent down and picked up the paper.

"What have you got there?" Mrs. Kroll asked.

The business card. Dave Evans, land developer. His voice echoed in Zoe's memory. *"Keep the card all the same. You never know. I've already purchased several of your neighbors' properties. And I pay top dollar. The Krolls won't find a better deal anywhere."*

No. There had to be another, better solution. "Nothing. I'll look in on you when I get done in the barn." Zoe jammed the card back in her pocket.

FIVE

The morning breeze wafting through Pete's kitchen window carried a fading remnant of the nighttime's coolness, but already promised another miserable sultry summer day.

In a perfect world, the heat might keep folks from committing crimes—too steamy to move. In reality, tempers flared when the thermometer crept higher. Hot heads combined with hot temperatures made extra work for the police.

Showered and shaved, but still bleary-eyed from lack of sleep, Pete was pouring fresh coffee into a huge ceramic mug when someone pounded on his aluminum storm door. He turned to answer, but Sylvia Bassi didn't wait for an invitation.

"You look like hell." She tossed her oversized purse onto a chair by the door and crossed to the table.

"Good morning to you, too." Pete held up the pot. "Join me?"

"Of course." Sylvia, who could pass for the Pillsbury Doughboy's grandmother, had spent years as Vance Township's police secretary before circumstances drove her from the job and into a position on the township board of supervisors. Both jobs offered her abundant opportunity to keep Pete in line, and he adored her for it.

He filled a second cup and carried both to the table where Sylvia eased into her usual seat. "You're up early this morning," he said, and sipped the steaming brew.

"My phone woke me at six a.m. What's your excuse?"

"I'm always up early. You know that."

"Yeah, but you don't usually look like something from one of those zombie movies the kids like. Can I assume the mess up at the new housing plan has something to do with the bags under your eyes?"

Pete nodded. "No sooner did I sit down to write my reports last night than the call came in they'd found a body. I spent half of the night watching the fire investigators remove her and the rest of the night helping Franklin Marshall process the body before he took her to the morgue."

Sylvia raised an eyebrow. "Her?"

"Her. Him. We don't know for sure yet. The body was burned too badly to be identified. Marshall and Doc will do the autopsy this morning."

"You going?"

"To the autopsy?" Pete stared at the steam rising from his mug and pondered the question. "I was thinking about it."

Sylvia huffed a laugh. "Thinking about it? Right. Pete Adams, who are you trying to kid? You'll be there."

He feigned scratching his lip to cover his smile. She knew him too well.

"If the explosion was an accident, the death was accidental, too, so there's been no crime." She gave him a questioning look. "Has there?"

"Not officially. Not yet," he added. "Except for the criminal trespass issue."

"That's what the phone call I got this morning was about." Sylvia ran a stubby finger around the rim of the cup. "Well, and the explosion, of course. Howard Rankin is in an uproar. *How can something like this happen in our township?*" She mimicked the gruff voice of the township board's president.

"Something like *what* exactly?"

"Squatters. According to Howard '*this isn't the Wild West.*'" She once again slipped into the impersonation and added air quotes.

Pete recalled Holt Farabee's tortured face as he spoke about his wife the previous day. "What did you tell Howard?"

Sylvia slapped the table with her palm and thrust out her ample chest. "I told him to go get bucked."

Pete choked on his coffee. "Sylvia," he pretended to chide.

She beamed proudly. "He deserved it. You know darned well I like Howard, but he can be an insensitive jackass sometimes."

"You can assure him I plan to talk to someone at the bank about it today."

"After you get done at the morgue." Sylvia grinned knowingly as she picked up her cup, cradling it in her hands.

"*If* I go to the morgue. I have to check in at my office first. See what kind of cases night shift left me."

She rolled her eyes. "How long did we work together? I know better. You always have to have your nose in every aspect of an investigation. Including the autopsy." She sipped the coffee. "Besides, Zoe might be there."

There was that. Zoe had somehow gotten herself bound into assisting Marshall. Made a deal with the devil as she put it, although Pete hadn't been privy to the details of the bargain. Maybe he'd ask her about it at dinner later. Autopsies always made such romantic mealtime conversation.

"Hello?" Sylvia's singsong voice brought Pete out of his daydream.

"What?"

Sylvia climbed to her feet. "I said let me know what you find out." She shuffled across the room and deposited her empty mug in the sink.

"I'm not the only nosy one around here. Admit it. You miss working for me, don't you?"

Sylvia headed toward the door, but veered back to the table and stood next to him. "I do miss being in the thick of things. Knowing what's going on as soon as it happens." She patted his shoulder. "But now that I'm on the board of supervisors, technically *you* work for *me*. That part outweighs being one step removed from the front lines." With an evil chuckle, which contradicted her sweet, grandmotherly appearance, she made her exit, snagging her purse from the chair on her way out.

Pete smiled to himself and glanced at the clock on the wall. The smile faded as he contemplated the morning ahead. He did intend to drive to the county morgue, but contrary to what Sylvia believed, he hoped Zoe wasn't there. He didn't think this particular autopsy was one she should be involved in.

Zoe sat on the hallway floor outside the morgue, the cool polished block wall soothing against her back. She'd almost made it all the way through the autopsy. Almost.

She'd survived watching the techs wheel the stainless steel gurney from the cooler into the autopsy suite. She'd cringed when they unsealed the body bag and removed the severely burnt body. The mentholated ointment she dabbed under her nose did little to camouflage the odor and nothing to block out memories of another body burned beyond recognition.

Zoe hung in there when Franklin Marshall—cruel son of a bitch that he'd suddenly become—thrust a camera into her hands and insisted she photograph the body. He also gave her the job of collecting trace evidence, of which there was precious little, considering conditions. Combing the victim's singed hair nearly did Zoe in.

She even endured the initial "Y" incision. But she lost it when one of the techs cranked up the electric bone saw, adding a whole other element to the array of odors circulating the room. Choking, she bailed out, stripping off the disposable biohazard gown and tossing it in the red bin on her way out.

As Zoe inhaled the fresher air from the hallway, she drew her knees in and hugged them. Would she ever be able to fully participate in an autopsy? Did she really want to?

The soft slap of footsteps drew her gaze down the hall in time to see Pete round the bend and head toward her.

Great. She really did not want him to see her like this. "Zoe? What happened?"

She covered her face with her hands, massaging her forehead and the ache building there. "I wimped out."

Pete squatted next to her. "You?" he said, a smile in his voice.

"Blood doesn't bother me. Guts? Brains? No problem." She rested her arms on her knees. "I can even deal with maggots and flies."

"I know."

"But the damned smell."

"I know."

She turned her head to study Pete with his weather worn face—he'd probably been one of those pretty boys twenty or thirty years ago—long before she'd met him. But at forty-six, ten years her senior, he wore his age well. Rugged. Some gray mixing with his brown hair. A twinkle in his pale blue eyes. And she knew he'd continue to grow more handsome with the years. She'd met his father.

"What?" he asked, the smile in his voice turned to suspicion. "Do I have something in my teeth?"

She choked back a laugh. "No. How's Harry?"

A dark cloud shadowed Pete's face. He climbed to his feet with a grunt. "Pop's the same. Maybe a little worse for wear."

"Let me know the next time you go visit him. I'd like to tag along."

"He'd enjoy that. If he's having a good day. Last time I drove out there I don't think he knew who I was."

The sadness in Pete's voice matched the ache in her heart. Damned Alzheimer's. "Doesn't matter. I'd still like to see him. He saved my life, after all."

"For which I'll be eternally grateful." Pete reached a hand toward her.

She took it and let him help her up. They stood toe to toe, face to face, her focus locked onto his lips. His breath, warm on her skin, smelled of coffee. He leaned closer, and she lifted her face toward his...just as the door to the morgue swung open.

They both took big steps away from each other. Marshall breezed into the hallway, nodded to Pete, and handed Zoe a bottle of water. "How are you doing?" Marshall asked her.

For a moment, she thought he'd caught her and Pete in their almost-embrace. Her neck warmed. "What?" Her voice squeaked.

The coroner tipped his head toward the morgue door. "You looked a little green around the gills in there."

"Oh." The autopsy. She swallowed. "Well, I didn't throw up."

"Good. That's always a start."

She unscrewed the cap on the water bottle. "For what?"

"A career in the coroner's office," Marshall said matter-of-factly.

She froze with the water halfway to her lips. A career? In the coroner's office?

Before she had a chance to comment, Pete broke in. "What did you find out?"

"Come inside and we'll talk." Marshall turned and motioned for them to follow.

The morgue office was sparse, little more than a cubicle with a door. The gray metal desk showed signs of abuse. The chairs had sturdy steel frames, but tears in the vinyl seats revealed the yellow foam stuffing. Marshall slid into a creaking swivel chair behind the desk and tapped the crumb-covered keyboard.

"Dental records confirm the victim is Lillian Farabee. No surprise there. In fact, there weren't *any* surprises. Injuries are consistent with what would be sustained in a natural gas explosion. Head trauma, assorted fractures, lacerations, and contusions."

"Cause of death?" Pete asked.

"Undetermined until we get the lab results back. Several of her injuries could have been fatal, one skull fracture in particular. But she could have died from smoke inhalation, too. With the condition of the body, it's pretty hard to tell. The lab should tell us something more definitive."

Zoe recapped the water bottle. "So manner of death is undetermined, as well?"

Marshall looked up from the computer screen. "For now. If I were a gambling man, which I am not, I'd bet on accidental. But it's too early in the game to make those kinds of determinations."

"Right." Pete nodded thoughtfully. "Let me know as soon as you get the lab results."

"Of course."

Pete turned to Zoe, directing her to the door. She noted his frown.

"What are you thinking?" she asked once they were alone again in the hall.

"A few things." Before he could elaborate, a rift of music burst from his pocket. Zoe watched as he dug out his phone, frowned at the screen, silenced the music, and stuffed the cell phone back where he'd found it.

"You could have taken that," she said.

He shook his head. "Nothing important."

"So what were you going to say about the case?"

"First I have to see Holt Farabee and break the news about his wife."

"I don't think he'll be surprised. He already seemed to know she was dead."

"Yeah. But it doesn't make giving the news any easier."

"Or receiving it." Zoe thought about the daughter. "How old did he say his little girl was?"

"Ten."

Crap. Only two years older than Zoe had been when she'd lost her dad. "Mind if I come with you?"

"All right. But we'll have to take two vehicles. I have an appointment with a loan officer at the Monongahela National Bank at eleven."

"A loan officer? You borrowing money?"

A grin replaced the frown on Pete's face. "I'm a bad risk. I'm looking into this business about the Farabees staying in a house they'd been evicted from. For a month."

"The poor guy's just lost his wife, and you're gonna charge him with squatting?"

"It's criminal trespass. And I'm not charging him with anything yet. That's why we investigate these things."

"Okay. I'll take my truck. After we talk to Farabee, I'll head home." She sniffed the sleeve of her shirt and winced. "I need to wash off the stink of autopsy before our date."

"Are we still on for tonight?"

"Unless you want to cancel."

The corner of Pete's mouth slanted upward. "Not a chance. Farabee's staying at the Sleep EZ Motel over by the Interstate. I'll meet you there."

The Sleep EZ? Poor guy. But it was the daughter who broke Zoe's heart. Losing a parent and her home—and stuck in a cheap motel. Not the kind of life a ten-year-old girl should have to deal with.

SIX

The skinny, sallow kid working the front desk at the Sleep EZ Motel acted like he had caterpillars crawling up his back the moment he looked up from his smartphone and spotted Pete and his uniform. The kid, whose name badge identified him as Gerald, shot a nervous glance at the computer in front of him. Pete wondered how many illegal activities were going on behind the motel's assorted doors and which of the occupants had paid Gerald extra to give them a quick heads-up if the heat came calling.

"I need the room number for Holt Farabee." Pete doubted it would be that easy.

Gerald's bloodshot eyes bugged from their sockets. "Um. I don't think I can give you it, dude. Not without a—whachamacallit—warrant?"

"Look, Gerald. I'm not here to arrest anyone, so relax."

The kid's shoulders released a notch. "I still can't give you a room number, dude."

"Okay, *dude*. Can you call Mr. Farabee and tell him Chief Pete Adams is here and needs to talk to him?"

"Um." The kid appeared on the verge of spraining something if he had to think any harder. "I...um...guess I could do that."

When Gerald continued to stare, motionless, Pete pointed at the grungy phone sitting next to the computer keyboard.

The clerk's eyes widened as he apparently realized Pete had not only wondered if it was possible, but also wanted him to do it. "Oh. Okay."

Unlike the standard Sleep EZ resident, Holt Farabee gave Gerald permission to reveal his room number to Pete.

Zoe had waited outside the motel office, stating she'd had all the offensive odors she could stomach for one day. She fell into step beside Pete as he headed down the row of closed doors and drawn curtains toward the room Gerald had indicated. Near the end, one of the doors opened and Farabee stepped outside without closing it. He wore the same jeans from yesterday, still stained from the mud, although it appeared he'd made an effort to wash them—probably in the motel room's sink. From inside, a TV blared a canned laugh track.

"Chief?" Farabee extended a hand, which Pete shook. The man's gaze darted from Pete to Zoe as if searching for some sign the news might be good.

From inside came a small voice. "Daddy? Who is it?"

Pete held Farabee's gaze and watched the hope drain away as he read his answer in Pete's face.

"You watch your show, honey," Farabee called inside to his daughter. "I have to talk to this gentleman for a few minutes."

As Farabee reached to pull the door shut, Zoe spoke up. "Would you like me to sit with your daughter while you talk?"

He glanced into the room. Then to Pete and back to Zoe. "She doesn't know anything about what's happened yet." Farabee's voice was low and strained. "I've been making up excuses for where her mom is until—until I knew for sure."

"I won't say anything," Zoe assured him. "I'll just watch TV with her."

He nodded. "That would be great. Thanks." He took a step inside. "Maddie, honey, this is..." Farabee glanced back at them, his eyes wide in embarrassment.

"Zoe," she said gliding past him into the room. "Maddie, my name's Zoe. What are you watching?"

Farabee watched the two for a moment before pulling the door shut behind him and facing Pete. "The body in the fire. It was Lill, wasn't it?"

Pete had seen more bereaved spouses in his career in law enforcement than he could ever count. The anguish in Holt Farabee's eyes was as genuine as any Pete had witnessed. Or else the man was one of the best liars he'd encountered. "Yes, Mr. Farabee. I'm sorry, but the coroner's confirmed—"

Farabee slumped against the outside wall of the motel and covered his face with his hands, muffling the sobs.

Zoe perched next to the ten-year-old blond ponytailed Maddie Farabee on a bed that under ordinary circumstances, she wouldn't have touched without first putting on Latex gloves. The room's carpet was a flat gray marred with dark stains. Faded and peeling wallpaper appeared to have been applied back in the '80s. And was that a bullet hole above the ancient television set? The show on the TV was almost as old as the room's décor, featuring a wholesome teen girl's antics while the actress playing her had long since grown into a rebellious young woman. Zoe had gone through her own rebellion, but maturity led her to see the link between her bad choices and the tragedy which had shaped her life. She glanced at the youngster beside her and hoped Maddie wouldn't make those same kinds of mistakes.

"Dad's upset," Maddie said without taking her eyes from the screen. "He won't tell me what's wrong because he thinks I can't handle stuff."

What had Zoe been thinking when she offered to sit and watch TV with this kid? *I won't say anything,* she'd told the dad, forgetting about how perceptive kids were. Zoe ran several possible responses through her mind. Other than a flat-out fib, nothing sounded reassuring.

Maddie gave a huge sigh. "I hate this place."

Zoe looked around again. "It's...not very nice." Understatement.

"It sucks."

Zoe snorted. "Yeah. It does."

"And it stinks."

"That, too."

"I hate smelly stuff."

Zoe gave the girl a smile. "So do I."

"And I don't have any of my stuff with me." Maddie smoothed her ruffled pink skirt over a pair of aqua leggings. "Dad picked me up from my friend's house and brought me straight here. I don't know why we couldn't stop at *our* house so I could pack some clothes and get my games."

Zoe pictured the fire. Maddie no longer had any clothes or games.

"I hope my mom brings me some of my things when she gets here."

Maddie no longer had a mom, either.

The girl turned to face Zoe. "Is there something wrong with my mom?"

Zoe opened her mouth, but words failed her. Unlike earlier when Maddie had changed the subject and saved Zoe from an uncomfortable response, the girl was clearly waiting for an answer this time. Her large, wise-beyond-their-years brown eyes stared unblinking at Zoe.

The door swung open and a pale Holt Farabee took two uncertain steps into the room. "Thanks," he said to Zoe. "You can go now. I need to talk to my daughter."

"I can stick around if you need me to." Zoe heard the words and realized they were coming from her own mouth.

Farabee shook his head. "We'll be fine."

Relieved even if she didn't believe him, Zoe jumped up—and hesitated. She couldn't simply bolt from the room. Turning to Maddie, she looked down into those searching, innocent eyes. What should Zoe say? *See ya* didn't sound right. *Nice chatting with you?* No.

Zoe glanced around the room, her gaze settling on the cheap veneered desk.

She crossed to it and picked up the motel's promotional pen to jot her name and number on the complimentary notepad. Ripping off the top sheet, she returned to kneel in front of the ten-year-old. She pressed the paper into Maddie's hand. "I live on a horse farm and give riding lessons. If you ever want to come out and go for a ride, give me a call."

Maddie's eyes widened. "I love horses."

Zoe would have bet on that. Most little girls did.

Maddie looked at her father. "Can I, Dad?"

Farabee's shell-shocked expression didn't waver. "We'll see."

Zoe patted the girl's knee and rose.

"Do you want to tell me what that was all about?" Pete demanded as he and Zoe walked to their vehicles.

She stopped short. "What was *what* all about?"

"Pony rides? That little girl isn't a stray puppy or kitten you can pick up and take home with you."

Zoe stared at him, a perplexed scowl on that beautiful face, her lips open, but no words coming from them.

She had a soft spot for kids. It had gotten her into trouble before. But this wasn't a friend's daughter. This was the child of a stranger—a man Pete wasn't at all sure he trusted.

Zoe closed her mouth and made a deliberate production of crossing her arms and cocking one hip before speaking. "You think I don't know the difference between a little girl who's lost a parent and a stray dog?"

Her sharp tone brought his own stupidity into focus. Chagrined, he removed his Vance Twp PD ball cap and ran a hand through his hair. "Of course you do. But you can't save everyone."

"I'm not trying to. Look, I know what Maddie Farabee's about to go through. I've been there."

Pete knew all that and tried to interrupt, but Zoe shut him up with the wave of a hand.

"If I can do something as simple as taking her for a horseback ride or two, give her some sense of self-worth and control, maybe she won't go all renegade like I did."

"As long as it stops with a horseback ride. Or two."

"Or three." A fleeting grin crossed Zoe's face. "Come on, Pete. Tell me you don't feel a little helpless where that kid's concerned."

He struck his official law enforcement pose. The one with the best intimidation factor. "You've been in the business long enough to know you can't get personally involved in a case. It'll break your heart."

Zoe showed no sign of being the least bit intimidated. "Maybe you've been in the business too long and have gotten jaded. Putting a kid on a pony isn't going to break anything, least of all my heart."

This probably wasn't the time for a quip about bucking broncs and potential broken bones. Maybe Zoe was right. Maybe she could make a positive difference in Maddie Farabee's life and leave it at that.

And maybe—as much as he hated the thought—maybe she was right about him, too. He thought about the phone message. The one he hadn't responded to. Yet. He jammed his cap back on his head. "All right. You win." Besides, odds were good Farabee would pack up his meager belongings and move with his daughter to someplace closer to family. "I have to go meet with the loan officer at MNB." Half afraid to hear the answer, he asked, "Are we still on for tonight?"

Zoe continued to glare at him for a moment. Then the corner of her mouth twitched. "That's the second time you've asked me. You must expect me to back out."

"Maybe."

She ducked her head, but not before he caught a glimpse of the smile she attempted to hide. "We're still on."

"I'll pick you up at six," he called after her as she strode to her truck.

"Don't be late."

Pete watched her drive away before climbing into his SUV. He sat behind the wheel, his hand on the key in the ignition. What was it about Holt Farabee that set his nerves on edge? The man seemed genuine enough. He'd almost charged into the fire yesterday. His heartbreak afterwards in the ambulance and again just now when Pete had told him about the positive ID of his wife's body all felt real. Even the criminal trespass charge seemed reasonable under the circumstances. Still a felony. But hardly worth the unease in Pete's gut.

Maybe the bank could offer some answers—or at least an insight into how a man with a wife and daughter could become a squatter.

Monongahela National Bank was headquartered in a relatively new multistory brick building in downtown Brunswick. Pete found a parking space in the lot behind the structure.

A young teller at the first window directed him to an office in the rear of the building. A statuesque redhead in a gray skirt and jacket met him at the door, introducing herself as Mary Lawson, Loan Manager.

She directed him to take a seat as she closed the door behind them and slid into the chair behind her methodically tidy desk. "How can I help you, Chief Adams?"

Pete crossed an ankle over one knee and fished his notepad and pen from his pocket. "Are you familiar with Scenic Hilltop Estates in Vance Township?"

"That's where the horrible explosion was yesterday."

"I understand your bank holds the mortgage on the homes there."

Lawson leaned forward, skimming her fingers over the keyboard. "Correct. The developer set up an arrangement for anyone planning to purchase property there to be financed through us."

"Is that common practice?"

She scowled. "I don't understand your question."

"Is it common practice for the developer of a housing plan to arrange the buyers' mortgages?"

Lawson leaned back in her chair and folded her arms. "It's not unusual."

"The house that exploded yesterday had been owned by Holt and Lillian Farabee."

Mary Lawson may have had flaming red hair, but her demeanor was cool as ice as she held Pete's gaze.

"Had been," Pete stressed. "Your bank had them evicted."

A crease appeared in the woman's forehead. "I wasn't aware. That's too bad."

"You weren't aware? Aren't you in charge of loans?"

"Loans, yes. But if the family had fallen into arrears, their case would have gone to our collections department."

Pete jotted a note. "Collections department?"

"Yes." Lawson leaned forward, resting her arms on her desk, her manicured fingers loosely intertwined. "Chief Adams, it behooves no one to repossess a home. The bank much prefers to work with our clients, make whatever arrangements necessary for them to repay their loans. We're interested in getting our money back. Not in dispossessing homeowners."

"Were you aware a woman was killed in yesterday's explosion?"

"I believe I heard something on the news."

"Doesn't it seem strange to you someone was inside the house when it exploded?"

Lawson's icy façade developed a crack as one eye twitched. "Until you told me the house in question had been repossessed, I wasn't aware of the situation."

Pete wasn't at all sure he bought Ms. Lawson's total ignorance of the Farabees' plight. "Now that you know, does it seem strange?"

Her chest rose and fell with a long breath, but otherwise she remained completely still. Pete imagined her brain, on the other hand, was churning in high gear. After a long silence, she replied, "I don't suppose it's all that strange. The victim was likely a real estate agent preparing the home for the market."

"The victim," Pete said, "was Lillian Farabee."

Lawson's eyes widened. "Oh. I—I—" She closed her mouth and made a visible effort to regain her composure. When she spoke again, the icy veneer was back in place. "The newscast didn't give her name."

Because Pete had only informed the next of kin less than an hour ago. "How can you explain the owner's wife being back in the house after your bank evicted her?"

Mary Lawson hadn't had an answer for Pete's last question. Instead, she directed him upstairs to another office—the collections department. After being bounced from one harried secretary to another, he found himself in the cubicle of one Dennis Spangler. In stark contrast to Lawson's cool persona and meticulously neat desk, Spangler's tie hung loose at his throat, the top button of his rumpled shirt unbuttoned, and his sleeves rolled haphazardly up to this elbows. Files and papers stacked a foot deep on either side of his computer threatened to avalanche at any moment. The greasy smell of a hamburger and fries signaled lunch had been eaten at his desk. Pete smiled. This man reminded him of some of the detectives he'd worked with in the city. Too much work. Too little time.

"How can I help you?" Spangler asked without lifting his gaze above the badge on Pete's shirt.

Pete was tired of repeating the same questions, giving the same explanation over and over only to be directed to another bank employee. "Are you in charge of the Holt and Lillian Farabee case?"

Spangler's fingers stopped tapping on his keyboard. He leaned back in his chair and looked up to meet Pete's eyes. "I am."

Finally.

Spangler motioned to the chair across from him. "Have a seat."

Pete lowered into it. "I assume you've heard about the explosion."

Spangler nodded cautiously. "Have you identified the body yet?"

Pete had a feeling Spangler had already guessed. "Lillian Farabee."

Spangler swore. "I was afraid of that."

"Why?"

The rumpled bank employee's face revealed a number of emotions crossing his mind, but he seemed unable to settle on one. Nor did he answer.

"Mr. Spangler?"

The man blew out a breath. "I'm in trouble, aren't I?"

"I don't know. Are you?"

Spangler shifted his weight in the chair and it creaked in protest. "I knew about the Farabees moving back into the house."

Pete waited.

"I was supposed to go there and secure the house after they moved out. And I intended to. But my caseload has become overwhelming." Spangler swept his arm over the piles of folders and papers on his desk. "By the time I got to the property, I saw someone was living there. I confirmed it was the homeowners. Former homeowners. And they didn't seem to be trashing the place. Some people do, you know. They're angry about being put out of their house so they vandalize it out of spite. That wasn't the case here."

"What did you do?"

"Nothing. I did nothing. I felt bad for them, okay? I mean, they had a little kid and all. Besides, a lot of these vacant foreclosures fall victim to vandals and thieves. You know?"

Of course Pete knew, but he kept quiet. Spangler's floodgates had opened and Pete wasn't about to risk having him clam up.

"Anyhow, I decided to look the other way. For now. I have plenty of other cases to keep me busy. And the Farabee place wasn't set to go up for sheriff's sale for another couple of months. I figured, what's the harm? Let the previous owners babysit the property for a little longer." Spangler pressed a hand to his forehead and eyes. Pete wasn't sure if the man was about to cry or simply had the mother of all headaches. Or both.

"Did you talk to the Farabees?"

Spangler dropped his hand from his face. "No."

"Had you met them before?"

"Not face-to-face. I've spoken to Mr. Farabee on the phone a number of times. Trying to arrange some sort of payment plan which would allow them to keep their house."

Pete jotted a note. "How did you know it was them in the house?"

"Stephen Tierney. Their neighbor. He's a bank employee. He told me."

Pete closed his notebook and thanked Dennis Spangler for his time, assuring him if he was in any trouble, it was with his own bosses, not the law.

But Pete wasn't so sure the same held true for Stephen Tierney.

SEVEN

Three hours of stripping and re-bedding stalls when the thermometer read eighty-eight degrees resulted in a perspiration-soaked t-shirt and jeans, but the combined stench of sweat and manure still didn't mask the smell of the autopsy. Ordinarily, Zoe's favorite meal was a cheeseburger from Parson's Roadhouse, but after being around Lillian Farabee's burnt cadaver, Zoe prayed Pete's plans for them didn't include a restaurant that served burgers or steaks. Bring on the pasta.

She stepped out of her ratty barn sneakers on the back porch before letting herself into the house. With a couple of hours before her date, the first item on her agenda was a shower. It might take the rest of the afternoon to wash off the eau de barn.

Zoe loved her bathroom, the only completely remodeled room in the entire house. A reproduction clawfoot tub made for luxurious long soaks, but the walk-in shower in one corner received the most use, especially in the summer. Zoe skimmed off the t-shirt and tossed it into the wicker hamper. The sweaty jeans felt glued to her legs and had to be peeled off.

The temperature of the water pelting her was perfect. Not too hot, not too cold. She let it drench her hair before soaping up. After the intense heat and work in the barn, the tepid shower spray felt almost too cool. As she worked shampoo into a lather with one hand, she cranked up the hot water with the other. But it seemed slow to warm up. In fact, she shivered. She squinted through the soap to make sure she hadn't accidently turned the wrong dial. No. Not the problem.

Zoe spun the hot water spigot all the way up, expecting to be scalded. Instead, she shivered in the icy stream.

No hot water.

And with a head full of shampoo, she couldn't simply quit mid-shower. Gritting her teeth, she did her best to stand back and keep only her head under the spray. She'd always thought you had to actually eat ice cream to get an ice cream headache. Now she knew better. When she couldn't stand it any longer, she slammed the spigot off, hoping she'd washed out most of the soap.

Twenty minutes later, after drying her hair and slipping into a tank top and shorts, she headed down to the basement for the second time in as many days. At least this time there was light, courtesy of a few bare bulbs along the low ceilings.

She opened the breaker box and studied the switches. None appeared to be tripped. But she found the one tagged "Hot Water" and flipped it off and back on again. Nothing happened. She stepped over to the ancient tank and glared at it as if she could intimidate it into working. Nothing. No hum or gurgle or hiss. She gave the tank a whack with the heel of her hand. Still nothing.

What Zoe knew about these things could fit in a shot glass and leave plenty of room for whiskey. Should she call an electrician? Or a plumber? Mr. Kroll would know. But would *Mrs.* Kroll? Probably not.

With a sigh, Zoe trudged up the basement stairs. At the top, she hesitated and glanced at the door to her side of the house on the left then frowned at the one on the right. She reached for the knob and eased it open, peering into the empty center hallway.

"Mrs. Kroll?" she called.

From somewhere in the house, her landlady replied, "Zoe?"

"Yeah. I'm in the hall at the basement door. Where are you?"

A moment passed before Zoe heard footsteps on the main staircase. She slipped the rest of the way into the hall as Mrs. Kroll made her way down the steps. "What's wrong, dear? Did the power go out again?"

"No, but have you tried to use any hot water lately?"

Mrs. Kroll reached the bottom of the stairs and hobbled toward Zoe. "I washed up a few dishes after lunch. Why?"

"Did the water seem...cool?"

The woman brought a gnarled finger to her cheek and tapped thoughtfully. "Hmm. Now that you mention it, I did think the water wasn't as hot as it should've been."

"Something's wrong with the hot water tank. I just had a cold shower."

"Oh, dear. Now what do we do? Wait. Maybe it's a breaker like it was yesterday."

"I already checked. Have you had problems with it before? Maybe there was something Mr. Kroll did to reset the heater?"

Mrs. Kroll shook her head. "No, never. We've had that tank for at least thirty years and never had a bit of trouble with it. Why now?"

Probably because you've had it for at least thirty years, Zoe thought. "I'll make some phone calls and try to get a serviceman out here. In the meantime, we'll have to pretend to be hardy pioneer women and heat water on the stove."

"A serviceman," Mrs. Kroll echoed. "More bills. I don't know where I'm going to come up with the money."

Zoe watched her landlady turn and shuffle away, shoulders slumped. "I'll try to think of something," Zoe called after her.

Zoe ducked through the passageway under the main staircase back to her side of the house. Within those few steps, the seed of an idea sprouted. Two women living alone in a mid-nineteenth century farmhouse, which was quickly falling into a state of disrepair. Bills mounted. Income didn't. One possible solution—the business card still in Zoe's dirty jeans' pocket—didn't appeal to her at all. But fifteen miles away, in a scummy motel room, a little girl and her out-of-work carpenter father needed a place to stay.

Pete stopped at the explosion site on his way home from the county seat. Yellow tape encircled Farabee's property. The state fire marshal's team continued to sift through the debris. A dozen or so onlookers stood off to one side, snapping pictures of Monongahela County's newest tourist spot.

One of the investigators broke away from his work long enough to update Pete on their findings, which amounted to zilch. So far.

He climbed into his SUV and drove through the narrow opening in Stephen Tierney's privacy fence, parking in front of the garage. Pete strode up the sidewalk noting the drawn blinds in the windows. He suspected Tierney was still out of town, but rang the doorbell anyway.

He was greeted with total silence. No footsteps. No shuffling to indicate someone might be home but pretending otherwise.

After pounding on the door produced identical results, Pete returned to the Explorer. He hated being lied to, and Tierney had told him a whopper. Even worse, he'd told it convincingly. Pete would catch up to him later.

At the station, Nancy looked up from her computer as Pete walked through the front door. "Hey, Chief."

"Anything going on that I need to know about?" he asked.

"Nothing urgent. Dad called and wanted me to let you know Ryan still hasn't trimmed his hedges. You have a message from..." Nancy paused to check her notes. "...from Chuck Delano asking you to return his call at your convenience. I put his number on your desk. That's about it. I guess we're getting a reprieve after yesterday."

Pete grunted. "Thanks. Coffee?"

"Fresh pot in your office."

"Remind me to give you a raise."

She choked out a short laugh. "Yeah, right."

He ambled down the hall to his office, poured a cup of coffee, and slid into his chair. After a sip of the steaming brew, he shuffled through the pink while-you-were-out notes stacked neatly on his desk. Jack Naeser and those damned shrubs. Pete made a mental note to stop in and talk to Mancinelli. Maybe he'd make more progress if he caught the guy at a calmer time when chainsaws weren't a threat.

The last note bore the name Chuck Delano and the number he'd left for Pete four times now. What was up with Delano anyway?

Pete picked up the phone and punched in the number. Delano answered on the second ring.

"Petey, you old hound dog," he shouted through the line after Pete identified himself. "About time you called me back. I was beginning to think you were dodging me."

Possibly because he was. "I'd never dodge you, Delano. What's so important that you keep leaving messages for me all over the county?"

"I told you. I have a job offer."

"I'm already gainfully employed. You know that."

Delano made a disgusted sound over the phone. "Chief of Police in Podunk, Pennsylvania? You call that a job?"

Pete pinned the receiver between his ear and his shoulder and straightened a pile of papers threatening to take a dive onto the floor. "Big fish. Little pond. I like it."

Delano chuckled. "Beats being a small fish in a big pond, huh?"

"You know it."

The line fell silent for a moment and Pete wondered if they'd been disconnected. Before he could ask, Delano spoke again. "How would you like to be a big fish in a big pond? A very warm and sunny pond."

"It's ninety degrees here right now. Warm isn't much of a draw."

"It would be in the middle of January, though."

"What are you babbling about, Chuck?"

"Maui. I'm talking about Maui."

Maui? "As in Hawaii?"

"Only one I know, Petey. Look, I've gotten myself into a sweet gig. Head of security for the Grand Lahaina Resort. The group who owns it also owns another big hotel down the beach called the Maalaea Bay Grand Hotel. The head of security there is retiring the end of next month and they're looking for a replacement. They came to me asking if I could recommend anyone and I thought of you, buddy. What do you think?"

Hawaii? Pete's mind stalled on an image of sandy beaches and hula dancers.

"And did I mention the salary? Six figures, Petey boy. Six. Figures."

Pete caught the phone receiver as it slipped from his ear and sat back in his chair.

His gaze fell on the note about Naeser and his son-in-law's hedges. A luxury resort in Hawaii probably didn't have that kind of excitement. Six figures?

Speaking of figures...a luxury resort in Hawaii didn't have Zoe either.

"I don't think I'm interested," Pete said.

Another silence. This time Pete was pretty sure they hadn't been disconnected. He was right. "Are you out of your mind?" Delano's gruff voice had gone up an octave. "Did you hear what I said?"

"I heard. I like it here. I like my job. I like the people. I even like the weather." Well, most of the weather anyway.

"You *are* out of your mind. Listen, I'm not going to say anything to my boss one way or the other. You have some time to come to your senses about this. Just don't lose my number. And try to get back to me within a week or two."

"Do whatever you want, but I'm passing on the job offer. Appreciate you thinking about me though."

Delano muttered something and clicked off.

Pete dropped the receiver back onto its cradle. He fingered the pink slip with his old partner's 808 area code number—and crumpled it. He reached to toss it into the trash can, but hesitated.

Maui. Six figures. Might be nice to think about it. Dream a little.

Pete set the wadded note on his desk and smoothed it out before shoving it under one of the paper mountains.

"Where are we going?" Zoe asked as Pete held the door of the Ford Edge, his personal vehicle, for her.

"I thought I'd take you into the city for dinner."

"Brunswick?" At least the county seat offered more restaurant choices.

He shot her a look. "Pittsburgh."

"Oh." She slid into the passenger seat and reassessed her choice of attire. Wranglers—albeit a pair still too new to be downgraded to barn jeans status—and a clingy black Gap tank top were suitable for any local eatery or the pizza joint in downtown Brunswick, but hardly seemed proper for a *real* restaurant. Pete, she noticed, had on khaki Dockers and a short-sleeved button down shirt. Not exactly a suit, but a step up from his usual off-duty faded jeans and t-shirt. "Where in Pittsburgh? Should I change into something dressier?"

He settled into the driver's seat and gave her a long, appreciative inspection. "You look fantastic."

Her neck warmed, and she glanced away to hide her smile. "Thanks, but that doesn't answer my question."

Pete fired up the Edge. "What are you hungry for?"

"Anything other than meat."

He choked. "You going vegetarian on me?"

"No. I'm just not in the mood for steak or burgers."

They'd reached the bottom of the farm lane before Pete jammed the brakes and laughed. "I get it. The smell from autopsy is still bothering you."

Zoe slouched in her seat. "I may have to swear off anything roasted or grilled for a while."

"Understood."

An hour later they sat at a small table at Bahama Cove, a small, well-hidden restaurant in Pittsburgh's Strip District with a décor that made Zoe feel like she was in the Caribbean, or at least what she imagined the Caribbean felt like. Although the Cove, as it was known to the locals, was situated on a corner of a narrow alley, the food always drew a crowd. The place was packed. They were lucky to get a table, even though it meant squeezing in between two others, which were occupied on one side by a large, tattooed man, his wife and brood of three children, and on the other side by a quartet of what Zoe guessed to be frat boys.

Pete eyed her over his menu. "How's this?"

She breathed in aromas of island spices and herbs. "Perfect."

He chuckled. "I still don't believe you can't face a steak after a little thing like an autopsy. You and I have sat down to the spaghetti lunch at the Phillipsburg Diner after some pretty gory accident calls. You've never flinched."

He had a point. But this was different somehow.

Zoe studied the menu while Pete ordered a couple of drafts and a plate of Jamaican Jerk Wings.

"All right. What's bothering you?" he asked once the waiter had gone.

Where to start? "This morning. The autopsy."

Pete folded his arms and leaned back in his chair. "I was only teasing you about the steak. I don't blame you a bit. In fact, I'd be surprised if this kind of autopsy *didn't* affect you."

"You mean because of my dad?"

Pete raised an eyebrow in a silent "of course."

"It's more than that."

"Okay. Tell me."

She drew a breath. "When I signed on to be a deputy coroner, I didn't know what it really involved. I thought it would be—I don't know—fun. I imagined I'd be out in the field collecting evidence, solving crimes."

"In other words, *my* job."

Zoe fought a grin. "Maybe."

Pete grew serious. "Investigating deaths *is* part of your job."

"But it's the one part I rarely get to do. Franklin loves that part of it, too, and he's the boss, so he makes a point of being on the scene every time something's going down." She heard the whine in her voice and stopped to compose herself. "Most of what I do is pronouncing time of death on old folks who die in their sleep. And now there's this autopsy thing."

"Autopsy thing?"

"Franklin's pushing for me to assist on more of them. Six to be precise. And I'm not sure he's gonna count Lillian Farabee since I bailed out halfway through."

"Why six?"

"It was a deal I made with him last month."

"The so-called 'deal with the devil' you mentioned?"

"That's the one. He promoted me to chief deputy coroner so I could get into the old records room at the courthouse to investigate my dad's death. In exchange I had to agree to assist with six autopsies."

Pete stared at her for a moment and then snorted. "The old scoundrel."

"It's not funny. You heard him mention my future with the coroner's office. The promotion wasn't supposed to be real. At least I didn't think it was."

The waiter returned with their beers and the appetizer and asked if they were ready to order. Zoe realized nothing on the menu had registered in her brain, and she gave it another quick perusal.

"Do you want me to order for you?" Pete asked.

She tossed the menu down. "You know what I like better than I do."

"Two grilled salmon," he told the waiter, who collected the menus and retreated. Pete picked up one of the wings and studied it intently. "Do you *want* the promotion to be real?"

Leave it to Pete to cut through the crap and come to the heart of her conundrum. She opened her mouth to say *no*, but the simple word stuck. Did she want to be chief deputy coroner? Possibly coroner one day? "Want? I don't know. I don't think I can do it."

"Of course you can." He took a bite and chewed. "This case isn't a good indicator. If you want a career in the coroner's office, I think you'd be damned good at it."

There was that "career in the coroner's office" line again. Had Franklin enlisted Pete to help lure her? But it still came down to *want*. She loved working on the ambulance. Working to save the living. The side gig of deputy coroner had seemed like a good fit. Working to find answers for the dead.

As long as it didn't involve the morgue.

Pete must have been watching the indecision play across her face. "You don't have to make up your mind anytime soon. But I do think you ought to keep your options open. Pay your debt to Marshall."

She ran a finger around the rim of the glass of beer. "You mean...do the six autopsies?"

"Yep. Six is a good number." Pete finished the wing in two bites. "Afterwards you'll have a better idea of whether you're cut out for that life or not. You'll either be immune to the smell or you won't ever want to set foot inside the county morgue again."

Zoe noticed the tattooed man at the table behind Pete had turned in his chair and was giving them the evil eye. "Uh, maybe we should change the subject. I think our conversation is carrying to the folks around us."

"Oh?" Pete shifted in his seat and was met head-on with a venomous glare. After apologizing for the inappropriate dinnertime topic, he hailed the waiter and ordered refills of cocktails for the offended couple and soft drinks for their kids be placed on his tab. Beverages apparently appeased the family's lost appetites, and Pete turned back to Zoe. "One more reason not to discuss work on our off time."

"No work talk?" She thought of the other subject she wanted to discuss with him. Technically, it was work related, too. "Might make for a quiet evening."

"Are you insinuating I'm a workaholic?"

"Pretty much. Yeah."

Pete laughed and took a draw on his brew. "Have some wings."

She obliged, savoring the blend of sweet and spice while mentally testing her foray into the other subject she wanted to broach. After swallowing, she said, "I—Mrs. Kroll and I—need a repairman at the farm."

"Why?" he asked around a mouthful of chicken.

"Since Mr. Kroll's been laid up, stuff's falling apart right and left. There's a leak in the roof. My kitchen sink is dripping. One of the window panes in Mrs. Kroll's front room is cracked. Yesterday the main breaker tripped. And today the water heater died."

Pete scowled as he wiped his fingers on a napkin. "Your water heater's electric, right? It probably blew an element. That's what kicked the main."

"Possibly. But how do you replace an element?"

"I could come over this weekend."

"Don't be silly. We could have you there full-time for the next week to get everything fixed. And then something else would go. Did I mention I need some boards nailed back up in the barn? And the whole farm needs to be mowed."

"Do you want me to find someone for you?" Pete dropped the last bare bone on the plate as the waiter arrived with two steaming plates of salmon.

"I already have someone in mind."

Pete moved his small appetizer plate out of the way so the waiter could set down the entrée. "Who?"

Zoe swallowed. "Holt Farabee."

EIGHT

The appetizer plate nearly slipped from Pete's fingers, but he made a good save, juggling it and allowing only one scoured wing bone to hit the table. "Holt Farabee? Have you lost your mind?"

Zoe didn't reply other than getting that stubborn-as-a-mule look on her face.

Pete should have seen this coming with all her talk about the little girl and horseback rides. "You yourself pointed out the man seemed to have his wife already dead and buried before we'd found a body. Yet you're willing to let him in your house to do repairs?"

An odd look flitted across Zoe's face. Pete had seen it before, when she was hiding something. "Well, why not?" she said. "He's an out-of-work carpenter with a child to feed. Obviously he can't afford a decent room for the two of them. He needs work. I need repair work done. It seems like a good fit."

"Good fit, my ass."

Zoe glanced over his shoulder and gave the tattooed eavesdropper an apologetic grin.

Pete lowered his voice. "There are a number of unemployed carpenters in the area. Not to mention handymen who hire out for just this kind of work. Let me ask around. I'll get you a list of names."

That look crossed Zoe's face again. She picked up her fork and poked at her dinner. "If you want. But I still think Holt needs the work more than anyone else."

"You're trying to save the world again. First you want to give the kid pony rides. Now you want to give her father a job."

Zoe skewered a piece of fish and popped it in her mouth, chewing slowly. Was she intentionally avoiding a response? After a long rumination, she lowered her fork to her plate. "Haven't you heard? When you save a life, you're responsible for it?"

"Bullshit. You save lives all the time."

Something slammed behind him. A hand on a table, perhaps. A chair scraped on the floor, ramming into the back of Pete's, jostling him. "Excuse me," said an irritated voice.

Zoe grabbed her fork and dug into her salmon. "You're right. We shouldn't talk business at dinner."

Pete climbed to his feet and turned slowly to face the tattooed man. Or rather, face the man's chest. The guy had to be pushing seven feet tall. Pete looked up without surrendering his law-enforcement-officer-in-charge expression.

"My family and I are trying to have a quiet, pleasant dinner," the man growled, "and your big mouth is ruining it for us."

Pete held back a desire to inform the irate diner his own romantic dinner plans were sinking faster than the Titanic, too. He considered a subtle flash of his badge, but this guy didn't look the type to be the least bit intimidated by a cop. One wrong word or move could escalate an uncomfortable encounter into thrown punches. Getting thrown out of one of his favorite restaurants lacked appeal. Other patrons had stopped eating and were watching the two men facing each other down. Pete could imagine tomorrow's headline. "Local Police Chief Creates Scene in City Dining Establishment." Complete with a photo from one of the other patron's cell phone. The job offer in Hawaii might become his only option.

Pete eyed the half-eaten dinners on the neighbors' table. Nothing too extravagant. "Would your evening be salvaged if I picked up your check?"

The man's hard glare softened. "Well, I suppose that might be all right. Thanks."

Pete turned back to his own dinner to find Zoe staring wide-eyed at him. "This just became a very expensive date for you," she said.

He waved her off and dug into his fish. She was right, though. Especially considering he had little hope of getting anything more than dinner out of the effort.

"Let me pay for half of it."

He glared at her. "No."

She shifted her gaze toward the next table. "It's my fault as much as yours. I shouldn't have said anything."

Some of Pete's irritation subsided. Here he was, finally on a date with the girl he'd been harboring lustful fantasies about for years, and she now felt like she couldn't say anything to him without raising his hackles. Good job, Pete. Way to go. "You're not paying for me not knowing how to behave in public." He shot a sheepish grin at her.

She grinned back. God, she was beautiful. Maybe the evening could be salvaged after all.

His pocket vibrated. "Damn it," he muttered as he dug for his phone. No matter who it was would have to wait. He was off duty.

Except the screen read Franklin Marshall.

Pete answered the call. "What have you got?"

"Thought you should know. The fire investigator just informed me they found something at the Farabee house."

Pete glanced at Zoe who had questions in her eyes. "What did they find?" he asked the coroner.

"I don't know all the details, but they're saying the explosion may have been intentional. They're ruling the cause of the fire as suspicious. Looks like maybe the undetermined cause of death for Lillian Farabee has just been reclassified as a homicide."

Zoe wasn't unfamiliar with crappy dates. She'd been on more than her share. But she never expected a real date with Pete would end up on her top ten bad dates list. The next morning, she mulled it over while feeding the horses. Pete had looked good. Real good. The food had been incredible. But the conversation sucked. She never should have brought up the Farabees. Any of them. In fact, she should have begged off the date after her bad experience in autopsy. It had put a pall over the entire day.

This day wasn't faring much better. Seven a.m. and already sweat trickled down her back. There wasn't even a trace of a breeze. As the horses finished their morning grain, Zoe slipped plastic mesh fly masks over their eyes and faces before opening each stall door and letting them out. Too sluggish to kick up their heels, each freed horse ambled out the big door at the end of the barn. She'd leave it open in case they chose to hang out in the indoor arena, but they'd probably wander down to the creek and loiter in the shade of the willow trees.

By eight o'clock, Zoe kicked off her barn sneakers on the back porch and stepped into the relative cool of the farmhouse. Hot, sweaty, and dusty, she longed for a cool shower. Cool. Not ice cold, which was the only kind available at the moment.

Muttering to herself, she pushed through the swinging door to the kitchen, hauled her biggest soup pot from the cupboard, and positioned it under the spigot in her sink. A spot bath wasn't going to do the trick, but would have to suffice for now. She was on duty later and intended to arrive early to take advantage of the crew shower facility.

The pot was less than half full when a knock at the back door interrupted. She cut the tap and padded across the hardwood floor to answer the door. Through the lace curtain hanging on the door's window, she made out an unfamiliar man's form. She swept the curtain aside for a better look and was greeted with an eager smile.

Dave Evans. The cheerful land developer who seemed intent on making her homeless.

"Ms. Chambers, isn't it?" He extended a hand the moment she opened the door.

She reached for the hand, but hesitated and pulled back. "Sorry. I just came from the barn and I'm pretty disgusting."

"Oh. Right." He stuffed both hands into the pockets of his wrinkled khaki trousers. "I don't mean to bother you. I'm looking for the owner. Mrs. Kroll. You gave her my card, didn't you?"

"I forgot." Sort of.

"No problem. I'll give her one in person. Is she home?"

"I told you before. The farm isn't for sale." But one look at the overgrown Boy Scout's eager smile, and she knew she'd never dissuade him. "She's home, but Mrs. Kroll isn't an early riser. You'll need to come back later."

The man's smile faded into disappointment. "Of course I don't want to disturb the poor woman from her rest." He held up another business card, pinched between his index and middle fingers. "Please make sure you give this one to her. I can offer her top dollar for this farm. A lot of the local farmers are eager to make a deal with me. Mrs.

Kroll would probably kick herself if she missed such a golden opportunity." Evans gave Zoe another big smile. The kind the used car dealers used in their television commercials.

Zoe watched him glance back over his shoulder at her as he climbed the path to his car. Why, she wondered, was Dave Evans so interested in acquiring more property when the development he'd already started remained largely vacant?

She waited until he'd driven down the lane and turned onto Route 15 before she returned to her kitchen to wash her hands. The second card went into the trash. Then she hurried out her door and across the porch to Mrs. Kroll's door. Zoe knew full well her landlady was always up at dawn unless she was sick.

Mrs. Kroll answered within seconds. "Who was that man?"

"Just some salesman who's been hanging around."

"Well, I'm glad you got rid of him."

"Do you mind if I come in for a couple minutes? There's something I wanted to discuss with you."

Mrs. Kroll stepped aside. "Please, please come in. I'm happy for the company. I hate being alone here all day."

Zoe passed through the kitchen into the dining room. "That's kind of what I wanted to talk to you about."

After accepting a cup of coffee, she took a seat at the table. "Now," Mrs. Kroll said, settling into her chair. "What's on your mind?"

Zoe ran the scenario through her mind one more time, mapping out her plan while imagining Pete's reaction when he found out. "You know about the explosion over at the housing development..."

"Yes, of course. Terrible thing. Just terrible."

"The man who lived there, whose wife was killed, he and his little girl are staying at an awful motel in Brunswick. He's lost his job, too."

Mrs. Kroll's face was a study in compassion as she silently listened, her frail fingers curled against her chin.

Zoe took a deep breath. "He's a carpenter. An out-of-work carpenter with a ten-year-old daughter and no place to stay. We have a bunch of stuff around here that needs to be fixed. I was thinking..."

Mrs. Kroll brought her hand down to the table with a soft thud. "You want to take in this poor man and his daughter in exchange for him doing some repairs."

"Yes," Zoe said, unable to read whether the older woman was appalled by the idea or approved.

"You've met this man?"

"I tackled him when he tried to run into the fire to save his wife. And I went with Pete yesterday to the Sleep EZ to tell him it really was his wife's body in the rubble."

Mrs. Kroll fixed her with a glare, which included one raised eyebrow. "The Sleep EZ? That man is staying at the Sleep EZ? With his little daughter?"

Zoe nodded. "It's pretty hideous."

"Hideous? I read the *Monongahela Review*. That place is in the news almost every day. Drug dealers. People getting shot. Mercy me. I can't imagine a child in that dump."

"So you wouldn't mind if I let them stay here? One of them can have the sleeper sofa and the other can sleep in my recliner."

Mrs. Kroll waved her hand as if shooing a fly. "No one is going to sleep in your recliner. Or on your sofa. I have a perfectly good guest room. And there's one of those air mattresses in a box in the attic so the little girl can have her own bed. They can stay as long as they need to. He can work on repairs here in exchange for room and board. If he runs out of things to fix..." She chortled. "Well, we'll deal with that possibility when and if it ever happens."

Zoe smiled. The guest room had been her preference, too, but she hadn't felt right suggesting she bring a stranger into the Krolls' home, especially their half of it. But since it was Mrs. Kroll's idea..."How soon can I tell them?"

"As soon as you can. Right now. The guest room is all made up. I changed the linens after our son stayed here for a few days following Marvin's accident."

"Great." Zoe finished her coffee. "I'll get washed up and give Mr. Farabee a call."

As she headed for the door, Mrs. Kroll called after her. "Tell him to bring a hot water tank with him."

The acrid odor of burnt building materials, more chemical than wood, still lingered on the air around Scenic Hilltop Estates. Pete stood on the road next to the flattened house and gazed across the valley dotted with cattle to the barn on the distant hill. Zoe's barn.

He'd been a damned fool.

How long had he waited for a chance to take Zoe out? Years. He'd finally—*finally*—convinced her they should try a romantic relationship, that it wouldn't mess up the friendship they both valued so much. And he'd screwed it up royally. By the time he dropped her off at the farm last night, she didn't even give him a chance to walk her to the door, let alone kiss her goodnight.

Maybe she'd been right all along. They should have remained just friends.

"Damn," he muttered.

"What?" Fire Chief Bruce Yancy asked.

Pete's attention snapped back to the small group of men standing behind him. "Nothing. What were you saying, Reggie?"

Reggie O'Brien, the state fire marshal, leaned on the hood of his pickup, which was currently doubling as a desk. He'd spread a series of photographs out for the others to view. "I said as devastating as the fire was, it didn't destroy this bit of evidence." He tapped one of the photos. "Someone disconnected the gas dryer and broke the valve."

Wayne Baronick picked up the picture in question and studied it. "Whoever did this planned to kill Mrs. Farabee?"

"Not necessarily."

"What's that supposed to mean, Reggie?" Pete asked. "'Not necessarily?'"

The fire investigator shifted to face Pete, but continued to brace one hip against his truck as if he didn't have the energy to stand without support. "You have to understand. There are gas explosions leveling houses all the time, but using it to murder someone is difficult to pull off with any degree of reliability. There are too many variables."

"You couldn't be sure how much bang you'd get for your buck," Yancy said.

Baronick replaced the photo and shuffled through the others. "You're saying there are more dependable methods of murder."

"Exactly," Reggie said.

Pete gazed at the broken lumber, bits of insulation, a door blown off its hinges…"What triggered the explosion?"

"Hard to say." Reggie gathered his photos into a neat stack. "We're lucky we found the source of the leak. We'll likely never know what sparked it."

"Educated guess?" Pete asked. "Did Mrs. Farabee come home and hit a light switch?"

The fire investigator shook his head. "A gas explosion probably wouldn't be initiated by a light switch spark. The switches are inside the walls, reasonably well sealed, and covered by a plate. There are always the other potential ignition spots. Pilot lights on the water heater or furnace. But in a new home like this, those wouldn't be on unless needed."

Baronick slipped out of his sports jacket. "And it's the middle of summer, so we can rule out the furnace."

"Which leaves the water heater." Pete glanced across the valley toward the Kroll farm and another troublesome hot water tank. "Mrs. Farabee comes home from her job interview. She turns on the hot water tap..."

"The pilot light kicks on," Baronick added.

"And boom." Yancy opened both hands as if an illustration was needed.

"Yeah." Pete stepped away from the others, once again transfixed on the farm in the distance. "Boom." There might be easier, more reliable methods to commit murder, but if a man wanted to make his wife's death appear to be a tragic accident, a gas explosion would fit the bill.

And Zoe was intent on playing the Good Samaritan by bringing the man into her home.

"Over my dead body," Pete muttered.

NINE

Holt Farabee had been oddly reluctant to accept Zoe's offer when she'd
phoned him. Male pride, she guessed. But when she'd brought up
Maddie and the difference between his daughter staying in a sleazy
motel versus a farmhouse, even one currently without hot water, he
acquiesced.

As Zoe waited for the Farabees to arrive, she thought about the
little girl who had complained because her dad hadn't let her stop at
home to pick up her stuff and the sad fact she no longer had anything
to pick up. Zoe jogged out to the barn where a small group of her
boarders, mostly young teens, were busy saddling their horses for a
ride. She told them about the girl and her father and how they'd lost
everything. The kids started buzzing with ideas. Clothes they'd
outgrown and their moms had packed away. Toys their younger
siblings never played with.

Within a half hour, the kids had found an empty can and made a
label for it. *Donations for Maddie Farabee.*

They set the can on a table in the tack room where everyone who
came and went could see it. And they emptied their pockets, starting
the collection with almost twenty-five dollars.

Zoe scrawled out a notice on the dry-erase board, which usually
bore notes about horses needing special care or a change of feed.
Today, it carried a plea for donations to be left on the back porch.

The group finally mounted and rode off, chattering about setting
up a benefit trail ride. Zoe smiled after them. She loved horse kids.

She returned to the house in time to see a red Ford crew cab
pickup with tool boxes attached to the rim of the bed climbing the farm
lane. Holt and Maddie Farabee.

Zoe strolled up the path to meet them. Holt parked next to Zoe's Chevy and stepped out of his truck, attired in faded, ill-fitting jeans, a plain white t-shirt, and a black ball cap with a blue UK emblem. Maddie clambered over the center console, and her dad helped her down.

"Welcome." Zoe spread her arms to indicate the house and surrounding property. "I'm glad you agreed to come."

A matched set of dark circles framed Holt's eyes, but he managed a weak smile. "Thanks for the offer." He reached into the rear seat and came up with a plastic grocery bag. "Our luggage. I managed to scrape up enough cash for a stop at the Goodwill store and a change of clothes for each of us."

Maddie wore a summery yellow floral tank top and pink leggings, but her young face looked haunted enough for Halloween. Zoe bent down in front of her. "I'm working on getting you some games and things to play with. But for now I'm afraid all I can offer you is a barn full of horses."

The girl slipped her tiny hand into her father's large but gentle-looking one. "I'll be okay. I don't need anything."

Zoe stood up and shot a helpless look at Holt. A brave, stoic ten-year-old with her grieving father. A farmhouse with a broken water heater, even boasting a barn and horses, seemed woefully inadequate. "Come on. I'll take you inside and introduce you to my landlady."

Mrs. Kroll opened her door before Zoe had a chance to knock.

After introductions, Mrs. Kroll ushered everyone into the dining room. "I'm so glad you're going to help us out, Mr. Farabee. I've been at a loss since my husband was hurt. Zoe's been wonderful, of course, but—"

"But I'm useless at anything more involved than hammering a nail or drilling a hole," Zoe said.

"You're the one helping me out." Holt gazed around the room and up at the thirteen-foot ceilings. "This is a beautiful old house. They don't make them like this anymore. I'll bet it's post and beam construction."

Mrs. Kroll shot a questioning look at Zoe, who could only shrug.

"I'll have to take your word for that, young man," Mrs. Kroll said. "Let me show you to your room and then Zoe can show you where the water heater is. That's the only priority right now. For yours and little Miss Maddie's sake as well as ours. Everything else can wait until you have a chance to...well...to get your feet under you."

"To be honest, ma'am, the work will be a welcome distraction. But I do have to make arrangements."

"Of course." Mrs. Kroll led the way into the center hall and up the grand staircase.

Zoe tagged along behind. She'd lived here for years, but had only climbed these steps a handful of times. Unlike the dark, steep, narrow enclosed back staircase on her side of the house, these were wide and open with a landing two-thirds of the way up.

The second floor was split in half same as the first. The two rooms behind closed doors on the right side were Zoe's bedroom and bath. On the left, the first door stood wide open.

Mrs. Kroll stopped outside it. "This will be your room, Mr. Farabee."

"Please. Call me Holt." With Maddie still clinging to his hand, he paused in the doorway and looked around. "It's—" His voice wavered. "It's nice. Really nice."

Mrs. Kroll motioned as if to shoo him in. "Go on."

"Where will I sleep?" Maddie asked.

Mrs. Kroll crooked a finger at the little girl, beckoning her to the other side of the bed and pointing to a box on the floor. In response to Maddie's perplexed scowl, Mrs. Kroll said, "It's an air mattress." She looked at Zoe. "Maddie and I can set this up. Why don't you and Mr. Farabee—"

"Holt," he corrected.

Mrs. Kroll nodded. "Why don't you take Holt downstairs and show him the water heater? Maddie can decide where she wants her bed and help me with the sheets and such." She turned toward the little girl. "Then I have cookies in the kitchen. Do you like cookies?"

Maddie seemed to give the question serious consideration. "What kind are they?"

"Chocolate chip."

For the first time since she'd arrived, her face softened. Not quite a smile, but close. "I like chocolate chip."

Zoe relaxed. This might work out after all.

Leaving Mrs. Kroll and Maddie with the air mattress project, Zoe led Holt down the staircase and the basement steps.

"This is a great old house," he said, touching the fieldstone foundation walls. "It's amazing what men could do before the advent of bulldozers and power tools."

"I hadn't thought about it, but I guess you're right."

"When was this built?"

"Around 1850, from what I've been told."

He nodded in approval.

Zoe stopped at the doorway to the room she'd been frequenting as of late. "The water heater's in there."

Holt ducked the low-clearance header and surveyed the electrical panel, the oil tanks for the furnace, and the hot water heater. "Looks like the electrical service has been updated at least. Lots of these old houses still have fuse boxes. But this—" He placed a hand on the water tank and whistled. "This is truly an antique."

"Can you fix it?"

"Fix? Well, yeah. I could replace the heating element. Clean out the tank. But this thing is on borrowed time. A patch job might last a year, or it might last a week before something else goes bad." He raised an eyebrow at her. "You need a new one."

"But that's a lot more work, isn't it?" Not to mention money. "Mrs. Kroll and I know you have a lot to deal with for the next few days."

Holt breathed a loud sigh. "Like burying my wife, you mean."

Zoe leaned against the dusty door frame, but didn't answer. What could she possibly say? The man looked like a raw nerve, held together with muscle and sinew, but ready to implode at any moment.

He kept his gaze on the broken heater. "I almost turned you down when you offered Maddie and me a place to stay."

"Why? Anything would have to be better than the Sleep EZ. Even a dilapidated old farmhouse."

He huffed a laugh, but didn't smile. "True. But to come back to Vance Township, so close to our home. Our life. Mine and Lillian's." He gazed toward the small window, but Zoe suspected he was seeing something other than dust motes. "She was beautiful. And smart. The best mom a kid could have. Lill had a beautiful voice. She sang Maddie to sleep every night of her life. Until..."

Until two days ago.

"That house was supposed to be our dream home. The place we grew old together. Maybe have another child." His voice grew frayed. "After the explosion I never wanted to come near this area again."

Another thing Zoe hadn't thought about. "I'm sorry."

Holt lifted a hand to stop her. "No. Don't apologize. You're right. That dump of a motel was no place for Maddie." He lifted his gaze, as if he could see through the beams above his head to his daughter. "And your landlady and chocolate chip cookies? Sure beats being alone with junk from a vending machine. Especially right now."

"Mrs. Kroll doesn't have any grandkids, so I think she has a lot of grandma skills she's just dying to use."

This time, Holt's short laugh was accompanied by a hint of a smile. He moved around the water tank and fingered the pipes and the shut-off valve. "Our family, what's left of it, is all in Kentucky. Lill's folks died when she was young, and I don't have much contact with mine. So Maddie's never had grandparents around." He tapped the pipe. "I'll eventually replace all of this, too. Bring it up to code."

Zoe started doing the math. Her live-in handyman idea might cost more money than she'd counted on. "I hate to tell you to cut corners, but Mrs. Kroll is having a tough time of it financially."

A strange look crossed his face. Zoe wondered if he'd cut his finger on a sharp edge. But he didn't draw back. Instead, he gazed into the distance, his jaw clenched.

"I just mean don't feel you have to do the entire job at one time."

Holt gave his head a quick shake. "Don't worry about it. Some of the local stores give me discounts on materials. I'll bring the job in under budget." He grinned at her, whatever had darkened his mood forgotten. Or at least buried. "I can run back into Brunswick this afternoon and pick up what I need. Would it be okay to leave Maddie here with you and Mrs. Kroll?"

"Uh. Sure. I guess." Zoe wasn't comfortable volunteering her landlady without asking first. "Mrs. Kroll will be leaving to visit her husband at rehab in a little while. And I'm on duty at the ambulance garage starting at four this afternoon. But I'll be here until then."

Holt continued to study the pipes. "That'll be fine. I'll be back before you leave." He brushed his hands together, knocking off the dirt, and turned to face her. "I'd take Maddie with me except I also need to stop at the Marshall Funeral Home and sign some papers. I'd rather not drag her along for that."

"Marshall." As in Franklin Marshall, the county coroner. "He'll take good care of you." Zoe winced at her word choice. "I'm sorry. I just mean..." What did she mean? "I know the mortician. He's a good man."

Holt's mood had darkened again. "I'm sure. But I'm not giving him much work to do."

"What do you mean?"

"I'm having Lill cremated, and I'm not having a viewing or whatever you call it. I figure it'll be easier for Maddie to just move on."

"Not necessarily. Trying to shelter her from the reality of losing her mother won't make it easier. On either of you."

He studied her for several long moments. "You sound like you have personal experience in the matter."

"Yeah, I do." She wanted to tell him about losing her dad when she was only eight, but she had a hard enough time sharing that pain with her oldest and dearest friends. "Suffice it to say you can't protect her by avoiding the grieving process."

Holt's jaw tightened. "She's *grieving* right now. I don't see the point in prolonging it with a public display." He patted the old water tank one more time. "Now if you'll excuse me, I think it's time I head to the hardware store."

He brushed past Zoe. As she watched him disappear up the basement stairs, a nagging sense of unease tiptoed across the back of her mind.

The state fire investigator and the township fire chief continued to discuss percentages and weights of propane versus natural gas. Since their discussion was hypothetical, Pete tuned them out and strolled back to his Explorer.

Wayne Baronick caught up to him. "Something's on your mind. Care to share?"

"No."

The county detective caught Pete's arm and stepped in front, blocking his path. "If it's about this case, I'm afraid I have to insist."

Pete glared at him. "Are you taking over my case again, Wayne? It's been a while."

Baronick crossed his arms and fixed Pete with an annoyed stare. "I'm not taking over the case. But this isn't an accidental explosion anymore. It's a homicide investigation. You don't have the manpower or lab facilities to properly handle the case solo."

Pete released a growling breath. He knew that. It was the one big downfall of running a small department. And the one time he missed working on the Pittsburgh Bureau of Police. There was no use getting possessive or territorial with a case.

But he had no intention of sharing his concerns about Zoe with Baronick. There was, however, another person of interest. Pete nodded at the house with the stout fence. "Remember I told you Stephen Tierney worked for MNB?"

"Yeah?"

"He also claimed he didn't know the Farabees had moved back in."

"From the way you say 'claimed,' I assume you've found out otherwise."

Pete recounted his talk with the collections agent at the bank.

Baronick whistled. "Why did Tierney lie?"

"Good question."

Baronick checked his watch. "I'm going back to Brunswick. I'll stop at the Sleep EZ and talk to Holt Farabee—try to get some information on their marriage and their families. You take Tierney. Personally, I like the husband for this, but I'd sure be interested in what the neighbor's game is."

Pete thought about Tierney's odd reaction to hearing Lillian might have been in the house. "He may not be home yet, but I'll stop over there now and check. Either way, I'll dig into his background." Like why someone who clearly despised the country would move to rural Vance Township.

"Sounds like a plan. How about we meet at your station later this afternoon to compare notes. Say around six?"

Pete moved past the detective, heading for Fort Tierney. "Make it five," he said over his shoulder.

TEN

Pete had been right about Tierney not being home and wondered how long this business trip would last. Or was he even on a business trip? He'd already lied about one thing. Pete jotted a note to himself to call Mary Lawson at the bank.

In the meantime, he took a stroll through Scenic Hilltop Estates, knocking on the doors of the other four houses. There was no answer at one. He learned damned little at the remaining three.

Stephen Tierney kept to himself. He didn't even wave to his neighbors, much less engage them in conversation. If he had a dog, he never walked it. If he had a cat or a parakeet or a fish, he never asked anyone to feed it while he was away. He never accepted invitations to parties or picnics. And no one had ever been invited to his home.

Pete asked about any possible connection between Tierney and the Farabees, Lillian in particular, and received the same non-information. No one knew anything.

Stephen Tierney was a ghost who lived in a fort.

With a farewell shout to Bruce Yancy and the state fire marshal, Pete climbed into his SUV and headed back to Dillard.

"Messages?" he asked Nancy as he breezed past the front office.

"My dad called," she said after him. "He wants you to know Ryan still hasn't touched those hedges. The rest are on your desk."

Pete swore under his breath. He might just have to grab a pair of loppers and do the job himself.

With a cup of coffee in front of him, he thumbed through the handful of pink notes. The standard minor complaints. And one from Chuck Delano.

Nancy had scrawled, "He said to tell you he was going snorkeling. Whatever that's supposed to mean."

Pete laughed to himself. He crumpled the note and tossed it in the trash. Then he picked up the phone and punched in the number for Mary Lawson at MNB. Lawson's sultry voice carried a note of impatience after Pete had identified himself. Yes, she knew Stephen Tierney. No, she didn't know anything about him. They ran in different social circles. No, she didn't know about his travel itinerary. However, she happily transferred Pete to Tierney's office.

At the same time Tierney's phone was ringing in Pete's ear, the station's other line also rang. Pete let Nancy get it.

Instead of a secretary or another—what was he?—Investment Group Manager picking up, Pete's call went to Tierney's voicemail, which stated he would be back in the office Monday morning. That was more information than he'd gotten from anyone else.

Nancy appeared in his doorway as he hung up the phone. "Detective Baronick is on line two."

"What's wrong with the intercom?" Pete asked.

"It's broken." She turned on her heel and clomped away.

Pete sighed. He punched the button for the other line and picked up. "You're fast. What have you got?"

"Nothing."

Apparently Baronick was having as much luck as he was. "No one home?" Pete couldn't imagine why anyone wouldn't want to spend all day lounging around a room at that dump.

"He's checked out."

Pete sat up. "What do you mean? He claimed he didn't have anyplace else to go."

"He does now. The kid at the front desk didn't know squat, but I managed to persuade him to fork over the phone number Farabee had given him."

"Give it to me. I'll call him."

"You don't have to. I already did."

"And?"

"He answered."

Pete pressed his fingers into the center of his forehead. "Damn it, Wayne, quit playing games."

Baronick chuckled. "You're gonna love this. He's moved in with your girlfriend."

* * *

Zoe stood in the feed room doorway watching as Maddie brushed George, the schooling pony.

After Holt had left for the hardware store and Mrs. Kroll had gone to visit her husband at rehab, Zoe discovered she had little to amuse a ten-year-old girl other than more of her landlady's cookies. So she and Maddie walked out to the barn. Zoe distracted the girl by pointing out a circling hawk, a groundhog out in the pasture, one of the boarders riding off in the distance—anything to keep her from looking across the valley toward Scenic Hilltop Estates.

The chocolate palomino gelding had been loafing in one cool corner of the indoor arena, swishing flies with his flaxen tail. He offered no resistance when Zoe approached him, halter in hand. Small enough to not intimidate, big enough that even a small adult could take him for a spin, good old George could be trusted with youngsters who didn't know you shouldn't hug a horse's back leg, as well as rank beginner riders. He was probably close to thirty years old and had seen it all, done it all.

Maddie started out shy and standoffish with him. But after Zoe showed her how to hold a peppermint candy flat on her palm and George gently lipped it from the girl's hand, Maddie was enthralled.

Zoe handed her a brush and rubber curry and showed her how to groom the already spotless pony.

Next, Zoe demonstrated how to saddle him and put on the bridle telling the girl to watch closely because tomorrow, she'd have to do it herself.

Maddie's first riding lesson consisted of learning to steer and the importance of "whoa." The girl's ear-to-ear smile told Zoe she'd made the right decision bringing her here. As a treat, Zoe clipped the long lunge line to George's bridle, taking control from her student, and clucked him into a jog. Maddie's giggles floated into the rafters as she clutched the saddle horn and bounced around and around the circle.

Lesson over, Zoe stripped the tack from the pony, tied him to a metal ring on the wall, and stood back while Maddie groomed away the saddle marks.

The young Miss Farabee beamed at Zoe. "That was fun."

The other boarders started drifting in as Zoe helped Maddie put George in his stall. Perfect timing. Initial spills and mishaps tended to be less painful when there wasn't a crowd of seasoned riders watching. Zoe always preferred the first few lessons with a greenhorn be private. However, with the pony munching some hay, Maddie busied herself meeting the other kids. And the other kids had a chance to see who their donations would be helping. Thankfully, they were wise enough to not mention Maddie's recent traumas.

Zoe glanced at her watch. Three o'clock. The afternoon had gotten away from her. "Come on, Maddie. Time to get back to the house." Zoe hoped Holt had returned. She had to be at the ambulance garage in Phillipsburg by four.

They strolled the farm lane from the barn back to the house rather than the overgrown footpath.

"My mom would've liked it here," Maddie said.

For a moment, Zoe tried to think of some way to change the subject, but her own advice to Holt came back to her. "What was she like?"

Maddie paused to pluck a wildflower. "She was pretty. And she liked to be outside." Clutching the blossom, Maddie extended both arms and spun as if pretending to be a helicopter. "Mom hated when I played my computer games. 'Go outside and be a kid,' she'd say. I bet she'd like to ride George."

"I hear she liked to sing to you."

"Uh-huh." Maddie stopped spinning and staggered a little. "When I was little, she sang songs from cartoons to me. But she sang grownup songs, too. I kinda like those better." She stopped for a moment and fingered the flower. "You know, sometimes I think I'm gonna turn around and she's still gonna be here. Everyone tells me she died, but I don't feel like she's really gone."

The old emptiness Zoe was so familiar with sucker punched her in the solar plexus. Again. "I know what you mean. I lost my dad when I was little. Littler than you. And I still feel that way some days."

"Really?"

"Uh-huh."

Maddie sighed. "I never got to say goodbye. I hope she knows I love her."

Zoe swallowed the lump of tears in her throat. "She knows." Zoe put a hand on the girl's shoulder, and they walked the rest of the way in silence.

When they topped the hill behind the house, Zoe spotted Holt's red Ford.

"Dad's back," Maddie said, her voice light once again. "Wait until he hears what I did today." She took off at a run.

Zoe followed, but after a few yards, the girl stopped and stiffened. Zoe slowed and eased up beside her. "What's wrong?"

Holt's Ford was parked next to Zoe's Chevy. Angled behind both trucks idled a white Lexus. A man wearing an expensive-looking business suit stood at the open driver's side door, a few feet in front of Holt, who had his fists planted on his hips and his jaw jutted.

At that distance, Zoe couldn't hear what the two men were saying, but it was clear they weren't discussing the weather. Holt Farabee looked like he was on the verge of throwing a right hook, while the other guy appeared to be trying to talk him out of it.

"Who is that?" Zoe whispered, more to herself than to Maddie.

"Mr. Tierney," the girl replied in a voice low and remarkably full of venom for one so young. "Our neighbor."

Zoe eyed Maddie. "Tierney? The guy in the fort?"

Maddie blinked. "Huh?"

Zoe shook her head. "The house with the big fence."

"Yeah. Dad hates him."

Zoe stared down at the girl who didn't take her eyes from the two men. "Why does your dad hate Mr. Tierney?"

Maddie puckered her mouth. "I don't know for sure. I've just heard Mom and Dad mention his name when they were fighting. But as soon as they knew I was in the room they'd quit. When I ask questions, they say it's nothing for me to worry about. Or it's grownup stuff. Like I'm too little to understand."

While they watched, Tierney put up both hands as if surrendering—or preparing to block a punch. He said something else, slid into the Lexus, and headed down the farm lane toward Route 15.

Maddie took off down the hill at a gallop. "Dad!"

By the time Zoe reached Holt, he'd swept his daughter into his arms, lifting her off the ground.

For a moment, the girl hugged him tightly, but then she squirmed free. "I'm too old for that now, Dad."

The fury had vanished from Holt's face, replaced by the love of a father. "Excuse me. I forgot." He playfully tugged Maddie's ponytail. "What'd you and Zoe do today?"

She started chattering away, telling him about George and brushing and saddling and riding and trotting... Zoe didn't think Maddie bothered to take a breath. Holt shot a furtive glance at Zoe with a hint of a grateful smile on his face.

Maddie continued to prattle on about everything and everyone she'd encountered in the past few hours as Holt reached into one of his toolboxes, removing a bag from Brunswick Hardware and Plumbing Supply. He punctuated his daughter's rambling with an occasional "Uh-huh."

Zoe tagged along behind them toward the back porch. She had a long list of questions for her new housemate. Was he able to find a water heater and all the supplies he needed? How much would it cost?

What was going on between him and the fort guy?

But she would wait until Maddie wound down for the first ones and was out of earshot completely for the last one.

Zoe's chance came as soon as they stepped into the center hallway.

"All right, munchkin," Holt said to his flush-faced daughter. "Why don't you go upstairs and get cleaned up? I have to take some stuff down to the basement. Then you can tell me the rest over some of those cookies—if you didn't already eat them all."

"No, there're some left. I'll be right back." Maddie turned and charged up the staircase with all the grace and delicacy of a herd of stampeding elephants.

Holt turned to Zoe. "Thank you. It seems like a long time since I've seen her like that."

"My pleasure." Zoe feigned a bow. "I have to get ready for my shift at the ambulance. Is there anything I can help you with?"

"Nope. I got everything I need at the store."

Which answered one question.

"And I have a dolly in the back of my truck, so I shouldn't have any problems getting the tank down to the house."

"There's an outside entrance to the basement. You'll only have to go down two steps instead of the whole flight, which is probably a better way to get it inside."

"Great."

"I'll go out and unlatch the door."

Holt scowled. "Out?"

"There're old wooden bulkhead doors secured with a hasp and a pin from the exterior. Then there's the interior door with a slide bolt you can open from the inside."

Holt shook his head. "You gotta love old houses."

Zoe started to turn away, but her curiosity stopped her. "Holt?"

"Yeah?"

"Maddie and I saw you talking to that man in the Lexus. Is everything all right?"

Zoe caught a glimpse of a deep crease between Holt's eyes before he ducked his face away from her. "Everything's fine. He's our old neighbor. Must have spotted my truck and stopped to express his condolences."

Something about the tone of Holt's voice made the words sound sour on his tongue. Zoe wanted to press him, but she doubted he'd share anything more.

Confirming her suspicion, he turned and strode toward the basement stairs. "Go ahead and open those outer doors, okay?"

"Yeah."

Zoe headed outside. As she started around the side of the house, the rumble of an engine and the crunch of tires on the gravel lane drew her back. Vance Township PD's Ford Explorer with Pete at the wheel pulled in behind Holt's truck. She watched as Pete stepped out and stormed down the path to the backyard. His posture and the look on his face would have scared the crap out of her if she'd been a criminal.

"Where is he?" Pete demanded.

"Who?"

"You know damned well 'who.' Farabee."

"He's in the basement getting ready to put in a new water heater." Provided she opened the outer doors for him. "What's wrong?"

Pete loomed over her, striking his I-mean-business pose. "Putting in a new water heater? As I understand it, you've moved him in here."

"Well...yeah."

"First it's pony rides for the kid. Then you want to hire him to do some work. I recall I warned you against both of those ideas."

Zoe's spine stiffened. "*Warned* me against them?"

"And now you've taken him and his kid in like a couple of stray cats."

She opened her mouth to give Pete a large piece of her mind when she caught movement out of the corner of her eye. Beyond Pete, Maddie stepped off the porch, her eyes wide.

Pete had only started unloading on Zoe when he noticed her gaze shift and her face go white. He followed her gaze and saw the little girl.

Damn it. How much of his stupid rant had she overheard?

Zoe stepped around him, tucking her shoulder to completely avoid any possibility of brushing against him as she passed. "Maddie? Are you okay?"

From the look on the kid's face, she'd definitely overheard part of what Pete had said.

"Dad hollered up from the cellar. He needs you to unlock the door," she said to Zoe without shifting her gaze from Pete.

"Go back inside and tell him I'm on my way."

The girl continued to watch Pete for a moment then disappeared back inside.

Zoe spun on him. "You happy now?"

"I didn't know she was there."

Zoe stomped past him, again giving him wide berth. He followed her alongside the house to a pair of sloped and weathered wooden doors. A vintage wood wheelbarrow was propped against the stone foundation next to them. She yanked what appeared to be a broken screwdriver from the hasp securing the doors and flung one open with a *whomp*.

Inside, Holt Farabee pushed the second one open. "I thought you got lost," he quipped but caught sight of Pete and froze. "Chief Adams?"

The picture of the two of them, Farabee and Zoe, standing there at the cellar door, at ease with one another—and both perturbed with him—sent a stabbing pain through Pete's temple. "Farabee, I need you to come down to the station. I have some questions for you."

Zoe crossed her arms and stepped between them as if shielding her new best friend. "What kind of questions?"

"Zoe—"

"What. Kind. Of questions?"

The soft thud of footsteps behind him drew Pete's attention.

"Dad?" The little Farabee girl jogged up to join her father and Zoe.

Oh, great. Nothing like a ten-year-old in a ponytail to make Pete feel like an ogre. He fixed Zoe with a look he hoped said, *Work with me here.* Lowering his voice he told her, "The kind of questions I don't want to ask in front of his daughter."

ELEVEN

"It's okay, honey." Farabee climbed the stone steps out of the basement. "You go back inside."

"No." Maddie stomped her foot. "What's going on?"

The pain in Pete's temple pierced his brain and pressed into his eyes. Just what he needed. A ten-year-old acting like a four-year-old throwing a temper tantrum. "Zoe, can you watch Madison while I take him down to the station?"

"No," Zoe said, sounding a lot like the little girl. At least Zoe didn't stomp her feet. "I'm on duty tonight. In fact, I'm going to be late if I don't get out of here in a few minutes."

"Where's Mrs. Kroll?"

"Visiting her husband." Zoe moved toward Pete and lowered her voice. "What's going on? Are you arresting Holt?"

"Arresting?" Farabee's daughter said, her voice growing taut and damp. Damn, the kid had good ears. "Dad?"

Farabee knelt and pulled the girl into his arms. "It's okay, honey. No one's going to arrest me."

Pete wished Holt hadn't told her that.

While Farabee soothed his daughter, Zoe stepped closer to Pete. "What's happened?" she demanded in a whisper.

He did not want to discuss Zoe's idiotic decision to bring Holt Farabee into her home with the man standing right there anymore than he wanted to question him about his wife's homicide in front of Zoe. And he sure as hell didn't want to discuss either topic with the little girl around.

"Go get ready for work. We'll talk later."

Zoe crossed her arms. "We'll talk now."

Terrific. It wasn't the little girl on the verge of throwing a tantrum. It was Zoe. "Stop being a stubborn jackass. If you want to help, take the girl inside with you."

"Why? What's going on?"

"I'd like to know the answer to that, too," Farabee said. He'd climbed to his feet and rested one hand on his daughter's shoulder.

Pete rubbed his temple. Fine. If they both insisted he deliver his news with the girl standing right there... "The fire investigators have determined the explosion was not an accident."

Zoe looked like she'd been slapped.

The color drained from Farabee's face. He moved his hand from his daughter's shoulder to the top of her blond head. "Honey, go inside now. I'll be there in a minute."

"But, Dad—"

"No buts. Zoe? Take her inside, please."

Zoe nodded. "Come on, Maddie." She shot a glance at Pete which he interpreted to mean, "I'll deal with you later."

The fact that Zoe accommodated Farabee's appeal when she'd flat-out refused the same request from Pete wasn't lost on him either.

"All right, Chief," Farabee said once the girls had disappeared around the corner. "Ask your questions."

They retreated to the shade of a massive locust tree at the edge of the yard. Pete dug his notebook and pen from his pocket. "Who had access to your house?"

"You mean a key?"

Pete shrugged.

"No one. Lill and I were the only ones."

"None of your neighbors?"

"No."

Pete made a note. Someone else had a key. The bank. But he wasn't going to offer Farabee an easy way out. "The morning of the explosion. Take me through it."

Farabee stared at him. Was he trying to think up a story? Or was he hesitant to revisit the day he'd lost his wife?

"You and your wife got up and had breakfast," Pete prompted.

Farabee blinked. "Oh. Yeah. Lill had a job interview in Brunswick, and I was supposed to meet someone about giving an estimate."

Pete checked his notes. "Mr. Smith?"

Farabee winced. "Yeah. I'm a sucker, falling for that one, huh?"

Seth had looked into the information Farabee had provided regarding the elusive Smith. The phone number belonged to a photographer who swore he hadn't called anyone that day. The address was a vacant lot. "Where in Brunswick was your wife's job interview?"

"At the Home Depot. She left for Brunswick. I dropped Maddie off at her friend's house and headed out to meet the guy about the estimate."

"What time did your wife leave the house?"

"Must have been close to eight-fifteen, eight-thirty."

"And what time did *you* leave?"

"Five or ten minutes later. Maddie was dragging her feet and I was afraid I was going to be late."

Pete jotted the times in his notebook. "You dropped Maddie off...when?"

"Her friend lives in Dillard, so it only took maybe five minutes to get there. I didn't even get out of the truck."

"You left Dillard at about eight-forty-five?"

"Sounds about right. I was supposed to meet Smith at nine. I was a few minutes late, but there wasn't anyone there. I waited until nine-thirty and then called the number he gave me. It was some photography studio up in Butler County. The guy who answered the phone thought I was nuts."

So far, Farabee's story matched what Pete had already learned. "Then what?"

"I was pissed. Like I really need to waste gas on a wild goose chase." Farabee ran a hand across his mouth, took a couple of steps, and turned to pace back. "I called Lill on her cell. She was all excited. Happier than I'd heard her in a long time. She'd gotten the job." Farabee's expression changed from relived anger to agony. "She wanted to stay in town and do some shopping. Get herself some clothes for work and something for Maddie. We haven't had any money for so long, we've been doing without."

Pete gave him a minute, watching him struggle with raw emotion.

When Farabee continued, his voice was ragged. "I was so damned frustrated about everything, I told her not to spend money we didn't have yet. But I needed some materials for a cabinet I was building. I asked her to pick up a few things for *me* and to come straight home." He rubbed his forehead, covering his eyes for a moment. "If only I hadn't been such a... If only I'd let her do her shopping. If only I'd been the one to go straight home. It would have been *me* in the house. It *should* have been me."

"You didn't go straight home?"

"No. I should have. But I was angry and knew I needed to cool down. I drove around a while."

"Did you stop anywhere?"

"No."

"Did anyone see you?"

Realization spread across Farabee's face. "You're asking if I have an alibi?"

Pete shrugged. "One wouldn't hurt."

Farabee looked at Pete as if he had sprouted a second head. "You honestly think I'm responsible—that I had anything to do with—?" Shaking his head, Farabee stalked away, turned, and came back toward Pete with a clenched fist. "I loved my wife, Chief Adams."

"All marriages have rough spots."

"We would have gotten through this—" Farabee must have caught his slip and clamped his jaw shut.

Pete pretended he hadn't noticed, but he jotted a note to go back to Scenic Hilltop Estates and ask Farabee's neighbors specifically about problems they might have been having. "Is there anyone who might have wanted to do harm to your wife?"

"No," Farabee snapped.

"You didn't give a lot of thought to that question."

Before Farabee had a chance to respond, the screen door on the side of the house slammed, and Zoe, dressed in her paramedic's uniform, stormed out from what Pete knew was her kitchen. "Stop," she said as she approached them. "Pete, are you interrogating him without a lawyer?"

Damn it, Zoe. "I'm just getting some information for my investigation."

"Uh-huh," she said doubtfully. She pointed a finger at Farabee. "Don't answer any more questions without your lawyer."

"I don't have a lawyer."

Zoe glared at Pete but directed her words at her new housemate. "I'll give you the number for one."

Pete sighed and closed his notebook.

"Where's Maddie?" Farabee asked.

"In my kitchen having a peanut butter sandwich." Zoe hoisted a thumb toward the door she'd just come from.

"I'm gonna check on her." Farabee raised an eyebrow at Pete. "If we're done here?"

"We're done," Pete muttered.

As soon as Farabee had disappeared into the house, Zoe planted her fists on her hips. "Will you please tell me what's going on?"

"I could ask you the same question. Why are you protecting him?"

"I'm not protecting him. I'm protecting Maddie."

"And right now, that's pretty much the same thing?"

"I guess so. She's just lost her mom. He's all she has."

"Hasn't it occurred to you he might be the reason that little girl's lost her mom?"

Zoe wavered. "Maybe at first. But not now."

"At first? You mean at the fire. When you questioned why he was acting like his wife was dead when we didn't even have a body yet. When you were thinking like a cop," he reminded her.

"Before I had a chance to get to know him."

"Know him?" Pete didn't like the sound of this at all. "You *don't* know him. You feel sorry for the kid. But you don't *know* Holt Farabee. You've invited a total stranger into your home. A man you met two days ago. A man who may have rigged his house to blow up, killing his wife."

"I don't believe that."

"Why? Because you don't want to believe it?"

"You trust in your gut all the time. Well, *my* gut says he didn't have anything to do with the explosion."

"Your gut." Pete wanted to grab her and shake some sense into her. "In other words you're trusting your gut, evidence be damned."

"Evidence? What evidence?"

Pete lowered his voice in case Farabee might be listening through the screen door. "The gas line into the dryer had been tampered with.

Farabee has the handyman skills to do that. He has no alibi for the time prior to the explosion." Zoe opened her mouth to protest, but Pete held up one hand, shushing her. "And I have a sneaking suspicion he and his wife weren't as happily-ever-after as he'd like everyone to believe."

Zoe sputtered through several false starts at refuting Pete. Finally, she blew out an angry grunt. "None of that is evidence. A halfway decent defense attorney would laugh you out of court if that's all you have."

"I've just gotten started."

"You're only going after Holt because you don't like him."

"And you do?"

She pulled up short. Drew a breath. "Yeah. I do."

There it was. Zoe had held Pete at arm's length for months—years. And yet within two days, she was sharing her house with Holt Farabee, trusting his word over Pete's, and admitting she had feelings for the man. "All right." Pete nodded. "You go ahead and trust your gut. After all, it's done a fine job of guiding you with regards to men in the past."

And without waiting for her reaction, which he assumed would be a slap across his face, Pete stormed past her, heading for his vehicle.

Zoe stood, trembling in the shade of the old locust tree. Chills wracked her body while hot, furious unshed tears burned her eyes. The problem with falling in love with her best friend was he knew about all her skeletons. And he knew which buttons to push to cut the deepest.

She didn't even realize she'd walked back to her kitchen door. She didn't remember opening it, stepping inside, or letting it slam behind her. But she blinked and came back to her senses when she looked up and saw Maddie perched on the stool she kept in the corner at the far end of the long narrow room. Holt leaned against the counter next to his daughter, his forehead creased.

"Are you okay?" He sounded as though he expected her to drop dead at any second.

Maddie had stopped eating what was left of her sandwich and stared wide-eyed at Zoe. Did she look that bad?

With a glance at her watch—crap—she said, "I'm late for my shift. There's a Rolodex on my desk in the other room." She waved in the general direction of her office. "Look under 'I' for Imperatore. Anthony Imperatore. He's a lawyer and a good one. Give him a call."

"Zoe, I didn't—" Holt shot a look at Maddie. "I didn't do what Chief Adams clearly thinks I did."

"I know." Did she? "All the more reason to call Mr. Imperatore and put a stop to this nonsense now rather than later."

"You're right. Thanks."

"I really am late. Lock up when you're done in here." Zoe headed for the swinging door into her dining room/living room, but stopped next to Maddie and gave her ponytail a gentle tug. "I'm on duty until Monday morning. Tomorrow, you take your dad out to the barn and introduce him to George, okay?"

The little girl brightened. "Okay. Can I show Dad how to brush him?"

Zoe smiled. "You bet."

As she hit the door, swinging it open, Holt called out to her. "Zoe?"

She turned to him.

"Thanks." He tipped his head toward Maddie. "For everything."

Zoe nodded and pressed on through the door. She grabbed her keys from the table and paused. Had she just traded her long-time friendship with Pete to protect a man she knew nothing about? Did she really trust her gut that much?

Could Pete's words have hurt this deeply if she didn't somehow fear he might be right?

TWELVE

Wayne Baronick showed up at the Vance Township Police Station a few minutes after five. Pete gathered the county detective and Officer Kevin Piacenza, who had Friday's four-to-midnight shift, into the conference room to share and compare notes from the day.

Pete settled into a chair at the end of the long table, his notebook and a cup of coffee in front of him. "Did you find out anything about the Farabees?"

Baronick pulled his phone from a pocket. "You should be answering that question, since he'd moved to friendlier digs by the time I got to the motel."

Pete noticed the puzzled look on Kevin's face, but his officer knew enough to keep his mouth shut. "Are you telling me you didn't accomplish anything this afternoon?" Pete growled.

Baronick chuckled. "You know me better than that." He clicked his phone's screen and read from his notes. "Holt and Lillian Farabee were married twelve years ago in Ashland, Kentucky. Her parents are both deceased. His mother and father are still living in that area. I tracked down their phone number and reached the old man, but he basically told me to get lost. Only not in that nice of terms. Said he hadn't spoken to his son since shortly after the wedding. He's never even seen his granddaughter and didn't sound like he cared to, either."

"Nice guy," Pete muttered.

"Not from the sound of it. When I told him about his daughter-in-law's death, he didn't seem to care one way or the other. Nor did he care where his son and granddaughter were right now. He had no idea where they'd lived after they moved from Kentucky." Baronick tapped the screen again. "I, however, found out anyway."

Pete had no doubt. Baronick might be as annoying as hell most of the time, but he was a go-getter.

"Holt and Lillian Farabee moved from Ashland to Columbus, Ohio, which is where their only child was born. They bounced around to a half dozen locations in Ohio and Indiana, following big construction jobs, before moving to Monongahela County four years ago. He's worked on a handful of building projects here and in Allegheny County, some big, some small."

"What about the wife?"

Baronick scrolled through his notes. "She must have been a stay-at-home mom for a while because I couldn't find any employment records on her until they moved here. She worked as a secretary for the Monongahela Technical Institute until two years ago when she got laid off. Since then, she's had a few part time gigs at different shops in the mall. Nothing substantial or long-term. And I couldn't find anything at all in the last seven months."

Pete tapped his pen on his notebook. "Check the Home Depot in Brunswick."

"Oh?" Baronick shifted in his chair. "Why?"

"According to Farabee, his wife had a job interview there the morning of the explosion, and they'd hired her."

Baronick tapped out a note on his phone. "Learn anything else from him?"

Pete briefed the detective and Kevin on his interview with the grieving husband—leaving out any reference to Zoe.

"So he has no alibi for the time of the explosion," Kevin said.

Pete shrugged. "Even if he had met with someone, he was still the last person to leave the house. He had plenty of time to disconnect the dryer and open the valve after his wife left."

"And he had the know-how," Baronick added. "Although it doesn't necessarily take a skilled plumber or carpenter."

Scowling, Kevin rubbed his chin. "But why kill his wife?"

Pete thought of Farabee's slip-up. *We would have gotten through this.* "I have a feeling there was a lot of strain between them over money."

"But a lot of couples fight over money," Kevin said. "They don't generally kill each other, though."

"True." But Farabee was hiding something, possibly flat-out lying, where his wife was concerned. Pete would bet his career on it. He was already betting his relationship with Zoe on it. "Dig around," he said to both men. "I want to know what kind of marriage Holt and Lillian Farabee had and if anything had changed recently." Pete aimed his pen at Baronick. "And see what you can find out about insurance."

The detective tapped out a note on his phone. "If Farabee had a nice-sized policy on the wife, it could solve all his money troubles."

"Check his homeowner's policy, too."

"But they'd been evicted," Kevin said. "Would the policy still be in effect?"

Baronick rubbed his nose. "I'll find out. What about the neighbor who lied about knowing they were occupying the house? Tierney?"

"He wasn't home yet. According to his work voicemail, he'll be back at his desk on Monday. I'm going to keep checking at his house every time I go past." Pete pointed at Kevin. "If you see anyone around when you're on patrol, call me. And brief Seth when he comes on duty, too."

"Roger that, Chief."

The police radios on Pete's and Kevin's duty belts squawked. Kevin quickly turned the volume on his down so they wouldn't be faced with stereo transmissions. "Vance Base, this is Mon Dispatch."

Nancy had left for the day, so Pete keyed his mic. "Dispatch, this is Vance Unit Thirty."

"Unit Thirty, respond to a traffic collision with injuries. Thirteen forty-eight Phillipsburg Road."

Good thing Nancy wasn't there. "Ten-four, Dispatch. Units Thirty and Thirty-one responding."

Kevin was on his feet even before Pete. "Isn't that...?"

"Yeah," Pete growled.

Baronick remained seated. "Someone you know?"

"I hope not. But we're familiar with the address. It belongs to my secretary's parents." Pete followed Kevin out the door, calling back over his shoulder, "And there's been an ongoing argument about hedges."

* * *

Hot water was a marvelous thing, even when the temperatures outside sizzled. Hair damp, but the rest of her clean and dressed in a fresh uniform, Zoe stepped out of the crew shower room at the Monongahela County EMS and nearly collided with her partner.

"I was just about to knock and ask how long you were gonna be." Earl Kolter crooked a finger at her. "We're up."

She jogged after him, through the front office and into the garage, grabbing her ball cap from the peg on the wall. "What have we got?"

Earl circled around to the driver's side of Medic Two. "Traffic accident with injuries."

She leaped into the passenger seat, and Earl tossed her the note with the address so she could start filling out a run report. As the ambulance rocked out of the bay and onto Main Street, Zoe grabbed the mic. "Control, this is Medic Two. We're en route to..." She checked the note. "...thirteen forty-eight Phillipsburg Road."

"Ten-four, Medic Two. Seventeen-twenty-three."

Zoe jotted the time—the military version of 5:23 p.m.—on the run report and started filling in the little information they had at this point.

Earl flipped on the siren through town, easing around the cars that moved out of their way. "You want to tell me what's going on?" he asked over the wail.

Zoe pretended to focus on the form on the clipboard. "What do you mean?"

"Coming in late? That's not like you. What's up?"

She fingered her damp curls. "The water heater at home is broken."

"I got that much. All the more reason to come in early."

"I intended to."

She and Earl had been partners for years. On the job, they knew each other's strengths and weaknesses. They'd developed a kind of communication shorthand, and working on a patient became a well-choreographed dance.

Between calls, they shared an easy friendship born of having each other's backs in the trenches. On slow nights, they were hard-to-beat euchre partners against the other crew members. Off duty, she attended his kids' birthday parties. He was part of the poker gang, which also included Pete, Sylvia, Seth, and Yancy.

Earl knew about her lousy romantic history, but was smart enough to not ask for details. When he fell quiet, she assumed he was going to let the matter of her tardiness drop.

As they reached the edge of Phillipsburg, for a moment traffic cleared. He reached over and silenced the siren. "You want to talk about it?"

So much for letting it drop. "Not really."

Even keeping her eyes on the report, she caught the glance he shot her. "Does it have anything to do with Pete?"

She wanted to snap at him. Mind your own business. But getting snippy on the way to a call wasn't exactly professional. Instead, she kept quiet.

Earl whooped the siren as they approached Dillard. "I'll take that as a yes."

She thumbed through the copies of old reports stashed in a pocket on the aluminum clipboard's lid for no reason other than avoidance.

"Look. I don't know what happened between you two, and you sure don't have to tell me. But it's like ambulance crew romances. Everything is hunky dory until you have a spat and have to face the other person at work."

As if punctuating the point, they blew past the Vance Township Police Department. Zoe noticed Pete's SUV wasn't in the lot. It was late enough he should be off duty. In fact, with any luck, she wouldn't have to face him all weekend. Maybe by Monday, she'd have sorted through this mess and could track him down and apologize.

Better yet...he could apologize to her.

Pete encountered stopped traffic and brake lights a half mile back, which was never a good sign. The knot in his stomach cranked tighter as he topped the hill a quarter mile shy of the scene and was treated to his first look at the accident.

Except for Kevin's vehicle in Pete's rearview mirror, there wasn't an emergency strobe in sight. They were first on2 the scene. A southbound semi was jackknifed across both lanes, blocking Pete's view. Damn. He hoped the tractor trailer had gotten in that position trying to stop as opposed to having collided with something. Or someone.

With traffic unable to get through coming from the other side of the crash, Pete cruised along the clear northbound lane, passed the stopped southbound traffic, and braked to a stop on the berm. Kevin parked behind him and met him as he stepped out. The whoop of distant sirens rising above the throaty rumble of idling vehicles told him they wouldn't have to man the scene alone for long.

A few of the cars had shut off their engines and their occupants stood together in the road, talking in hushed tones. With Kevin on his heels, Pete jogged around the semi, noting the heavy black skid marks on the pavement as the trucker had made every effort to stop.

Besides the tractor trailer, three other vehicles with varying degrees of damage littered the two-lane road. It wasn't hard to guess what had happened. Jack Naeser had nosed his Hyundai out a tad too far in order to see around those hedges. A white pickup had clipped his front fender, knocking the car into Naeser's yard and sending the pickup into a 180, which left its back bumper rammed against the hillside across the road. A third vehicle, a black Toyota Rav4, must have slammed on its brakes to avoid hitting the truck only to be rear-ended by the jackknifing semi. If obvious damage was any indicator, the entire scene could have been much, much worse.

A woman remained behind the wheel of the Rav4. A concerned-looking heavy-set man stood at her passenger window and waved at the officers. Pete guessed he was the trucker and motioned to his officer. "Kevin, check them out."

"Got it, Chief."

The white pickup with the mashed right front fender was empty, so Pete headed for Naeser's car. A familiar and noisy crowd had gathered next to it.

Jack Naeser sat on the ground leaning against the Hyundai's driver's door. He pressed his left hand to the side of his head, blood trailing down his face. Mrs. Naeser was on her knees next to him, weeping. Ryan Mancinelli, the hedge-loving son-in-law, stood over him, bellowing at Ashley, who raged right back at her husband. A tall man Pete didn't recognize stood holding a cowboy hat and looking like he'd pay a small fortune to be anywhere except where he was at the moment.

Pete waded into the middle of the group and summoned his take-charge voice. The one that cut through most turmoil. "Ryan. Ashley. Give it a rest." They both fell quiet, and Pete knelt beside the Naesers. "Jack? How bad are you hurt?"

Naeser lowered his bloodied hand to reveal a gash above his left temple. "I don't know. Must've whacked my head pretty good when that guy creamed me."

"I'm really sorry," the cowboy sputtered, worrying the rim of his hat. "He pulled out smack dab in front of me. I never even had a chance to hit my brakes until it was too late."

"It's those damned hedges," Mrs. Naeser said, her voice shaky.

"Look," Ryan Mancinelli said, "I told you how awful I feel. What more do you want me to say?"

And then Mancinelli's wife and mother-in-law launched into a renewed tirade about hedges being more important than Naeser's life and stubborn jackasses and would-haves and should-haves.

The cowboy clearly would have preferred to face a raging bull. He took a big step back.

Pete's take-charge voice wasn't going to cut it. He stood, brought his finger and thumb to his lips and let loose with a piercing whistle that silenced everyone. He pointed to Mancinelli and his wife then to their house. "You two go wait on your porch. I'll talk to you shortly."

Chagrined, they nodded and headed away. Mancinelli reached for his wife's arm, but she jerked it free. Pete shook his head. Happily ever after? Yeah. Right.

From the sounds of the sirens winding down on the other side of the jackknifed semi, he guessed medical help had arrived. He looked at the cowboy. "How about you? Are you hurt?"

"No, sir, I'm fine."

"I need to talk to you as soon as we get Mr. Naeser taken care of."

The cowboy gave his pickup a dejected glance and sighed. "I ain't goin' anywhere."

Pete checked the progress of the emergency medical response and spotted Zoe and Earl speaking with the driver of the Rav4 through her window.

Zoe. Damn it. Every other time they'd worked a scene together, he'd been happy to see her. This evening, he didn't have the luxury of sorting through the debacle their relationship had become. He had to stay focused on the accident scene. At least it was less messy.

"Chief?" Mrs. Naeser said.

Pete squatted next to her and her husband. "Yes, ma'am?"

The worry in her dark eyes had sparked into anger. "I want you to arrest my son-in-law."

"Arrest? Ma'am, I'm afraid not trimming his hedges isn't against the law."

Bitter tears glistened. "I don't want you to arrest him for not trimming his hedges. I want you to arrest him for attempted murder."

"My neck hurts. A little."

The redhead behind the wheel of the Toyota Rav4 seemed more scared than injured when Zoe asked her if she was all right. But any indication of possible whiplash couldn't be ignored. "Anything else? How about your back? Your legs?"

The woman moved her lower extremities in response. "No. I'm fine. Except for my neck. And it doesn't hurt much. I'm probably fine. Right?"

Zoe smiled. "Probably. But you should let us take you to the hospital and get it checked out anyway."

The redhead took a trembling breath. "Okay."

Earl touched Zoe's shoulder. "I'm gonna call for a second ambulance. Then I'll get the collar and backboard and take her vitals. You check on the guy over there." He motioned toward Pete and a man sitting next to one of the other cars.

Zoe shot a look at her partner. The last person she'd wanted to see was Pete, and Earl knew that. But he'd turned his back and headed to the ambulance at a trot. Thanks, pal. Payback was gonna be a bitch.

"You sit tight," she told the woman in the car. "My partner will be right back. I'm going to see if the gentleman over there needs treatment."

Zoe grabbed the jump kit and strode toward the Hyundai with the mashed fender. A man she recognized as Jack Naeser sat on the ground next to his car. Pete was engaged in an intense conversation with Naeser's wife.

"There has to be something you can do," the woman was pleading as Zoe arrived.

Pete looked exhausted. He met Zoe's eye for the briefest moment before shaking his head at Mrs. Naeser. "I'm afraid not. Ryan hasn't broken any law."

The woman opened her mouth to reply, but Pete held up a hand. "You help the paramedics tend to your husband. I'll go get a statement from your son-in-law. That's the best I can do."

If Pete made any gesture to Zoe, she didn't see it. Instead, she dropped to her knees beside her patient and gently took his wrist, fingering a pulse. "How are you feeling, Mr. Naeser?"

"Like I've been hit by a truck, how do you *think* I feel?"

"Jack," his wife scolded gently. "Be nice."

"Can you tell me what happened here?" Zoe asked, as much to determine his cognition as to learn the details of the crash.

While Naeser spewed his story of overgrown hedges and not being able to see to pull out of his own goddamned driveway, Zoe opened the jump kit and ripped into a stack of sterile gauze pads, using them to blot away some of the blood. Head wounds bled excessively and this one didn't look quite so bad once she'd cleaned him up a bit.

She tore into three more of the 4x4 squares and pressed them against the gash. "Hold these." She took his hand and positioned it over the bandage.

He winced but obeyed.

Zoe plucked her penlight from a pocket in her cargo pants to check his pupils. Equal and reactive. Naeser continued his story, and she continued her eval, taking his blood pressure—elevated—and his respirations.

"Do you have any history of heart disease or stroke?"

"No," Naeser barked.

"Yes," his wife said. "He refuses to admit it, but he had a TIA a little over a year ago."

Transient Ischemic Attack. Mini-stroke.

Naeser snorted. "I was just overly tired is all."

Mrs. Naeser narrowed her eyes. "That's not what the doctor said."

Indignant, Naeser pushed away from the car, drawing one leg in, moving to stand up. "You think I got hit because I had some kind of spell?"

Zoe put both hands on his shoulders, blocking him gently. "Not at all. I just have to ask."

He sat back. "Oh."

Zoe added more sterile squares to the blood-soaked ones and opened a package of sterile bandaging. "Are you on any prescription drugs?"

"Yeah, but I don't know what they are."

"I have a list in my purse," Mrs. Naeser said.

"Good." Zoe touched Mr. Naeser's arm. "Your vitals are fine, but I think you should let us transport you to the hospital to be checked out."

"I don't need an ambulance."

She shifted her gaze to the wife. "At the very least, he'll need some stitches. But head injuries can be serious. You really want to rule out a concussion." Or something worse. Zoe raised an eyebrow at Mrs. Naeser, hoping the wife got the message without making Zoe say it out loud. She didn't want to further rile the man if she could avoid it.

Mrs. Naeser crossed her arms and fixed her husband with a hard stare. "Let them take you in the ambulance, Jack. I don't want to drive you to the hospital and have you pass out halfway there."

The man mumbled something Zoe couldn't quite make out.

She hid her smile. Poor Jack Naeser didn't stand a chance.

THIRTEEN

"Your mother-in-law wants me to arrest you for attempted murder." Pete dropped the bomb without letting Ryan Mancinelli know the charge was ridiculous. Scare the guy a little. Maybe a little fear, even unfounded, might be what it took to get him to trim those damned hedges.

"Attempted murder?" Mancinelli's reaction was exactly what Pete had hoped. Panic. "She—you—can't do that. Can you?"

The correct answer was *no*, but Pete leaned on the Mancinelli's porch railing and kept mum.

Mancinelli turned to his wife, who stood at their front door, her arms crossed and shoulders hunched. "You need to talk to your mother. Tell her. I—I never intended—" He waved at the Hyundai and the pickup. "This was just an accident. I never wanted your father to get hurt. I sure didn't want to *murder* him!"

Ashley's lower lip trembled. Pete wasn't certain if her tears were a result of anger at her husband or fear for her dad. She uncrossed her arms, although her fists stayed balled, and looked at Pete. "Do it. Arrest him. I'll give a statement or testify or whatever you need me to do." She turned on her husband. "Just don't expect me to post your bail."

Anger. Definitely tears of anger.

She wheeled and slammed through her front door.

Clearly stunned, Mancinelli stared after her, his jaw slack.

Pete hadn't anticipated the wife's reaction, but decided to go with it. "Look, Ryan. I know you never meant for this to happen. And the court systems are overwhelmed. No one wants to add to the burden."

Mancinelli's mouth had clamped shut—the exact opposite of his eyes—and he nodded then shook his head.

"The way I see it," Pete went on with his good cop routine, "you have an easy way out."

"I do?"

Damn, the guy was dense. Or maybe terror had dulled his brain cells. Pete gripped Mancinelli by one shoulder and gave him a wake-up shake. "Cut the hedges."

Mancinelli reacted as if the idea was entirely new to him. "Oh. Yeah. I guess I should."

"Yeah. You should."

"If I promise to trim them will you not arrest me?"

Pete pretended to give the proposition serious thought. "All right." He neglected to add he wasn't going to arrest Mancinelli either way. "I think if you do that, I can even talk your mother-in-law out of pressing charges." Mancinelli's wife was another matter, but she wasn't Pete's problem.

Mancinelli blew out a breath. "Okay. I'll do it. I promise. I'll go get my trimmer right now."

"You should wait until we clear the wreckage."

"Sure. No problem." He gazed past Pete and tipped his head. "I think someone's looking for you."

Pete turned to see Zoe striding his way. For a second he forgot they weren't getting along and smiled, descending the porch steps to greet her. Then the memory of Holt Farabee living under Zoe's roof slapped the smile off his face.

"We have a second ambulance on the way." Zoe hooked her thumbs in the front pockets of her pants and cocked one hip. "The lady in the SUV is complaining of neck pain. Mr. Naeser probably just needs stitches, but I can't rule out a concussion or a closed head injury."

Pete shifted his position to keep an eye on Mancinelli. With the threat of an arrest off his shoulders, the guy had slouched into a chair on the porch. Keeping his voice low, Pete asked her, "Has Naeser's wife calmed down any?"

Zoe glanced toward the Hyundai. "She's not letting him back out of going to the hospital, if that's what you mean."

It wasn't. But as long as she'd quit ranting about attempted murder charges, maybe Pete could see that the offending hedges were trimmed before the Naesers returned from the hospital.

One item off his caseload. "Zoe, we need to talk."

Her jaw jutted. "I have to get back to my patient."

Pete caught her arm as she spun away from him. "I'm sorry," he said, lowering his voice. He'd prefer to keep his personal business personal, but suspected Ryan Mancinelli's ears had perked up. "I had no right to say what I did."

Her eyes, filled with steely resolve, met his, but she didn't say a thing.

"You know I respect your instincts. But you're letting that little girl cloud your judgment."

Zoe bristled. "And you have tunnel vision where Holt's concerned."

Pete winced. He should have stopped after the *respect your instincts* comment. "Will you at least consider the possibility he might be involved in his wife's death?"

"What happened to innocent until proven guilty?"

"I'm a cop, not a lawyer. Not a judge or a jury. Neither are you. If you want to be a coroner and investigate homicides, you better learn that."

"So you have free rein to railroad someone just because you don't like them?"

"No." Pete sputtered. "I'm not railroading Holt Farabee. I'm investigating his wife's death. He may or may not have played a part in it. But until I clear him, I'd prefer the woman I love not live under the same roof with the man."

Zoe's eyes widened, and a hush fell over the entire accident scene with the exception of the idling motors of stopped traffic and rescue vehicles.

Pete realized his voice had risen more than he'd been aware. The Naesers at the end of their driveway, the cowboy by his pickup, Earl, two firefighters, and the truck driver standing next to the Rav4 all stared at him. Pete glanced at Ryan Mancinelli, whose face had gone ashen.

Damn it. Pete had just professed his love for Zoe in the worst possible manner. He wished she'd slap him. Hard. "Zoe, I'm sorry..."

She wrenched free from his grasp and walked away without another word. Pete closed his eyes and gave himself a silent tongue lashing. Idiot. Moron. Stupid son of a bitch. Could he possibly screw up his chances with her any worse?

Mortified, Zoe strode toward the Rav4 and her partner. "What's the second unit's ETA?"

Ever the voice of reason and the face of calm, Earl checked his watch. "Should be here any minute now. In fact, I think I hear them coming."

Over the roar inside her head, she made out the faint siren in the distance. She nodded at the two Vance Township firefighters staring at her. "You have enough help extricating her from the car, right?"

"Right."

"Okay, then I'll keep an eye on Mr. Naeser until the other ambulance arrives. Holler if you need a hand."

"We're fine."

Zoe rubbed at the stabbing pain piercing her skull above her left eyebrow as she made her way back to the wrecked Hyundai while keeping her gaze on the ground in front of her. The last thing she wanted was to make eye contact with anyone.

Had Pete just said he loved her?

Had he then *apologized* for it?

Why on earth had she thought they could be anything more than friends? She'd known better. Or should have. Never. Again.

And yet... He loved her.

She'd been crazy about him for years. Wanting him. Fantasizing about him. Resisting her feelings for him...

"Ma'am?"

Zoe looked up into the concerned face of the guy in the cowboy hat and boots. She winced. *Ma'am?* When had she ceased being a *Miss?* And when had she stopped walking?

"Are you all right?" With that drawl, he was definitely not a local boy.

"I'm fine," she muttered and brushed past him.

She risked a glance toward Ryan Mancinelli's front porch.

Pete was no longer there, but Mancinelli leaned against one of the pillars, watching her.

She wondered if *everyone* was watching her, and her face burned.

She dropped to her knees beside Jack Naeser, noting the bandage on his head had soaked through. "How are you doing?" She caught his wrist, palpating his pulse. Focus on the patient. Put everything else out of her mind.

The man scowled. "I've got a whopper of a headache."

"I don't doubt it." His heart rate was slightly elevated.

"His head's still bleeding," Mrs. Naeser said.

"I see. Head wounds do tend to bleed profusely." But Zoe didn't like the looks of him. He was paler than before and a sheen of sweat glistened on his face. "Mrs. Naeser, those prescriptions he's on, are any of them blood thinners?"

"Yes. I think it's called war—war something."

"Warfarin."

"That's it."

Crap. "You might want to get your purse and that list now." Zoe looked toward the semi, relieved to see Tony DeLuca and Vickie Spencer, the crew from Medic One, dragging a gurney around the jackknifed rig. She waved them toward her.

Before they reached Zoe and her patient, a younger woman, who Zoe recognized as the Naesers' daughter, jogged up. "What's going on? Is Dad going to be all right?"

Zoe caught Mrs. Naeser's gaze. "Why don't you both go get her purse?"

"Okay," Mrs. Naeser said, but Zoe noticed the woman and her daughter didn't budge.

"What've you got?" Tony DeLuca asked.

Zoe fired off a quick summary on the patient, including the warfarin. "I want a new BP. And let's get him on the gurney and elevate his legs."

The three medics didn't need to say it out loud. They all knew they were dealing with a patient who was getting shocky.

As a team, they moved the gurney next to Naeser, took a new set of vitals which revealed, as Zoe had suspected, a lowered blood pressure, and started him on oxygen. Tony helped him onto the cot with a pillow under his lower legs, and Zoe and Vickie covered him with a light blanket and strapped him down.

The daughter's voice rose over the stethoscope plugged into Zoe's ears as she rechecked Naeser's BP. "What's going on?"

Zoe looked up. Mother and daughter clung to each other, both wide-eyed. She held up one finger to them and finished listening to the thud-dub of Naeser's heart while releasing the blood pressure cuff's valve. "One-oh-eight over fifty-six," she announced to Vickie. Zoe turned to the worried pair. "He's bleeding a little heavier than normal because of the warfarin. Tony and Vickie will be taking him to Brunswick. He's in excellent hands."

Both women nodded.

Zoe focused on the daughter. "Can you drive your mother to the hospital?"

"Yeah."

Tony clapped Zoe on the back. "We're taking off. We'll get an IV started once we get him in the ambulance."

Zoe waved, and Tony and Vickie wheeled the gurney and patient away.

"We'll be right behind you, Dad," the daughter called after them.

"Drive safely, okay?" Zoe told her.

The young woman gave her a weak smile, but her gaze shifted over Zoe's shoulder, and the smile faded.

Zoe turned to see Ryan Mancinelli headed their way.

"I need to talk to you," he said.

Zoe could have sworn his words were directed at her instead of his wife or mother-in-law.

But his wife strode toward him and gave him a shove that staggered him. "Stay away from me and my family, you bastard. I don't ever want to see you again. Do you hear me? We're through!"

In the next moment, both women were screaming at Mancinelli, who held up his hands in surrender and babbled apologies to no avail. Zoe looked around frantically for Pete. She was still furious with him, but she feared a murder was imminent unless someone intervened. Preferably someone big and commanding, carrying a sidearm.

Instead of Pete, Kevin trotted their way. At the same time, she heard her name being called. Earl waved at her from beside the Rav4. He and the two firefighters had their patient stabilized on a backboard and gurney.

Without waiting for more blood to be shed, Zoe grabbed her jump kit and ran.

Saturday was supposed to be Pete's day off.

Sleep had been sparse. He never needed a reason for insomnia, but the look on Zoe's face last night haunted him into the wee hours of the morning. When he did drift off, he dreamed he was in the center of an angry mob closing in. By five a.m., he was showered and shaved. By six, he'd had breakfast and three cups of coffee and was sitting in his basement workshop.

He worked a third coat of linseed oil and beeswax into the heavy stock of the reproduction Jaeger flintlock rifle he'd been building for almost a year. With any luck, it would be ready for this fall's deer season.

Fall. Three months away. To be quickly followed by winter. Bitter cold, icy, snowy, blustery winter.

Unless he took Chuck up on his offer.

Pete brushed an arm across his forehead. No way. Maui would not be good fit. He wasn't cut out to live in paradise.

Was he?

He dipped his rag in the small can holding the oil, letting the excess drip off. He stared at the amber droplets and replayed recent events in his mind. How could one man so completely derail a relationship in only two days?

He'd handled everything wrong. Everything. From criticizing Zoe's interest in helping a little girl to dredging up her less-than-stellar history with men—as if his history with women was anything to brag on—to last night's angry outburst, which very publicly humiliated both of them.

Damn.

Pete smoothed the oil onto the stock and watched the grain pattern darken. If only he could oil his brain and bring a solution to his stupidity to the surface.

His cell phone rang, interrupting his thoughts. Thank heavens. He draped the oily rag on a hook, wiped his hands on a paper towel, and picked up the phone. The station's number filled the screen.

"Chief," Seth said when Pete answered. "I'm sorry to bother you so early, but Ryan Mancinelli called here for you. Said he needs to talk to you. And he sounded like it was pretty important."

"I don't suppose he said what it was about."

"No, sir. I asked. He said he didn't want to get into it on the phone."

Pete rubbed his right temple. "Any word on Jack Naeser's condition?" If anything had happened to Naeser, Mancinelli might be seeking protective custody.

"No. Do you want me to call the hospital and find out?"

"That won't be necessary. Do you have a call-back number on Mancinelli?"

Pete jotted down the number as Seth read it to him. Five minutes later, after washing his oily hands, Pete placed the call to the township's hedge lover.

"This is Chief Adams," he said when Mancinelli answered. "I understand you wanted to talk to me."

"Yeah, I do." His voice sounded tight over the phone. "Can I meet you at the station?"

Pete checked the clock on the wall. "How soon?"

"Eight o'clock?"

"Fine. How's your father-in-law?"

There was silence on the line for a moment, and Pete thought they might have been cut off. But he heard Mancinelli take a breath. "I don't know. My wife isn't answering her phone. At least, she isn't answering for me."

Pete wasn't the only one screwing up relationships this week. "Is that what you want to talk to me about?"

Pete was prepared to assure the kid his mother-in-law could not press attempted murder charges, but Mancinelli replied, "No. That's not it at all." There was another long silence before he said, "I have information about Holt and Lillian Farabee."

FOURTEEN

Groggy from a Friday night of nonstop calls and little sleep, Zoe sat in the ambulance garage office at the desk, filling out the last incident report. The coffee in front of her would do nothing to hinder slumber if she could only manage to sneak off to the bunkroom. The morning sunshine streamed through the large picture window, promising a gorgeous Saturday. Which meant folks would be outside, playing sports, riding motorcycles—and getting injured.

Her cell phone buzzed in her cargo pants pocket. She pulled it out and checked the screen, but didn't recognize the number. For a moment, she considered ignoring it, but touched the button to answer the call instead.

"Zoe? It's Holt."

The grim tone of his voice tightened her chest. "Holt? Is something wrong?"

"No, no. I'm sorry. I didn't mean to scare you. I have some business I need to attend to today, and Mrs. Kroll will be visiting her husband. I was wondering if you know of someone dependable who could watch Maddie for a few hours."

A babysitter? Zoe rubbed the space between her eyes, trying to coax her brain into action. With Patsy Greene in Florida and Rose Bassi still somewhere out west, her first two choices weren't available. But an even better choice leapt to mind. "Sylvia," Zoe said.

"Who?"

"Sylvia Bassi. She loves kids."

"Is she..." His voice sounded strained. Cautious. "...reliable?"

Zoe laughed. "As reliable as they come."

A shadow swept the room as a pedestrian passed the window.

"I hate to be a pest," Holt said, "but if I call her, she won't know me from Adam."

"I'll call her and have her phone you at the house." The front door to the office scraped open, and Zoe looked up to see Pete with the sun at his back. In a flash, all her conflicted emotions steamrolled over her. Joy. Longing. Pain. Heartbreak. She turned her attention back to the phone. "Unless you'd rather have her call your cell?"

"Either is fine."

"And if I can't reach her, I'll call you back and let you know."

Holt, sounding relieved, thanked her and hung up.

Zoe hesitated, staring at the screen and the End button. Clicking it would mean having to deal with Pete. She could feel his gaze on her. And no footsteps from the back indicated anyone else was coming to invite him in. She tapped the screen and rose to face him.

Deep creases furrowed Pete's brow. Wearing a faded t-shirt and jeans, he stood with a hand on the doorknob as if unsure whether he was coming or going. Or staying.

Zoe let the phone slide back into her pocket before crossing her arms. "Did you want something?"

He winced. Opened his mouth. Closed it again. And stepped the rest of the way inside, shutting the door behind him. "How about a do-over?"

He looked so uncomfortable, Zoe had to resist an urge to smile. "A do-over? Of what?"

"Of yesterday. And Thursday night if I can get two."

Zoe pretended to consider it. "Nope. No do-overs."

He lowered his gaze. "Damn." Raised an eyebrow in her direction. "Well then, can you just throw something at me? Or punch me? I deserve it."

"Is this your way of saying you're sorry?"

"God, no. I tried that last night and it made things worse."

They stared at each other for several long moments, the silence only broken by the staticky transmissions from the scanner on the shelf above the desk. Zoe unfolded her arms, planting her hands on her hips instead. "You really suck at apologies, you know."

"I do. Yeah." He gave her a hint of a grin. "But what they lack in quality, they make up for in sincerity. I really am sorry."

"For what?" There was the little profession of love he'd already apologized for.

He must have thought of that, too, because he took a moment to weigh his words. "For being a jackass?"

Zoe gave him an exaggerated eye roll. "I guess that'll do."

He stepped toward her with an extended hand. "Friends?"

She looked at the hand. Friends? So they were back to that? Well, maybe it was for the best. She slipped her hand into his. "Friends."

But he held onto it for longer than a friendly handshake, and the heat of his skin against hers sent a flush of warmth all the way up to her cheeks.

Gently slipping from his grasp, she said, "You're out and about early on a Saturday."

"I'm meeting someone at the station at eight. I thought I'd swing by here on my way."

"On your way?" The police station was a little more than two blocks up the hill from Pete's house in Dillard. The ambulance garage was two miles away at the other end of Phillipsburg.

Pete grinned sheepishly. "Okay, I took the long way around. I hated the way I left things with you yesterday."

"Who are you meeting?" Zoe thought of Holt saying he had *business* to attend to. *Police* business?

A fleeting scowl crossed Pete's face. "Ryan Mancinelli wants to see me."

Zoe hid her relief. "How's his father-in-law doing?"

"I haven't heard."

"Keep me posted, okay? He had me a little worried."

Pete's eyes had grown guarded again and he glanced at his watch. "Okay. I'd better go or I'll be late." He gave her a look she couldn't quite decipher before leaving.

She watched him pass in front of the big window. He may have apologized, in his own way, but he was keeping her at arm's length about something. And she suspected the *something* was Holt.

Which reminded her... She pulled her phone back out and scrolled through her address book in search of Sylvia's number.

* * *

No way was Pete going down that rabbit hole again. Zoe didn't need to know the reason he was meeting Ryan Mancinelli was because he claimed to have information about Holt and Lillian Farabee.

Pete slid behind the wheel of the Explorer, fired it up, and headed back to Dillard.

Zoe hadn't exactly accepted his fumbling excuse of an apology with wild abandon. But had he really expected she would? While he might have hoped she'd run sobbing into his arms, offering her own request for forgiveness—along with a promise to give Farabee the boot and never see him again—Pete knew better. As long as Farabee was in the picture, Pete had two options. Prove the widower was indeed guilty, followed by refraining from any and all I-told-you-sos. Or prove Zoe was right and Farabee had nothing to do with the explosion, followed by the biggest apology of Pete's life, which may, or may not, have the desired effect.

Something else bugged him. Who was she on the phone with when he'd arrived? He'd wanted to ask. Casually. And up until a few days ago, he would have. He was a cop. Being nosy was a hazard of the job. Zoe understood. Or used to. But he had a feeling he knew who she was talking to. And if that was the case, her answer would have put an end to any kind of reconciliation he'd been attempting.

His SUV's dashboard clock read 7:56 as he wheeled into the lot in front of the station and parked in his usual spot. A shiny, but dented Impala with the Vance Township insignia took up another slot, and a massive black Ram pickup with "Ryan Mancinelli Building and Remodeling" painted on the side took up two others.

Bells on the front door jangled as Pete pushed through, his travel mug of coffee in hand. Seth sat at Nancy's desk, sifting through some papers. He looked up. "Hey, Chief. I put Ryan Mancinelli in the conference room."

"Good. Any word on Naeser?"

"I haven't heard anything. Do you want me to call Nancy and ask about him?"

"Yeah. Anything else going on around here I need to know about?"

Seth grinned. "It's your day off, or have you forgotten?"

Pete glared at his officer. "Smartass." As chief of police, days off were little more than wishful thinking.

"It was a busy night. Besides the pile-up involving Naeser and Mancinelli, there was a minor car versus tree on Covered Bridge Road. Drunk driver had a nice goose-egg, but wasn't feeling any pain." Seth ticked off a half dozen other relatively minor calls before tipping his head toward the rear of the building. "Nate's back in the bullpen getting ready to head out on patrol. I'm looking for some phone numbers in Nancy's stuff so I can finish one more report and then I'm outta here."

Pete nodded approval. "Do me a favor. Catch Nate before he leaves and tell him to wait for me. I want to talk to him."

"Yes, sir."

Ryan Mancinelli sat at the conference table, facing the door, and rose when Pete entered. He swayed as if he'd caught a breeze, and his bloodshot eyes widened, leading Pete to wonder if the kid had been drinking.

Pete motioned for Mancinelli to sit and eased into the chair across from him. "You said you had information on the Farabees?" Unblinking, Mancinelli gave a quick nod. When he didn't respond, Pete asked, "What kind of information?"

Mancinelli looked down at his hands, which were clasped on the table in front of him, as if he were praying. "They were having problems."

Pete waited for more, but Mancinelli simply stared at his fingers. "What kind of problems?"

Mancinelli flinched. "Marital problems. Holt found out his wife was having an affair. It made him crazy. He threatened her."

"He threatened her, how?"

Mancinelli shot a glance at Pete before once again examining his hands. "He said he'd kill her."

Pete studied what he could see of Ryan Mancinelli's face, which wasn't much. But the man's entire body appeared so tightly strung, Pete wouldn't have been surprised if he keeled over at any second. "Did you hear him threaten her?"

"Yes."

"When?"

Mancinelli sneaked another look at Pete. "I don't know. A couple of different times."

"You're friends with Farabee?"

Mancinelli opened his mouth, but no sound came out for a moment. Then he said, "Yes." And nothing more.

"How long have you been friends?"

"I don't know. About three years, I guess."

"You say Farabee threatened to kill his wife. Do you believe he did?"

Mancinelli looked up at Pete and held his gaze this time. The look on his face was pained, almost pleading. "Yes."

"I don't suppose you know with whom Lillian Farabee was supposedly having this affair?"

Mancinelli gave a quick nod. "Their neighbor. Stephen Tierney."

The fort dweller.

After ascertaining Mancinelli had nothing else to share, Pete thanked him and watched as the man bolted out the door. Pete leaned back in the chair, took a sip of his coffee, and pondered the story. Mancinelli had confirmed several of Pete's suspicions about the events at Scenic Hilltop Estates. He'd verified Holt Farabee was a viable murder suspect.

The problem nagging at Pete now was simple.

He was pretty damned sure Ryan Mancinelli was lying through his teeth.

"Seth said you wanted to see me, Chief?" Officer Nate Williams took up most of the doorway to the front office. If there was ever a police officer who could settle an altercation by simply stepping out of the cruiser, it was Nate. No one in their right mind wanted to mess with this guy.

"I gather Seth updated you on what's been going on?"

"Yeah." There was an air of caution in that one word.

Pete wondered how much detail Seth had shared regarding Farabee's current living arrangements. "I want to talk to Stephen Tierney."

"The dude who lives behind the big fence?"

"That's the one. He's been out of town on business and I know he's supposed to be back at work on Monday. What I don't know is when he's coming home. I'm heading there now to check on his house. I'll call you if he's there. If not, make an extra effort to patrol the area, and let me know if you spot him."

"Is this an official BOLO?"

Pete thought about it. "No. Be on the lookout, but not officially. Not yet."

One corner of Nate's mouth tipped up. "Got it, Chief."

A few minutes later, Nate was heading north in the old Impala, and Pete headed south along Route 15 toward the Kroll farm—by way of Scenic Hilltop Estates.

Nothing much had changed at the remains of Farabee's house. Yellow caution tape marked the perimeter. The state fire marshal's car sat at the edge of the road, and Pete recognized Reggie O'Brien still combing through the debris along with another uniformed man.

Reggie spotted him and waved. Pete powered down his window, letting in a blast of sultry air. "Hey, Reggie. Anything new?"

The fire marshal picked his way through the shards of wood and glass toward the tape. "Nope. Nothing that would interest you, anyway."

Pete pointed toward the fort. "Don't suppose you've seen anyone coming or going over there, have you?"

"I haven't noticed. But I've been busy."

Pete thanked him and eased the SUV into Tierney's driveway. Nothing had changed there either. Still, Pete climbed out of his vehicle and strolled around the house. No one responded when he knocked on the door. He peered through the window, shielding his eyes from the glare. What he could see of the interior looked spotless and impersonal. It could easily have been a display model rather than a lived-in home.

If he wasn't going to get any answers from Tierney about this alleged affair, he'd get them from Farabee. At least this time, Pete wouldn't have to deal with Zoe's interference. But how was he going to question the father without the girl overhearing? Maybe he could get Mrs. Kroll to keep an eye on the kid. One way or the other, he intended on getting those answers. And he was going to get them today.

FIFTEEN

Pete's plans started to unravel when he bounced up the rutted farm lane and spotted a white Ford Escort instead of Farabee's red pickup parked on the slope behind the house. What was Sylvia doing there? And where was Farabee?

As expected, his former secretary opened the door when he knocked. "Pete? What are you doing here?"

"I was wondering the same thing about you."

She stepped aside letting him in. Maddie sat in the dining room with a sketch pad and some pencils. She had a too-big black ball cap perched on her head, and after looking at him with a pair of dark brown eyes overflowing with loathing, she lowered her head so the bill of the cap hid her face from him.

"What have you got there?" Pete asked, keeping his voice light. He had miles of ground to make up for with this child after their last encounter.

She mumbled something.

"Maddie," Sylvia said in a soothing, but no-nonsense tone. "Don't be rude to Chief Adams."

The little girl gave a dramatic sigh and lifted her face again. Her eyes were no less accusatory—*you want to arrest my daddy*—but she spoke with polite composure suitable for one much older. "Mrs. Bassi brought me a sketch pad and some..." Maddie looked to Sylvia for help.

Sylvia lowered into a chair across from the girl. "Charcoal pencils."

Maddie gave her quick nod. "Charcoal pencils," she said to Pete. "I lost all my coloring books and markers when my house burnt down, so I'm using these to draw pictures of George."

"George?" Pete couldn't recall anyone named George having been mentioned before.

Maddie turned the pad around and held up a pretty damned good rendering of a fat pony.

"Oh. *That* George." Pete slid into the chair next to Sylvia.

Maddie gazed at him from under the brim of the cap with a look that clearly stated he was too stupid to live.

He certainly had a way with women lately. Not giving up yet, he reached over and tapped the ball cap. "Your hat's a little big. I could adjust it for you."

"No, thank you. It's my dad's." She touched the stitched UK on the front of it. "University of Kentucky. His alma mater."

Pete almost asked her if she knew what an alma mater was, but decided he didn't want to be on the receiving end of the "duh" look again.

Sylvia patted the table with her palm to turn the girl's attention to her. "Why don't you take the pad and pencils up to your room and finish your drawing there?"

"Okay." Maddie gathered the pencils and gingerly placed them into their box. "I'll be careful with them."

"I'm sure you will be, dear. But they're yours to keep."

Maddie's eyes widened. "Really?"

"Really."

"Thanks!" She gave Sylvia a smile that could melt Siberia. No wonder Zoe had fallen in love with this kid. Tossing her dad's ball cap onto the table and scooping up her new art supplies, Maddie scampered out of the room.

Sylvia sighed. "That stuff belonged to Allison." Her teenaged granddaughter.

"Have you had any word on when Rose and the kids are coming home?"

"In time for the start of school. Rose has them out in New Mexico somewhere. No TV. No cell phones. No computers." Sylvia rolled her eyes. "Computers are what got them into trouble in the first place."

How well he knew. "So what are you doing here?"

"What's it look like? I'm babysitting." She glanced to the doorway. "Although heaven help me if Maddie heard me calling her a baby."

"I didn't realize you were acquainted with the Farabees."

"I wasn't. Zoe called me and asked if I could come over and keep an eye on the child."

"Zoe? When?"

"This morning. Holt had something he needed to do, and Mrs. Kroll had a meeting early this morning with the staff at the rehab center. Holt didn't know anyone, so he asked Zoe." Sylvia spread her arms. "And here I am."

"Any idea when Farabee'll be back?"

"A couple hours, I believe."

A small voice rang from the hallway. "He said he's bringing back pizza for lunch."

Both Pete and Sylvia leaned to look through the doorway at Maddie, who peered at them through the spindles of the banister on the staircase.

"Upstairs, Missy." Sylvia hoisted one finger skyward.

The retreating *thump thump* proved she'd obeyed this time.

Nevertheless, Pete kept his voice low. Just in case. "I'm glad I didn't say anything."

Sylvia lowered hers as well. "What's going on? Maddie obviously isn't your biggest fan."

Pete snorted.

Sylvia glanced toward the staircase again before continuing. "Last we talked, you were looking into the question of him and his wife being guilty of illegal trespass."

"That's been overshadowed by the revelation about the explosion being no accident." Pete tipped his head in the direction Maddie had disappeared. "The kid happened to be present when I broke the news to her father. And there was some mention about me possibly arresting him."

"Which didn't go over real well, I imagine."

"You imagine correctly."

"But you don't really believe he had anything to do with his wife's death, do you?"

Pete weighed his answer. "Possibly."

"Holt? That nice young man?"

"Nice young men can sometimes be cold-blooded killers."

Narrowing her eyes, Sylvia stared at Pete with an intensity that made him believe she had psychic skills. Her mental probe produced one word. "Zoe."

Pete rubbed a seed of a headache sprouting behind one eyebrow. "Don't go there, Sylvia."

She ignored him. "Zoe brought him into her home. Clearly she doesn't believe he's capable of harming his wife."

"Zoe took one look at that little girl and completely lost her mind."

Sylvia's eyes remained in mind-reading mode. "You see Zoe in the company of a nice-looking man and you lose yours."

Pete slammed a hand down on the table hard enough to make the UK ball cap jump. "Apparently I'm the only one around here who's capable of keeping an open mind right now."

Sylvia shushed him, and he realized he was on the verge of shouting. "You keep thinking and talking like that and forget about losing your mind. You're going to lose that girl."

He stood, shoving the heavy chair back so hard it nearly tipped. "Too late. When Farabee gets home—" Pete choked. He still couldn't stomach thinking of Zoe's home as Farabee's, too. "Back. When he gets *back*, tell him I need to talk to him."

Pete stomped through the kitchen and was almost to the back porch door when Sylvia's stern voice stopped him. "Pete Adams, you listen to me. If Holt Farabee killed his wife, fine. You go after him with everything you've got. But don't let your feelings about Zoe keep you from seeing that someone *else* might be responsible, and you might be letting *that* person get away with murder."

In spite of the unusually crystal clear skies for a Saturday afternoon in late July, there had only been two emergency calls, one for chest pains and another for an elderly woman who had fallen and possibly fractured a hip.

Zoe had declined an invitation to take part in the latest euchre tournament, and instead sprawled on the lumpy sofa in the crew lounge with dreams of catching a power nap to make up for last night's sleep deprivation. Tony and Vickie were up for the next call, so Zoe kept her eyes closed when the tones from EOC went off. After some initial scuffling noises from the front office, the station fell quiet for a moment. Then the door between the crew quarters and the office slammed open.

"Zoe." Earl's voice sounded oddly tense.

She rolled to one side, hoisting herself up on an elbow. Earl's tight jaw matched his voice. "What?" she asked warily.

"Come on. We're gonna take this one."

"Why?" But she was already climbing to her feet, knowing Earl wouldn't shift the rotation unless it was important.

"Fire standby," he said. Shorthand for being at the scene of a fire in case they were needed.

"Where?"

But he'd already disappeared back through the office. Zoe jogged to catch up. Tony and Vickie wore the same anxious expressions as Earl as she darted past them on the way to the ambulance bay.

Her partner had the motor fired up, and she climbed into the passenger seat. "Earl, what's going on?"

He tossed an aluminum clipboard onto her lap, shifted into drive, and flipped on the siren.

Zoe picked up the clipboard. The call sheet was still blank, but a sticky note was attached to it containing all the information Vickie had taken down from the Emergency Operations Center. Zoe's eyes blurred when she read the details and the location.

Barn fire. At the Kroll farm.

The drive from the ambulance garage took less than ten minutes, but felt like an hour to Zoe.

The barn. With all the horses. Her own gelding, Windstar. The schooling pony, George. Jazzel. She knew them all by name. In her mind she pictured the barn engulfed, the horses trapped, terrified.

She forced her clenched muscles to relax. It was a beautiful day. No reason for the horses to be inside. Someone would have turned them out into the pasture.

Please, God, let someone have turned them out.

Which left hay—highly flammable hay—stacked to the rafters. Hay baled while it was still damp had the potential to spontaneously combust. Zoe had always been extremely cautious about only buying properly cured hay. But sometimes one or two bad bales slipped into a load.

Route 15 split the Kroll farm in half, overgrown fields and timber on the western side, the house, barn, outbuildings, and horse pastures on the eastern side. Zoe craned her neck as the barn, at least five hundred yards up the hill from the road, came into view. She counted four fire trucks with lights flashing parked next to it. Smoke billowed over the roof from the far side. The structure remained standing. But she could see flames reaching over the roof and the arc of water from the fire hoses trying to knock them down.

Her stomach knotted, only slightly eased by the sight of horses gathered in the shade of willows next to the creek. She tried to count. Were they all out? She couldn't tell.

Earl gunned the medic unit as he steered off the road and up the graveled farm lane. The parking area behind the house was empty. Was Mrs. Kroll home yet? This latest disaster would be enough to give the poor woman a heart attack.

And Maddie. The little girl had to be scared to death. Another fire...

Earl gunned the medic unit over the rise. The ambulance bounced and pitched over the ruts in the gravel lane. The fire engines and two first responders' vehicles blocked access to the barn. Zoe recognized a pair of SUVs, which belonged to boarders, and both Vance Township police vehicles parked in the grass on either side of the lane. A momentary memory from a little more than a month ago flashed across her mind. A call to this same location for a shooting. The victim had been Mr. Kroll.

She closed her eyes against the image of her stepfather, bloodied up to his elbows, holding pressure on the wound. She opened them again as Earl jammed the brakes. The ambulance hadn't reached a complete stop before she flung the passenger door open.

"Zoe!" Earl called after her.

But she ignored him and sprinted toward the barn, maneuvering the maze of emergency vehicles to get her first good view of the barn.

Holt's red Ford crew cab was backed up to one of the two big doors. Hoses snaked from a tanker around the upper side of the barn, the side not visible on their approach from the road. The snap and hiss of flames and the thrum of water striking the outside of the building came from the same direction. Choking smoke continued to billow over and around, as if trying to embrace the structure. Disregarding the assorted shouts from firefighters, she sprinted into the barn.

The stalls at the far end glowed from crackling flames flickering through their windows. Smoke drifted in, but every stall door stood open, every stall empty.

Zoe released a breath she'd been holding longer than she realized and doubled over in relief, bracing her hands against her knees.

With an explosive pop, one of the windows lit by flame burst.

Zoe's heart jumped. She leapt backwards and spun smack into a brick wall named Pete.

He grabbed her by the arm and dragged her outside, shouting, "What the hell do you think you're doing?"

A wave of smoke rolled over them from around the side of the barn, sending her into a coughing fit. "I—had to—make sure—there weren't any—horses inside."

"I already checked. So did Yancy."

She met his steely blue eyes. Concern and anger stared back at her. Nothing unusual there. For a moment, she forgot she was mad at him. "How did it start?"

He aimed a thumb toward the barn wall farthest from the road. "The round bales stacked back there."

Before Mr. Kroll had been injured, he'd positioned a half a dozen large round bales of hay against the outside of the barn. Next winter, he would use his tractor's fork lift to move them into the pasture as needed.

Provided he was well enough.

"We must have gotten a bad bale."

For a moment, Pete didn't respond. When he did, his voice was low. "It wasn't a bad bale."

She wasn't sure she'd heard him, and his expression offered nothing. "What?"

"It's arson." He crooked a finger at her and, keeping hold of her arm, drew her around the corner.

Arson? Her throat closed and not because of the smoke.

Four firefighters manned the hose, pouring water on the smoky flames lapping at the side of the barn. Three others used long poles with hooks on the ends to break apart the bale, dragging as much of it away from the structure as possible. Bruce Yancy and several other firefighters in turnout gear, VTVFD emblazoned across their coats, stood with their backs to her like a barricade. Farther up the hillside, a trio of teens watched the proceedings with wide eyes.

Pete led her toward the human barricade and called out to Yancy. He turned and the firefighters with him shifted, giving her a view of Nate Williams—and a handcuffed Holt Farabee.

SIXTEEN

Zoe froze mid-stride. "What's going on?"

Holt's jaw looked tight enough to snap. "Zoe, Maddie's in the house with Mrs. Kroll. I don't want her seeing me like this."

Zoe shot a glance at Pete, remembering all too clearly why she was angry with him. Was that a hint of a smirk on his face? When had he become such a jerk? She shifted her attention back to Holt and Nate. Wrestling her arm free from Pete's grasp, she stormed toward them. "What happened?"

Yancy stepped in front of her, blocking her advance. "When the first responders got here, they found this guy trying to catch the barn on fire."

Holt let out a muffled growl. "I told you I was trying to put the fire *out*."

Zoe threw a shoulder into Yancy's arm. Considering their size difference, she should have bounced off the fire chief, but determination counted for something. She plowed past him, stopping in front of Nate and his prisoner. Behind her, she heard the soft thud of footsteps and knew Pete was going to try to stop her. She half spun, shooting him a look she'd learned as a child from her mother. *Back off and shut up.*

It worked.

She turned back to Holt. "What happened?" she asked again, keeping her voice conspiratorially low. The last thing she wanted was Holt incriminating himself—provided he was innocent.

"I was going to replace those broken boards in the stalls. I scrounged up some lumber from a friend who had it left over from a job. I was all set to unload when I smelled smoke. I went looking for where it was coming from and when I came around the back, I spotted the fire. I ran to my truck to get my fire extinguisher—"

"Convenient cover," Pete said.

Crap. She'd forgotten about his exceptional hearing. And his ability to read lips.

Holt swung on Pete. "I told you, I didn't do this." To Zoe he said, "I would never do something like this. I tried to put it out, but it was burning too hot. Too fast. I called 9-1-1. You can check my cell phone."

"We will, believe me," Pete said.

Another window exploded from the heat, sending Zoe's heart somewhere into her throat, choking her. When she regained her voice, she demanded, "Why are you so sure it's arson? And what makes you think Holt had anything to do with it?"

Pete dug a plastic bag from his back pocket and held it up for her to see. A scorched lighter. "Go ahead and look. You want to be an investigator."

Zoe took the bag from him and turned it over in her hand.

"One of the firemen found it on the ground over there when they first arrived."

Smoothing the plastic over the lighter's surface, she was able to make out the lettering. *Holt Farabee, Carpenter.* And a phone number.

"I had a thousand of those made for promotion," Holt said. "Half the people in the county have them."

"Including you," Pete added.

Holt stuffed one of his cuffed hands into his jeans pocket and pulled out another lighter. Same design, same lettering, different color. "Yeah, including me. See? I still have mine."

Pete took the bag from Zoe and shook it at Holt. "Tell me something, Farabee. How many more of these do you have lying around?"

Holt's jaw tensed. "A few."

"If I check your truck right now, how many will I find?"

Holt met Zoe's gaze for a moment, defeated. "I guess I better use my right to remain silent."

"Good idea." Pete pointed at the group of frightened boarders watching from the hillside. "Nate, question those kids about what and who they might have seen. I'm taking Farabee down to the station."

Nate gave a terse nod. "On it, Chief."

Pete closed a hand around Farabee's bicep. "Let's go."

Holt stood firm. "Zoe, take care of Maddie for me." He glanced around as if searching for...what? "I don't want strangers around her. I don't know if Mrs. Kroll is able to protect her."

Protect her? From what? But before Zoe could ask, Pete gave his suspect a tug. "Don't worry about Maddie," she told Holt. "And don't say anything else. I'll have Mr. Imperatore meet you down there."

The tension in Holt's face eased a little. He bent his head toward her and in a soft southern voice too low for anyone else, except maybe Pete, to hear, he whispered, "Thank you."

Pete stepped between them. "Zoe—" He opened his mouth, but words didn't come. Instead he clenched his fist, as if wanting to grab her and shake her, and let out a growl.

"Excuse me, Chief." She stressed *Chief*, something she hadn't called him since their first meeting. "I have to go make sure Maddie's distracted so she doesn't happen to see her father being carted off to jail in a police car." Zoe took one more look at the barn. Smoke lifted from the blackened siding, but the fire company had soaked it down and dragged what was left of the burning round bale away from the structure. Disaster averted.

She wheeled and took off at a lope, away from the fire and away from the questions whispering in the back of her mind. Why did Holt want her taking care of Maddie instead of "strangers" when *she* had been a total stranger four days ago? What was she supposed to protect Maddie from?

And the big one. Could Pete's cop gut be right about him?

Zoe found Earl leaning against the front of the ambulance, arms crossed. "What's going on?" he asked.

She gave him the Cliff's Notes version of the fire. "They've arrested Holt for arson. I need to get back to the house to make sure Maddie doesn't see her dad in the back of Pete's police car."

Earl's eyes narrowed. "Okay," he said, dragging the word out. "I'll pick you up at the house on the way out. And I'll call your cell if we get an emergency."

Zoe glanced back at the police SUV as Pete opened the back door for his passenger. "Holt asked me to watch Maddie."

"You're on duty."

As if she needed to be reminded. For a moment she contemplated taking Maddie with them. Kids love sirens. She'd probably think it was grand fun. On the other hand, Holt has specifically said he didn't want her around strangers. Taking the girl to hang out at the ambulance garage would definitely go against the *No Strangers* edict.

Earl coughed.

She looked at him. He held her gaze and coughed again, obviously faking. "What's wrong with you?" she asked.

He rolled his eyes, nodded toward the barn, and coughed again.

Slowly, his attempt to help her out of her jam dawned on her. "Oh." She feigned a cough.

Earl smiled. "Standing too close to the fire, Zoe. You took a lungful of smoke. I could put you on some oxygen, but you probably just need to rest for a while. Maybe the rest of the day. And night."

In spite of Pete, in spite of Holt, in spite of burning bales of hay, Zoe laughed, triggering a real cough. "Maybe I really did inhale some smoke."

"Go watch the little girl."

"Thanks, Earl."

He shrugged one shoulder. "I have three kids of my own, remember? I'd want someone keeping an eye on them if I got busted for something I didn't do."

Anthony Imperatore was arguably the best attorney in Monongahela County. He was also a helluva nice man. But when the lawyer marched Holt Farabee out the front door of the police station a mere hour after he'd hauled him in, Pete wished he could have the man disbarred.

Imperatore had calmly pointed out a promotional lighter as the only evidence at the scene was laughable, especially when the attorney himself pulled an identical one from his pocket. The worst part of it? Imperatore was right. Pete didn't have a case. Not yet. Farabee stuck to his story about trying to put the fire out. Otherwise, he'd followed Zoe's and the attorney's advice to not say anything.

Sitting alone in his office, Pete slammed his hand down on his desk. Damn it, Zoe.

Chief. She'd called him *Chief.*

"Chief?" Nate stood in the doorway, his thumbs hooked in his service belt.

Pete rubbed his forehead. "Did you talk to the kids at the barn?"

Nate stepped into the small office and eased into the chair across from Pete. "No one claimed to see anything, but they'd just come back from riding. Said the bale was already on fire when they got there. They put their horses in one of the round pens out back and checked to make sure there weren't any other horses inside."

"Did they say anything about Farabee?"

"He was using a fire extinguisher on the hay when they first arrived. The extinguisher wasn't doing much. By the time they'd taken care of the horses, the first fire truck was pulling up."

Pete raked his fingers through his hair. "So the kids basically backed up his statement."

"Pretty much."

Damn. "Don't suppose they mentioned seeing anyone else there, did they?"

"They said some other riders had been there earlier. They were done riding and were putting stuff away while these kids were saddling up." Nate pulled his notebook from his hip pocket. "I got the names and numbers of those other kids. Want me to call them or do you wanna do it?"

Pete held out his palm. "I'll do it."

Nate ripped out the page and handed it to him. "I was gonna head out on patrol. You need anything else?"

That do-over starting with Thursday? "No. Thanks."

Nate stood but made no move to leave.

"What?"

"Don't worry, Chief. He'll slip up at some point. We'll get him."

At least someone around here agreed with Pete. "Thanks."

Nate disappeared from the doorway. A moment later, bells jingled, indicating he'd left the station. Pete glanced at the clock on the wall. Seven p.m. He was missing the poker game and had nothing to show for it. Yet. He smoothed the note paper on his desk and reached for the phone. The bells jangled again. What now? He climbed to his feet and stepped into the hallway, nearly colliding with Nate.

"Sorry, Chief. I was on my out and I ran into them in the parking lot." The officer shifted to one side and thumbed over his shoulder at Jack Naeser, his wife, and their daughter, Ashley. "They wanted to talk to you."

Pete resisted sighing. No matter how upset the Naeser family was with Ryan Mancinelli, he still hadn't broken any laws, and Pete could not arrest him for attempted murder. He crossed the hall, opened the door to the conference room, and flipped the light switch. "Come on in, folks."

With Nate once again headed out on patrol and the Naeser family seated around the big table, Pete pulled out a chair and settled into it. He assessed Jack who sported a bandage on his head. "Other than your odd-looking headgear, you don't look too worse for wear."

Naeser fingered the left side of the bandage and winced. "I must look better than I feel then."

Pete leaned back. "What can I do for you?"

Mrs. Naeser folded her hands on the table. "We want you to arrest my son-in-law."

Pete had guessed right. "We talked about this before. I can't arrest him for refusing to trim his hedges. And refusing to do so doesn't constitute attempted murder."

The three exchanged wary looks. Mrs. Naeser ran a tongue over her lips. "We realize that. But to be honest, Ryan is acting crazy."

"How so?"

The older woman glanced at her daughter before speaking. "Ashley has left Ryan and moved back in with us."

All of one door away. One of the downfalls of living next to your parents.

"Ryan isn't taking it very well," Mrs. Naeser continued. "I think he's been drinking nonstop since the accident last night."

Pete thought back to suspecting as much during his own meeting with Mancinelli earlier in the morning. "Has he gotten behind the wheel?"

"No. Well, he was out this morning for a little while, but he's been home the rest of the day."

"Mrs. Naeser, I'm afraid there isn't anything illegal about getting drunk in your own home."

The woman looked like she wanted to slug Pete. Which would be illegal. "I know, but he's doing stuff over there. We can hear glass breaking. Crashing noises. I think he's tearing the house apart inside."

Pete eyed Ashley Mancinelli. "Has he hurt or threatened you?"

"No," she said. "Never."

Mrs. Naeser appeared ready to climb across the table. "But he still might hurt her. Hurt us. He's crazy. And drunk. Surely there has to be something you can do."

Pete rocked back in his chair and studied the trio across the table. Was this visit a case of the Naesers disliking their son-in-law so intensely they would do anything to get their daughter away from him? Ashley had tears in her eyes and certainly didn't appear to be as gung-ho to see Ryan behind bars as her folks were. Pete came forward again and directed his words at her. "If you're feeling threatened in any way, I could start the proceedings to get you a temporary PFA—Protection From Abuse order."

She ran a trembling finger beneath one glistening eye, catching a tear. "No. He would never hurt me."

Her mother put an arm around the girl's shoulders. "You don't know that. When he's drunk, he's not himself."

Pete held Ashley's gaze. "There's also a 302D. Involuntary commitment."

Her already wide doe eyes widened even more. "Commitment?"

"If you think he's a danger and he's acting bizarre, he'd be taken in and held for observation."

Jack Naeser nodded enthusiastically. "That's what we want."

"No." Ashley sounded on the verge of hysteria. "It's not. Chief, can't you just go check on him? Make sure he's okay? Maybe talk to him. He respects you. He'll listen."

Pete wasn't so sure about the last part. "Absolutely. And I'll ask my men to swing by on patrol more often."

Mrs. Naeser let her arm fall away from her daughter's shoulders. The three of them again exchanged looks. "Okay. If that's what Ashley wants, we'd appreciate you stopping by and talking to him. But I'm still afraid he'll do...*something*."

"If he does or if Ashley changes her mind, all you have to do is call and I'll come right out."

The Naeser delegation rose in unison. Jack extended a hand to Pete. "I wish he'd use all that energy on cutting down those danged hedges."

Pete nodded his agreement.

Mrs. Naeser followed her husband out of the conference room. The young Mrs. Mancinelli brought up the rear, pausing at the door. "He was like this before, you know."

"No, I didn't know," Pete said. "When?"

"After he got back from Afghanistan. He had PTSD pretty bad. But I thought that nightmare was behind us."

Pete rested a hand on her shoulder. "The stress of the accident last night..." And losing his wife, Pete thought, but decided not to say. "...probably triggered it again. I'll talk to him. If he's a vet, maybe we can get him some outpatient help through the VA."

The girl managed a weak smile and a nod before trailing after her parents.

Once they'd left, Pete looked back at his office. Should he call the other boarders at the farm? Or check on Ryan Mancinelli? Blowing out a breath, he grabbed his ball cap before heading out to see what was left of the Mancinelli home.

SEVENTEEN

The drought-stunted grass crunched under Pete's feet as he approached Ryan Mancinelli's front porch. He wasn't sure what to expect, which meant preparing for anything. He'd never known Mancinelli to be violent, but until a half hour ago, he hadn't known Mancinelli suffered from posttraumatic stress either.

From outside, the house appeared no different than it had every other time Pete had been there, including during last night's accident. Even those damned hedges remained exactly as they had always been.

He climbed the steps and pressed the button next to the door. From inside, he could hear chimes. And nothing else.

He pounded the wood-framed screen door. Still nothing.

"Ryan," Pete called. "It's Chief Adams. I'd like to talk to you."

Only silence responded.

Pete tried the latch. It clicked open. He grasped the knob on the ornate wood and glass door. It turned easily and the door swung open.

"Ryan?" Pete called again.

Nothing.

Pete stepped inside, his hand on his sidearm.

While the outside of the house was pristine, the inside looked like a bomb had gone off.

A throw rug was bunched in the entryway. A decorative painting was smashed on the newel post, which now wore the frame like a gaudy necklace. A hole had been bashed through one wall. The entire place reeked of cigarette smoke. Pete eased toward the back of the house and the kitchen. White cabinets gaped open. Canned goods had been dumped onto the floor. Glassware smashed on the gleaming black granite countertops.

An empty bottle of whiskey lay on its side on the stove, which thankfully was off.

"Ryan?" Pete called again.

Still nothing.

Pete continued around to the left into the family room. A large flat screen TV hung on the wall, shattered. Books had been tossed from their shelves. Two floor lamps sprawled on the Berber carpet. Another empty whiskey bottle rested against one of them. And a third almost empty bottle dripped its contents onto the rug from the coffee table. Next to the damp spot, a half-smoked cigarette and a burn mark.

He stepped through the archway into the room and spotted Ryan Mancinelli, prone on the couch, his head turned to one side, his mouth hanging open.

Pete stepped over one of the lamps and leaned down to slide his fingers into the groove in Ryan's neck.

The pulse was strong and steady. Pete blew out his breath.

"Ryan? Hey. Ryan." Pete gave him a shake.

The man moaned.

Pete grabbed him by his shoulders and rolled him none-too-gently onto his back. "Hey! Ryan!"

He winced and groaned. "Lea'me alone."

Pete straightened, planted his fists on his hips, and surveyed the trashed room again. "Oh, man. Ryan, my boy, you may be alive now, but when your wife sees her house you'll wish you weren't."

Next to the couch, an ashtray overflowed with butts. The idiot was lucky he hadn't burned his house down. Just what Vance Township needed. Another fire.

Something tucked against the ashtray caught his eye. He squinted and bent down for a closer look before picking the thing up.

He pulled out his reading glasses and turned the small disposable lighter over in his hand. Printed on the side—*Holt Farabee, Carpenter.*

After the Weekend From Hell, Zoe thought Monday morning would never get there. Once the day crew shuffled in, she bolted for home. On the drive, she thought about the half dozen phone calls she'd fielded on her cell. Word had spread about the fire and Holt's arrest. Boarders didn't want their kids being exposed to an arsonist. Or a killer. She'd tried to explain the accusations were merely rumors. But there was talk of moving their horses elsewhere. At least two of them were already actively looking for another facility.

By eight-thirty, Zoe stood on the hillside above the barn, inspecting the scorched siding and broken windows. Two round bales had been reduced to charred marks on the ground. A blackened strip up the tin roof mapped the flames' path.

"It could have been a lot worse."

Zoe flinched, startled by Holt's voice even though she'd seen his truck parked in front of the barn.

He strolled toward her. "Sorry. Didn't mean to scare you."

"You didn't. I'm just jumpy."

"Because of me?"

"No." Was she lying? She wasn't sure.

"I wanted to thank you for watching Maddie for me Saturday afternoon."

Zoe shoved her hands into her pants pockets. "No problem. Maddie's a great kid." She studied Holt's profile as he scowled at the barn. At another time under different circumstances, she might have harbored some seriously lustful thoughts about the man. Now all she saw was the devastation and grief in his eyes. "I'm glad they didn't keep you." She didn't tack on *in jail.*

He huffed a humorless laugh. "Me, too."

"And thanks for giving me a lift back to the ambulance garage."

"I guess we're even."

"Where's Maddie now?"

He glanced toward the farmhouse. "She was still in bed when I came out here. I should warn you...she's fixing to hit you up for a riding lesson later today."

Zoe smiled at the thought of the giggling ten-year-old jogging around the arena on George's back. "I think I can arrange that."

Holt took off his hat and swiped it across his forehead before replacing it. "I fixed those boards in the stalls. You can inspect my work if you want."

"Not necessary. Right now I just want a shower." She raised an eyebrow at him. "Provided we have hot water."

"Absolutely. I had the new water heater installed Friday night."
He took a deep breath and blew it out. "I guess I should start on this
now." He pointed at the fire damage. "I can tear the siding off, but you
won't be able to use those stalls until I can get new stuff."

Dollar signs appeared in Zoe's mind. "We still owe you for the
water heater."

He waved a hand. "I put it on my account at the hardware store. I
don't need the money until the first of the month. And the boards I
used for the stalls were headed for the dumpster, so there's no charge
there. But this..." He shook his head. "I'm afraid my accounts at all the
lumber yards are maxed out. And I doubt I can scrounge up extra barn
siding for free."

All the talk of money made Zoe think her forehead was in the
grasp of a vice. "I don't necessarily need the stalls, but I hate to have a
big hole in the side of the barn. The weather forecast is calling for
severe storms by midweek and tarping the opening might not be
enough."

Holt rubbed his chin. "Do you have some plywood lying around?"

"Not enough for that."

"How about for the busted out windows?"

"Oh. Yeah."

After directing Holt to the tool shed where she'd spotted some
scraps he could use, she shuffled to her truck and drove back to the
house. No sooner had she stepped into the enclosed porch than Mrs.
Kroll opened her door.

"Zoe, I've been watching for you to come home. Can I talk to you
for a minute?"

Something in the woman's face made the vice grip on Zoe's brain
tighten down even more. "Sure." She crossed the porch and stepped
into Mrs. Kroll's kitchen.

Instead of leading Zoe into the dining room as her landlady
usually did, Mrs. Kroll sat down on one of two wooden chairs. Zoe took
the other. "Maddie's in there eating her breakfast and playing one of
those...things." Mrs. Kroll held out her hand, palm up.

"Handheld video games?" Zoe offered.

Mrs. Kroll sighed. "I guess that's what it is. It's been so long since
I had a young one in the house. And times have changed. I think the

poor child was bored to death most of the weekend. No cable TV. No computer. Thank heavens your kids from the barn brought her some toys and gadgets yesterday."

Her kids from the barn.

If Holt stayed much longer, she'd have some serious damage control to do.

"Anyhow, I wanted to talk to you," Mrs. Kroll said.

The anxiety in her voice sent Zoe's mind racing. Did the older woman want Holt gone, just like those nervous parents? Just like Pete? Had something happened to Mr. Kroll? Had there been bad news during the nursing staff meeting the other day?

"I've been thinking about something. I need to discuss it with Marvin first, of course. But with everything that's happened and all the expenses... Now the fire is going to cost quite a bit. Well, I had a visitor, and I think he may have the best solution." Mrs. Kroll held out a small white card.

Zoe recognized it. Hesitantly, she took the business card and looked at it, although she didn't need to.

David Evans. Evans Land Development. Baltimore, Maryland.

"When did he...?"

"He said he's been trying to reach me for a while."

Duh. Yeah.

"Yesterday. He stopped in yesterday afternoon. Maddie and her dad were out at the barn, so we had a nice chat." Mrs. Kroll broke into a nervous smile. "He offered me quite a lot of money for our property."

"But—but—" Zoe stopped. Ran her tongue over her dry lips. "You and Mr. Kroll love this place."

"Yes, I know. Mr. Evans explained we could keep the house and the yard. Or he could bulldoze it and build us a lovely new modern house on the lot. Marvin's not getting any younger. He's not going to be able to do things around here like he used to. And we can't expect you to pick up all the slack."

Inside Zoe's head, she screamed *Yes, you can!*

"I think it would be nice having a new house. New things. And never have to worry about money ever again. I could pay off Marvin's doctors' bills. We'd be completely out of debt."

"And the barn?" Zoe squeaked. But she knew the answer.

"Oh." The exaggerated enthusiasm melted from Mrs. Kroll's voice. "Well, of course, they would tear it down to make room for all the new homes."

Of course. Tear down the barn. Bulldoze the farmhouse. Bring in the earth-moving equipment to alter the landscape. So city people like the Fort Guy could move to the country.

But that was only a small part of the death knell chiming inside Zoe's head. The Krolls would have a new home and new things. Zoe—and her horse and her cats—on the other hand, would be homeless.

Mrs. Kroll must have read Zoe's face. "It will take a while to make happen. You'll have plenty of time to find another place to live."

Mrs. Kroll kept talking, but Zoe didn't hear a word of it until a small voice filtered through. "Mrs. Kroll?" Maddie stood in the doorway between the kitchen and dining room with her nose crinkled. "Oh, hi, Zoe."

"What is it, dear?" the older woman asked.

Maddie made a face again. "I keep smelling something funny."

Mrs. Kroll sighed. "Yes. I've been smelling it, too."

"What are you talking about?" Zoe asked.

"Remember last summer when that groundhog died in the crawlspace under the kitchen?" Mrs. Kroll pointed at the floor.

How could Zoe forget? The whole house had stunk like the morgue.

Mr. Kroll could see the source of the eau de decomp by lying on his belly and shining a flashlight through the gap in the stone foundation, but there was no way to reach the poor creature. Its dried, and eventually odorless, carcass was probably still down there. But she didn't notice the smell they were talking about now.

"I saw a mouse when I was down in the basement the other day and set a couple traps. I'll check to see if there's anything in them." Although Zoe doubted a tiny dead mouse would cause enough of a stink to make its way upstairs.

Maddie's face had relaxed. "I don't smell it here."

"Neither do I," Mrs. Kroll said. "I only get a whiff every now and again."

Zoe stood, preferring to think about checking mouse traps rather than contemplating finding a new home.

Maddie stepped toward her. "Zoe? Do you think you could take me riding today?"

Holt had been right. "Sure thing. Let me check those traps and grab something to eat. I'll come get you in about an hour."

"Okay. Thanks." Maddie spun and disappeared back into the dining room.

Mrs. Kroll climbed to her feet and breathed a heavy sigh. "Mice in the basement. Dead groundhogs under the kitchen. More reasons to tear this old house down and start new."

Zoe tried to appear happy for her landlady, but couldn't do it. All she could think about was how hard it had been to find a place for her and her animals five years ago and how happy she'd been to strike a deal with the Krolls.

Reeling, she made her way across the porch and into her side of the house. Home. Her home. But for how long?

Jade and Merlin sat next to the door as she stepped inside. She leaned down to stroke both orange tabbies. "Are you guys hungry?" she cooed. "Want kitty food?"

While Jade continued to rub her face against Zoe's leg, Merlin trotted to his bowl, which was still half full, and looked back at her.

"Who said cats can't communicate?" Zoe started to unlace one boot. But a familiar smell stopped her. "What the...?" Maddie and Mrs. Kroll hadn't been kidding.

She retied her boot and opened the basement door. The stench staggered her. Something had definitely died down there. Another groundhog must have found its way in, probably while Holt had the outer doors open.

Zoe flipped on the light switch and picked her way down the stairs. She stretched her collar over her mouth and nose to filter the odor. It helped. A little.

The mousetrap under the staircase remained baited and un-tripped. Still clutching the fabric of her uniform shirt to her face, she passed the ancient canned goods and the root cellar and glanced at the shiny new water heater. She'd placed the second trap near the furnace, on the stone ledge created by the foundation. It had been tripped, but the sneaky mouse had escaped. The smell was not a result of a small rodent.

But she already knew that.

Zoe glanced around the basement. Her gaze settled on the root cellar. She recalled the time when an odor had almost driven her out of her own kitchen...until she'd discovered a couple of rotten potatoes in her pantry. Could a whole bin-full be the culprit this time, too?

She backtracked to the root cellar and stepped inside, knowing full well rotten potatoes didn't smell like this. Nor did they draw a swarm of flies.

With her stomach pressing upward against her throat, she yanked the pull-string attached to a bare bulb in the ceiling.

EIGHTEEN

Pete carried his coffee and a stack of reports into the conference room to find Wayne Baronick already seated with his feet propped on the table.

Nate sat across from him, leaning on his forearms. "Hey, Chief."

"Have you stopped at Ryan Mancinelli's house this morning?" Saturday night, Pete had covered the inebriated hedge-lover with a blanket and left him to sleep off his binge. Yesterday, he'd checked in and found him hungover to the point of begging for sudden death.

"I banged on his door about an hour ago, but didn't get an answer. I figure he must've sobered up enough to go to work."

"I'll stop at his in-laws and make sure everything's okay." With one deft movement, Pete swept Baronick's feet from the table. They hit the floor with a thud.

The detective responded with an impish grin. "Sorry, Mom."

Pete slid into the chair at the head of the table. "Since you're the big county detective and made the drive here from Brunswick, I assume you have something to contribute?"

"You assume correctly. And I'll have you know getting information about insurance policies on a weekend is a real bitch. But—" Baronick thumped himself proudly on the chest. "I did it. It's a good-news-bad-news-good-news thing."

Pete waited for the detective to continue, but he only flashed that annoying smile. "Well?"

"Good news. Farabee did indeed carry a life insurance policy on his wife. Bad news. It's barely enough to cover burial costs. If he builds her casket himself."

"So he didn't kill his wife for the money."

Baronick held up one finger. "I said good news, bad news, *good* news. I'm not finished."

"Get on with it already."

Baronick clucked his tongue. "My. Aren't we a little crabby this morning?" He winked at Nate. "And I hear he practically proposed to Zoe at a traffic accident Friday night. She must have turned him down."

Pete launched out of his chair and slammed both hands on the table in front of the smug son of a bitch. None of the retorts that came to mind seemed adequate.

Slugging him would be gratifying, but probably wouldn't have the best long-term results.

Baronick must have been able to read Pete's thoughts. The detective cleared his throat, his smile fading. "Uh, I don't think we should write off the murder for money motive just yet."

Pete held his intimidating position for another few moments, secretly enjoying the sight of Baronick squirming. "Out with it."

"I expected to find the house insurance policy to be held by the bank, but it turns out Farabee was the one paying on the policy, so he's the beneficiary."

Pete took his seat again. "And?"

"And it's substantial. He had the place insured for a cool 1.5 mil."

Nate whistled. "I'd say that's motive with a capital M."

Baronick rocked back in his chair and started to swing one foot onto the table again.

Pete glared at him and he reconsidered.

"It's possible this guy never intended to kill his wife. Maybe he just wanted to collect on the homeowner's policy. Lillian Farabee was collateral damage."

"Possibly." But Pete wasn't buying it. There was still the accusation of infidelity to deal with. "Nate, any sign of Stephen Tierney?"

"None. I cruised through the development at least a half dozen times this weekend. I never saw any indications of life behind his fence."

"He's supposed to be back at work today." Pete's cell phone rang. "I'll catch him there."

Baronick climbed to his feet. "Tierney works at the Brunswick branch, right? I'm headed back to the city. I can stop in and have a chat with him."

"No." Pete dug his phone from his pocket. "Tierney's mine."

The detective moved toward the door. "I could meet you there if you want."

Zoe's name flashed on the screen, and Pete's gut tightened. Until a few days ago, a call from her would have brightened his day. Now it filled him with dread. "No, thanks. I'll handle Tierney on my own."

Pete answered the call. The hysteria in Zoe's voice sent a chill up his neck and into his brain. Baronick had a hand on the doorknob, and Pete snapped his fingers at him. The detective stopped. Frowned.

"Slow down," Pete told Zoe. "Say that again."

In his ear, he heard her take a breath. And in a voice stretched so tight it sounded like it would break, she said, "I have a dead body in my basement."

Zoe had seen some macabre things in her work on the Monongahela County EMS, but a dead body buried in a potato bin had to be some kind of pinnacle of weirdness.

The "bins" in the root cellar had always reminded her of bunk beds. The remains of last year's crop of onions occupied one, a few dried-up carrots another. Potatoes filled a third. Except today the spuds appeared piled higher than usual. Sprouting eyes reached out like pale tentacles straining to find soil—and had been joined by a human arm.

She'd checked for a pulse, but the gray skin tone and the deafening buzz of flies let her know the man was dead before she ever touched the cold flesh.

Desperate for fresh air, she thudded up the wooden stairs and out onto the porch where she leaned against the outside wall of the house gulping breaths.

She'd placed the call to Pete before pounding on Mrs. Kroll's door, telling her to stay put. Neither she nor Maddie was to go into the basement under any circumstances. Zoe had dodged her landlady's demands for an explanation, but she'd probably guessed pretty darn close. After locking Jade and Merlin in her office, Zoe had perched on the back porch to wait.

She heard them coming before she saw them. Sirens echoed through the valley, growing louder. Closer. They fell silent when they hit the bottom of the lane, and Zoe looked up to watch Pete's Explorer followed by the township's cruiser and a black unmarked sedan crawl up the gravel driveway. The three vehicles parked behind her Chevy.

A canvas bag slung over one shoulder, Pete made his way down the path toward Zoe. Nate trailed him with Wayne Baronick bringing up the rear. She stood, ramming her hands into her uniform pants pockets and stepped back, allowing them to enter the enclosed porch.

Pete stopped only inches in front of her. She met and held his gaze, surprised and relieved the awkward tension seemed, for the moment, to have dissipated.

"Are you all right?" he asked, his voice low.

"Terrific. With the exception of having a dead man in my basement."

"Where is he?"

Zoe motioned for Pete to follow and led them into the house. As she reached for the knob for the basement door, Pete gently caught her wrist.

"Just tell us where to find the body," he said.

Puzzled, Zoe glanced from Pete to the others. Three cops. Three poker faces. "It'd be easier for me to show you."

Pete didn't release her. Instead he drew her back from the door. "I need you to stay up here with Nate and let Baronick and me handle this."

"But—"

"The County Crime Scene Unit is on the way," Baronick said. "And Officer Williamson has some questions for you."

Zoe narrowed her eyes at the detective. "I'm a deputy coroner." She might not like the morgue part of the job, but here was a murder investigation in her own house. No way was she going to be relegated to filling in the blanks of an incident report.

Pete moved his hand to her shoulder and gave a squeeze. "We know you are. But you also live here."

"So?"

He turned her toward him and fixed her with a stern stare. "Think about it a minute."

She didn't want to. So much for the tension between them having dissipated. "You know I had nothing to do with this. I don't even know who he is."

"I know that. But your house is a crime scene and you discovered the body. I can't let you work on the investigation."

"But—"

"But nothing. I need to know where you found the body."

She held his gaze. When had she lost the ability to read him? "At the bottom of the basement stairs, first doorway on the left. He's pretty much buried by potatoes, but you can't miss him."

"Potatoes?" Baronick said.

"It's a root cellar."

Pete tipped his head toward her drawing her focus back to him. "What did you do when you found the body? Did you go near it?"

"I checked for a pulse."

"You touched the body?"

"Just his wrist. Nothing else. Then I came upstairs to call you and to tell Mrs. Kroll not to go down here."

"Good girl." Pete gently bumped her chin with his fist. "Give a preliminary statement to Nate. Direct the crime scene unit guys and Franklin Marshall down here once they arrive."

She wanted to argue. Stomp her feet. Throw a tantrum. But in her heart she knew better. At least Pete wasn't pointing out the obvious.

Until they cleared her, she was a suspect.

Pete set the canvas bag on the hard-packed dirt floor and removed a camera from one compartment. Zoe had handled being kept out of her own basement and off the case surprisingly well. For a moment he'd seen a flash of anger in her eyes and thought *here we go again*. But then she'd clamped her mouth shut and moved out of their way. Pete snapped photos—several overall shots and then a number of closer, more detailed angles of the arm protruding from the mountain of potatoes. Baronick measured and sketched the room. By the time they were done with the overview, Franklin Marshall had arrived.

"Zoe's not very happy with you," the coroner told Pete.

Baronick laughed. When Pete shot a look at him, he covered his mouth and pretended it was a cough.

"Yeah, well," Pete said, "that's become status quo."

Marshall grunted. "She said she checked for a pulse and pronounced him dead, but I suppose for propriety sake, I should confirm her findings."

Pete eyed the bluish-gray hand and huffed. "Not that there's any question, but for the official record, yeah."

As the coroner did his thing, the ceiling above them vibrated with heavy footsteps. Voices drifted down. A moment later, the county crime guys clomped down the stairs and took charge.

Pete, Baronick, and Marshall stepped out of the way as the county unit spread out a sheet and began moving potatoes onto it from the bin with the painstaking precision of an archeological dig.

The detective crossed his arms. "How long do you think he's been there?" he asked Marshall.

The coroner gave him a dark look. "Estimate a TOD by the appearance of one limb? You're kidding, right?"

"Just asking."

Marshall narrowed his eyes, studying the corpse. "Although I can tell you this much. He's gone out of rigor. And considering the visible insect activity and rather advanced state of decomp in this nice cool basement, I think it's safe to say he's been here a while. Possibly a week."

Baronick elbowed Pete. "Any idea who Mr. Potato Head is?"

Pete had been trying not to think about it.

"I mean, I know you can't tell by just an arm. But has anyone been reported missing?"

"No." Which troubled Pete as much as anything. It also narrowed down the possibilities.

The man's blue shirt became visible. Then the back of his head, his hair, dusted with fine soil from the potatoes. But lying prone, his identity remained concealed.

"Hey, Franklin," one of the investigators called, waving the coroner toward them. Pete went with him, hanging back, but staying close enough for a good look.

Marshall leaned over the victim touching his head with a gloved hand. Then the coroner stepped aside. "Photographs, please."

One of the investigators positioned a measuring marker next to what appeared to be a deep indentation in the man's hair and held it as another CSI tripped the shutter.

"Skull fracture?" Pete asked.

Marshall kept his eyes on the proceedings. "I would say so."

"Cause of death?"

"Possibly. But I won't know until I do the autopsy. You know that."

"We're ready to turn him," one of the CSIs said.

Marshall nodded. "Do it. Let's see who we've got here."

Moving with as much care as if the dead man were alive and suffering a spinal injury, the investigators log-rolled the body. One of the investigators grunted. "This is messy. I hope no one planned on using the rest of these potatoes."

Pete shifted closer without moving his feet. Milky, unseeing eyes looked out of a bloated, pale gray face. In death, the man was almost unrecognizable. Almost.

"I don't know him," Baronick said from over Pete's shoulder.

"I do." Pete let out a breath. "It's Stephen Tierney."

What was taking them so long?

Zoe sat at Mrs. Kroll's table playing a half-hearted game of Go Fish with Maddie. Zoe had opened all the windows—not an easy task considering they were original to the house—to help alleviate the odor wafting through the floorboards. She'd pleaded with Nate to let her take the little girl outside, but he'd insisted they stay where he could see them while he sat in the parlor with Mrs. Kroll, asking questions in tones too low for Zoe to make out the words.

He'd already questioned Zoe. *Questioned* sounded better than interrogated. Where had she been the last few days? At the ambulance garage. Could anyone verify that? The rest of the crew. What had she done, where had she gone since she got off duty? Zoe retraced her steps for Nate, who wrote down everything she said while offering no indication of whether or not he believed her.

More police had arrived. County detectives. State troopers. Milling around on the back porch, tromping through Zoe's side of the house. Good thing she'd locked the cats in her office.

"Is there really a dead guy in the basement?" Maddie asked, her nose wrinkled in disgust.

"Yeah, there really is." Zoe forced herself to focus on her hand. "Got any eights?"

Maddie scowled at her cards and removed one, handing it to Zoe. "I didn't want it to be a groundhog. They're kinda cute. But I didn't want anyone else to be dead either."

"I know." Anyone else. Who was the "anyone else" in her basement? How had he gotten there? And who had killed him?

"At least it isn't my dad."

Zoe looked up. "Huh?"

Maddie sighed. "My mom's dead." A simple, calm statement of fact. "I don't think I could stand it if something happened to my dad, too."

The girl's straightforward pronouncement, spoken without a hint of a tear, twisted Zoe's heart into a knot. She reached across the table to lay a hand on Maddie's thin arm. "I'm not going to let anything happen to your dad."

From outside voices grew louder. Footsteps pounded across the porch. A scuffle. Maddie's eyes widened and she dropped her cards. Zoe set hers down as well and rose, crossing to the window. Two Pennsylvania State Police troopers held Holt by his arms as he tried to wrestle free.

Zoe spun and pointed an authoritative finger at the girl. "Stay right there." With a don't-dare-to-stop-me glance at Nate, she stormed through the kitchen and onto the porch.

Wild-eyed, Holt looked at her. "Has something happened to Maddie?"

"Maddie's fine." Zoe took two big strides toward Holt and the troopers. "Let him go. He lives here."

"We're simply securing the crime scene, ma'am," one of the troopers said. "No one in or out."

"Crime scene?" Holt twisted, trying again to break the troopers' hold. "What crime scene?"

"There's a dead body in the basement," Zoe said.

A small yelp behind Zoe spun her around.

Maddie stood in the kitchen doorway, her dark eyes in stark contrast to skin that had lost all color. "*Dad!*" she shrieked and bolted past Zoe.

The troopers released Holt, and he dropped to his knees to catch his hysterical daughter in his arms.

Zoe caught movement beyond the troopers. Pete emerged from her side of the house. He appeared to assess the situation for a moment before striding toward them.

"Pete. Did you find out who the victim is?" She winced. "Was?"

He stole a glance at Maddie, his shoulders sagged ever so slightly as he shifted his eyes to Zoe. "I think you better take her inside."

Holt climbed to his feet. Maddie clung to him, and he kept one protective arm around her. "What's going on?"

"Zoe," Pete said, his voice low, but insistent. "Get her out of here."

Maddie dug in her heels. "I'm staying with my dad."

Zoe hadn't noticed Nate and Mrs. Kroll were standing in the kitchen doorway until her landlady spoke up. "Come on, Maddie dear. Let's leave the grownups to sort this thing out."

Maddie looked up at her father, pleading. Holt tipped his head toward the older woman. "Go on, baby. I'll be okay."

The girl's lower lip jutted and tears glistened on her dark lower lashes, but she released her grip on her dad. Shoving her hands into her pockets, she shuffled past Zoe and into the kitchen.

Once the door was closed, Zoe spun on Pete. "Now tell me. Who is the dead man in my basement?"

Pete's gaze locked on Holt. "Would you care to answer her question?"

Holt shook his head at Pete. "I have no idea what you're talking about. I just came in from the barn and saw all the cop cars."

Zoe had seen the look on Pete's face before, when everyone had shown their hands at poker, and he knew his was the best. "It's your neighbor. Stephen Tierney."

"Tierney?" Visions raced across Zoe's mind. Tierney. The guy in the fort. The man she'd seen arguing with Holt three days ago. Maddie's words, *Dad hates him.*

NINETEEN

Farabee grew still. His face might as well have turned to concrete for all the better Pete could read it. He kept his gaze on Farabee and closed the distance between them until they were nose-to-nose. "Thanks for your help," Pete told the troopers. "I've got it from here."

They nodded and left Pete, Holt, and Zoe alone on the porch.

"Zoe," Pete said, "you can go, too."

"Not on your life."

He figured as much. Without acknowledging her smartass retort, he honed in on Farabee, close enough to feel the man's breath. Close enough to smell his nervous sweat. "You and I are going down to the station to have a little talk. You have the right to remain silent—"

The door at the far end of the porch crashed open, interrupting the Miranda warning. Wayne Baronick, a brown evidence bag in his gloved hand charged toward them. "Good. You're still here. You're gonna want to see this."

Pete took a step back from his murder suspect. "What have you got?"

Baronick opened the bag. "The boys found something besides a dead body in the potato bin." He reached into the bag and removed a black ball cap.

A black ball cap with a blue UK stitched on it. Just like the one Farabee's daughter had been wearing on Saturday.

Pete closed in on Farabee, whose stone-faced façade had started to crack. "Do you recognize that hat?"

Farabee's eyes had widened, locked on the hat. Pete could almost hear the whir of the man's mind processing his predicament. Farabee opened his mouth.

From behind him, Zoe cleared her throat. "You were about to Mirandize him, weren't you?"

Damn.

She continued where Pete had left off. "Anything you say can and will be used against you."

"Zoe," Pete warned.

"So shut up."

Farabee gave a barely discernible nod. "I think I will."

Pete resisted the urge to snarl at Zoe. *Stop helping.* Instead he shrugged. "Fine." There would be plenty of time to get the truth. Baronick dropped the cap back into the evidence bag while Pete unclipped a pair of handcuffs from his duty belt. "Holt Farabee, you're under arrest for the murder of Stephen Tierney."

Farabee made no effort to resist, but as Pete closed the cuffs on the man's wrists, he turned his head toward Zoe. "Maddie."

"Mrs. Kroll and I'll take care of her. I'll call Mr. Imperatore, too."

"Not Mrs. Kroll. You. I need *you* to protect her. Don't let her out of your sight." Farabee's voice sounded strangled. "Promise me. Don't let anything happen to my little girl."

Zoe watched Pete and Holt from the bank of windows on the back porch. Pete put Holt in the Explorer's backseat, climbed behind the wheel, and drove away. Downstairs, Franklin Marshall and the Monongahela County Crime Scene Unit along with Wayne and his county detectives processed her basement. Unless they'd removed Stephen Tierney's body through the outside doors, he was still down there, too. The assorted police jurisdictions remained on the premises, some talking among themselves outside, some moving in and out of her side of the house. Yet the commotion all around seemed muffled by the noise inside her mind.

Protect Maddie.

Holt didn't say watch. Or keep an eye on her. He said *protect.*

Why did that word stick inside Zoe's head like a burr to her jeans after a ride through the brush?

Then there was the ball cap. She'd seen him wear it a number of times since he'd moved in. But when was the last time? When he'd argued with Tierney on Friday. After that she had no way of knowing. She'd been on duty. What on earth had happened here while she'd been out trying to save lives?

She turned away from the window to fix her gaze on the closed door to Mrs. Kroll's kitchen. Behind it waited the landlady and Nate. And Maddie. What was she supposed to say to Maddie? *Your dad's been arrested for murder. But everything will be okay because he didn't do it.*

Or had he?

Had Zoe invited a killer into her home? Hers and the Krolls'. Had she not only put herself in danger, but that sweet old woman as well? Had Zoe been blinded by her need to shelter Maddie? Had she refused to consider Holt's guilt because he happened to be good-looking?

Handsome men had blinded her to their fatal flaws in the past, too. It was a weakness. One Pete had pointed out. Zoe pressed her hands to her face, massaging her forehead and covering her eyes as if that would block out the images of all her mistakes. Right now she had to check on Maddie and call the attorney for Holt.

Protect Maddie.

From what?

"You can't be serious." Anthony Imperatore thumped his briefcase down on Pete's desk after the attorney's meeting with Farabee.

Pete leaned back in his chair. "Can't I? Your client's personal belongings keep popping up at crime scenes. Did he give you a viable explanation?"

Imperatore gave him a tight smile. "You know any discussion I have with Mr. Farabee is subject to attorney/client privilege. Besides, he doesn't have to. The burden's on you and the DA to prove guilt. And if all you have is a Kentucky Wildcats ball cap and a promotional lighter, your case is a tad malnourished."

Imperatore was right, unfortunately. For now. "I have a few questions for him, which might help me fatten it up a bit."

The attorney sniffed. "Not if I have anything to say about it. I've told Mr. Farabee he shouldn't speak to you at all, but he says he wants to clear his name." Imperatore jerked his head toward the door.

Pete pushed up from his seat and led the way down the hall to the interrogation room.

Farabee sat motionless, his hands folded on the table. Imperatore took the empty chair next to his client. Pete lowered into the one across from them. For a long moment, he studied Farabee, his clenched jaw, his eyes glazed.

Pete had sat across this table or others just like it more times than he could count. He'd seen cocky criminals convinced they were too smart to get tripped up by a stupid cop. He'd seen suspects who were clearly innocent and those who clearly were not, but tried to act that way. He'd even encountered a few with unreadable faces, stoic as statues.

Farabee didn't fit any of those categories. He seemed to be shooting for impassive, but there was a hurricane of activity below the surface of his eyes. If Pete had to make a guess, he'd say the man was scared out of his wits.

Pete turned on the recorder between them and made his routine statement of who was in the room and confirming Farabee had been read his rights.

With the preliminaries out of the way, Pete sat back. "How long have you known Stephen Tierney?"

It was a simple question, but long seconds ticked off before Farabee answered. "Four, maybe five years."

"He was your neighbor?"

"Yes."

"Did you know him before you moved to Scenic Hilltop Estates?"

"No."

"Did your wife know him before you moved to Scenic Hilltop Estates?"

"No," Farabee said tersely, his eyes darkening.

Farabee's reaction confirmed Pete's suspicion. The topic of Stephen Tierney and Lillian Farabee was clearly a trigger. "Would you say you were friends with him?"

"Friends?" Farabee's voice deepened. "No."

"How would you classify your relationship with him?"

Farabee fixed Pete with an unwavering glare. "Neighbors."

"How did your wife get along with Mr. Tierney?"

Farabee's folded hands tightened, his knuckles turning a mottled crimson and white.

"Don't answer that," Imperatore said.

The hands relaxed.

"All right." Pete turned a page in his notebook. "When was the last time you saw Mr. Tierney?"

One of Farabee's fingers started tapping the opposite knuckle. "I'm not sure of the exact date. Before the fire."

"Had you talked to him since you moved back in?"

"Talked to him? No. I saw him coming and going is all."

Interesting. Pete wished like hell he could have asked Tierney a few questions before someone shut him up permanently. "Can you explain how your ball cap ended up with Mr. Tierney's dead body?"

Farabee's hands remained relaxed, and he opened his mouth to reply, but Imperatore touched his arm. "Now, Chief. We don't even know for certain the hat belonged to my client."

Pete eyed Farabee.

All three men knew the hat belonged to him. But Imperatore had been right earlier. It wasn't enough.

A knock at the interrogation room door distracted Pete from contemplating his next question. He pocketed his notebook and clicked off the recorder. "Excuse me for a moment."

He opened the door to Baronick, who motioned him into the hall. "What?" Pete snapped.

"Thought you'd like an update. The coroner is transporting the body to Brunswick and will do the autopsy either tonight or tomorrow, depending on when he can get Doc Abercrombie to come in."

"That's it?"

"Not entirely. I pressed him for a guess about how long Tierney's been dead. Marshall says since the decomp is so far along, he'd clearly been dead several days to a week. Maybe even a little longer."

Typical Franklin Marshall. Never one to give clear cut information prematurely. "Anything else?"

"The Crime Scene Unit and my detectives are still there picking through the basement. I asked Zoe if we could search the house."

Pete battled a grin. "I have a pretty good idea of her reply."

Baronick huffed.

"Actually it was pretty tame. The little girl was in the room. So unless we come up with probable cause for a search warrant, we aren't getting access beyond the basement."

"I doubt we'd find anything anyway."

Baronick tipped his head toward the interrogation room. "You getting anything useful?"

"Not with his attorney sitting next to him."

"At least we have his ball cap."

"Imperatore has pointed out we don't know for certain it belongs to Farabee."

Baronick snorted. "Who else around here went to the University of Kentucky? We can test it for DNA if need be."

Pete breathed a soft growl. "Yeah." If need be.

The detective narrowed his eyes. "I know that look. What's wrong? You know we've got our man."

Did they?

Pete wasn't so sure anymore.

The coroner's van had pulled out, signaling to Zoe that Stephen Tierney's body no longer occupied the potato bin. Nate Williamson and most of the police and news media vehicles had also vacated the premises. However, the crime scene truck and a pair of unmarked sedans belonging to the county detectives remained parked behind the house. Footsteps and sounds of scuffling still floated up from the basement.

Zoe found Maddie curled up with a book on the couch in the parlor. "How are you doing?"

The girl looked up, her eyes red and weepy. "When's my dad coming back?"

Zoe wished she knew. She searched for words that wouldn't offer false hope, but wouldn't scare the child either.

Before Zoe could come up with a suitable answer, Maddie must have seen it in her eyes. "I don't want to sleep in our room all by myself. Can I stay with you?"

Holt's words echoed in Zoe's head. *You. I need you to protect her. Don't let her out of your sight.*

"Absolutely. If your dad isn't home before bedtime, we'll just move your bed across the hall into my room."

Maddie seemed appeased. She lowered her eyes to her book.

But Zoe suspected the girl didn't comprehend a word of it. "Hey, why don't we go out to the barn? We can saddle up George and Windstar and go for a little ride."

Maddie drew her puckered mouth to one side of her face, contemplating. "No, thanks. I don't feel like it."

In Zoe's experience, it was never good when a girl turned down a chance to go riding. If equine therapy wasn't going to work, maybe feline therapy would. "Then can you do me a favor?"

"What?"

"Merlin and Jade are locked in my office because of all the hubbub. I want to move them upstairs and put them in the bathroom instead. You know. In case one of those guys opens the office door."

"You don't want your cats getting out. They might run away."

"Exactly."

Maddie placed her bookmark and closed the book. "Okay."

Zoe dug her key from her pocket and motioned for Maddie to follow.

They crossed the wide center hallway, Zoe unlocked the door at the base of the front staircase, and they stepped into her office. Jade stood there as if she'd been waiting for them, her tail twitching. Merlin gazed at them from the sunny windowsill next to the fireplace.

Zoe scooped up Jade and deposited her into Maddie's eager arms. Then Zoe squeezed around her recliner to retrieve Merlin from his sunspot. Cats in hand, they returned to the hall and climbed the main staircase, slipping into Zoe's bedroom at the top.

With the felines contained securely in the bathroom, Maddie hopped onto Zoe's bed. "I like your room."

"Thanks." She took a seat next to the girl. "Everything's going to be all right, you know. Mr. Imperatore will bring your dad back as soon as Pete's done talking to him. They might even be on their way now. Or it may take until tomorrow morning."

Maddie scowled at her hands, neatly folded in her lap. "I don't know." She looked up at Zoe. "The police think my dad killed Mr. Tierney, don't they?"

A knot formed in Zoe's throat. "They're just trying to find the truth. It might take a little while to sort it out, but they'll figure out who really did it."

A troubled line creased Maddie's smooth forehead. "That's what I'm afraid of. What if my dad *did* do it?"

TWENTY

"Do us all a favor." Imperatore glowered over his glasses at Pete. "Next time you get an urge to drag my client down here, just come to me first. It'll save everyone some aggravation and gas money."

"Yeah, yeah." Pete watched as the attorney escorted Holt Farabee down the hall and out of the police station.

Baronick leaned against the doorjamb to Pete's office. "I can't believe you let him go."

"What choice did I have? Imperatore said we had a flimsy case, and he was right." Pete had jumped the gun. Again. Slapping handcuffs on a suspect every time a new shred of evidence showed up was a damned stupid move. He'd known better than that when he was a rookie. Of course, Zoe hadn't been twisting him up inside like a lovesick teenager when he'd been a rookie either. "We have to build a solid case before we ask the DA to press charges. And I'm not convinced we *have* a case."

"I had the feeling you were hedging back there. What's eating you?"

Pete brushed past the detective and slid into his chair. "Holt Farabee is no fool. I have a hard time believing he'd kill a man and then hide the body in the house where he's living."

Baronick took the chair across the desk. "Obviously it wasn't planned that way. I figure Tierney showed up at the farm. They got into it. Farabee whacked him and hid him there until he could move the body." The detective shrugged. "Zoe found it first."

"Hide him in the basement? Two floors down from where he and his little girl are sleeping?" Pete shook his head. "You don't shit where you eat."

Baronick's phone jingled and he dug in his pocket for it. "He didn't drag it in there. For some reason he and Tierney happened to be in the basement. That's where Farabee killed him."

"And hid him in the root cellar?" Pete huffed. "Why the root cellar?"

The question was for himself as much as the detective. And it pertained to the killer in general, Farabee or not. Why had the killer buried the body in the potato bin of all places?

Baronick frowned at the message on his phone. "I may have to take back what I just said. It looks like Farabee *did* drag Tierney into the basement."

"What'd they find?" As soon as Pete asked the question he waved away Baronick's response. "Never mind. You can tell me on our way out. I want to see for myself what your county detectives found."

Zoe put an arm around the little girl's shoulders. "Why would you think your dad would hurt Mr. Tierney?"

The little girl toyed with her fingernails as if trying to decide whether a manicure was in order. "Dad hated him."

"You said that once before." When Zoe had witnessed a confrontation between Holt and the man she'd thought of as the guy from the fort on Friday. This was Monday. Considering the stench of the body and the subsequent rate of decomp, it was very likely Tierney had died shortly after the encounter.

How shortly?

Maddie sighed. "I used to hear Mom and Dad arguing. They said it wasn't anything important. Grownup stuff. They said I'd understand when I was older. And I guess it was okay because I'd see them getting all kissy and lovey dovey afterwards. But lately it was different. A couple of times, Dad was really mad. *Really* mad. They weren't just arguing. Dad was yelling. Loud."

"What about?"

"I don't know exactly. But I remember Dad yelling about Mom and Mr. Tierney. Dad called him bad names." Maddie swallowed hard. Her eyes brimmed with tears, and her voice wavered when she said, "One time, he called Mom a bad name, too."

Zoe tried to picture troubled, bereaved Holt calling his late wife a name their daughter couldn't repeat. "Sometimes adults say stupid stuff. Things they don't mean."

Maddie met her gaze, the little girl's dark eyes wide with sorrow. "He said—one time, he said—if he ever saw Mom and Mr. Tierney together again—he'd kill them both."

The mental image created a knot in Zoe's heart. She shoved the picture away. Before she could think of a response to sooth Maddie, a door slammed beneath them followed by the rapid thump of boots on the staircase.

"Maddie?" Holt's voice echoed up to them.

"Dad!" Fear and worry forgotten, Maddie tore out of Zoe's bedroom and into the hallway.

By the time Zoe reached her door, Holt had made it almost to the top of the stairs, and Maddie had flung herself into her father's arms. He crushed her to him, smothering her with kisses. As Zoe watched the father-daughter reunion, faded memories of similar moments with her own dad threatened to rip open the old scar yet again.

Holt met Zoe's gaze over Maddie's blond head. He mouthed the words, "Thank you."

Zoe responded with a tight smile. "They let you go, I see."

He set Maddie down, but kept a hand on her shoulder. "They don't have a case and everyone knows it."

Everyone. Except Zoe.

Holt dropped to one knee and cupped his daughter's face in his hands. "Sweetheart, I want you to go in our room and pack up all the nice stuff Zoe's friends have given you. And then pack the clothes we brought with us."

"But why?"

Zoe wondered the same thing.

"We've taken advantage of Zoe's and Mrs. Kroll's hospitality long enough."

"You're leaving?" Zoe asked.

He looked up at her and nodded once. "I don't feel right taking all this stuff from your boarders. I'm sure you can see it gets back where it belongs."

"Don't be silly. No one wants their things back."

"I know, but—"

"It was an act of kindness on their parts. Returning toys and clothes that Maddie enjoys... They'd take it as an insult."

Holt appeared to reconsider.

Maddie tugged at the front of his shirt. "Please, Dad."

His face softened. "All right. Pack up everything."

"Where are we going?"

From the look on Holt's face, Zoe guessed he hadn't gotten that far.

"Just go pack. I have to talk to Zoe."

Maddie shot a forlorn glance at her before darting into the room across the hall. Holt climbed to his feet and closed the distance between him and Zoe.

He made a couple of false starts before he finally said, "Thank you for everything you've done. I'm sorry I can't stick around and finish the repairs."

She studied his face.

It was a handsome face. Strong jaw. Tortured eyes. They didn't look like a killer's eyes. But then again, she'd been fooled before. "Did you kill Tierney?" she whispered.

"No." His voice sounded like it had been roughed up with 12-grit sandpaper. He held her gaze and the creases in his forehead deepened. "I could never..." He shook his head. "But I can't expect you to believe me."

"I want to. But if you didn't, why are you running?"

His eyes shifted toward the room across the hall for a millisecond. "I can't explain. Not now. I have something I need to take care of." His face grew hard. Dark.

For a moment, Zoe thought back to the mental picture of Holt threatening his wife. It was so hard to imagine. "What do you need to take care of?"

"Something I've put off too long."

She really didn't like the sound of that. "Then leave Maddie here," Zoe said, hearing the desperation in her own voice.

He gave his head a quick shake, and Zoe thought she caught a glimpse of tears in his eyes. "I can't." He took a deep breath. Blew it out. "Look. I really appreciate everything you've done, from saving my life to helping my daughter through losing her mom. But the best thing I can do right now to repay you is to get out of your house."

"But Maddie—"

"Stays with me."

Zoe could tell there would be no arguing with him. Besides, maybe it was for the best. Bringing the Farabees into her life and into her house had all but destroyed her relationship with Pete. And yet, the idea of never seeing them again, especially Maddie, left a yawning ache in her heart. "Can you promise to let me know where you are? That you and Maddie are okay?"

A sad smile crossed Holt's lips. "Promise? I can't promise anything. But I'll try." He reached out and brushed her cheek with his fingertips before turning and disappearing into the guest room with his daughter.

Zoe retreated into her room and closed the door to the second-floor hallway. If only she could shut the door to her fears as easily.

"Chief." Pete's secretary called out to him before he could make it out of the station. "Wait."

"What is it?"

Nancy waved her personal cell phone at him. "My sister just called me."

"Let me guess. Her husband and father are duking it out again with hedge clippers."

"Huh?" Baronick clearly wasn't up to speed on the local hedge feud.

"Not exactly. She's worried to death about Ryan, though. Said she hasn't seen or heard from him since Saturday."

The trashed house. Ryan Mancinelli passed out on the couch. "Did she try going over and knocking on the door?"

"No one answered."

Pete closed his eyes with a sigh. Opening them again, he turned to a perplexed Baronick. "I need to check on this guy. It's on the way."

"Need backup?"

"I don't think so." He nodded to Nancy. "Tell your sister I'm on my way."

The secretary was already thumbing her phone's screen. "Thanks, Chief."

Pete and Baronick stepped out into the suffocating heat. Pete paused in the shade of the building before venturing into the broiling sunshine. "Tell me what your detective found."

"A wheelbarrow."

"It's a farm. There have to be a half a dozen wheelbarrows around the place."

"This one happened to be leaning outside the basement's exterior doors."

Pete remembered the day he'd had the confrontation with Zoe outside those doors, and the vintage wheelbarrow leaning against the foundation. "Yeah. So?"

"It also appears to have some...leakage on it."

"Leakage? You mean blood?"

"Not really. Let's just say body fluids and leave it at that until the lab gets a look."

Body fluids. On the ancient wheelbarrow. Pete pressed his fingers into his left eyebrow, behind which a killer headache lurked. "Wonderful. You heading back out there?"

"Absolutely."

Pete nodded. "I'll catch up to you after I make sure Ryan Mancinelli hasn't crawled into a bottle and drowned."

From the outside, the Mancinelli house looked no different than it had in recent days. When Pete had stopped by to check on Ryan on Sunday, the kid had met him on the porch. Red-eyed and pale-skinned, he'd insisted he was fine.

Today, one day later, no one responded when Pete pressed the doorbell. Pounding on the door didn't help either.

Pete backed away from the house to look around and spotted Ashley Mancinelli standing on her parents' porch next door. She waved and headed his way.

"Thanks for coming. My folks are ready to write Ryan off, but I'm worried about him."

"I understand. Do you have the key?"

She held up a loaded key ring with one of them singled out.

Pete took it and unlocked the door. Pushing it open, he called out, "Ryan, it's Chief Adams. Are you in there?" Pete's words reverberated through the spacious entryway, the slight echo the only response. He stepped inside.

Ashley followed. "Ryan, honey? It's me." Still no answer. She caught sight of the smashed painting and the hole in the wall. "Oh my God."

"It was like this Saturday night when I looked in on him."

She sniffed and wrinkled her nose. "He started smoking again."

"The rest of the place isn't any better. Stay behind me."

"Okay."

Nothing else inside the house had changed, either. Except for the couch in the living room. The blanket Pete had covered Ryan with was lumped at one end.

Ashley only made it as far as her kitchen. Or what remained of it. She covered her mouth with one trembling hand and surveyed the shards of her dinnerware scattered across the counter and floor. A sob broke through.

"I'm going to check the rest of the house," Pete said.

She nodded without meeting his eyes.

From what Pete could tell, Ryan hadn't taken his trail of destruction upstairs. The rooms there—a vacant bedroom with the beds made and another one set up as an office—were spotless. The basement likewise appeared unharmed.

And no potato bin with a body in it.

Ashley stood in the spot where Pete had left her. "He's not here." She looked up at him. "Is his truck in the garage?"

"Let's check." Pete escorted her outside and around to the three-bay industrial-sized garage which doubled as Ryan's workshop.

Ashley punched in a code for the garage door opener. They stood back as the door clanked and rose to reveal an empty bay.

Pete swept both arms open toward the void. "See? He probably slept it off and went to work this morning."

She nodded, but looked unconvinced. "I hope so. But it's never been that easy. The PTSD, I mean. And the accident didn't trigger it. The explosion did."

"Explosion? You mean the Farabee house?"

"Yeah. He got pretty weird when he saw it on the news. I guess because he'd dealt with that sort of thing so much."

Pete's gut started gnawing at him. "What 'sort of thing' do you mean?"

"I thought you knew. Ryan was an EOD Specialist."

TWENTY-ONE

Even before Holt and Maddie were packed, Zoe had been on the phone to Franklin Marshall. She learned he and Doc Abercrombie were setting up to do the autopsy on Stephen Tierney. She also learned she wasn't welcome. No surprise. She already knew she was still technically a suspect.

Welcome or not, the minute the Farabees drove away from the farm, Zoe jumped into her truck and headed to Brunswick. Forty-five minutes later, she stood in the morgue's office with Franklin, who was decked out in his scrubs.

The coroner planted his fists on his narrow hips. "Good lord, Zoe. Every time I've tried to get you to assist with an autopsy, you pull every trick in the book to get out of it. This one I can't possibly allow you to be anywhere near, and here you are."

"I don't want to assist. I just want to know what you find."

"I'll call you."

"I'll save you the trouble."

"Zoe..."

"I found him in *my* basement."

"Precisely."

They stood nose-to-nose. Zoe wasn't backing down. Especially when she noticed Franklin's eye twitch.

The coroner sighed. "I'm serious, Zoe. I can't let you in there. A defense attorney would have a field day throwing out any evidence we might provide."

"Then let me sit here. I won't set foot inside the autopsy room."

"You could sit upstairs in the hospital's snack bar. I'll call you as soon as we finish."

"C'mon, Franklin." Zoe let a touch of a whine creep into her voice for effect. "This guy died in my house. I need to know why." And who did it, but "why" would be a start. "The cops won't let me work on the case. I get that. But I can't just stand back and be an impassive observer."

He shook a bony finger in her face. "You don't have a choice." But he dropped his hand to his side and huffed at her. "Fine. You can sit here. But do not set foot through that door."

The truth was she'd have settled for sitting in the hallway. "Okay. Thanks."

The coroner muttered something she couldn't quite make out as he shuffled from the office to the autopsy room.

Zoe walked to the window and peered through the slats in the blinds. Stephen Tierney's body lay on the stainless steel table. She could make out the marbled discoloration to skin stretched too tight from bloating. The forensic pathologist looked up as Franklin approached and nodded. As Doc Abercrombie prepared to make the first incision, Zoe let the slats close and turned to sit in one of the worn vinyl chairs that graced the office. No, she definitely did not want to be in the autopsy room for this one.

"Ryan was an EOD specialist?" Pete echoed Ashley Mancinelli's words. EOD. Explosive Ordnance Disposal.

"Yes." She turned away from the empty garage bay. "He'd blown up so many devices in the war, any kind of loud noise would send him into a panic attack."

Pete scanned the contents of the garage, looking for—what? The makings of a bomb? So far the person he was looking for hadn't needed one. Natural gas. Hay. A lighter. Who needed an incendiary device when materials abounded? "Don't suppose you know where Ryan's working today, do you?"

"No." She nodded toward the house. "But he keeps his schedule on his computer. Do you want me to look it up?"

"Please."

Ashley led the way back inside, keeping her head down to avoid looking at the mess. Upstairs, she pressed a button to power up the computer. As it hummed and whined, she looked around the room, hugging herself as if she was cold. "He should be home soon."

Good. Then Pete wouldn't have to track him down to ask him a few questions.

"It wasn't always like this. We used to be so good together. And Ryan and my folks used to get along great. Ryan and Dad would sit for hours and talk about the wars. Dad had been in the Gulf War. The first one. He wouldn't talk to Mom or me about it. Only Ryan."

"When did things start changing?"

Ashley shook her head. "It happened gradually. I can't really put a date on it. But this business with the hedges..." She sighed.

The computer played a short ditty as a white bar appeared, asking for a password. Ashley slid into the leather swivel chair and typed a few strokes. The computer binged and a new screen appeared. Within a minute, she'd pulled up an appointment book. "That's odd."

Pete leaned down to look over her shoulder. "What?"

"There's nothing here. It's blank."

"For today?"

She scrolled down. "For the last week. I don't understand. He's been going to work everyday."

Pete touched her shoulder. "Do you mind?"

"Not at all." She vacated the chair so he could take her place.

Pete scrolled further back through Ryan's calendar. There were a number of small jobs. New roof. Room addition. Replacement windows. The man had kept busy. Pete was about to quit when he spotted a block of months marked only as SHE. "Um. Who is *she*?"

"Excuse me?"

Pete hoped he wasn't about to drive the final nail into the Mancinelli marriage's coffin as he pointed to the screen. "She. Who is she?"

Ashley laughed. "Those are initials. His shorthand for Scenic Hilltop Estates. He worked up there on and off for almost two years."

Pete left orders with Ashley Mancinelli to call his cell phone as soon as her husband returned home and headed to Zoe's farm, currently known as the crime scene. The crowd had thinned out considerably.

The crime scene boys appeared to be packing it in. Baronick was engaging one of the investigators in conversation next to the county CSU truck. Obvious by their absence were Zoe's and Farabee's pickups. Pete parked next to the detective's unmarked sedan and climbed out. "What have we got?"

The crime scene investigator gave a short laugh lacking amusement. "A truck full of evidence that's probably nothing more than a century's worth of garbage."

Baronick flashed his too-big smile. "Maybe you've bagged the next big Antiques Roadshow find and don't even realize it."

"Right." The CSI didn't sound optimistic. "We'll start sorting through everything as soon as we get back to the lab. I'll let you both know if we find anything of importance."

They shook hands, and the crime scene guys piled into their truck.

"Where's Zoe?" Pete asked Baronick as the CSU rig bounced down the lane.

"She was gone by the time I got here. Farabee and the kid, too." Baronick hoisted a thumb toward the house. "The old lady says the Farabees have flown the coop permanently. Packed their meager belongings and vamoosed."

"Did he happen to say where he was going?"

"Not to the old lady. Maybe he told Zoe." Baronick waggled a suggestive eyebrow. "Maybe she's helping him move."

The thought chilled what had been a warm realization. Farabee no longer shared Zoe's house. But had the change in address come too late to sever the bond that had developed?

"Or," Baronick continued. "She might be at the autopsy. Franklin called me a little while ago to say he and Doc were gonna get started on it..." The detective checked his phone. "Right about now."

"Zoe can't assist with this one. Franklin knows that."

"But does Zoe?"

Any other time, she'd have found an array of excuses to avoid the morgue. But under the circumstances...

"How about you? Did you find your secretary's brother-in-law?"

"Not exactly." Pete relayed the tidbit about Ryan Mancinelli's work history at Scenic Hilltop Estates.

Baronick whistled. "Any connection to Lillian Farabee?"

"I intend to find out. One more thing. He was an EOD specialist in Iraq."

"Get out. An explosives expert who worked at a housing development where there happened to be an explosion. I think I want a long talk with that man."

"Me, too. His wife's supposed to call as soon as he gets home."

"Don't suppose he's flown the coop, too, do you?"

"I hope not." Pete dug his phone from his pocket and checked the time. A little after five. Technically, he was off duty. He punched in Kevin's number. "I'm going to update my officer and tell him to keep an eye out for Mancinelli," he told Baronick before pressing send. "Then I'm going to check in on Tierney's autopsy." And he wasn't sure if he hoped to find Zoe there or not.

Zoe paced the small office. Stopped to peer through the blinds. Made another loop around the desk. Stopped and checked her phone. No call or text from Holt. Not that she'd expected one. But she'd like to know Maddie was okay.

Zoe pulled up his number from her address book.

The call rang twice and went to voicemail. She hung up without leaving a message.

The door swung open, and she wheeled, coming face-to-face with Pete. A blanket of regret settled over her when she met his icy blues. Until a few days ago, there would have been a sparkle in them. This evening, there was only guarded disappointment.

She backed against the dented steel desk, half sitting on it, half leaning. "Hey."

"You aren't supposed to be here."

"Nice to see you, too."

He heaved a sigh. "You know what I mean. This case is off limits."

"So I've been told." She shot a glance at the closed blinds. "I haven't gone near the body. In fact this is as close as I've gotten to it since I checked him for a pulse when he was just an arm among the eyes."

"Huh?"

City boys. "His arm. The potatoes' eyes. Never mind."

"I got it." Pete cast a quick look at the same closed blinds. "Any idea what they've found?"

"Nope. I'm behaving. Really. All I know is what I can see when I peek, which isn't much."

Pete seemed to be pondering whether to leave her there to check their progress for himself or to stay where he was. He crossed his arms. "Your housemates left."

It was a statement of fact more than a question, so she saw no need to respond.

"Where'd they go?"

"I have no idea."

Pete raised a doubting eyebrow.

"I don't. To be honest, I don't think Holt knew either."

"Why'd he leave?"

Zoe figured Pete already guessed one possible reason—guilt—so she didn't mention it. "He said he needed to take care of something he'd put off too long."

Pete frowned. "And you don't know what he meant by that?"

"He didn't confide in me." Zoe pushed away from the desk and hooked her thumbs in the belt loops of her uniform pants. She'd been off duty all day, but still hadn't found time to change clothes. "Look, I owe you an apology."

That eyebrow shot up again, but this time in surprise. "You do?"

She looked down at her boots. Caught her lower lip in her teeth for a moment. "You may have been right about him. I should have listened to you instead of inviting him to stay with me and Mrs. Kroll."

She could feel Pete watching her and looked up to see his reaction. She expected an I told you so. Or a self-satisfied smirk. Instead, he was scowling.

"What?"

He shook his head. "I was about to say I've changed my mind about Farabee. I don't think he killed Tierney. And probably not his wife either."

The admission startled Zoe into silence. For a moment, at least. "Why not?"

"I don't think the man's a complete idiot. And he'd have to be to hide the body of a man he'd killed in his own basement." Pete made a sour face. "Or the basement of the house where he was living at the time."

"What about his ball cap?"

Pete shrugged. "I don't have answers. Just a lot of puzzle pieces. And the ones involving Farabee don't fit."

Before Zoe could add a few more spare pieces to the puzzle, the office door swung open, and Franklin Marshall breezed through. He'd shed the gloves and scrubs.

"You missed all the fun," he said to Pete.

"Not all of it. Did you find anything?"

Franklin eyed Zoe. "Perhaps she should leave before we discuss business."

"For crying out loud." She planted her fists on her hips. "Do you seriously consider me a suspect?"

"No," both men said simultaneously.

She raised both hands, palms up, imploring.

The coroner rolled his eyes. Pete grinned. "What'd you find, Franklin?"

He walked around the desk and leaned down, tapping the computer keyboard. Zoe positioned herself so she could peer over his shoulder. After a few mouse clicks, a page of photo thumbnails opened. "This body tells quite a story," Franklin said with a tired sigh. "And it's considerably different than that of the police report."

"How so?" Pete moved next to Zoe. "And in English, please."

Franklin enlarged one photo. He tapped the screen with his pen, indicating a greenish pattern on the torso. "This is called venous marbling. And this..." He pointed the pen at red and white mottling over the rest of the body. "This is the set livor and blanching which show the positioning of the body when he was killed."

Zoe's pulse raced. "That's not right."

Franklin and Pete turned to look at her.

"He was lying on potatoes. There should be white marks on his chest and abdomen from lying face down on potatoes."

A smile teased Franklin's lips. "You're right. If he'd fallen onto those potatoes or even been placed there immediately after he was killed, the blanching and lividity would show it. This man had been on his side. The body was moved after his livor was set. Also, if I were to believe this gentleman had died where he was found, which was a cool dark basement, I'd say he'd been dead for quite some time. Perhaps a week or more."

Zoe nodded. "Because decomp would have been slowed down."

"Exactly."

Pete pulled out his reading glasses, settled them on his face, and took another look at the photo. "Do you have a cause of death?"

"There was a compressed fracture to the posterior aspect of the right parietal bone." Franklin's fingers went to the spot on his own head. "I'd say someone struck him from behind with something smaller than a baseball bat. A pipe perhaps. And there's something else, too." The coroner clicked the mouse, zooming in on the photo. "See this area of blanching?"

Zoe squinted at a whitish band circling Tierney's midsection with a matching mark on both arms. "Was he tied up?"

"Possibly." Franklin winked at her. "I'll make a coroner out of you yet."

A flash of pride was quickly nullified by doubt. Was that a good thing or a bad thing?

Pete either didn't catch Franklin's comment or pretended not to. "Do you have a time of death?"

"Hard to say since the body was clearly moved." Franklin lowered into his chair. "Could have been any time from last Thursday to Saturday. It would help if you knew when he was last seen."

"He's been out of town on business." Pete said. "As far as I can tell, the last time anyone saw him was last Wednesday after the explosion."

"I saw him on Friday." Zoe braced for an explosion of a different sort as both men looked at her. She met Pete's withering glare. "Right before you showed up. In fact, you just missed him."

"What," Pete asked, his jaw tight, "was Stephen Tierney doing at your house?"

"He was arguing with Holt."

TWENTY-TWO

Pete caught Zoe by her arm. "Would you excuse us?" he said to the coroner as he escorted the woman he'd *thought* he knew into the hallway.

Zoe trotted along with him, but wrenched her arm free the moment the doors closed behind them. "Ouch." She rubbed the spot he'd been holding and glared at him. "What's wrong with you?"

"What's wrong with *me*? What's wrong with *you*? Why didn't you tell me Stephen Tierney was at your house?"

"You never asked."

"You knew I was looking for him."

"No, I didn't."

Pete started to insist she did, but the wounded look on her face stopped him, made him think. He and his men had been working the case with Wayne Baronick and the county police detectives. Zoe, however, had been out of the official loop. Pete had kept her on the outside. Holt Farabee had become a fence between them, keeping them from seeing eye-to-eye just as surely as Tierney's fence had kept him from seeing the rural beauty around him.

Pete reached for the spot on Zoe's arm that he'd gripped too tight, but stopped short of touching it. "I'm sorry."

She continued to glare at him. "You've said that before."

He sensed the anger in her words masked a heavy dose of disappointment. In him. He gave her an apologetic grin. "Yeah. Is it possible to say I'm sorry for saying I'm sorry?"

The bitterness in her eyes softened, but didn't disappear.

He sighed. "Look. Can we sit down and talk? Preferably without arguing."

"Is there anything left to talk about?"

Somehow he didn't think she meant the homicide cases. "I hope so."

Zoe lowered her gaze as if searching for answers on the toes of her boots. "I'm hungry. I'm tired. I'm going home to change out of my work clothes." She looked up at him. "Provided I'm allowed into my house."

"As long as you stay out of the basement."

She rolled her eyes. "Fine. If you want to talk, I'll be home."

"I'll bring pizza."

Zoe backed up a step, studying him the way she sometimes did when they played poker. Then she turned. Over her shoulder, she said, "Extra pepperoni. And don't forget the beer."

Pete kept his gaze on her ass as she swaggered away. And smiled.

Zoe lifted the cardboard lid of the pizza box and breathed in the aroma of pepperoni, cheese, and herbs. Her stomach let out an eager rumble. She picked up a slice, flopped it onto a paper plate, and pinched the string of mozzarella tethering the wedge to the rest of the pie.

Pete leaned against her kitchen counter. "Have you eaten today?"

She thought about it. "No." The cheese stretched thinner and finally broke. She dropped the savory thread onto the slice and offered the plate to Pete.

He shook his head. "You take it."

She was too famished to argue. Grabbing a cold beer from the six pack, she nudged open the swinging door separating the kitchen and dining/living room with her hip and flopped into a chair at the table. She'd wolfed down a large portion of the wedge before Pete had a chance to join her.

He looked at her and chuckled.

"What?" she mumbled around the mouthful of pizza.

Pete clamped his mouth shut and shook his head. "Nothing."

Zoe washed the not-so-ladylike bite down with a slug of beer. "I told you. I'm hungry."

"I didn't say a word."

They ate in silence for a few minutes. By the time Zoe had stuffed the crust into her mouth, her stomach had stopped complaining. She chewed slowly, wiping her fingers on a paper napkin. After swallowing, she leaned back in the chair. "I honestly didn't know you were looking for Tierney. I'd have told you about the argument between him and Holt if I had."

"Tell me now."

She took a deep breath, thinking back to Friday. "I'd had Maddie out in the barn playing with George. The schooling pony. When we were coming back to the house, I saw Holt's truck and a white car. He was talking to a man." Zoe licked one finger and used it to capture a few stray crumbs on the grease-stained paper plate. "I couldn't hear what they were saying, but it was pretty obvious Holt was pissed. I didn't realize who the other guy was until Maddie said it was their neighbor."

"What else did Maddie say?"

Zoe looked at Pete. He'd finished his slice, too, and was watching her suck the captured crumbs from her fingers. "She said her dad hated Tierney."

The expected outburst of "I told you so" or "I knew it," never came. Zoe went on to tell him about the arguments Maddie had overheard between her mom and dad. "She said her dad threatened to kill Tierney."

Pete continued his silence. After a moment, he stood and held out a hand. "Do you want another slice?"

Zoe handed him her plate. "Please." She watched him disappear into the kitchen and sipped her beer while she waited for his return. Was he being deferential about the news out of respect for her feelings? She'd expected him to jump on his phone and put out a BOLO the second he'd heard about the threats. Instead, he was playing waiter.

Pete emerged from the kitchen and set her plate piled with two more slices in front of her before sinking back into his chair. "How long was Tierney at your place?"

Zoe picked up a wedge. "I don't know how long he was there before Maddie and I came back from the barn. But he didn't stay long afterwards." She took a bite. Savored the salty tang. "And he was alive when he left."

Pete grinned at her snippy comment. "Did Farabee say anything to you about his visitor?"

"I asked him about Tierney, but all Holt said was he'd stopped by to express his condolences. I didn't believe him."

"Did you see Tierney after that?"

"No."

"That sets time of death somewhere between Friday late afternoon and this morning."

The thought of the smell and the condition of Tierney's body turned the pizza sour on her tongue. She dropped the slice on her plate. "Closer to Friday, I'd think. I'm surprised you aren't running out of here to arrest Holt again."

While Zoe's appetite may have spoiled, Pete's seemed unaffected. He shoved half a piece into his mouth and chewed. After taking a sip of his beer and swallowing, he shook his head. "I still don't think he did it."

"What? You said that before. Now I've told you about this animosity between him and the victim and you still don't think he's responsible?"

"Do you?"

She blew out a breath. Turned the paper plate around a couple of times, as if studying the slices from different angles might give her a clearer view of her own feelings. "I don't know. I liked him. He seemed like a nice guy who'd lost his wife. But I've always had a sense he's been hiding things, too. There's something he's holding back. Something...dark." Zoe looked up at Pete. "Your turn. Why don't you think he's guilty?"

Pete finished his supper and wiped his fingers on a crumpled napkin. "I agree he's hiding something. Farabee's smart. Too smart to kill a man he clearly despises and then leave the body in his basement. And definitely too smart to kill him elsewhere and move him *into* his basement."

"You don't think he just hid him in the potato bin until he could dump the body?"

Pete shoved his plate to the side and leaned forward. "What was he waiting for? You were out of the house all weekend. He had ample time to dispose of the body. Besides, the CSU went over every square inch of your basement. There is no evidence indicating he was killed there."

Zoe leaned back. "Why would someone kill Stephen Tierney elsewhere and sneak him into my house?" The reality of the scenario destroyed what was left of her appetite. "To frame Holt?"

"It's one possibility."

"But who would want to frame Holt for murder? The only person I ever saw him angry with is *dead*."

Pete shifted back. "What do you know about Ryan Mancinelli?"

Zoe rolled the name over in her mind. "The wreck on Friday..." The one where Pete had said he loved her and then apologized. She quickly decided the accident in front of Ryan Mancinelli's house was a bad frame of reference. "He's married to Jack Naeser's daughter, right?"

"Yeah. What else do you know about him?"

"Not much. He's a carpenter. Wait. Do you think there's a connection between him and Holt because they're both carpenters?"

Pete shrugged. "Possibly. Did Farabee ever mention him?"

"No. Why? What's Ryan got to do with Stephen Tierney? Or Lillian Farabee?"

"For starters, Ryan Mancinelli worked on the Scenic Hilltop Estates project for a couple of years."

Zoe's pulse kicked up a notch. "So he knows—knew—both of them."

"I intend to ask him." Pete glanced at his watch. "Which reminds me." He pulled out his phone and scowled at the screen. "His wife was supposed to call me when he got home."

Zoe watched Pete key in a phone number.

Ryan Mancinelli.

She didn't know him, but there was something about the name. Something she'd read or heard. Had he done work for the Krolls at some point? What was it she couldn't put her finger on?

Pete didn't need to put his phone on speaker for Zoe to hear Ashley's side of the conversation. The girl was clearly frantic. "He hasn't come home yet. I'm afraid something's happened to him."

"Don't panic," Pete told her. "I'll have my men check the bars and keep an eye out for him. I'm sure he'll be fine." After telling her to call if Mancinelli showed, Pete hung up.

"You think he's been drinking?" Zoe asked.

"Saturday night, he was passed out on his couch, surrounded by empty whiskey bottles. Yeah. I think he's drinking." Pete made another call, this one to Kevin, placing an unofficial BOLO on Mancinelli.

Zoe gave up trying to force the memory out of hiding. "I still don't see why you would think Ryan Mancinelli has anything to do with this," she said after Pete set his phone on the table. "There were probably a hundred men who worked over there in the last few years. Do you suspect all of them?"

"Only those with a history of handling explosives. Ryan Mancinelli was an EOD specialist in Afghanistan. His wife thinks the blast last week triggered his posttraumatic stress disorder and his subsequent tumble off the AA wagon."

The memory jumped back into center ring, but remained veiled.

Pete must have noticed the look on her face. "What is it?"

She wished she knew. "I can't quite grasp it, but I have a feeling I've heard something about Ryan Mancinelli before."

"Like what?"

She narrowed her eyes at Pete. "I told you I can't remember."

He stood up. "Well, let me know if you do." He pointed at her uneaten pizza. "Are you gonna finish that?"

"No." Whatever was stuck in her subconscious was screaming to be let out. "You said Ryan was what kind of specialist?"

"EOD." Pete scooped up his empty plate and her full one and headed for the kitchen. "Explosive Ordnance Disposal."

"Explosive—*what?*" Zoe launched out of her chair and punched through the swinging door after him. "Bombs? Ryan Mancinelli handled bombs?"

Pete slid her uneaten pizza back into the box and deposited the paper plates in the trash can. "He handled explosives. One of the ways they get rid of bombs and suspicious packages is to blow them up."

"Do you think—could he have blown up Holt's house?"

Pete washed his hands, dried them, and turned to lean back against the sink, facing her, his expression impassive. "I haven't ruled it out. But it's a pretty big jump. There was no evidence of a bomb or detonating device found in the debris. All signs point to it being a gas explosion. And you don't have to be a demolitions expert to disconnect a dryer and turn on a valve."

The veil blanketing Zoe's memory lifted. "No, you don't. But if you like fires, any old explosion would probably do."

"What are you talking about?"

"I've been trying to remember why Ryan Mancinelli's name seemed so familiar. Years ago, before you moved here, Ryan was a junior firefighter on the Vance Township Fire Department. At least, he was until he got busted for starting fires just so he could go put them out."

The internal chatter in Pete's mind fell deadly quiet. "Why is it I'm just now hearing about this?"

"He was only a kid. Maybe fifteen at the time." Zoe ran her fingers through her blond curls as if she could massage details from her scalp. "He was tried as a juvenile. As far as I know, that was the only time he was in trouble, so it's probably not in his adult record. I'd completely forgotten about the incident."

Ryan Mancinelli, a fire bug. With intimate knowledge of explosives. The Farabee house. The Krolls' barn...

But why kill Stephen Tierney and plant the body in Zoe's basement?

Pete needed to step up the search for Ryan Mancinelli. He pushed off from the kitchen counter and shouldered his way through the door to snatch his phone from the table and key in Kevin's number.

"Have you located Mancinelli yet?" Pete demanded when his officer answered.

"You only told me to keep a lookout for him like five minutes ago," Kevin complained. "No, I haven't located him yet."

"I want to talk to him, now. Find him. Bring him down to the station. And call me. I want to hear about it the second you track him down." Pete hung up before the young officer could respond.

From behind him, Zoe said, "So Holt's really innocent."

The softness of her voice when she said it sliced through Pete's heart. "I'm not a jury, but it looks that way."

He didn't turn to look at her. Didn't think he could stand to see the brightness of her eyes when she thought of another man. He heard her inhale and then release a loud sigh.

Her fingertips touched his back, so lightly he thought maybe he imagined it. Wished her caress into reality.

"Pete?" Her voice was soft this time, too, but it carried a note of sadness, heartache echoing his own agony.

He turned to her. Her fingers that had brushed his shirt and connected to his soul hovered in the vibrating air between them.

She curled those fingers into an uncertain, unclenched fist. "I'm sorry," she whispered. "I've been an ass."

His throat threatened to close. He forced a grin and what he hoped was a nonchalant shrug. "Well, as asses go, yours is rather cute."

Her eyes widened in momentary surprise. Then she snorted a laugh. "Yours isn't bad either, Chief Adams."

Swallowing against the lump in his throat, he broke one of his own rules and asked a question he didn't really want to know the answer to. "What about you and Holt Farabee?"

A pained scowl carved a crease in her perfect forehead. "There is no me and Holt Farabee. Yeah, I like him. My heart breaks for his little girl. But he just lost his wife, and I..." The crease deepened and she lowered her face so all he could see was the top of her blond head. "I'm kinda hung up on another guy."

The temperature in the room cranked up at least ten degrees. "Oh?"

She looked up, meeting his gaze, unwavering, no more scowl. "Yeah."

A thousand thoughts ripped through him the way the explosion had torn through the house at Scenic Hilltop Estates. Smartass quips formed and faded on his tongue. In his mind, he visualized taking her right there on the table. Instead, he cupped her face in both hands, her skin soft against the roughness of his. He allowed himself the luxury of looking at her. Really looking at her instead of the stolen glances he'd become so good at over the years. He brushed one thumb across her lips and then bent down to meet her mouth, warm, wet, inviting.

Her strong arms around his waist pulled him against her. He kissed her, devoured her, cradling the back of her head with one hand, fingers twining through her hair. With his other hand, he traced the line of her jaw, down the long curve of her throat, to the collar of her v-neck t-shirt.

He hesitated. Broke the kiss and drew back to look at her. How far was she going to let him go before stopping this?

She was breathing hard, and she held his gaze for only a moment then leaned in and brushed his cheek with her lips, her breath warm on his ear, her kiss soft on his neck.

Pete's breathing matched hers. He leaned his face against her hair as his fingers continued their southbound journey from the collar of her shirt, over the curve of her breast.

In response, she gasped and, like a cat bringing out her claws, dug her nails into his back.

Without thinking, he slipped his hand under her t-shirt, palm against her flat, toned stomach, sliding his fingers up to touch her bra.

Swallowing hard, he drew her head back and looked down into her questioning eyes. "If you intend to red-light this," he said, his voice ragged in his own ears, "you'd better do it now."

The questions in her baby blues faded into a smile as she grabbed the hem of his shirt and skimmed it over his head.

TWENTY-THREE

Zoe opened her eyes to the pale light of early morning sun through her lace curtains. Her curtains. Her room. Her bed. Yet even before her mind kicked into gear, she sensed something was very different. Then last night cut through the brain fog.

She rolled slowly from her side to her back and snuck a covert peek. Pete.

He faced away from her, still asleep. The sheets...her sheets...covered him from the waist down, but his broad, muscled back held her appreciative gaze.

The sweet and sultry memory of last night stirred a flutter, like bird wings, inside her chest.

She lay back against her pillow and blew out a long breath. It had been incredible.

They'd denied their passions for so long, and once released, those passions had nearly consumed both of them.

She smiled recalling the trail of clothes they'd shed in her living room before she'd taken his hand and lured him up the back staircase to her bed.

Wow.

But now what?

She drank in one more look at Pete's bare back before rolling away from him and gingerly sitting up.

Merlin sat on the floor staring at her in disapproval, his tail swishing from side to side. Zoe looked around for Jade and found her curled up at Pete's feet. Clearly Merlin was the only judgmental one.

Zoe tiptoed into her bathroom with Merlin trailing along behind. Jade appeared perfectly content to keep an eye on their guest from the foot of the bed. The door squeaked as Zoe eased it shut, and she shushed it. Pete didn't stir.

Running the shower would be too noisy. It could wait until after the morning's barn work. She dug through the hamper for some not-too-terribly-dirty clothes to slip into. Her fuzzy tongue tasted like the stuff she scraped off her boots, but the old pipes in the even older house tended to elicit an assortment of whistles and bangs. Sounds she had grown accustomed to and didn't even hear anymore, but which would no doubt wake the man slumbering in the next room. She snatched her toothbrush and paste. She could brush her teeth in the kitchen sink.

Pausing to look in the mirror, she groaned. Her short blond curls suffered a severe case of bed head. Her hairbrush did little to tame them. A red line creased her face where she'd had it buried in her pillow. She offered up a little prayer Pete wouldn't wake up until she was already out in the barn. Not only because she looked horrible, but also because she needed to think.

Something she should have done—but didn't—last night.

She turned the bathroom doorknob as quietly as possible until it clicked open. Pete had rolled onto his stomach. The sheet had slipped even lower. Heaven help her, he looked good out of uniform. *Way* out of uniform.

With Merlin underfoot, she padded toward the stairs. Jade stood and gave a long feline stretch before dropping to the floor with a soft thud. Still Pete didn't budge.

Zoe touched the plain pipe handrail at the top of her staircase, and the phone rang. Pete flopped over onto one side, pushing up onto one elbow. Zoe did a shuffle-step around the cats to grab the cordless handset on the mantle.

"Zoe? It's Wayne. I've been trying to reach Pete, but he's not answering his cell. Do you happen to know where he is?"

She thought of Pete's cell phone still on her table downstairs. But how on earth did Wayne Baronick know to call her house? She glanced at Pete, now sitting up in her bed, looking rugged and rumpled and incredibly sexy. "Yeah, I do," she said into the phone before tossing it to him.

Clutching her toothbrush and paste, she bolted down the steps.

*   *   *

Zoe reconsidered her retreat to the barn. With the cats fed and her mouth tasting like Colgate instead of dried mud, she scooped her favorite mix of light roast and French vanilla into the Mr. Coffee and filled the reservoir with water. Leaving it to brew, she returned to the living room to gather Pete's clothes, and hers, from last night and headed back upstairs.

The bed was empty, sheets strewn to the side. Her phone was back in its nest on the mantle. The shower she'd taken a pass on was running in the other room.

For a fleeting moment, she contemplated joining Pete, but she had no problem playing the choice out in her mind. It would end with them back in bed. And she still had her doubts as to the wisdom of that move the first time.

She deposited her clothes on a chair and his on the bed and slipped downstairs again.

Her cell phone was in its usual spot with her keys on the small catch-all table next to the door. She snatched it up on her way to the kitchen. The screen indicated two missed calls. One voicemail. Probably Baronick in his attempt to track down Pete. She'd listen to the message later. Right now she needed to think, and the best way to do that was by cooking breakfast.

As she cracked eggs into a stoneware mixing bowl, she replayed last night. After years of waiting and longing, being with Pete had been close to perfect. Close. There was still the little matter of the last few days when they'd been at each others' throats. Did one night, even one unbelievable night, mean everything between them was copacetic?

Yeah. Right.

Zoe whisked the eggs into a froth. By the time Pete swung open the kitchen door, she had the makings of an omelet sizzling on the stove.

"Hungry?" she asked over her shoulder, her voice entirely too cheerful.

When he didn't answer, she risked a glance at him.

She'd hoped to see a smile. A twinkle in his ice-blue eyes. The expression she saw instead was one she'd never witnessed before.

Troubled creases carved his forehead, his eyes were wide with...what? Worry? Regret? Trepidation? His slightly lopsided mouth seemed torn between admiration and lament. Definitely not the in-charge poker-faced Pete Adams Zoe was familiar with.

Since he still hadn't responded to her question, she pointed to the skillet. "I'm making omelets."

Pete blinked. Offered an apologetic smile. "It smells great. I wish I could stay. But—" He motioned over his shoulder. "I have to go."

She should be relieved he was leaving. She wouldn't have to make sense of her jumbled feelings with him sitting across the table. Instead, her chest felt hollow.

He aimed a thumb at the Mr. Coffee. "Do you mind?"

"Of course not." Pete had never asked permission before. The fact he was asking now left Zoe convinced the void between them had not been bridged by sex.

He opened the cabinet door where she kept her cups and pulled out a travel mug, which he held up to show her. "I'll get it back to you."

A lump was growing in her throat. "Don't worry about it." She tossed a handful of cheese on the eggs and folded the omelet. Not that she had any appetite left. "What did Wayne want?"

Pete filled the mug and replaced the pot on its warmer. "He's heading to the station so we can have an early meeting."

With everything that had transpired, she'd almost forgotten about the body in the potato bin. At least the odor had dissipated. "Has he learned anything about Tierney's murder?"

"I don't know yet. That's why we're meeting."

He was dodging her questions. This was how it was going to be? A one-night stand? The lump continued to press upward, squeezing her brain. She kept her eyes on the skillet, switching off the heat to the electric stove.

Pete moved behind her. She hoped, prayed, he was going to turn her to face him, apologize for being an ass, and kiss her long and hard like he had last night. Instead, she felt his presence, the heat of his closeness. His fingers lightly touched her shoulder and he pressed a brief kiss into her hair on the back of her head. Then he took his coffee and walked out of her kitchen. A moment later, the back door slammed.

Zoe swept a hand across her face. No. She would not cry.

She slid the omelet onto a plate. Nothing about it appealed to her at the moment. Maybe later. Or maybe she'd feed it to the cats. What she really needed was to talk to her best friend Rose. Unfortunately, Rose was out west somewhere with her kids and had sworn off electronics for the summer.

Zoe scooped up her phone. Perhaps this one time, Rose would have her cell turned on. Zoe keyed in the number, but the call went directly to voicemail. With a guttural growl, she contemplated hurling the useless thing across the room, but remembered the two missed calls.

The first one, as expected, was from Wayne's number. The second was from Holt's. The lump in her throat returned. Had something happened to Maddie? She played the message, but it was the detective. "If you see Pete, have him call me." Zoe deleted it.

No message from Holt.

She dialed his number. Like her call to Rose, it went straight to voicemail.

"Holt, this is Zoe. I see you called." What else should she say? "I hope you and Maddie are all right. Call me back. Okay?" After she hung up, she held onto the phone and asked it the question she'd really wanted to ask Holt. "Where the hell are you?"

Had it been possible to kick himself all the way to Dillard, Pete wouldn't have needed his SUV to get to the station. He was a damned idiot. He'd finally, *finally*, made love with Zoe. It had been better than he'd ever imagined. He'd dreamed about her for years. Wanted her for years. He'd had their first time all planned out. Romantic dinner. Perhaps dancing. Taking her back to his place. A little wine. And then slow and sweet.

Instead, he'd practically ripped her clothes off in a primal zealous rush to claim her as his own like some frigging caveman.

He could have...might have...redeemed himself this morning if he'd simply talked to her. The second part of his dream. The afterglow. A languid morning of mimosas and French toast, sharing laughter and conversation in each other's arms.

She'd fixed breakfast for him. Not French toast, but omelets she'd prepared herself. She'd wanted him to stick around. That was huge.

He'd wanted to stay. Longed to stay and take her in his arms again. Instead, coward that he was, he bolted.

For a moment, he contemplated turning the Explorer around and heading back to the farm. And Zoe.

But there was the blasted phone call from Baronick.

"I think we may have been too quick to dismiss Farabee as a suspect."

Pete didn't want Zoe to suspect Holt might once again be on his radar. Not until he knew what Baronick had dug up. And the detective had refused to discuss it over the phone.

Zoe could read Pete all too well. If he'd stayed for breakfast and conversation, she'd have known immediately he was keeping something from her.

So, he'd left without telling her what he'd intended to say.

I love you, Zoe.

Pete slammed the steering wheel with his palm. He was an idiot, plain and simple.

Baronick was already seated in the conference room with two cups from Starbucks when Pete arrived. The detective slid one of the cups toward him. "Morning, Pete."

He eyed the Starbucks brew then the travel mug of Zoe's French vanilla crap. He loved the woman. Hated her coffee. Swapping cups, he took a seat across from Baronick. "What's so damned intriguing you couldn't discuss it on the phone?"

"Whoa there, big fella. First things first." He hiked his eyebrows suggestively. "How was your evening?"

Pete fixed him with *The Stare*. The one that withered criminals and put his officers in their place when needed.

Baronick was a little tougher and took a little longer, but he eventually backed down. "Fine. You don't wanna be the kiss and tell type. Hey, I'm cool with that." He picked up his phone and did some swiping and tapping. "I did some digging into our EOD Specialist Ryan Mancinelli. Honorable discharge. Treated at the VA in Pittsburgh for PTSD. Nothing new there. So I checked him out with the Monongahela County Builders Association where he's a member in good standing. All four and five star ratings for his work. But no one has any idea what job he's been on lately."

Pete turned the Starbucks cup around and around. "Builders Association. Don't suppose you asked whether Holt Farabee was a member."

The smug grin returned. "I did indeed. And that's where it got interesting. Farabee's also highly thought of. Good worker. His customers are happy."

"That's interesting?"

"No, but the guy I talked to told me Farabee and Mancinelli are best buds from way back."

"Really?"

Baronick swiped the screen again. "They always sat together at meetings. Most of the time, they rode to meetings together and went out for burgers afterwards."

Pete mulled it over. "So? They live in the same township. They share the same profession. They'll either be friends or competitors."

"True. Let's move on to my next tidbit. I decided to have a talk with Dennis Spangler."

It took a moment for the name to register in Pete's brain. "The guy from the collections department at MNB?"

"Yeah. I wanted to touch base with him now that Tierney's dead."

Pete should have thought of that. If he wasn't so damned twisted up about Zoe... "And?"

Baronick leaned back, interlacing his fingers behind his head and giving Pete a triumphant grin. "He told me the eviction for the Farabees had been hurried along. Holt and Lillian should have been given at least six more months to get caught up on their payments, but one bank employee somehow managed to expedite the whole process."

The space behind Pete's eyes cooled. "Stephen Tierney."

"Give the man a cigar."

"Did Farabee know?"

Baronick shrugged. "Spangler says he never met Farabee and has no idea how much he knew about the eviction being fast-tracked. But Farabee doesn't come across to me as someone who would go quietly. I'd bet a month's salary he knew he should have had more time and the reason he didn't get it."

Exactly what Pete was thinking. "Stephen Tierney has an affair with Lillian Farabee. He knows Holt and Lillian are having money problems and it's driving a wedge between them, so he helps matters along by having them evicted. Holt finds out. Now, not only is he pissed at Tierney for taking his wife, but also for taking his home."

"Pretty strong motive for murder." Baronick drained his cup and wiped the back of his hand across his mouth. "One thing that's bothered me is the whole moving the body thing."

"The added motive still doesn't help explain that."

"True. But hear me out. You kill someone and want or need to move the body. Easier said than done, right? Okay so Tierney's a small man. He's still dead weight. Farabee may be strong, but strong enough to lug a dead man into the basement? I doubt it."

Pete knew where Baronick was headed. "Unless he had help."

"You guessed it. Here's what I'm thinking. Farabee kills Tierney. I don't know where he killed him, but after a few days he has to move the body. Maybe it's about to be discovered. He decides to hide the body in a nice cool root cellar, just until he can figure something else out. He gets on the phone and calls his good buddy, Ryan Mancinelli, to lend him a hand."

Pete picked up the story. "Farabee knows how to get into the basement from the outside. The two of them bury the body in the potato bin. Mancinelli's conscience starts to get the better of him, so he drinks himself into a stupor. The explosion didn't trigger his fall off the wagon. Having a hand in moving Tierney's body did."

Baronick came forward in his chair again, planting his forearms on the table. "I'd sure love to get my hands on Mancinelli and have him confirm our theory."

"That's not the only reason we need to find him."

"Oh?"

Pete hated what he was thinking. "Mancinelli's a loose end. Friend or not, if Mancinelli's drinking, Farabee has to be afraid he's going to spill his guts."

"Which means Farabee might be looking to shut him up for good."

"Yeah." Pete pushed his half-full cup of coffee away, his stomach soured. "If he hasn't already."

TWENTY-FOUR

The milky blue sky offered no hint of relief from the dry spell. As Zoe took the footpath back to the house after finishing her morning barn work, sweat glued her shirt to her back. She'd worked twice as hard as she'd needed to, taking out her frustration on bales of hay and piles of manure.

She entered the house through her kitchen, bracing the wooden door open with an antique iron to let a faint breeze waft into the room. Although the farmhouse didn't have air conditioning, the first floor stayed surprisingly cool all summer long. Those thick post and beam walls must provide some serious insulation. They didn't make homes like this anymore.

Zoe wondered what kind of place she'd have to live in after Mrs. Kroll sold the farm and the bulldozers made quick work of this lovely old structure.

Her phone rang, interrupting her train of thought...a train she was happy to derail. The name on the screen made her pulse quicken.

"Holt? Where are you?"

"I'd rather not say." His voice sounded strained. Gruff.

"Are you and Maddie okay?"

A pause. "Yeah. For now."

"What does *that* mean? For now? Holt, what's going on?"

She heard him release a heavy breath. "You're better off not knowing."

"Listen. The cops don't believe you had anything to do with your wife's or Tierney's deaths anymore." Zoe bumped through the swinging door into the living room. "If you're hiding out—"

"The cops are the least of my concerns."

All this cryptic nonsense was wearing on Zoe's last nerve. "Just tell me what you're doing. You said you had to take care of something. What is it?"

Another pause. "I can't risk telling you. For your own sake. But I do need a favor."

"What?"

"If anything happens to me, I want you to make sure Maddie is taken care of."

Zoe dropped into one of her upholstered chairs in front of the fireplace. For a moment she sputtered, torn between which question to ask first. "What do you think is gonna happen to you, Holt?"

"I don't know. Hopefully nothing. But just in case, I need to know someone I trust will take care of my daughter."

"Take care of? You know I will, but what exactly are you asking? Maddie isn't a stray kitten or puppy you need me to feed. I don't know what you expect me to do. Or what I *can* do."

There was some scraping noises and a soft thud on the other end of the line. "Look. You've been a good friend to us when we both needed one." He'd lowered his voice to a clandestine level, as if someone else had come into the room. Maddie perhaps? "You're the only person I can trust," he said, his voice dropping to a barely audible whisper, "to protect my little girl."

There was a faint click on the line. "Holt?" Zoe said.

Only dead air greeted her.

"*Holt?*"

Nothing. She looked at the phone. He'd either hung up or they'd been cut off. She tried calling him back, but got his voicemail.

Zoe leaned back into the chair and turned her phone over and over in her hand as she turned Holt's words over and over in her head.

"*If anything happens to me, I want you to make sure Maddie is taken care of.*"

"Oh my God," she whispered. Whatever Holt was planning to do, he didn't expect to survive.

Pete hammered on the Mancinellis' front door having gotten no response to leaning on the doorbell. Finding Ryan Mancinelli drunk, but alive, would be the best possible scenario right about now. Of course, he didn't expect it to be that easy. And it wasn't.

Pete trudged across the drought-stricken lawn and through the gap in the hedges to the Naeser residence. Ashley, wearing a matched set of luggage under her eyes, stepped onto their porch before he made it up the steps.

"Chief, have you found Ryan?"

"Not yet. I was hoping you might have heard from him."

She shook her head vehemently. "I'd have called you if I had."

"Nothing? No texts or emails?"

"No. I'm really worried."

Pete was, too, but had no intentions of sharing his concerns or the reasons behind them with Mancinelli's fragile wife. "If it's any comfort, my officer checked all the bars and called the local hospitals. He hasn't shown up at the emergency room." Or the morgue.

She didn't appear reassured. "I've called all his buddies. They haven't heard from him either."

All his buddies? Pete struck his casual pose. "Ashley, do you know Holt Farabee?"

"The man who lost his wife in the explosion last week? No."

"Did Ryan?"

Her eyes shifted side to side as if scanning her memory. "I don't believe so. He never mentioned him to me. Why do you ask?"

Pete gave her a nonchalant smile. "Just wondering. They're both carpenters. Ryan worked at Scenic Hilltop Estates."

Ashley apparently had completed the search of her memory and shrugged. "Sorry. If Ryan ever said anything about him, I don't remember."

Pete's cell phone rang and he reached in his pocket for it. "No problem," he told Ashley. "But please, if you hear anything from him or think of anything that might shed some light on his whereabouts, let me know immediately."

"I will. Thanks."

Pete turned away and glanced at the cell's screen before answering it. Zoe. He prepared to answer with the litany of apologies he'd been rehearsing, but her frantic voice on the other end stemmed his attempt at contrition.

"Pete, I just had a really strange phone call from Holt. I'm afraid he's in danger."

For the second time in as many days, Pete and Zoe stood face-to-face in her living room, although she was pretty sure this conversation wasn't going to end with them in each other's arms.

He had struck his all-business pose as she related the phone call from Holt including his request that she take care of Maddie if something happened to him.

Pete's eyes narrowed, and he showed none of the concern for Holt's safety that Zoe had hoped he would.

"Did he say where he was?"

"No."

"And you don't have any idea what he was talking about when he said he had something he needed to take care of?"

"None."

"Did he ever mention Ryan Mancinelli to you?"

"Ryan? No. But I did tell Holt you didn't suspect him of killing his wife or Stephen Tierney anymore."

Pete winced, but tried to cover it.

"Pete?" If she didn't know better, she'd have thought he was squirming. "What's going on? Did you find Ryan?"

"No." Pete looked pained as he met and held her gaze. "When Baronick and I met this morning, he had some information."

Zoe didn't think she was going to like whatever information Baronick had uncovered. "About Ryan?" she ventured.

"About Ryan—and Farabee."

Zoe listened as Pete told her about the friendship between the two builders.

By the time he got to the part about Stephen Tierney's role in evicting the Farabees from their home, she'd dropped into one of the chairs at her dining table. "Now you're back to thinking Holt's the killer?"

"I just want to talk to him."

"You don't have any more evidence than you did the last two times you talked to him." Zoe shook her head. "Honestly, Pete, you're giving me whiplash. First you think Holt did it, and then you think Ryan did it. And now you think Holt did it."

"It's not up to me to determine who murdered two people. That's up to a jury. My job right now is to keep a killer from striking again."

Zoe choked out a humorless laugh. "Who do you think he's out to kill now?" She didn't expect him to have an answer, but from the look on his face, she was wrong. "Pete?"

With a sigh, he sat down across from her. "Ryan Mancinelli's missing."

"You just said they were friends. Why would Holt want to kill him?"

"Maybe Mancinelli was helping out his buddy. I don't know how deeply he was involved with the explosion that killed Lillian, but suppose he helped Farabee kill Tierney. Helped him hide the body in your nice cool root cellar until they could figure out what to do with it."

"None of which explains why you think Holt wants Ryan dead."

Pete held up a hand, palm toward her. "Hear me out. Mancinelli doesn't have the stomach for murder and starts drinking again. Farabee starts worrying Mancinelli will spill his guts. You said yourself Farabee had something he needed to take care of. Maybe the 'something' is Ryan Mancinelli."

Zoe tried to wrap her mind around Pete's words. Tried to fit Holt into the mold Pete had built for him. Although for a brief moment she'd considered the possibility, she'd leapt at the reasoning that Holt would not hide a body under the house where he was living with Maddie. She shook her head. "No."

"Zoe, Mancinelli's been missing for at least two days now. He could know Farabee's gunning for him and is hiding. Or—" Pete reached out and put a hand on hers. "Or Mancinelli could already be dead."

"No," she repeated to herself as much as to Pete. Her own spin on the scenario started forming in her mind. "It could be the other way around, too. Ryan killed Lillian and Tierney and now is after Holt. He told me if anything happened to him, I'm to take care of Maddie. Holt's afraid someone is after *him*."

Pete closed his fingers around her hand. "Or he knows he's going to jail for the rest of his life."

"I don't believe that."

"You don't *want* to believe it. Zoe, you're wrong about Holt Farabee. You saved his life the day of the fire. Hell, maybe he even set you up to *think* you saved his life. We don't know he was really going to run into those flames. He might have been trying to make himself look like the frantic, grieving husband."

Her chest ached as she struggled to control her breathing. She remembered that moment. A man—panicked, hysterical—charging toward the raging fire consuming the house where his wife had perished. Pete chasing him, but she'd known Pete wasn't going to catch him in time. The man—Holt—showed no signs of stopping or even slowing. She remembered tackling him. They both went down into the mud.

Could that man have been responsible for the fire? For his wife's death? Had she saved the life of a cold-blooded murderer?

"No." She pulled her hand from Pete's grasp. "I was there. He wasn't going to stop."

"I was there, too, and I can't say that for sure."

She fixed Pete with a hard stare, pleading him to hear her. To believe her. "Holt did not kill his wife. Or Tierney. He's in trouble and needs help."

Pete sighed. "Zoe..." he said, his voice thick with disappointment.

"You need to trust my gut on this."

He shook his head. "Zoe, I love you. I do. But your gut isn't exactly trustworthy."

Her gut, trustworthy or not, felt as if a block of ice had formed in it. She wished the ice could cool the heat of tears she refused to shed. Jaw clenched, she stood and nodded. "Thank you for clearing things up for me." She stalked to her back door and opened it, standing to one side. "You can go now."

Pete climbed to his feet, a little unsteady. "Don't do this."

She pointed outside. "I want you to leave."

He moved as if he'd taken a bullet and stopped in front of her. "You need to listen to me."

"Why? Because you know better than me? Because your gut instincts count and mine don't? Because my feelings aren't to be trusted?"

"That's not what I meant."

"Funny. I think that's exactly what you meant."

"Zoe—"

She pointed again. "Go. And don't worry about me bothering you anymore. We're done."

She felt him trying to draw her eyes to him. But she refused to meet his gaze.

With a soft groan, he stuffed his ball cap onto his head and left.

Zoe slammed the door. The glass pane in its upper half rattled, but didn't shatter. Her heart, on the other hand, was another matter.

TWENTY-FIVE

Pete blew past Nancy's office on his way into the station. Her exclamation of surprise trailed after him down the hallway and into his own office. He slammed the door so hard it didn't catch and bounced back open as if wanting to knock some sense into him. Not willing to give a slab of wood the final word, he slammed it a second time.

It gave up and stayed closed.

Zoe had thrown him out. Out of her house. Out of her life. He wasn't sure who he was angrier with—himself, Zoe, or Holt Farabee.

Pete had burned his last bridge where Zoe was concerned. There was no going back, no making amends. He, Pete Adams, was an ass.

All there was left to do was solve this case. Find out who killed Lillian Farabee and Stephen Tierney. If, as he expected, it turned out to be Holt, he could at least be satisfied he'd been right.

Not that vindication would keep him warm at night.

He looked around his desk for something to take out his frustration on. He settled on a defenseless stapler, picked it up, and hurtled it across the room. The Swingline bashed into the wall next to his door just as Nancy timidly opened it.

She flinched. "I'm sorry," she whispered, backing out of the office. "I'll come back another time."

"No, no." Pete leapt to his feet. "I'm sorry. Come in." He stepped around his desk to retrieve the stapler. "I'm having a bad day. I'm really sorry."

Nancy stood there, wide-eyed and unwilling to venture further into the lion's den. "My fault. I should have knocked."

Pete replaced the stapler on his desk. Gently. "It's not your fault. What can I do for you?"

Without crossing the threshold, she held out two pink slips of paper to him. "You had a couple of phone calls." Her hand was shaking.

He took the messages from her. "Thanks. Have you heard anything else from your sister?"

"She told me you were over there earlier."

"Nothing since then? She hasn't heard from her husband?"

Nancy shook her head.

"Okay. Thanks."

She reached to pull the door closed behind her, but Pete held up a hand.

"Leave it open."

She withdrew her hand as if he might whack her knuckles if she dared touch the knob.

Yes, he—Pete Adams—was an ass.

After his terrified secretary had retreated to the relative safety of the front desk, he flopped into his chair and studied the two messages. The first one was from Deborah Vallina, the mother of two of the girls who had been at the Kroll farm Saturday before the fire, and the only two potential witnesses he hadn't been able to reach yet. No one else had seen anything or anyone unusual. Odds are the Vallina kids hadn't either. The second message was from Chuck Delano and marked *urgent*.

Pete set both slips of paper in front of him. Chuck Delano. Hawaii. Palm trees. Pristine beaches. Major pay increase. Major.

Girls in bikinis.

Pete sighed, picked up the phone and called Deborah Vallina.

After three rings, the now familiar recorded voice answered. Phone tag. At the beep, he left his name and another request to return his call.

He pressed the button on the phone base, disconnecting, and held it while eyeing the note from Delano. Urgent.

Pete released the button and punched in the number to paradise.

"Hey, Petey," came the gruff voice across the miles. "I expected you to ignore me. Again."

"I've been busy."

"I'm sure you have. Look, I'd love to be able to give you more time to think about this job offer, but my boss needs to fill the opening—"

"I'll take it."

"—and he needs to know by the end of business today if you—"

"I said I'll take it."

There was forty-six hundred miles of silence on the line, followed by a cough. "You—what?"

"I'll take the damned job. Unless this was all one of your practical jokes."

"No. No joke. I just never thought you'd really...Hey, this is great! I'll have the big guy fax you all the paperwork."

"I need to turn in my resignation." And put his house up for sale. And tell his sister and father. And Zoe. Not that she'd care at this point.

"Not a problem. As long as they know you're taking the job."

"And I need to solve the case I'm working on right now."

Another stretch of silence. "How long do you expect *that* to take?"

"Not long." It had already taken too long.

Pete listened to Chuck prattle on about the Maalaea Bay Grand Hotel and all the perks and benefits of the job and the island lifestyle until the other phone line rang.

"Chuck," he interrupted. "I have to get back to work if I'm ever going to clear this murder case."

"Murder? Oh. Yeah. Watch for the fax. And I'll email you."

Pete hung up and hit the button for the other line at the same time Nancy did. They spoke over each other saying, "Vance Township Police Department."

There was a pause at the other end before a feminine voice replied, "Uh, this is Deborah Vallina."

"I've got it, Nancy," Pete said. He heard the other line click. "Mrs. Vallina?

"Yes?"

"Sorry about that. Thanks for calling back."

"You said in one of your messages you had some questions about strangers or if anything suspicious happened while my kids were at the barn on Saturday?"

Pete dug out his notebook and pen to cross off the Vallinas from his list. "That's right."

"I talked to my girls about it. They said it was pretty much a normal Saturday."

Which was exactly what everyone else had reported. Another dead end. Pete closed the notebook.

"Except for that one guy."

Pete opened it again. "What guy?"

"My oldest girl said there was a man walking around the barn, looking at the stalls and such. He asked her a few questions about whether she liked boarding her horse there, how well it was cared for. That sort of thing. Said he was considering moving his horse there and wanted to check the place out."

"Did she say what the guy looked like?"

Deborah Vallina laughed. "She said he was old. But for her that means anyone over the age of eighteen."

"Would you be willing to bring her to the station to look at a few photos?"

"I plan to take the girls out to the farm after supper. We could stop on the way."

"That will be fine. Thanks." Pete hung up. "After supper" meant staying late for Pete, but he had a lot of paperwork to take care of anyway. Especially if he was about to pack up his life and move to Maui. And if the Vallina girl could identify a photo of Ryan Mancinelli, Pete would be one step closer to solving an arson and two murders.

Once again in uniform and ready for a sixteen-hour shift, Zoe poured out extra cat food into the large bowl next to the kitchen door. Jade and Merlin dug in like two starved beasts even though there had been a considerable amount of kibble there before Zoe added fresh. She stroked both purring felines and stashed the bag before shifting her gaze toward the Krolls' half of the house. Taking a deep breath, as if she could draw in a healthy dose of courage with the oxygen, she headed out onto the porch and across to Mrs. Kroll's kitchen.

The older woman answered almost immediately. "Zoe dear. Please come in." Her voice sounded even more tired than usual.

"Thanks." The room smelled faintly of chicken and, as Zoe stepped inside, a microwave beeper went off.

"My dinner," Mrs. Kroll said fluttering a hand at the machine. "It can wait." She waved for Zoe to follow her into the dining room.

"I don't want to interrupt your meal."

Her landlady blew a short raspberry. "If it gets cold, I'll just microwave it some more. It's not like it's real food anyway." She slumped into a chair at the table. "Sit."

Zoe obeyed. "I can't stay long. But I wanted to look in on you."

Mrs. Kroll lowered her gaze to her clasped hands. "That's nice." She breathed a loud sigh. "I had a meeting with Marvin's care team at the rehab facility today."

"Oh?" From the look on Mrs. Kroll's face, it wasn't good.

"He's making progress. But slow. And they still don't know how complete his recovery will be." She made air quotes around "complete."

Zoe rested a hand on her landlady's folded ones. "He's a fighter. He'll get better."

"I know he will. But we've had to face facts." Mrs. Kroll looked around the room, and Zoe spotted a glint of tears in her eyes. "This house, this farm is too much for us. The bills for Marvin's care are stacking up. And I still owe Holt for the water heater. Plus now that he and Maddie have left there's no one to handle the repairs."

"I'll find someone else." Zoe heard a hint of panic in her voice, fearing where the older woman was going with all this.

"No. I've had to come to accept it's time to downsize." For a fleeting moment, Mrs. Kroll met Zoe's eyes before looking down again. "Marvin and I talked about it for a long time, and we've accepted that land developer fellow's offer. We're selling the farm."

"All right, I'm here." Sylvia tossed her handbag onto Pete's desk with a thud. "What's so important I had to drop everything and come to your office?"

Pete eyed the handbag and recalled a time Sylvia had used it as a weapon. The damned thing was huge and would no doubt send him sprawling if she swung it at him. He pulled an envelope from his desk drawer and handed it to her.

"What's this?"

"My letter of resignation."

"Your *what*?"

He held her gaze while keeping his peripheral vision on the purse.

Sylvia ripped into the envelope, pulled out the contents, and unfolded it. She pressed one finger to her lips as she read. Her blue-gray eyes raised from the page to lock onto him. "No."

"No?"

"No, I'm not accepting this. Not without some kind of explanation."

"It's not up to you to accept it. There are two other members of the board of supervisors who have a say."

She shook the letter at him. "But you handed this to me."

"I wanted you to be the first to know."

Sylvia flopped into one of the chairs across from him. "You're serious?"

Pete moved her handbag on the premise of clearing their line of sight. He also made sure it was just out of her reach. What the hell did she keep in there? It had to weigh twenty pounds. "If I wasn't serious, I'd never have written the letter."

"Why? You love it here."

Pete's chair squeaked as he rocked back in it. "I do. But I've been offered a better job."

She raised an eyebrow. "Better? How?"

"Head of security for a resort. In Maui. Six figure salary."

Sylvia let out a low whistle. She reread the letter. "Well, don't expect Vance Township to try to match that kind of pay increase."

"I wasn't fishing for a raise."

She folded the letter and fitted it back into the envelope. "I know you, Pete Adams. You aren't the sun-and-sand type. And money doesn't mean squat to you. It's what makes you a good, honest cop. What's this really about?"

Pete looked at his desk, but was thinking back to the last conversation he and Sylvia had. That day at the farm. Sylvia had been babysitting Maddie and had been chastising him about his fixation on Farabee as the killer. Sylvia's prophetic words echoed in his mind. *You're going to lose that girl.*

"Zoe."

"Hmm?" He looked up.

"Zoe. She's the only reason you'd pack up and move half a world away. What happened?"

Good question. What happened? Holt Farabee happened. Pete's own stubborn stupidity happened. "We...she..." He sighed. "It's over. That's all."

Sylvia looked as though she was winding up to give him a massive portion of her mind, but the bells on the station's front door saved him.

"I still have a couple cases to work." Pete stood, scooped up a file in front of him, and circled the desk to plant a kiss on Sylvia's gray head. "I'll miss you."

She was mumbling something as he strode out of the office and headed toward the front of the station. Nancy had left for the day, so Deborah Vallina and her two dark-haired daughters stood just inside the entrance. The mother gave Pete a nervous smile as he approached.

"Thank you for coming in." He ushered them into the conference room.

Sylvia, her head high and shoulders back, passed him on her way out. "I'm not done with you yet," she said through a clenched jaw. But he noticed the letter sticking out of her handbag.

Once the Vallinas and Pete were settled around the conference table, he placed the unopened folder in front of him. "You talked to someone at the barn on Saturday who said he was interested in boarding there?"

"I did." The older girl, who had been introduced as Brianna, appeared to be around twelve or thirteen. Her long hair was braided around her face and down her back, and while she wore jeans and riding boots appropriate for an evening in the saddle, she also wore enough makeup to qualify her for a modeling session.

"Can you tell me what the guy looked like?"

She shrugged. "He was old."

"How old?"

"Old enough to be a dad." She squinted at Pete. "Not as old as you, though."

He stared at the girl, trying to determine if she was a clueless kid or a brat.

"Brianna," Mrs. Vallina snapped, clearly appalled. "I'm so sorry, Chief."

"What?" The girl held out both arms. "I don't know how old the guy was."

Clueless kid, Pete decided. "Okay. Would you recognize him if I showed you a photo?"

"Yeah, I guess."

Pete opened the file and pulled out a photo of Ryan Mancinelli, which Ashley had provided, sliding it in front of Brianna.

The girl took the photo. Repositioned it on the table as if to get a better view. She braced an elbow on the table next to the picture, resting her chin in her hand, and made a series of faces.

Pete's opinion started to waver toward brat.

"No," Brianna said after an extensive study of the picture. "That's not him."

"Are you sure?"

"Positive." She held up the picture to her younger sister who shook her head, then handed it back to Pete.

He exchanged it for a photocopy of Holt Farabee's driver's license. "How about this guy?"

The girl brightened. "That's Maddie's dad. No, he wasn't the man looking at the barn."

The younger sister craned her neck to look at Farabee's photo. "Mr. Farabee's nice," she said.

Brittany nodded. "We like him. Maddie, too."

Great. Pete retrieved the picture and tucked both of them back into the folder. "All right. Thanks, girls. Thank you, Mrs. Vallina, for bringing them in. Do me a favor. The guy who was at the barn? If you see him again, call me immediately."

The Vallinas agreed, and Pete walked them to the door. As he watched them climb into their minivan, he released a frustrated sigh. Whoever had been hanging around Zoe's barn the afternoon before the fire wasn't Ryan Mancinelli or Holt Farabee. So who then? Or maybe he really was just checking out the facilities before asking to board his horse there. For a moment, Pete thought about calling Zoe and asking her if she'd had any inquiries about a new boarder. He reached for his phone. The reality of the situation stopped him cold. She probably wouldn't answer the call if she saw it was from him.

He keyed in another number.

"Kevin," he said when his officer answered. "I need you to do something for me."

TWENTY-SIX

The thermometer on the bank down the street from the ambulance garage read ninety-four degrees, and the humidity was so thick, Zoe thought she was breathing soup. Added to a need to work off her frustrations, circumstances were perfect for washing an already clean Medic Two.

"You were smart marrying a teacher," she said to Earl as she balanced on a stepladder, scrubbing the roof of the ambulance's cab.

He trained a stream of water from the garden hose on the already soaped up hood. "You mean because my wife has the summer off?"

Zoe shot him a look. "No. Because you don't work together." She went back to slopping suds, not caring the front of her overalls were getting soaked. "Never ever get involved with someone you work with."

"Technically you don't work with Pete. He's a cop. You're a paramedic."

"Doesn't matter." She paused. "Although, since I have to move, I suppose I could look for a place outside of Vance Township."

"Just don't transfer out of Phillipsburg. I don't wanna have to train a new partner."

Zoe backed down the ladder. "Your level of empathy and compassion is astounding." She plopped the sponge into the bucket of soapy water and hoisted a thumb toward the ambulance's roof. "Hit it."

Earl aimed the hose at the top of the cab.

The overspray misted Zoe and felt heavenly against the heat of early evening.

"I knew better than to get involved with Pete." She leaned down to retrieve the sponge and wrung it out. "He was my best friend. Now we're less than nothing."

"Just give it a rest. Once he finds out who killed Farabee's wife and your potato guy, things will settle down and you two can start over."

Zoe let the sponge drip around her fingers. "I wonder who did kill them."

Earl released the trigger on the sprayer. "Holt Farabee?"

She wound up to blast her partner with the sponge. He raised an arm to block the toss, but she stopped before releasing it. "I don't know. I hope not. Do you know Ryan Mancinelli?"

"He installed new windows for my in-laws. Nice work. But personally? No." Earl hit the ambulance's passenger door with a quick blast. "Why?"

"He might be involved somehow."

A horn blast jarred Zoe, and a white Ford Escort braked to a stop in front of the garage's front window. Sylvia hoisted herself out of the car and stormed toward them, her massive handbag slung over her shoulder.

"What's wrong?" Zoe asked her.

"You tell me." Sylvia huffed. "What on God's green earth has gotten into you and Pete?"

"Uh-oh," Earl said under his breath. He set the hose on the sidewalk. "The word is out. I think I'll go find some paperwork to do."

"You stay put." Sylvia shook a finger at him. "I won't be here that long." She swung back to Zoe and yanked an envelope from her purse. "I don't know what happened between you two, but I want you to fix it."

Zoe sighed. "I don't think that's possible."

Sylvia waved the envelope in Zoe's face. "Don't tell me it's impossible. You want to know what's impossible? I'll tell you, missy. Finding a new police chief with Pete's credentials and heart. *That's* impossible."

"Finding a new—what?" Zoe snatched the envelope.

Sylvia stood in front of her, breathing as hard as if she'd jogged the two miles between the Vance Township Police Station in Dillard and the Monongahela County EMS garage in Phillipsburg.

Zoe removed the letter and unfolded it. Earl sidled up to her and read it over her shoulder. The words made no sense. She reread them, but they didn't change. Pete? Resigning from the force? She met Sylvia's eyes and knew it was true. "But—" Zoe stuttered. "Why?"

"Why do you think? No matter what he tries to tell me, he's not leaving just because of a high paying job he's been offered in Hawaii. He's leaving because of *you*."

Zoe felt the blood drain from her head and her heart on its way to her feet. Medic Two, the garage, Sylvia, and Earl all spun around her. For a moment she thought she was going to hit the pavement. Earl must have thought so, too, because he caught her, bracing her against him.

"Hawaii?" she squeaked.

Sylvia's ferocity had softened. "You didn't know?"

"No."

Earl rubbed Zoe's back, encouraging some of the earthbound blood to flow back into the brain. "Hey, look at it this way. If he moves to Hawaii, you don't have to worry about leaving Vance Township."

Zoe glared at him. "You aren't funny."

He gave her a cock-eyed grin and a shrug.

Sylvia reclaimed the letter, which Zoe had forgotten she was still clutching. "Pete Adams may be a hardheaded jackass from time to time, but he's as good a man as they come. And he loves you." Sylvia reached out and took Zoe's hand. "And I know as sure as I'm standing here that you love him, too. Whatever's come between you two isn't worth losing each other over." She released Zoe and turned, tottering back to her car.

Zoe eased away from her partner. "Hawaii."

Earl's grin faded. He crossed his arms and fixed her with a hard stare. "That's a heck of a long way to go to escape. Pete must figure you have a pretty strong pull on him to have to run that far away."

She let out a breath and sat down on the ambulance's running boards. "It's also a pretty strong statement." She met Earl's gaze. "Quitting his job? Moving to the end of the earth? If that isn't the final farewell, I don't know what is."

"He's not gone yet."

Earl's words hung in the sultry air around Zoe, echoing in her mind. Yet. Pete wasn't gone yet. Before she could ponder a way back to the point before things had gone sideways, her cell phone rang from its perch inside the ambulance bay. She climbed to her feet and jogged inside to grab it.

The number wasn't familiar.

"Hello?"

"Zoe? This is Kevin Piacenza." Pete's officer. Her heart froze. Had something happened to Pete? "Is everything okay?"

"Uh, yeah. I'm...uh...on duty and working on the arson out at your barn." He ended the sentence in an upbeat, as if it were a question.

Immediately Zoe knew what was really going on. Pete had a question but was sending his officer to ask it. "And?"

"One of the kids...a, uh..." Zoe could almost hear him reading his notes. Or Pete's notes. "Brianna Vallina...said she talked to a man in the barn on Saturday who claimed to be looking to possibly board his horses there. She didn't recognize him and couldn't give much of a description. Have you had any inquiries from potential new boarders lately?"

"No." And there wouldn't be any new boarders either, but she didn't think Kevin cared to hear her problems. "Sorry. I can't help you. Do you think he might be the one who set the hay on fire?"

"I really don't know. Just covering all bases." Kevin's nervous laugh filtered through the phone. He thanked her and hung up.

"What's going on?" Earl asked.

"Someone was asking about boarding at the farm Saturday. Which reminds me. I need to start telling everyone they'll need to move their horses out." Zoe's eyes grew hot, and she considered sitting down on the pavement next to the ambulance and having a good cry. "I don't know where they're all gonna go. I don't know what I'm gonna do with Windstar." She flung up her arms. "And I sure don't know where I'm gonna go."

Earl, ever the big, brotherly partner, put an arm around her squeezing a little too hard. "You can sleep on my couch. My wife won't mind. And the kids will love having their Auntie Zoe around."

She grunted. "And what about the cats and my horse?"

Earl waved away her concerns. "The cats will get along fine with our dog. And Lilly's been bugging us for a pony for at least a year. Your horse can sleep in her bedroom. She'll be thrilled."

Zoe laughed in spite of herself. "I can see it now." She gave him a playful shove. "We'd better finish washing the ambulance." She opened the unit's door to toss her phone inside when it rang again. "Now what?"

The number on the display was a Brunswick exchange.

She tapped the screen to answer. "Hello?"

Silence greeted her, followed by a groan.

"Who is this?"

A sharp intake of breath came through the line. "Zoe?"

"Holt?"

His voice was little more than a hoarse whisper. "I need help."

Zoe grabbed a clipboard from the center console of the medic unit and flipped to a blank call sheet. "Where are you? Are you hurt?"

Another gasping breath. "I've been shot." A pause. "Sleep EZ— room fourteen."

The same dump where he'd been staying with Maddie before Zoe had invited them to live at the farm. "I'll get an ambulance there right away."

The only response was a thunk.

"Holt? *Holt?*"

Nothing. Zoe grabbed the bucket and heaved it out of the way while holding her phone to her ear in case he replied.

Earl was already reaching for the driver's door. "What's going on?"

"We're going to Brunswick. Gunshot wound." Zoe stuck her head into the empty office. "Tony!"

Footsteps thudded from the crew quarters, and Crew Chief Tony DeLuca appeared in the doorway, munching chips from a bag in his hand.

"Radio Control for a police and medic response to the Brunswick Sleep EZ Motel, room fourteen. Gunshot wound. Earl and I are headed there, too."

"What?" Tony chewed and swallowed. "Why? We're a half hour away. They'll respond a unit from the downtown garage."

"Because the victim is a friend."

Tony appeared on the verge of arguing, but instead waved at her. "Go. I'll call it in."

*   *   *

With Earl behind the wheel, lights and sirens the entire way, they made the thirty-minute trip to Brunswick in twenty—still not fast enough to suit Zoe. Where was Maddie? Was Holt all right?

Police vehicles and news trucks choked the motel's parking lot. A police officer waved Medic Two through the line they'd established to keep onlookers at bay.

Another Monongahela County EMS unit was backed up to room fourteen, its back doors standing wide open. Earl wheeled their ambulance alongside. Zoe leapt out before they'd come to a complete stop. He yelled after her, but she didn't catch his words and didn't go back to ask him to repeat them. She sprinted to the motel room's doorway. And froze.

Police officers in uniforms from an assortment of jurisdictions— City of Brunswick, Monongahela County, Pennsylvania State Police— gathered around the periphery. At the center of the room, two paramedics from the downtown station knelt over their patient, blocking her view of him. Dark red pools and streaks marred the already stained carpeting. The phone from the nightstand sprawled on the floor, the corded handset lying next to it.

Zoe scanned faces. Across the room, Wayne Baronick watched her, his expression grim. A few other officers looked vaguely familiar.

No Maddie.

Zoe stepped inside, careful to avoid the blood on the floor. Wayne skirted the rescue effort in the center of the room and caught her before she could reach the paramedics.

"What are you doing here?" he asked.

She craned her neck, trying to see the patient. "Holt called me. He said he'd been shot."

The detective grabbed her arm. "What else did he say?"

"He told me where he was, but that's it." She tried to pull free. "Let go."

"No. You need to stand down, Zoe."

The paramedics shifted. "Let's do it," one of them said. The other one moved their gurney closer. They moved around the patient, one to the head of the backboard to which he was strapped, one to his feet.

It was Holt all right, pale, his clothes bloodied. IV lines, oxygen tubing, and EKG cables trailed from his motionless body. The heart monitor showed a rhythm, and his chest rose and fell with each breath.

Zoe shoved away from Wayne to move to Holt's side. She and another police officer bent down to grasp the edge of the backboard.

"On three," one of the paramedics said. He counted, and they hoisted the backboard and Holt up and onto the gurney.

As the other paramedics strapped him down, Zoe leaned closer. "Holt?"

His eyes fluttered open. "Zoe?" His voice rasped with the effort.

She touched his arm. "I'm here. Where's Maddie?"

He squeezed his eyes closed in a pained grimace. "You have to find her. He's going after her."

"Who? Ryan Mancinelli?"

"Let's go," one of the medics shouted.

"Wait," Zoe called as they started to wheel the gurney away.

"There's no time," the medic said.

And looking at Holt, she knew there was no use either. His eyelids had drifted open as his eyes rolled back in his head. He wasn't going to answer any more questions right now. She only hoped he'd be alive to answer them later.

Zoe trotted along behind as they rushed him out of the room and into the waiting ambulance. A very big part of her longed to climb into the patient compartment with the other crew and stay at Holt's side. Biting her lip, she resisted, watching as they closed the doors. Holt was getting the best care. His little girl, on the other hand...

"We have to find Maddie."

Wayne held up a wait-a-minute finger at Zoe as he phoned in the latest development. Maddie Farabee was missing. Someone—a man—was going after her.

Why?

None of this made sense. If only Holt had stayed conscious long enough to tell her *who* was going after his little girl.

While Wayne continued his conversation, Zoe took another look around. The same crime scene unit guys who had crawled all over her basement yesterday morning were now photographing the motel room. A gun lay on the floor near where the ambulance crew had worked on Holt. She hadn't noticed it before, probably because it had been hidden from her view by the medics. And once they'd moved, the only thing Zoe had focused on was Holt.

"Zoe." Wayne interrupted her thoughts.

"Huh?"

"Don't suppose you have a picture of the girl, do you?"

"No. Check Holt's phone. I'm sure he has some on it."

Wayne shook his head. "His phone isn't here. It wasn't on him either."

Zoe glanced at the room's phone on the floor next to the bedside table. The unfamiliar number on her caller ID. "Whoever shot him must have taken it."

"That's what I figured, too. But I need a photo of the girl to put out to law enforcement and the media."

Why hadn't she taken any pictures of Maddie when she'd been at the farm? Maybe some of the other kids had caught her in one. But it would take time they didn't have to call every boarder and ask around. "Wait. The day of the explosion, Holt had left Maddie at a friend's house."

"A friend of Holt's?"

"No, Maddie's friend. I bet they'd have pictures."

"Give me a name."

"I don't know. Pete would. Or Seth Metzger. He drove Holt from the fire to go pick up Maddie."

Wayne gave her a thumbs-up. "Great. Do me a favor and call Pete. Tell him what's happened and ask him to get a photo and send it to me ASAP." The detective turned his back on her before she could explain that Pete Adams would probably not pick up the phone if he saw her name on the caller ID. An officer was dusting the room's phone for prints. She could go outside, find Earl, and borrow his.

Stop it. Maddie's life was at stake.

Zoe took a deep breath and keyed in Pete's number.

TWENTY-SEVEN

Pete had just stepped out of the shower when he heard his cell phone. Slinging a towel around his hips, he charged out of the bathroom and snatched the phone from his dresser. The clock next to his bed showed it was a few minutes past eight p.m. and the phone screen indicated the caller was his evening shift officer. "Kevin, what's up?"

"We may have a situation here."

"What kind of situation?"

"Mrs. Romanakis called to report a missing child."

Pete reached into his closet for a clean uniform. "Go on."

"She said she'd been babysitting and took the girl and her two kids to the pool at Phillipsburg Park. Says she only turned her back for a minute to get some ice cream at the concession stand and when she looked back, the girl was gone. She tried calling the girl's father, but there was no answer."

"Get the fire department out there to start a search. And get Seth and Nate to come in to help. I'll be there in ten minutes."

"Um, that's not all, Chief."

Pete stopped with one leg in his uniform trousers. "What?"

"This missing girl? It's Madison Farabee."

"Damn it," Pete muttered.

"And there's more."

"More?" What else could there be?

"A report just came over the air. There was a shooting at the Sleep EZ Motel in Brunswick."

Pete shifted the phone to his other ear as he pulled on his shirt. "There are *always* shootings at the Sleep EZ Motel in Brunswick."

"Yeah, but this time the victim is Holt Farabee."

Pete's jaw tightened. "What's his condition?"

"All I know is he's being transported to Brunswick Hospital."

In other words, he was alive. So far. Pete wondered if Zoe knew. "Any word on Ryan Mancinelli's whereabouts?"

"Nothing yet."

"Put out a statewide BOLO on him. Wanted for questioning in the shooting of Holt Farabee. And call Ashley to make sure he hasn't contacted her."

"On it, Chief."

Pete hung up and tossed the phone on his bed. He was tucking in his shirt when the phone rang again. Zoe's name came up on the screen. He hadn't expected to see that happen again anytime soon. Clearly she knew about either the shooting or Maddie's disappearance. Or both. "Hey," he answered.

"Holt's been shot." Her voice was so fragile it sounded as if it might shatter.

"I know."

"I need you to find out who he used for a babysitter for Maddie. Probably the one he'd left her with the day his house blew up." Zoe's words tumbled over each other. "I need a photograph of her. Before Holt lost consciousness, he told me someone was going after her, but he didn't get a chance to tell me who or where Maddie is. Wayne needs a photo—"

There were some muffled voices in the background and it sounded as though she'd dropped the phone. "Zoe?" Pete said. "Are you still there?" As he strained to make sense of the garble, one question echoed in the recesses of his brain. What the hell was Zoe doing with Farabee when he'd been shot?

More muddled, incomprehensible voices filtered through the phone before she came back on the line with a sob. "Wayne just told me he's received word Maddie's missing."

"Yeah. I'm on my way to the park now." Pete grabbed his duty belt and his Glock and strode out of the bedroom. "Zoe, what exactly did Farabee say to you after he was shot?"

"What I just told you. *He* is going after Maddie. But I don't know who 'he' is."

"Don't worry. We'll find her. Where are you?"

"At the Sleep EZ. But I'm coming back there to help with the search."

Pete slammed through the door between his kitchen and garage. "You're too upset. I don't want you behind the wheel."

"Earl's driving."

So she was there in an official capacity. "Good. I'll call you if I hear anything." When silence was the only response, Pete looked at the screen. She'd hung up. He let out a growling breath and climbed into his SUV.

Trees cast long shadows across the road as Earl gunned Medic Two north on Route 15, heading back to Phillipsburg. Zoe hung up her cell phone, all too aware the search for Maddie would be racing nightfall.

"What did your nurse friend say?" Earl asked.

"Holt made it to the Emergency Department alive, but he's in critical condition." Zoe stuffed the phone back in her pocket. "They're getting him ready for surgery."

"He'll make it."

Zoe glanced at Earl's profile. "You have a crystal ball?"

A brief smile played on his lips. "No. I have kids. He'll fight for every breath so he can get back to his daughter."

"I hope you're right."

Earl took his eyes from the road for a second to meet Zoe's. "We have to concentrate on finding her. He'll want her there when he comes out of surgery."

Zoe rested her forehead against the passenger window and watched the familiar scenery. What on earth was going on? First the gas explosion appeared accidental, but turned out to be rigged. Then the fire at the barn. Then Stephen Tierney's murder and his body moved into her basement. Now Holt was fighting for his life, and Maddie... Zoe closed her eyes. She couldn't let herself think about what Maddie might be going through right now.

Someone had it in for Holt. That much seemed clear. But who? And what did Tierney have to do with it? Holt may have had a motive to kill him, but who else? None of it made sense. Zoe opened her eyes again as they passed the Kroll farm. Home. For the moment. What would that beautiful hillside look like dotted with oversized, cookie-cutter houses populated by city folks who thought they wanted to live in the country?

What would Vance Township be like without Pete?

Zoe shifted away from the window and didn't realize she'd groaned out loud until Earl gave her a concerned glance. "Are you okay?"

"No. Not even close." But she wouldn't allow the pain of losing Pete and her home to distract her from what mattered most. Finding Maddie.

Less than ten minutes later, Earl turned into the park on the hill overlooking Phillipsburg.

Zoe had vague memories of her dad bringing her here when she was a tot, pushing her on the swings, catching her at the bottom of the sliding board. As a teen, the picnic benches in the grove of trees had been a prime make-out spot. And the pool was always a welcome reprieve in the heat of summer. This evening, the usually peaceful recreation spot had transformed into yet another major emergency response scenario.

Both the Phillipsburg borough's and Vance Township's fire departments were on scene. The volunteers weren't wearing bunker gear, but carried walkie-talkies and were working their way through the trees and underbrush bordering the park. State troopers, county police, Vance's and Phillipsburg's officers were scattered about, speaking with groups of picnickers, swimmers, and families, whose plans for the summer evening clearly had not included this.

Zoe picked up the mic. "Control, this is Medic Two. Show us on standby at the Phillipsburg Park."

"Ten-four, Medic Two. Twenty forty-two."

Almost nine o'clock. If Maddie was still here, somewhere, it would be dark soon.

Nausea slammed Zoe in the pit of her stomach. If Maddie was still here, what condition was she in? And if she wasn't here, who had her and what was he doing with her?

Earl took the mic from Zoe and clipped it to the dash. "Stop imagining the worst."

She looked at him. "You do have a crystal ball, don't you?"

He opened his door. "Nope. Like I said before. I have kids. If it was my daughter out there..." He shook his head as he climbed out.

Zoe fell into step at Earl's side. They headed toward the center of all the action where a pair of State Troopers, Bruce Yancy, and Pete gathered around a map spread on the hood of one of the county police vehicles.

"Is there anything we can do?" Zoe asked.

All the men glanced up, but her eyes stayed on Pete.

She expected him to chastise her for getting involved in the case, and she was ready to dig in yet again. But instead he asked, "Any word on Farabee?"

She relayed what she'd heard from Cindy.

The fire chief shook his head. "That family has been through hell in the last week." Yancy aimed a pencil at her and Earl. "You two should stay here at the staging area. If we find the girl and she needs medical help, I don't want to have to track you down and drag you out of the woods to treat her."

For once in his life, Yancy had the tact to not mention the possibility of needing her deputy coroner training.

"Chief Adams," someone called out.

They all turned. Seth was hurrying toward them, leading two women and three fair-haired little boys.

"What have you got?" Pete asked.

Seth motioned to one of the women, a short, rotund bleached blonde wearing a huge blue t-shirt, which hung almost to her knees and covered whatever shorts or bathing suit she had on under it. "Mrs. Carter may have seen Maddie."

Zoe's heart quickened. "Where? When?"

Pete held up a hand to her without looking away from the woman.

The blonde pointed in the direction of the pool. "Sherrie and I were sitting on a bench over there watching the boys swim. I spotted a man leaving with a little girl." She nodded to Seth. "The same little girl in the picture he showed me on his phone. I'm sure of it."

"What picture?" Zoe whispered.

Pete shushed her. "What time was this, Mrs. Carter?"

"About an hour ago. I thought it was odd because I'd seen the little girl with Bonnie Romanakis and her kids just before that and the man hadn't been around then. I just figured maybe the dad came to pick her up."

Zoe resisted telling her "the dad" was currently fighting for his life.

"What did the man look like?" Pete asked.

The blonde shrugged. "I didn't pay too much attention. He had on khakis, I think, and a dark polo shirt."

Pete produced a photo. Zoe caught enough of a glimpse of it to know the man in the picture was Ryan Mancinelli. "Is this the man?"

Mrs. Carter squinted at the photograph. "I honestly don't know. I only saw him walking away from me."

"But you're sure it was Maddie Farabee with him?"

"Positive. She turned and looked back as they were walking away and I thought she looked a little upset. Like she really didn't want to leave yet."

Or like she didn't want to go with this man. "Was she resisting him?" Zoe asked.

"You mean like he was taking her by force?" Mrs. Carter said. "Oh, no. He held her hand, and they walked away as nice as can be."

Pete moved closer to the woman. "Did you notice what kind of vehicle they got into?"

"Sorry. No."

"Is there anything else about this man you can tell us? Anything at all?"

She pondered the question. "Well, I did notice one thing."

"What?"

Mrs. Carter gave an apologetic grin. "He was very...nicely put together. You know? Like he worked out a lot."

Zoe pictured Ryan Mancinelli standing on his porch Friday night during the traffic accident in front of his house. Tanned and muscled from days of construction work in the hot sun, "nicely put together" definitely described the man.

One of the Phillipsburg police officers had located a second witness to Maddie's exit from the park. This witness, a teenaged girl, was equally positive the child in question was Maddie, but her description of the man was even vaguer than Mrs. Carter's. The teen did, however, see the vehicle they got into. A big pickup. Possibly black. Or maybe dark blue. Or it might have been brown. And it might have had printing on the side, although she wouldn't swear to it.

Pete knew Mancinelli drove a black Ram pickup, but as for make and model, the girl didn't even know what those terms meant.

Pete put out an Amber Alert with Maddie Farabee's photo, courtesy of the babysitter as Zoe had suggested. Included in the report going out across the tri-state area was the possibility she *might* be with Ryan Mancinelli in a dark-colored pickup.

The search was called off, although a few die-hard firefighters broke out their flashlights and continued traipsing through the underbrush on their own. Pete figured it was their way of managing the sense of helplessness.

The same helplessness he'd seen in Zoe's face when he'd sent her back to the ambulance garage with a promise to keep her in the loop. She'd promised the same.

Keeping each other in the loop was something they'd both failed at miserably as of late. Maybe if they'd done a little more sharing—no— if *he* had been a little less pig-headed, Maddie Farabee might not be in danger right now.

Pete was feeling his own share of helplessness. Instead of going back to the station, he called Nancy to come in and man the phones. She'd agreed without hesitation. No doubt she was suffering the same affliction as everyone else. Maybe worse, since her brother-in-law was involved. He'd asked her if she was okay with working under the circumstances, and she'd insisted her only concern was getting the missing girl back. From the tone of Nancy's voice, the legal system would be the least of Mancinelli's worries if he harmed a hair on little Maddie's head.

The night dragged on into early morning. Pete monitored the radio chatter while cruising the township. Activity was light, as though the entire county was holding its collective breath, waiting for a break in the case. The only emergency call came around three a.m. for a one-vehicle crash. Nate responded and radioed in only minor injuries to the driver, although the ambulance crew was transporting him to Brunswick just in case. The airwaves once again fell quiet.

Unlike Pete's brain.

Where would Ryan Mancinelli take Maddie? And why? This case was playing havoc with Pete's gut. He'd sensed something was hinky from the start, and nothing had happened in the last week to convince him otherwise.

His cell phone rang as he coasted to the stop sign next to Parson's Roadhouse. He dug in his pocket.

Wayne Baronick's name flashed on the screen. "Hey, Pete. I just spoke to the lab."

"At this hour?"

"Yeah, well, the tech owed me. The gun next to Holt Farabee in the motel room? Registered to Ryan Mancinelli."

Pete eased into the parking lot. "Guess their friendship went sour."

"There's something weird though."

Of course. "Weird? How?"

"No prints. The gun had been wiped clean."

Pete rolled that one around in his already upset gut. "If you're going to shoot your buddy with your own gun, why wipe it clean and leave it there for the cops to find?"

"Been wondering that myself. One other thing, although it may not mean much."

"What?"

"All the stuff we collected in Zoe's basement? Mostly it was trash. Old stuff. Probably been down there for eons."

"Why do I sense a 'but' in there?"

"*But* there was one scrap that seemed new. Clean. A torn piece of black plastic."

"What kind of black plastic?"

"Like from one of those big trash bags. Only heavy. Really heavy."

Pete's phone pinged. "Hold on a second. I've got another call." He tapped the screen. Incoming call from Nate. "What have you got?"

"What I've got," the officer said, "is Ryan Mancinelli."

The fact Pete's suspects kept turning up as victims crossed his mind. "Please tell me he isn't dead."

There was a long pause—too long—before Nate responded. "Well, not yet."

TWENTY-EIGHT

The clock in the ambulance service's office read a few minutes after four in the morning. Two crew members were asleep in their bunks. Two more were in Medic One heading for Brunswick Hospital with a patient who had crashed his car into a pine tree.

"I feel like I should be doing something." Zoe drummed a blank notepad with a pen while listening to snippets of static and conversations on the scanner. She'd taken a break from pacing the ambulance garage's office to sprawl in the chair at the dispatcher's desk.

"Every cop in the area is looking for her." Earl, eyes closed, slouched on the vinyl upholstered bench across the room, one ankle crossed over the other knee, his head resting against the window behind him. "There's nothing for us to do but wait."

The scanner hissed, stuck on one channel too weak to draw in anything comprehensible. Zoe turned down the volume and clicked a button, skipping the offending frequency and sending the radio through its loop again. "There's no reason for you to sit up with me. Go to bed."

"I can't sleep either."

"You can't keep your eyes open."

"And I can't shut my brain off."

She huffed. "I hear you. Maybe we could get in Medic Two and cruise the county. We can be on call while driving around."

"What do you think we'd see in the dark? We could pass Mancinelli's truck and never know it."

Zoe let out a growl.

How dare her partner be so rational—and right.

Someone tapped on the office's front door. Zoe jumped, and Earl sat up, blinking. Sylvia opened the door and stuck her head in. "I was driving around and saw the office light on. Do you mind?"

Zoe waved her in. "Welcome to the regularly unscheduled meeting of Insomniacs Anonymous."

"There's a fresh pot of coffee in the kitchen," Earl added, rubbing his eyes. "Can I get you a cup?"

Sylvia closed the door behind her. "That would be wonderful. Thanks."

Earl climbed to his feet and snatched Zoe's empty cup from the desk without bothering to ask. She smiled. He knew her all too well.

The scanner squawked out a garbled exchange between a police officer and a dispatcher on the other side of the county pertaining to downed power lines.

Zoe reached over to adjust the squelch dial. "Do I need to ask why you're driving around at four in the morning?"

"I couldn't sleep thinking about that darling little girl out there somewhere. And I couldn't just sit and wait for the phone to ring."

"I know the feeling."

Sylvia dropped her handbag onto the bench next to where Earl had been sitting and approached Zoe, wringing her hands. "I need to apologize to you—about earlier."

Pete was moving to Hawaii. Zoe had been pretending the conversation hadn't happened. It was a mistake. A misunderstanding. "You have nothing to apologize for."

"Yes, I do. I was mad at you. Blaming you for driving Pete away."

Zoe ducked her face away from Sylvia, busying herself with some wayward paperclips.

"I know it's not your fault," Sylvia continued. "When he stopped at your farm on Saturday, I told him he was going to lose you if he didn't watch out."

Zoe tried to respond. Wanted to act casual and unaffected by Pete's leaving. But words stuck in her throat. The scanner cycled back to the channel filled with nothing but static, and Zoe snapped the radio off.

Earl returned to the office with two steaming mugs and looked back and forth between the two women. "Did I miss something?"

Zoe stood up to take her coffee from him. "No."

"By the way," Sylvia said to Earl as he handed her a cup. "You mentioned something earlier I didn't understand."

"What?" he asked.

"You said Zoe wouldn't have to leave Vance Township since Pete was moving to Hawaii." Sylvia swung back to Zoe. "Were you planning to move too?"

Zoe sighed. "Yeah. Still am. The Krolls are selling the farm."

"Oh dear." Sylvia's eyes narrowed, and her focus seemed to shift somewhere far away. "I was afraid of that."

"He's inside and he's got a gun." Nate leaned against his cruiser, resting his forearms on its roof, keeping his gaze fixed on Ryan Mancinelli's house.

Pete was the second on the scene. Baronick had said he was on his way. Before long, the stretch of road in front of the Mancinelli and Naeser houses would be jammed with police vehicles from a variety of jurisdictions.

But for now, it was just Pete and Nate. "What about the girl?"

"Haven't seen her. And other than coming out on the porch with a revolver stuck in his pants and brandishing a shotgun, yelling for me to go away, I haven't seen anything else of *him* either. He sounded like he's been hitting the bottle pretty hard. "

Pete studied the dark house and thumbed toward the one next door. "What about his wife and in-laws?"

"I told them to stay inside with the doors locked. The women are in hysterics. Ashley claims she never saw him come in. Didn't know he was there."

"How did *you* know?"

Nate glanced at Pete without turning his head and chuckled. "I knocked on his door."

Pete huffed a short laugh.

"Figured it couldn't hurt. Didn't expect to get an answer. Sure didn't expect to hear someone chambering a round into a shotgun."

"It's a sound that gets the message across."

"Damn straight. I decided a hasty retreat was in order."

"Wise move." The last thing anyone wanted was shots fired if a ten-year-old girl was in the house with him. Pete pulled out his cell phone and punched in the number he had for Mancinelli. After four rings, a machine picked up with Ashley's cheery voice asking the caller to leave a message.

Pete hung up. "Give me your bullhorn."

Nate reached into the open window of his cruiser. "I was about to use it to contact him when you pulled up."

Sirens shrieking in the distance signaled backup was on its way.

Pete lifted the bullhorn. "Ryan Mancinelli. This is Chief Pete Adams. I'm trying to call you. Do yourself a big favor and answer this time." He handed the horn back to his officer and redialed Mancinelli's number.

This time he picked up. "Go away and leave me alone."

"You know we can't do that. Not while you have Maddie Farabee in there."

For a moment, Pete thought Ryan had hung up. Then he said, "What are you talking about?"

Pete's gut knotted. "Are you telling me you don't have her?"

He was greeted once again with silence, but this time it was broken by a strange keening wail. Or was that the sirens? No. Ryan Mancinelli was crying.

"Ryan? What's going on in there?"

"I screwed everything up. Now just go away and let me end it."

End it? Pete sure didn't like the sound of that. "Ryan, don't do anything foolish. As long as you haven't hurt the little girl, we can still get you out of this mess."

"Hurt her?" Mancinelli was in full-blown blubber mode. "I might as well have killed her myself."

"Is she in there with you?"

"No. I told you she wasn't."

"Is anyone else in there with you?"

"No, damn it."

Pete blew out a breath. They didn't have a hostage situation on their hands. "Do you know where Maddie is?"

"No." Mancinelli dragged the one word out into several syllables ending with an uptick, as though he were asking a question.

Pete felt his brain cool. "Do you know who has her?"

"I could have stopped this. I should have stopped this." Mancinelli's voice bubbled. He sniffed. "Tell Ashley I'm sorry and I love her."

"Wait. Ryan, listen to me. You said you could stop this. Then help me out. Let me come in and talk to you." In Pete's peripheral vision, he saw Nate wildly shaking his head. "I'll be unarmed."

"It's too late."

"You don't know that." Pete hoped.

He could hear the man breathing. Heavy. Wet. Pete never took his eyes off the dark house, but saw flashing blue and red lights dancing across the night's landscape. Sirens wound down and two state trooper vehicles pulled up. Additional units approached from both north and south.

Over the sounds of slamming car doors and crackling radio transmissions, Ryan Mancinelli's voice reached through Pete's phone. "Just you, Chief. No guns."

"This is crazy." Wayne Baronick had arrived as Pete removed his duty belt and slipped into a Kevlar vest. "You're taking his word he doesn't have the Farabee girl in there. Meanwhile, we do know he has at least two firearms."

Concealed behind his SUV, Pete checked his backup weapon strapped to his ankle and hoped Mancinelli wouldn't frisk him. "The only person he's interested in shooting is himself."

"At least let me slip around to the back of the house. He'll never see me, but I'll be close in case you need assistance."

Pete straightened. He met Baronick's concerned gaze and nodded. "You make a move without my okay and I'll shoot you myself."

"Roger that. But if I hear gunshots, all bets are off."

Pete grinned. "Deal." He picked up the bullhorn. "I'm coming in."

Aware that a dozen or so law enforcement officers lined the edge of the road, weapons trained on the Mancinelli house, Pete approached the front porch. He watched each window for movement or a glimpse of light reflecting off a shotgun barrel. Anything to warn him if Mancinelli decided to do more than simply talk.

With the sirens now silent, the crickets serenading the night from the woods behind the house sounded deafening. Nate had already heard Mancinelli pump a shell into the chamber, so there wouldn't be any warning.

He climbed the steps. Crossed the porch. Turned the knob. The unlocked door opened. "Ryan? It's me. Pete."

"I'm in the kitchen." The voice was slightly slurred, but no longer weepy.

The first gray light of dawn filtered through the windows, offering enough illumination to allow Pete to pick his way through the entryway without tripping over the wadded throw rug. The maid clearly had not come to visit since Ashley moved out and her husband had trashed the place.

Pete found him, as he'd said, in the kitchen. Mancinelli sat on a stool at the center island, holding up his head with one hand. The other rested on a revolver lying on the counter. A quick visual sweep revealed no other weapon. However if Pete's count was accurate, there were two more empty whiskey bottles than there had been on his last visit.

"Hey, Ryan," he said, keeping his voice soft. Like they were old buddies. "Where's the shotgun?"

Mancinelli tipped his head. "On the couch. I unloaded it."

"Okay. Good." Equally good, Mancinelli showed no interest in whether Pete had brought a concealed weapon to this little powwow. Still, the man's hand was on the only visible gun in the room—a large-frame Smith and Wesson .45. "I don't suppose you unloaded that one, too?"

Without meeting Pete's gaze, Mancinelli snorted softly. "No. I figure I still might wanna use it."

Not so good. Pete leaned against the kitchen island, doing his best to appear relaxed. "Let's talk."

For the first time since Pete had arrived, Mancinelli looked up at him. "Is Holt dead?"

"No." At least not the last time he'd checked. "What happened between you two in the motel room?"

Mancinelli blinked. "Between us? I wasn't there."

"You didn't shoot Farabee?"

"Hell no."

"The gun found next to him, the gun used to shoot him, was registered to you."

Mancinelli covered his eyes with his left hand—the right one still gripped the big revolver—and moaned. "I never should've let him take it."

"Who?" Pete put one foot up on the rung of one of the stools, bringing his backup pistol a little more in reach. "Let *who* take it?"

"Holt. He doesn't own a gun, but wanted one for this meeting. I offered to come along, but he insisted it was something he had to do by himself. So I gave him my Beretta."

"What meeting?"

Mancinelli lowered his hand, but kept his gaze on the revolver. "I told him it was a bad idea. I mean, this plan of his has sucked from the start. He should've listened to me and stayed away from the whole mess, but he thought he could handle it. Take the guy down. Instead, his wife ends up dead. That idiot Tierney, too." Mancinelli sniffed and swiped the back of his left hand across his nose. "Though God knows *he* was no great loss to humanity."

Pete tried to will Mancinelli into meeting his gaze. "Who are you talking about?"

But Mancinelli didn't seem to hear him. "This is all my fault. I'm the one who introduced them. I knew the asshole was bad news, but I didn't know how bad. I should've. I should've insisted Holt stop this crusade of his. Now it's too late. That bastard is gonna kill Maddie. And then Ashley."

Ashley?

Mancinelli lifted the revolver. Swung the big barrel up. But not at Pete.

Before Mancinelli could bring the muzzle to his own head, Pete reacted. Launched over the counter separating them. Grabbed Mancinelli's right hand. And twisted.

Just as the gun went off.

TWENTY-NINE

The concussion from the gunshot blast deafened Pete, but he could still hear the pounding of his own heart. A weeping Ryan Mancinelli sprawled on the floor among the broken glass from his rage days ago.

Wayne Baronick kicked through the back door, his weapon ready. He looked around, his questioning gaze settled on Pete. "What happened?"

Ears ringing, Pete read the detective's lips and motioned for him to put his firearm away. "No one's hurt." His voice sounded odd. Muffled. He held up the revolver. "It discharged while I was disarming him."

Baronick radioed in the all clear, and Pete knelt beside Mancinelli. "Now," Pete said, "can we talk without all the bullshit?"

Mancinelli nodded, and Pete helped him to his feet.

Minutes later, Pete, his hearing gradually returning, sat next to Mancinelli on the couch in the living room. Baronick leaned in the doorway, tapping notes into his phone. Nate and one of the county officers had gone through the house and reported finding nothing. Including the girl.

"Who has Maddie?" Pete asked.

Mancinelli started to tear up again. "It's my fault."

Pete wanted to slap the man, but settled for giving his shoulder a hard shake. "I don't care whose fault it is right now. I want to know where the girl is."

Mancinelli sniffed again. "I don't know."

Pete must have looked as homicidal as he felt because Mancinelli held up both hands in self-defense. "I don't know where she is. But I know who has her."

Pete and Baronick waited.

"Dave Evans."

Pete tried to process the name. He'd heard it, but where?

"Evans?" Baronick said, apparently also at a loss.

Ryan Mancinelli nodded. "From Evans Land Development."

Pete's hearing and brain cleared in the same moment. "Scenic Hilltop Estates."

Mancinelli stared at his folded hands in his lap. "I used to work for him in the early stages of the development. I'm the one who introduced Holt to him, before I found out what kind of deal it was."

"Deal?"

"Evans had grand ideas of being rich and powerful. You know. Make a fortune buying up farms for next to nothing, put up big-ass houses and sell them for major bucks. The problem started when he ordered us to use cheaper materials and to complete the jobs fast, no matter what."

"Sounds pretty typical of those kinds of housing projects," Baronick said.

"Yeah. Except Evans didn't want his developments to be thought of as chintzy." Mancinelli shook a finger at Baronick. "In fact, he'd go ballistic if anyone used the term *housing project*. Too demeaning."

A dozen questions crammed Pete's mind, but Mancinelli was on a roll.

"Holt had always wanted to build his dream house. Something to show off his skills as a carpenter. But he couldn't afford it. When Evans offered him one of the existing houses on the hill, Holt figured it beat the run-down double-wide he'd been renting." Mancinelli ran a hand across his lips. "Could I get some water?"

Pete raised an eyebrow at Baronick.

"Do I look like a waiter?"

Pete gave the detective a look.

"Fine." Baronick disappeared into the kitchen.

"Go on," Pete told Mancinelli.

"It didn't take long for Holt to discover he was expected to cut corners in his work, and his own house had been built with substandard materials. He complained to Evans, who is the king of apologies and excuses. Evans promised to have everything made right.

Which, of course, he didn't. So Holt started remodeling his place. Tearing out the shit and putting in quality stuff."

Baronick returned and handed a glass to Mancinelli. The detective turned to Pete. "Can I get you anything?" he asked, his voice oozing with sarcasm.

"No, thanks. I'm good."

Grumbling, Baronick returned to the doorway. Pete urged Mancinelli on.

He leaned forward, a light in his eyes. "In order to do all this remodeling, Holt had to post building permits. His neighbors on the hill saw them and started asking questions. Especially Stephen Tierney. Holt told them what he was finding. The house had been built using two-by-eights for joists instead of two-by-tens. And instead of using sixteen-inch center for the walls, they'd used twenty-four. Insulation was at a minimum. And don't get me started on the cheap shingles used on the roof. Anyhow, next thing Holt knows, Evans is pounding on his door, furious that he's daring to demean Evans' good reputation. Threatened to sue him for slander if he kept it up."

Mancinelli sipped at the water. From his expression, Pete suspected he wished it was something much stronger.

"Holt's complaints started putting a crimp in Evans' plans. Folks backed out on deals to buy lots. Others complained to the bank."

Baronick cleared his throat. "Speaking of the bank, wouldn't they come down hard on Evans for using substandard building materials?"

"They would," Pete answered for Mancinelli, sensing where this was going. "Except Stephen Tierney was Dave Evans' liaison with the bank."

Mancinelli's eyes brightened. "Right. Evans promised to give Tierney's house a complete upgrade if he kept a lid on Holt's claims. And when Holt didn't back down, Evans fired him and had him blacklisted so he couldn't get work."

"As a result, he fell behind in house payments and was evicted."

"Exactly. Holt tried to get Tierney to help him out with the bank, but he refused."

"Because Evans had promised to fix his house."

"More than that. Holt found out Evans promised to move Tierney into Holt's house."

Baronick looked up from his notes. "I imagine Farabee's house was pretty nice by now since he'd been upgrading things on his own."

"You got it." Mancinelli nodded. "Holt was getting desperate. He'd lost his house, couldn't get a decent job, his marriage was in rough shape. He decided he was going to take Evans down. He planned to go to the township supervisors and report him. Have all his permits pulled. Remember I said Evans was the king of apologies and excuses? Well, he's the *emperor* of threats. First he threatened to sue Holt for slander—"

"But it's not slander if it's true," Baronick said.

"Which is what Holt told him. So Evans got ugly." Mancinelli drained his water glass. When he continued, his voice had deepened. "He promised Holt would regret making trouble. Said if he lost his business, Holt would lose a helluva lot more. The next day..."

Pete's jaw ached. "The explosion?"

Mancinelli stared at his empty glass. "Yeah."

Baronick swore under his breath.

Pete jotted a note to himself. Look into the source of the phone call luring Holt away from his house the morning of the explosion. "Why didn't Holt tell us about all of this back then instead of letting us accuse him of killing his wife?"

Mancinelli's mouth drew into a thin, tight line. "Because Lillian wasn't the only thing Holt had to lose."

Pete's grip on his pen tightened. "Maddie."

"Yeah."

The son of a bitch had been threatening to harm the girl all along.

Baronick rubbed his upper lip. "Why kill Tierney?"

Mancinelli set the glass down next to one of the empty whiskey bottles. "I don't know for sure, but I have a pretty good idea. Evans had been controlling Tierney with the promise of giving him Holt's house."

Pete shook his head in amazement. "But then Evans blew it up, which probably didn't sit well with Tierney. He might have threatened to reveal what he knew, so Evans shut him up permanently and planted the body in the Krolls' basement to throw suspicion on Farabee."

"Plus it let Holt know how close Evans could really get to him," Mancinelli said. "And to Maddie."

It made sense.

"That's when Farabee moved out." Pete wondered if part of Farabee's leaving was to put distance between him and Zoe to protect her. If that were the case, Pete owed the man a debt of gratitude. She'd been in danger all right. But not because a killer was in the house. Holt was a target, not the murderer.

"Holt knew he had to do something drastic to catch Evans before anyone else got hurt. So he borrowed my gun."

Baronick scowled. "He planned to kill Evans?"

"No. The gun was for protection. Holt's plan was to meet with Evans and aggravate him into telling everything he'd done while Holt recorded it."

"Recorded? With what?"

"His cell phone."

"There was no cell phone at the scene," Baronick said.

"Evans must have figured out what he was doing," Mancinelli said. "That's when things probably went sour. Evans shot Holt. Took the cell phone. And went after Maddie."

"Which explains how Evans knew where to find Maddie, too," Pete said. "If Evans had Farabee's phone, he had all his contacts. Wouldn't take a genius to track down the girl's babysitter."

Mancinelli fidgeted with his wedding band. "Evans is sheer evil. You have to keep him away from Ashley."

He'd mentioned his wife earlier, prior to the gun going off. "Why Ashley?" Pete asked.

Mancinelli looked like a man whose world was on the verge of collapse. "Because Evans didn't just threaten Holt and his family. Why do you think I've never said anything about any of this? Why do you think I came to your station and told you all that crap about Holt killing Lill? I had no choice. Evans said he'd kill Ashley if I didn't help him frame Holt. Now...if he finds out I've talked to you..." Mancinelli doubled over, moaning.

Pete's head throbbed. "We're going to get this guy, Ryan. He's not going to have a chance to hurt Ashley."

"Hey, Pete." Baronick's brows were furrowed. "If Evans thought Holt was dead, why bother with the girl?"

"Maybe he didn't know if Farabee was dead. Or maybe Maddie knows something about it all and he wants to shut her up." Pete rubbed the ache in his forehead. "I just hope to heaven it's the first, because if that's the case, she's an insurance policy."

"And if it's the other," Baronick said, finishing Pete's thought, "she's a liability."

"And he's probably already killed her. We have to operate on the assumption she's still alive." Pete put a hand on Mancinelli's knee and squeezed. Hard. "Where would Evans take her?"

"I wish I knew. I don't."

"Think. You worked for the man. You might know more than you realize."

Mancinelli wiped a hand across his mouth. "Well...he does have his construction office outside of Dillard. He stores his big machinery there."

Of course. Pete should have thought of it sooner. "And he keeps a bunch of construction trailers parked at the back of the property."

Quarter after eight in the morning and already the temperature was inching well into the seventies with oppressive humidity. Zoe slid down from her pickup's air conditioned cab, exhausted from a sleepless night and wired from too much caffeine.

Once Medic One had returned to the garage, Zoe had stretched out in her bunk only to stare at the bottom of the one above her. As if Holt getting shot and Maddie missing wasn't enough to play on her mind, Sylvia's visit nagged at her.

Dave Evans had stopped at the farm to see Mrs. Kroll on Saturday while Sylvia had been watching Maddie. The man sure was persistent. But he'd accomplished what he'd set out to do. Once he finally tracked Mrs. Kroll down, he'd convinced her to sell.

Zoe knew she hadn't liked him since the day he'd interrupted her out in the barn.

On her way down the hill to the farmhouse, she called Brunswick Hospital to check on Holt's condition, but was told no information was being released.

Damned privacy laws.

She thought about calling Pete, but shook off the idea. He would've called her if they'd found Maddie.

Wouldn't he?

Stuffing the phone in her pocket, she stepped onto the back porch and crossed to the door at the far left. She wanted to make sure Mrs. Kroll was all right after yesterday's fiasco.

Zoe pounded on the door. No answer. No sound of movement inside. She knocked again. Still nothing. Odd. Mrs. Kroll was an early riser and shouldn't have left to visit her husband at rehab yet. Zoe tried the knob. Locked.

She stepped over to the window to the dining room and peered in. The room was dark. And empty.

It didn't feel right. But perhaps Mrs. Kroll's son, Alexander, had stopped by and taken his mother out to breakfast.

Still not convinced, Zoe went to her own door, unlocked it, and stepped inside. Jade and Merlin sat side-by-side waiting expectantly. At least that much of her morning was normal.

"Good morning, kittens." She deposited her keys and her phone on the table by the door. "You hungry?"

Jade meowed.

"Silly question, huh?" Zoe headed for the kitchen with both cats trotting along behind.

As she filled the cat food bowls, she ran her plans for the morning through her mind. Feed cats. Make coffee. Go to the barn to clean stalls. Shower. Sleep. Blessed sleep.

Oh, and try again to check on Mrs. Kroll.

With the cats happily chowing down, Zoe filled the Mr. Coffee's basket with her favorite blend. The one Pete hated. She shook her head. Stop thinking about Pete.

She filled the pot with water. Odd. The pressure seemed low. Great. One more thing going bad. Not that it mattered anymore. She wouldn't be living here much longer. The house—her beautiful, venerable mid-nineteenth century house—was going to fall to a bulldozer.

The thought soured her stomach.

She poured the water into the machine's reservoir and clicked the power button. The light didn't come on. What the heck? Zoe reached over and flipped the kitchen's light switch. Nothing. Crap. Was the power out all over the area? Or had the main breaker tripped again?

Grumbling to herself, she pressed through the swinging door, crossed her living room to the basement door. She stepped onto the landing at the top of the stairs. Without thinking, she tugged the pull-cord for the light and growled when nothing happened. "Idiot," she muttered into the darkness.

She turned to go back for her flashlight. But something—some sound—stopped her. A tiny whimper. From somewhere below.

Maddie?

Heart racing, Zoe started down into the total darkness of the basement.

There it was again. Weeping.

Putting aside her trepidation, she pounded down the next two steps.

But suddenly her foot found only air. She scrambled. Clawed for the railing.

And plunged into the black oblivion.

THIRTY

A check of the Pennsylvania Department of Transportation revealed Dave Evans owned a dark blue Ford F-250 pickup. Ryan Mancinelli confirmed Evans had his business name and phone number stenciled on the doors. Pete called in the updated information including license number to the Amber Alert and checked his watch. Evans had snatched Maddie over twelve hours ago. Twelve long hours.

Pete walked Ryan Mancinelli out of his house. Not even nine o'clock and the temperature was already sultry. Pete thought of those construction trailers Mancinelli had mentioned. A little girl locked in one of those wouldn't last long on a day like this.

Baronick jogged up to them. "The search warrant will be ready by the time we get there. One of my guys will meet us at Evans' office with it."

"Good." Pete crooked a finger at Kevin who hurried over to them. "Take Mr. Mancinelli down to the station and get him settled in our finest holding cell."

"Aw, Chief," Mancinelli started to complain.

Pete put up a hand to silence him. "You did threaten several police officers, myself included, with a firearm. But the bigger issue is Evans is still out there. He's trying to take out everyone he considers a threat of exposing him. You definitely fit the bill."

"What about Ashley?" Mancinelli said. "Evans threatened to go after her, too."

Pete spotted Mancinelli's wife and her parents standing on their porch next door. "I'll make sure an officer sticks around to keep an eye on her."

"Thanks, Chief."

Pete slapped Baronick on the back. "Let's go."

Within fifteen minutes, Pete, Baronick, Nate, Seth, and a couple dozen other law enforcement officers descended on the offices of Dave Evans Land Developing.

As promised, a county detective sat at the entrance gate, search warrant in hand.

The grounds were hauntingly quiet for a weekday morning. A dozen or so pieces of heavy machinery—bulldozers, backhoes, mammoth dump trucks, and the like—sat idle on the gravel lot. A gray Toyota Camry was parked in front of a construction trailer, which bore a sign labeling it as the office.

Pete and Baronick climbed the portable metal steps to the door, knocked, and entered without waiting for an invitation.

A wide-eyed woman in her late twenties wearing jeans and a short-sleeved plaid shirt was already on her feet, obviously having seen the cavalry coming through the gate. "Can I help you?" she chirped.

Baronick presented her with the warrant.

"Is your boss here?" Pete asked.

The woman's eyes flitted from the paper in her hand to Pete and Baronick. "Uh, no."

"Any idea where we can find him?"

"N-no. He called a little while ago and said he wouldn't be in. He said he was giving everyone the day off, but I had some paperwork to catch up on."

"Are those trailers in the back locked?"

"Um, yeah." She glanced toward a pegboard loaded with keys next to the office door. "But I can't let you into them."

Baronick pointed to the paper in her hand. "Warrant, ma'am. We need to search *everything*."

"Oh." She bit her lip. Then nodded toward the board. "The keys for the heavy equipment are all labeled. The trailer keys are the ones on the bottom row."

Pete scooped up the entire row of keys with one hand. "Come on." He paused at the door to point at the secretary. "You stay here."

He and Baronick charged out of the trailer.

"Seth, you search the office," Pete shouted to the waiting officers. "Everyone else, with us."

He doled out keys as they approached the eight trailers parked near the rear of the lot, and the officers split up. Numbered tabs on the key rings matched numbered plaques riveted onto each trailer.

Pete inserted the key for number three and climbed inside.

It only took a sweeping glance to see Maddie wasn't there. A couple of ladders hung on brackets next to coils of heavy duty extension cords and hoses. An eight-foot table and several folding chairs were secured to one wall. Shelves of tools lined another. Two large steel trunks sat at one end. Pete opened both to find them filled with tarps, ropes, and other assorted supplies. Exactly what you'd expect to find in a construction trailer.

He went back to the door and called out, "Clear!"

Six more calls of *clear* rang out up and down the row. He waited for the report from the last trailer. And waited.

After what felt like hours, Baronick's voice rang out. "Pete. You're gonna want to see this."

Zoe tried to push up from the cold, hard-packed dirt floor. She'd hit hard. Landed on her left side. Everything hurt like hell. As she maneuvered onto her hands and knees, pain tore through her left shoulder forcing her back on her knees. Only something sharp as a dagger cut into one of them.

She rolled to one hip, but that wasn't any better. Finally she staggered to her feet, swaying.

Her eyes acclimated to the low light enough to see the mess she'd fallen into. Except for the top treads, the entire staircase had been destroyed. Bashed. With what? The splintered remains of the heavy planks littered the basement floor. And she'd landed smack in the middle of it.

At least she could stand. Her legs weren't broken. But her left shoulder? She wasn't so sure. Any movement of that arm was met with searing pain. She undid one button of her uniform shirt just above her belt and tucked her hand and forearm inside to immobilize the shoulder a bit.

With her pain momentarily in check, she again became aware of the whimper she'd heard from the top of the stairs. The muted cries had escalated into full-blown sobbing along with what sounded like shushing sounds.

"Who's down here?" she called out while swiping cobwebs from her face with her functional right hand.

"Zoe?" That was Mrs. Kroll. Her voice sounded...odd.

"Yeah." Zoe took one staggering step toward the voice. Her left leg felt as if it had been torn from the hip, and she nearly ended up back on the cold earthen floor. Gasping, she regained her balance, keeping her weight off the offending leg. Through clenched teeth she said, "Where are you?"

"We're in here. *Hurry.*" The tiny weepy voice wasn't Mrs. Kroll.

"Maddie?"

"Help us!"

"Hang on." Zoe glanced around, searching for something to use as a crutch or a cane and found nothing. Not even a broom handle. Gritting her teeth, she hobbled through the dark cave of the basement. Without electricity, the only light filtered in through two small windows, protected on the outside by wooden slats and set high in the foundation walls—one on the far side of the basement and the other in the room ahead of her housing the water heater, fuel oil tanks, and electrical panel. "Where are you?" Zoe asked again.

A small familiar figure stepped out of the room. "In here," Maddie said. "Hurry. Mrs. Kroll is sick."

Doing her best to ignore the pain in her hip and shoulder, Zoe hopped one-legged to Maddie. "Are you okay?"

"I guess. But Mrs. Kroll isn't." The girl looked at Zoe. "And neither are you."

"Don't worry about me."

Maddie slipped an arm around Zoe. "Let me help."

The kid might be the next generation paramedic. Zoe leaned on her and limped into the room. She found her landlady dressed in a nightgown seated on the cold floor next to the water heater, leaning back against the stone foundation. "What's wrong? What happened?"

Mrs. Kroll managed a weak smile. "I'll be fine. I'm just upset. That awful man."

"Ryan Mancinelli?" Zoe glanced at Maddie.

"No." Mrs. Kroll groaned. "The man who wants to buy the farm."

"Dave Evans?"

"Yes. Horrible man. I was a fool to have showed him around the house, including this cellar, on Sunday."

Zoe eased to her knees beside the older woman. Even in the low light, she recognized there was more wrong with her landlady than she let on. "Tell me what happened."

Mrs. Kroll massaged her left arm and looked at Maddie.

Zoe gently took her landlady's hand. A simple act of comfort. Except Zoe's middle and ring fingers rested lightly on Mrs. Kroll's radial pulse. Zoe shot a quick look at the girl before resting her gaze on the sweep second hand of her watch. "Go ahead, Maddie."

The girl hugged herself, her shoulders hiked. "Mr. Evans came by the park last night when I was there with my friends. He said my dad had been hurt and had sent him to get me. I was scared, but he showed me he had Dad's phone, so I went. I guess I shouldn't have."

No, you shouldn't. But now wasn't the time for a scolding. "He brought you here?"

"Not at first. We rode around a while. He was acting really weird. I wondered where we were going. Where my dad was. When I asked, he got mean and yelled at me to be quiet. I guess I started crying. Anyway, he brought me here. I thought *good.* Dad had come back to the farm. But he hadn't."

"He brought you here last night?"

"Yes," Mrs. Kroll said, her voice weaker than usual. "He pounded on my door late. Must have been close to eleven o'clock."

"You mean you've been down here all night?"

"Yes. And it's none too comfortable, my old bones sitting on this cold floor, I can tell you."

Zoe slid her hand up to rest on Mrs. Kroll's forearm. Her skin was clammy even in the coolness of the basement. "How are you feeling?"

"I'm fine."

"No, she isn't," Maddie said. "She was dizzy and said her tummy was upset."

Zoe raised an eyebrow at her landlady. "Is that true?"

"Well...a little. But that awful man upset me so."

Zoe looked around. She didn't want to add to Mrs. Kroll's anxiety with the news the older woman was very likely having a heart attack.

"We need to get you out of here," she said, keeping her voice calm.

Mrs. Kroll gave a mildly hysterical laugh. "If only we could."

Maddie rocked from one foot to the other. "After Mr. Evans brought us down here, he took a sledge hammer to the stairs so we can't get back up."

Mrs. Kroll winced. "And he did something to the breaker box to kill the power. He went out the basement doors and latched them from the outside. We're trapped in here. When Maddie and I heard you at the top of the steps, we thought it was him coming back. If I'd known it was you, I'd have yelled to you to stay up there and get help."

Zoe braced one hand against the foundation and struggled to her feet, clamping her mouth shut to keep from crying out. Leaning on the wall for support, she hobbled to the electrical box. If Evans had simply flipped the main switch...but no. An empty hole glared back at her from where the main breaker should be.

"Do you have your cell phone?" Maddie asked.

Zoe put a hand on her pocket. Crap. She'd left her phone and her keys on the table upstairs. "Afraid not." She balanced precariously on one foot and scanned the room. A worn out broom leaned in one corner, enveloped in dusty spider webs.

She considered asking Maddie to fetch it, but doubted the girl would be willing to wrangle with arachnids to retrieve the makeshift cane. Zoe wasn't thrilled about the idea herself. She hopped across the room, each jolt sending pain up her spine to her shoulder, her neck, and her brain.

"Where are you going?" Maddie demanded.

Zoe paused, gritting her teeth. She pointed. "I need a crutch, but that will do."

"I'll get it." The ten-year-old scurried to the corner, reached through the web, and grabbed the broom, brushing it off as she brought it to Zoe.

"You're not afraid of spiders?"

"Nope. I've been bugging Dad to get me a pet tarantula."

Zoe eyed her. "*Bugging* him?"

Maddie didn't appear to catch her own pun. "He always said Mom would have a fit, but I think he's the one who's scared of them." The girl turned sullen at the mention of her mom.

"Well, you're braver than I am," Zoe said, hoping the praise would encourage continued bravery. She tested the broom handle to make sure it wasn't going to snap the moment she leaned on it. It held. But the wood surface was rough from age. She'd probably end up with a handful of splinters.

Then again, splinters were the least of her concern at the moment.

"Now where are you going?" Maddie asked as Zoe hobbled toward the door.

"We may not be as stuck as Mrs. Kroll thinks." Those outer basement doors, latched only with an old screwdriver through a hasp, were rickety and rotted. "You just stay here and rest," she told her landlady.

"Zoe?" Maddie's voice trembled.

"What, baby?"

"My dad? Where is he?"

Zoe swallowed. Put on the best poker face she could manage. "He has been hurt, but he's in the hospital, and they're taking really good care of him." She gave the girl a tight smile, turned, and limped out into the cavernous part of the basement before Maddie could question her further.

The oil furnace sat in a large pit in the center of the dark cave. Apparently when it or an earlier furnace had been installed, the beast had been too tall for the low clearance, and someone had dug out a two-foot deep, ten-foot wide crater to make room. Not keen on the idea of another fall, Zoe picked her way around the hole.

The inner door stood open, either left that way when Evans departed or opened by Maddie or Mrs. Kroll. The sloped bulkhead doors remained closed, rays of sunshine sneaking through the cracks between the boards.

Zoe put her good shoulder against the split where the two doors met, hoping the screws holding the hasp would pop loose with some pressure. She pushed, expecting some jiggle or give. There was none. She turned and braced her back against the doors, her feet on the first stone step, squeezing into the wedge of space.

Her legs—at least one of them—was strong.

She heaved, but the doors didn't give even a fraction of an inch. She gritted her teeth. Dug in hard as she could. Groaned against the stabbing pain in her hip and her quivering, protesting quads. The wood didn't so much as creak.

"I don't think that's gonna work," Maddie said.

Zoe hadn't realized the little girl had tagged along. "I'm not giving up yet. Maybe there's something here I can use to pry them open."

"I don't think so," Maddie repeated. "Mr. Evans went out that way and I heard him out there hammering. I think he nailed some boards across the outside."

Which would explain why there was no give to the rickety old doors. Zoe squinted at the gaps where the sun shone through. Maddie was right. Three boards blocked the striped pattern of light. "Okay." Zoe repositioned her left arm in its makeshift sling and stared into the darkness. "Time for Plan B."

"What's that?"

"I don't know yet."

"Zoe?" Mrs. Kroll's weak voice called out.

"Coming." Zoe tipped her head at Maddie and led the girl back to where they'd left the older woman.

Mrs. Kroll was still sitting on the floor, but she was clutching the front of her bathrobe.

Zoe knelt beside her. "Are you in pain?"

"Some," Mrs. Kroll whispered as if trying to keep Maddie from hearing. "But the thing is...I can't...breathe."

The metal steps had been removed from the trailer marked with the number six, so Pete had to hoist himself into the doorway. Inside, Baronick, wearing Latex gloves and holding a crowbar, had a look on his face that tied Pete's stomach into a knot. "What have you got?"

Baronick showed the heavy chunk of steel to Pete and pointed at a mark on it. "What's this look like to you?"

Pete pulled out his reading glasses. The stain was hard to see even with the magnification, but the bit of short brownish hair stuck to it was pretty clear. "The girl has long blond hair."

"I know. If I'm not mistaken, this doesn't look fresh." Baronick used the crowbar to point at a spot on the floor. "Neither does that."

Pete got down on one knee.

Definitely blood. Dried. And a lot of it. He looked over his shoulder at the officers standing outside the door. "Nate. Get the crime scene guys out here."

Nate gave a nod and backed away.

"Did you check the rest of the trailer?" Pete asked Baronick.

"Yeah. No sign of the girl. But look at this."

Pete stood and followed Baronick to a set of shelves built into one wall.

Tools and building supplies lined them in neat order. Except for a roll of black plastic trash bags, which appeared to have been yanked off the shelf and tossed back haphazardly.

Next to the bags, a roll of duct tape sat alone on the edge of the shelf while five similar rolls were stacked precisely aligned. "Someone with OCD organized these shelves."

"And someone in a big hurry or someone with no such compulsion borrowed some tape and a trash bag."

"Or two." Pete exchanged a look with the detective.

"Want to hear what I'm thinking?" Baronick said.

"Probably the same thing I am. Go ahead."

"Stephen Tierney came here to confront Evans. Maybe to complain about losing the house he wanted. Maybe he was fed up with Evans' scare tactics and threats. Either way, they had it out." Baronick held up the crowbar. "Evans whacks Tierney. Leaves him here in this trailer for a couple of days. Then decides he can kill the proverbial two birds with one crowbar. He bundles Tierney up in a couple of these heavy duty trash bags. Duct tapes them together to seal in all the body fluids that might leak out in his truck."

"Duct tape would explain the marks Franklin Marshall found during the autopsy. And the plastic would make it easier to slide a dead body." Pete turned toward the door and the missing steps. "Back the pickup right to the door and in you go."

"Drive the body to the farm where Holt Farabee's living and transfer it into the basement with the help of a convenient old wheelbarrow. But the plastic tears. Some body fluid leaks onto the wheelbarrow, and we find a scrap of the trash bag inside the basement. Evans, however, doesn't notice and thinks he's gotten rid of one troublemaker and framed the other one for murder."

Pete had to admit, it made more sense than anything else had lately. "Which is all well and good. One problem, though. It doesn't put us any closer to finding Maddie."

THIRTY-ONE

Even in the thin bands of sunlight filtering through the slats of the window above them, Zoe could see Mrs. Kroll didn't look good. Beads of perspiration glistened on her too pale face. She wore an almost constant grimace of pain and cradled her left arm as if it were broken.

Zoe checked her pulse again. Fast. Thready. "Try to stay calm and breathe slow."

Mrs. Kroll nodded.

Zoe patted her uniform cargo pants pockets even though she already knew what was there—two pairs of sheers, a pair of forceps, a penlight, and a pair of Latex gloves. She also knew what was *not* there—her phone, aspirin, and an oxygen tank.

If Mrs. Kroll wasn't having a heart attack, one was imminent. Zoe needed to get her out of there and to medical help immediately, if not sooner.

She struggled to her feet, gasping as what felt like a red hot dagger drove through her hip. Biting back the pain, she told Maddie, "Stay with Mrs. Kroll. I'm gonna look around for some way out of here. Holler if she gets worse."

When Zoe hobbled past Maddie, the girl reached out and caught Zoe's shirt. "Is Mrs. Kroll gonna die?" Maddie whispered.

Zoe spotted tears in the girl's eyes and brushed a finger over her cheek. "Not if I can help it."

Leaning heavily on the old broom, Zoe stumbled back toward the smashed staircase. On her way past, she gave the root cellar a quick glance. The potatoes remained piled on the floor, where the crime scene guys had left them. She pushed the memory of Stephen Tierney's arm sticking out of the pile of spuds from her mind.

She shuddered at the splintered remains of the stairs. As bad as the damage might be to her hip and shoulder, she was lucky she hadn't been impaled. While the basement might make a great location for a Halloween party, she was not a vampire and didn't need a wooden stake driven through her heart.

She looked up. The lowest surviving stair tread was at her eye level. Two steps above it, the door. And on the other side of it, her phone.

She rested the broom against the wall and reached up with her good arm. Chin-ups weren't her forte, but if she had the use of both arms, she could do it. She withdrew her left arm from its makeshift sling. Gingerly straightened the elbow, letting the arm hang at her side. The shoulder ached a little, but not bad. Maybe....

She lifted the arm—or tried to. The pain, like a hot spike being driven into her shoulder, took her breath away and left her clutching the arm against her side, doubled over and gasping.

So much for that idea.

As the agony subsided and she caught her breath, she noticed some odds and ends stashed farther back in the shadows. An even rattier broom than the one she'd enlisted as a cane leaned in a corner next to a galvanized bucket and a couple of cobwebby wooden chicken crates.

Zoe tucked her arm into her shirt again and collected her broom walking stick. What other forgotten tools and implements lurked down here? A ladder would have been too much to hope for. She knew all too well those were kept in one of the outbuildings.

She hobbled through the basement, her eyes becoming acclimated to the low light. She searched the walls and corners, hoping to find an ax, a pry bar, even the sledgehammer Evans had used on the stairs. Apparently, he took it with him. The rest of her wish list remained equally as illusive.

In the farthest corner, she found a rusted coal shovel, a relic from the pre-oil furnace days.

She reached through a veil of dusty spider webs and grabbed the shovel, hefting it. The thing weighed a ton, but was sturdier than the splintery broom. She swapped the two and used her new cane to hobble back to the bulkhead doors.

With one bum leg and one useless arm, handling the heavy coal shovel was awkward at best. Zoe shifted her weight until she felt reasonably steady. She tucked her bad arm a little more securely into her shirt. Picked up the shovel. Gave a couple of gentle test swings. And then hauled back and winged it as hard as she could muster.

It thunked against ungiving wood, jarring every electrified nerve in Zoe's body. The recoil as the shovel bounced back threw her off balance. She spun and hit the ground with a jolt.

Maddie must have heard either the thud of the shovel or the thud of Zoe biting the dust yet again and came running. "Are you okay?"

With the little girl present, Zoe couldn't even swear, except inside her head. "I'm...peachy," she muttered.

At least she'd landed on her right side, and as bad as it hurt, she didn't think she'd done damage. She stretched to grab the shovel and dragged it close, then struggled to get her knees under her. Bracing against her new crutch, and with Maddie's assistance, Zoe managed to regain her feet.

"Was that Plan B?" Maddie asked.

Zoe huffed. "Yeah." She leaned on the shovel and patted Maddie's blond head. "Let's go check on Mrs. Kroll while I think up a Plan C."

The older woman remained where Zoe had left her and looked about the same. "How are you?" Zoe asked.

Mrs. Kroll met Zoe's gaze, her eyes telling the tale. Not good.

Maddie hugged herself. "What are you gonna do now?"

Good question. Zoe blew out a breath. "Since we clearly can't get out through the doors, I figure the next best choice is the staircase."

"But it's all smashed," Maddie said.

As if she needed reminding. "I didn't say it was going to be easy. I'd try to haul myself up, but my shoulder won't let me." She fixed Maddie with a solemn stare. "I'm going to boost you up instead." Or at least she hoped she was.

The girl's eyes widened. "How?"

Zoe didn't let on she was making it up as she went. "Well, there are a couple of old chicken crates out there. We'll make sure they can hold your weight. You can climb on them and from there it'll be like me giving you a leg up onto a horse. Only you'll be getting on my shoulders. Doesn't your dad sometimes carry you on his shoulders?"

"Yeah." Maddie sounded doubtful.

"I can't lift you onto mine. But if we work at it, we can do it. Then you just climb the rest of the way onto the steps that are left. My phone's on the stand by my front door. You grab it and hand it down here to me." The plan sounded remarkably easy. As long as Zoe's hip didn't buckle and Maddie didn't fall. "Okay?"

Maddie looked apprehensive, but said, "It'll be like one of those acrobat shows at the circus."

Only without a net. "Exactly."

Maddie stood a little taller, planting her fists on her hips in a superhero pose. "Let's do it."

"Atta girl." Zoe knelt beside Mrs. Kroll to check her pulse once more. "You try to relax. We'll have help coming in a couple of minutes."

The old woman tried to smile, but her eyes reflected only pain and terror.

Phone first, but the second thing Zoe would send Maddie for was a bottle of aspirin.

Using the shovel and a hand on the foundation, Zoe climbed to her feet. She was about to turn away when movement outside the window caught her eye. She swiped a hand across the filthy window surface. A navy blue pickup with white lettering—the same truck she'd seen parked outside the barn the morning of the explosion—had made the turn off Route 15 into the farm lane.

Dave Evans was back.

"Now what?" Baronick asked as they walked back to the office, leaving Nate and Seth to string crime scene tape around the trailer.

"Find Maddie," Pete said. It was that simple. And that difficult.

"Any idea where to look next? We've already searched Evans' home. It's clear."

Pete's cell phone rang. The screen showed the incoming call was from the station. "Adams."

"Chief, the phone company just called with the information you wanted." Nancy's voice sounded strained. Probably because her brother-in-law was currently residing in the holding cell.

"And?"

"The call to Holt Farabee that sent him on a wild goose chase the day of the explosion came from a number registered to Dave Evans."

No big surprise. "Thanks, Nancy."

"What?" Baronick asked as Pete stuffed the phone back in his pocket.

Pete relayed the news. "Evans lured Farabee away from the house so he could slip in and tamper with the gas line to the dryer."

"The fire marshal said natural gas explosions are unpredictable. How would he know who would be home when it blew?"

Pete shrugged. "Maybe it didn't matter. If Farabee got killed, all Evans' problems with him would be solved. If he only got hurt or if his wife or daughter was hurt or killed, the message was sent. Ryan Mancinelli said the guy gets his jollies making threats." A thought occurred to him. He stopped and turned to Baronick. "Evans somehow got into Farabee's house to rig the explosion. He must keep keys to the houses he's built."

The detective scowled for a moment. Then his eyes widened. "The fort."

Pete slapped Baronick's arm. "Let's go."

No way was Zoe sending Maddie upstairs now. Not with Dave Evans out there. Somewhere.

But where?

He might not realize Zoe was in the basement with Mrs. Kroll and Maddie. She might be able to use the element of surprise to their benefit. She could hide in the shadows if he pried open the bulkhead doors to come in. Maybe she couldn't swing the shovel hard enough to shatter wood, but she could definitely swing it hard enough to flatten Evans.

Except her truck was parked in plain view. He might wonder if she was in the barn, but he'd be too cautious to be caught off guard.

"Okay, new plan," Zoe said after giving Mrs. Kroll and Maddie the bad news. She leaned on her shovel, fixing the whimpering ten-year-old with a determined stare. "I need you to give me a hand."

Sniffling, Maddie nodded. Zoe led the way back to the demolished stairs, praying Evans didn't choose that moment to open the door at the top. She stifled a groan as she eased her left arm from the stability of her shirt. Bending down, she took hold of one of the chicken crates with her left hand. She might not be able to lift the crate, but she managed to drag it. The shoulder still hurt like hell, but she didn't have the luxury of being a wimp right now. "Bring the other one and come on."

Maddie obeyed.

Zoe hoped Evans couldn't hear the thumping of the crate along the uneven earthen floor. She and Maddie lugged them to the edge of the pit. Zoe nudged hers into it, hoping the crate held together.

With Maddie's help Zoe managed to step down next to the furnace without falling. She lowered the second crate beside the first.

Within minutes, they'd stacked the crates under the window behind the furnace.

"What are you gonna do?" Maddie asked, her voice thin.

Zoe wished she had an answer for the girl. What was she gonna do? In her mind, she pictured climbing onto the stacked crates without falling and without the ancient wood cracking under her weight. She pictured bashing out the window and the sturdy-looking slats with the shovel. And she pictured herself disregarding the searing pain and hoisting herself up and out.

Basically, Plan D sucked.

"Go back and try to keep Mrs. Kroll calm," Zoe told Maddie. "And holler if she seems to be getting worse."

"Okay."

Once Maddie had climbed out of the pit and headed back to the older woman, Zoe steeled herself. Using the shovel for support, she attempted to step onto the crates. The hot spikes driving into her hip pierced her with an intensity that threatened to throw her to the ground. Instead, she tumbled into the stone wall of the foundation, jarring her shoulder.

Breathing hard, she waited for the pain to subside enough to try again. Wiser, this time, she sat on the crates instead of stepping up onto them. She scrambled onto her knees and worked her weight back onto her toes, thinking a beached whale probably looked more graceful. Longing to hurry, but having already experienced the less-than-stellar results of such foolishness, she wormed her way into a squat. Her hip throbbed, but was tolerable. Reaching out, she grabbed the shovel, which had also fallen against the foundation, and dragged it to her.

The crates creaked and trembled even more than her legs as she cautiously pushed up to standing. She'd never been surfing, but crashing under a wave had to be preferable to falling—again—onto the rock-hard dirt floor.

Zoe clawed out a hold on the window ledge to steady the swaying under her feet. So far, so good. She lifted the shovel. Brought the handle up to touch the window's surface. Turning her face away and closing her eyes, she drew the shovel back and slammed it against the pane.

The glass exploded, a few shards pelting the side of her face.

Plan D was going better than she expected.

She skimmed the handle around the frame, clearing jagged splinters of glass. Now for the slats.

She flipped the shovel, as if twirling a very heavy baton, bringing the business end of it up to the window, hoping to use the sharp edge to chop the wood.

A noise from above froze her before she had a chance to try. She held her breath and listened.

A familiar squeak. Her back door. She'd left it unlocked when she'd come home, which seemed like decades ago. Footsteps. Slow. Deliberate.

Dave Evans was in the house. Her side of it.

Do *not* touch Jade or Merlin.

As if she didn't already have enough to worry about with Maddie and Mrs. Kroll trapped in the basement with her, now she had a madman upstairs with her cats.

The footsteps continued deeper into the house. He wasn't moving toward the basement door. Was that good or bad?

With no time for prudence, Zoe grabbed the shovel with both hands and rammed the blade into the slats. Noise be damned. Paying no heed to the pain, she hacked. Again. And again. She squinted against the wood splinters flying in her face at every chop.

First one slat gave way. Then a second. She thought she heard the footsteps moving around upstairs, but she couldn't be sure with the twang of metal on wood and the crack of the slats coming apart ringing in her ears.

Finally the last one broke free. An opening—not a large one—to freedom.

Zoe let the shovel drop to the floor with a clatter, and for a moment there was silence. No thunk thunk thunk upstairs. Only the thud of her heart inside her chest and the rasp of her breath.

And a strange odor.

She sniffed.

Gasoline?

Before the totality of what it meant could take root, the sound of lighter, faster footfalls seized her attention.

"Zoe!" Maddie cried.

Still clinging to the stone window ledge, Zoe half turned.

"*Zoe!*" the girl shrieked again.

"We're gonna get out," Zoe said, hoping she sounded more confident than she felt.

"It's Mrs. Kroll. I don't think she's breathing."

THIRTY-TWO

Tierney's fortress appeared no different than it had the last time Pete had been there. He parked in front of the closed garage door. Baronick pulled his black unmarked sedan behind the Explorer.

Nothing stirred as Pete and the detective followed the sidewalk around to the front of the house. No movement of curtains to indicate someone peering out. No faint thumps of footsteps. Pete pounded on the front door rather than ringing the bell.

Somewhere nearby, a mourning dove *hoo-OO-hoo-hoo-hooed* its plaintive cry. A child's laughter rang out from a house farther up the hill. But from inside Tierney's house, silence.

Pete banged on the door again. "Police. Open up."

Baronick stepped into the mulch edging the house. Using both hands as a shield against the glare, he peered into a window. "It's a living room. Appears empty. No signs of a kid."

"What kind of signs are you looking for, Wayne? She was snatched from the park. She wouldn't have a bunch of toys with her."

"True." Baronick pulled a small case from one of his pockets. "Been a while since I've had a chance to use these." He withdrew a couple of metal picks.

Pete tried the knob. It opened. "It's gonna be a while longer, too." He swung the door open, keeping a hand on his sidearm. "Police. Hello? Anyone home?"

With Baronick on his heels, Pete stepped inside.

The house might as well have been a display model. Beige furniture, bland wood end tables with chrome lamps sat on laminate flooring with one ugly brown and white area rug. Not a single framed photo or knickknack.

Baronick headed for the kitchen, while Pete drifted toward a round coffee table. A fake plant sat next to an open book of wildlife photography. He skimmed a finger across the polished surface, leaving a clean trail in the dust. "Maid hasn't been in lately."

"But it looks like she might have been the last one here. The kitchen is spotless. Doesn't look like it's ever been used." Baronick opened a door. "Basement. I'll check it out."

Pete turned in a slow circle, taking in every detail. No artwork. No family pictures. No rings from beer cans marred the surfaces of the tables. No newspapers or magazines. Nothing to make the place feel like a home.

Baronick returned a few moments later. "Nothing down there either."

"They aren't here." Pete's head throbbed. If not here, where? What had Evans done with Maddie Farabee?

As they stepped outside and Pete pulled the door closed, his cell phone rang. Sylvia's name came up on the screen.

"Have you found Maddie?" she demanded.

"Not yet." In the background, Pete heard staticky conversation and the familiar beeps and boops of emergency tones going off. "Where are you?"

"Standing in your station," Sylvia said. "Have you talked to Zoe?"

Pete's headache cranked up a notch. "Now is not the time to lecture me on my lousy social skills."

"I know. I only meant...I went by the ambulance garage early this morning. Really early. I couldn't sleep."

"Lot of that going around."

A phone rang in the background of Sylvia's end of the call. "How well I know. Anyway, Zoe was up. Did you know the Krolls are planning to sell the farm to Dave Evans?"

"What?"

"I didn't think you did. When I was babysitting Maddie on Saturday, he stopped in looking for Mrs. Kroll. I got the impression it wasn't the first time he'd tried to catch her at home. He must have come back later."

"Saturday?" Pete's brain threatened to explode. "Dave Evans was at the farm on Saturday?"

"Yes."

"Why didn't you tell me this sooner?"

"You never asked. Why?"

Saturday. The fire at the barn. The man who claimed to be interested in boarding his horse there. "I'm an idiot," Pete muttered. He had known Sylvia had been at the farm that day. Hell, he'd sat in Mrs. Kroll's kitchen talking to her. And Maddie. About Holt's University of Kentucky ball cap. If Evans had been there the same day, it would have been a simple matter for him to pocket the hat and plant it near the body later.

Sylvia grunted. "You'll get no argument from me. Wait. What? Hold on."

"Sylvia?"

There was a muffled scratching noise on the phone, as if she was trying to mute the call with a hand over the speaker. From the valley below, distant sirens wailed. Now what?

The phone line cleared. "Oh my God," Sylvia said, gasping.

"What is it?"

"Pete, a fire call just came in. The Kroll farmhouse is burning."

Mrs. Kroll had slumped over. Adrenaline numbed Zoe's hip, and she raced to her landlady's side. As gently as possible, Zoe eased her onto her back and leaned over her, feeling for a carotid pulse and watching for some hint of breath.

There was neither.

Zoe pinched Mrs. Kroll's nostrils shut and blew two breaths into her mouth. Watched the woman's chest slowly fall as the air released. But there was no spontaneous inhalation.

Zoe scooted over, palpated the bottom edge of Mrs. Kroll's sternum, the xiphoid process, and, using it as a guide, positioned her hands for chest compressions. Behind her, Maddie sobbed. But Zoe didn't have time to comfort the girl. She counted each powerful downward thrust. One, two, three, four, five, six...

Her shoulder protested with every beat, but she blocked it from her mind. At thirty, she shifted for two more breaths before returning to compressions.

Half of her brain counted. She'd only performed CPR without the benefit of an ambulance and its advanced life support equipment once before. The time she'd been in the middle of a crowd at a flea market. An ambulance had been summoned and was on its way. She'd only needed to sustain life for a few minutes even though it had felt much longer.

This time there was no way to call for help. No one coming. No defibrillator. If Mrs. Kroll's heart didn't kick back into rhythm on its own...

...twenty-seven, twenty-eight, twenty-nine, thirty. Shift. Two breaths. Shift back. Pump and count.

How long could she keep this up? The rule was continue until skilled medical assistance arrived to take over. Or until you were physically exhausted and unable to continue.

...eighteen, nineteen, twenty...

No. She would *not* let Mrs. Kroll die.

...twenty-nine, thirty. Shift. Breathe. Shift. Compress and count.

She had only one hope. "Maddie."

The sobbing had stopped, but the little girl didn't answer.

Zoe risked a glance over her shoulder. She and Mrs. Kroll were alone.

...five, six, seven...

"Maddie?"

...ten, eleven, twelve...

Where on earth had the kid gone?

When Zoe completed the thirty compressions, she paused, taking a moment to check for a pulse. To watch for unassisted breathing. None.

"Maddie!" Zoe yelled.

Could she have somehow gone for help? Or had Evans gotten back into the basement and snatched her while Zoe focused on Mrs. Kroll?

Two more rescue breaths.

Before Zoe could decide whether to feel hope or despair, as she positioned her hands over her landlady's sternum for more compressions, a new concern crept into her consciousness.

She sniffed. No.

Good God, no.

Smoke.

The moment Pete drove clear of Tierney's fence, he stole a glance across the rolling hills toward the Kroll farm. Zoe's farm. A thin gray wisp rose above the towering pines that blocked his view of the house.

Zoe's house.

He flipped on the sirens. Mashed the gas pedal to the floor. And careened down the hill, Baronick's sedan on his back bumper. At the bottom, Pete checked for traffic and then blew through the stop sign hanging the left onto Route 15. Tires squealed, and the Explorer swayed, skidded, but held the road.

One lousy mile felt like a hundred. At least traffic was light. The two vehicles he roared up behind pulled out of his way. He glanced in the rearview mirror. Baronick was keeping up with him.

Zoe had been on duty last night. She'd be home now. Possibly asleep if she'd been up all night as Sylvia suggested. Did they have smoke detectors in the old house?

Pete dug his phone from his pocket. Speed-dialed Zoe's number. It rang five, six times before going to voicemail.

Damn it.

Maybe she was out in the barn. Maybe she wasn't home at all, but was out looking for Maddie. Surely Zoe would be okay.

Zoe *had* to be okay.

Pete cleared the final bend in the road and barreled down the straightaway. Massive old pines partially blocked his view of the house, but he could see the smoke drifting above them.

A tractor-trailer came around the turn just beyond the farm lane. Pete jammed his foot to the floor and veered across in front of the semi. The driver hit the brakes and the air horn. Pete muscled the SUV's steering wheel, fighting to maintain control against the ruts in the red-dog gravel. He didn't look back. Hoped Baronick was okay. But figured the detective could take care of himself.

As the lane swept around toward the back of the house, Pete got his first awful view of the Kroll farmhouse on fire. Flames engulfed the enclosed back porch, orange tongues lapping through the windows, reaching back over the tin roof toward the main body of the structure. Zoe's truck sat in its usual spot. Next to it, a navy pickup with the words *Dave Evans, Land Developer* stenciled on the side.

Pete dove out of his SUV. Where was Zoe? Her truck was here. If she was safe outside, she'd be doing something. Dragging out a garden hose to fight the fire.

She was inside the house. He knew it. Trying to save Mrs. Kroll or the cats. Or both. He started down the path, but a hand clamped onto his arm, stopping him. Baronick. "Let's be smart about this."

Above the crackle and pop of the hungry fire, sirens grew closer. The ancient timber of the old house wasn't going to wait to be saved by the fire department. "You be smart," Pete snapped. "I'm getting Zoe out of there."

"Do you know for certain she's in there?"

Pete gave him a look. Baronick had gotten to know Zoe well enough over the last six months. "What do *you* think?"

The detective let out a growl. "Yeah. But we aren't going through that." He tipped his head at the flames which were now blackening the one-story add-on, which housed Zoe's kitchen.

"The front door," Pete said.

Both men took off, charging down the hill, through the gate. A scream pierced the roar of the fire. Pete veered toward the sound, around the side of the house.

The sight of a man gripping a wriggling Maddie Farabee in one hand and a red gas can, the cap hanging open, in the other stopped Pete cold.

Baronick bumped him from behind as he pulled up short.

"Dave Evans, I presume." Pete said, forcing himself to stay calm. Behind him, he heard, sensed the detective un-holstering his weapon.

"Stay back," the man shouted.

Maddie strained against him. "Lemme go!"

"Do what she says, Evans." Pete kept his voice even, authoritative. "Let her go."

The man dropped the gas can softly at his feet. Readjusted his hold on the girl. "I can't do that."

"I'm going around," Baronick whispered and backed away.

"Don't move," Evans yelled.

But Baronick disregarded the order, spun, and bolted. Pete contained a smile. Evans didn't appear to have a gun or a knife. Just a squirming ten-year-old.

Pete held up both hands and took a step toward them. "You need to let her go. Now."

"And I told you. I can't." Evans held up his free hand.

Pete swore. No, Evans didn't have a gun or a knife. He had a lighter. And an open gas can at his feet.

Maddie twisted hard, nearly breaking his grip. "Lemme *go*."

Evans held fast, jerking her back against him. She let out a yelp.

Damn it. Pete didn't have time for hostage negotiations. A wave of smoke rolled over the roof of Zoe's kitchen. The sizzle and snap of flames grew louder, closer. He was vaguely aware of the throaty rumble of a fire engine grinding to a halt behind the burning house. And he was *keenly* aware Zoe was nowhere to be seen.

"Listen to me," Evans said. "You're going to back off and let me walk out of here with the girl."

"Not gonna happen."

He held the lighter above the gas can. "I've heard gas fumes from an empty tank are even more combustible than the gasoline itself. If I light this thing, there isn't gonna be much left of this little kid."

Pete's jaw ached. This was the kind of sick bastard he lived to put away. "The flaw to your plan is there won't be much left to you either."

"Doesn't matter. I imagine you know I've already killed two people."

Or more. "Yeah. I do. So what makes you think I'm gonna let you go and take her with you?"

"It's her only chance." Evans turned his head side to side, as if saying no in slow motion. "I never wanted to kill Lillian Farabee. I just wanted her old man to back off. She wasn't even supposed to be home."

"You wanted to kill Holt, but she died instead?"

Maddie let out a wail. Evans gave her a shake. "Shut up." To Pete he said, "I didn't intend to kill him either. I only wanted him to know I meant business. If he realized I could get into his house, he'd know I wasn't kidding."

Pete spotted Baronick, gun in hand, at the front of the house, behind Evans and Maddie. "Well, you proved your point, didn't you?"

"For all the good it's done me." Evans switched hands on Maddie, and for a moment Pete thought he might release her. Instead he grabbed her ponytail, wrapping it around the hand that wasn't holding the lighter.

The girl squealed.

"Pick up the can," he told her.

"No," she howled.

"Do it," he hissed.

This was his plan? Walk out of there with Maddie, the gas can, and a lighter. He might as well have a bomb strapped to her.

From the corner of Pete's eye, he knew the entire rear of the farmhouse was fully involved. Firefighters dragged hoses from the truck and shouted orders over the din. Additional fire apparatus rumbled past on Route 15 below, slowing to make the turn. But it wouldn't matter. The Kroll farmhouse was doomed.

Where was Zoe?

In one practiced move, Pete brought his Glock up, leveled at Dave Evans. "Are you a betting man?"

Evans froze, staring at the muzzle of the Glock, his mouth hanging open. But he held tight to Maddie's ponytail.

"I am," Pete said. "And I'm willing to bet I can make this shot before you can flick that Bic of yours."

Evans appeared to be considering his odds.

Pete glanced past Evans and the girl to Baronick who stood several yards behind them. "And," Pete went on. "If I miss, the county detective back there will definitely get you. One way or another, you are not leaving here with the child. Let. Her. Go."

Evans looked down for a moment. When he lifted his head again, he fixed Pete with a tired stare. "I'm not going to jail." He held out the hand with the lighter. His thumb twitched.

The two gunshots were nearly drowned out by the sharp crack of Zoe's kitchen's outer walls collapsing and the roof crashing into the inferno.

THIRTY-THREE

"Twenty-eight, twenty-nine, thirty." Zoe shifted and forced two labored breaths into Mrs. Kroll's lungs.

Smoke hung close to the basement's ceiling. Kneeling on the floor, Zoe remained beneath most of it. For now. Still, the air was getting hot, oxygen depleted. Her nose and throat burned.

The house above them was on fire. She knew that. Her beloved home. Her beloved cats.

She couldn't allow herself to think about her cats. Poor Jade and Merlin.

Eventually the house would collapse into the basement.

They never listed that as one of the reasons to stop CPR.

She shifted again, positioned her hands, and counted. Out loud now. She needed to focus on the sound, the rhythm of her own words, to keep going. "One. Two. Three..." She had to keep going.

Until she couldn't.

Somewhere above her, a crash. A roar. The beams supporting the house shuddered. A wave of thicker smoke rolled across the ceiling above her. Sagged lower. The stench choked her. It wouldn't be long now. Would she succumb to the smoke? The flames? Or be crushed by the floor caving in?

"Eight. Nine. Ten. I'm so sorry, Mrs. Kroll. Twelve."

Her arms ached. Not just the one she'd hurt in the fall. Her hip had long ago gone numb. She probably couldn't stand even if there was somewhere to go.

What had happened to Maddie?

Thirty. Two breaths.

Still no pulse or respiration. One, two, three...

The house creaked. Groaned. Protested against the fiery monster consuming it. The smoke, thicker, hung lower.

Zoe coughed. Wheezed. The room darkened. Or was it simply the soot in her eyes blinding her? She lost count. But kept pumping. Up. Down.

Above the other hideous noises, a loud ripping crack. But not from the rear of the house where she knew the fire raged.

"*Zoe?*"

Was that...Pete? She tried to yell, but choked again on the smoke. Don't...stop...compressions.

"Zoe!"

She pressed her face into her sleeve and fought to draw a breath. "Here," she yelled as loud as she could. The effort drove her into a coughing fit.

Suddenly Pete was next to her. Or was she hallucinating?

"Zoe." His arms were around her. "I've got them," he shouted to someone. "Help me get them out of here."

Someone else was in the room with them. Her oxygen-starved brain sensed she was being dragged away from Mrs. Kroll. Lifted into a pair of strong arms, jostled out of the room. Resting her head against Pete's shoulder, she whispered, "Save Jade, Merlin," before closing her eyes and letting go.

The hospital room smelled sterile and antiseptic, but the odor of burnt wood and wiring clung to the inside of Zoe's nose.

She sat in the bed with its head raised. A sling held her left arm immobile across her chest. A game show blared on the TV hanging high on the opposite wall. She stared at it, but wasn't seeing the host offering a new car to an excited player. In her mind's eye, all she saw was Mrs. Kroll's lifeless face. And smoke. Lots of smoke.

A knock at her open door jolted her out of the waking nightmare.

Sylvia clutched a stuffed plastic bag. "Are you up for some company?"

Zoe waved her in. "I hope you brought me some clothes. They're supposed to discharge me, but the stuff I wore in here smells like smoke." Then again, *everything* smelled like smoke.

Sylvia held up the bag. "I hope you can fit into some of Rose's things. You're taller than she is, so I picked out a pair of shorts and a t-shirt."

Rose's things. Of course. Everything Zoe owned had been destroyed in the fire.

Sylvia glanced back into the hospital's hallway with a grin and jerked her head. Maddie burst past her into the room. "Hi, Zoe."

Her hip kept her from leaping out of the bed to embrace the girl. Wincing, Zoe swung her legs over the side and pulled Maddie into a one-armed hug. "You have no idea how glad I am to see you." Zoe choked. "You know you saved my life."

A haunted look clouded the girl's eyes.

It had been slightly less than twenty-four hours since they'd been trapped together in the basement. Too soon to get the full story from Maddie.

Zoe had overheard Pete saying Maddie told him she and Mrs. Kroll were still inside the basement as the house above them burned. But most of the rest was a blur.

Sylvia ambled into the room and set the bag of clothes on Zoe's bedside table. "They need to open a Vance Township wing in this place." She nudged Maddie. "Tell Zoe about your dad."

Maddie brightened. "He's gonna be okay. We just came from seeing him. He's got tubes and stuff sticking out of him, but he was able to talk to me a little. He told me as soon as he gets out of here, we're gonna have a memorial service for my mom." She took Zoe's hand. "I hope you'll come."

Zoe leaned toward her, planting a kiss on the girl's blond head. "Count on it, sweetie."

Maddie hopped onto the bed beside her. "I'm staying with Aunt Sylvia until Dad gets out of the hospital."

Zoe raised an eyebrow at the older woman. *Aunt* Sylvia?

Sylvia smiled and shrugged one shoulder. "I miss Rose and the kids. It's nice having a youngster around. But—" She grew stern and thunked a key down on the tray in front of Zoe. "Your cats are making me sneeze."

"My...cats?" Zoe's voice broke over a sob. She'd been afraid to ask. Afraid to know what had become of Jade and Merlin.

"Yeah. You won't believe it. Wayne Baronick went into the house and rescued them." Sylvia shook her head. "I guess he's not such a bad guy after all."

"Both of them? Jade *and* Merlin?"

"Don't ask me which one is which, but there are definitely two of them."

Zoe stared at the key, blinking away grateful tears. "What's that for?"

"Rose's house. She and the kids won't be home for another month or so. I figure she won't mind if you and your cats stay there until you make other arrangements."

Other arrangements. Zoe was homeless without a stitch of clothes or a stick of furniture to her name. But she still had her cats and a barn full of horses to manage. She cast a wary glance at Maddie, afraid to broach another traumatic subject in her presence. "What about Mrs. Kroll?"

"I'm afraid I don't know," Sylvia said.

"Well, I do," came a familiar voice from the doorway. Pete.

She flushed at the memory of him scooping her up and carrying her out of the basement. Knight in shining armor stuff. "Hey."

He stepped inside, one hand behind his back. "Hey, yourself. How are you feeling this morning?"

She rubbed her shoulder. "Alive."

"Good."

"About Mrs. Kroll?"

"She's still in ICU, but stable. From what I was told, her prognosis for a full recovery is excellent. Looks like you saved another one."

Maddie let out a whoop. Hot tears of relief blinded Zoe. "Thank God," she whispered.

"That's wonderful news, Pete." Sylvia rested a hand on his shoulder. "And Maddie and I will leave the two of you alone."

"Wait," Zoe said. "Aren't you giving me a lift home?" She winced at the word *home*.

"I've got it covered," Pete said.

Sylvia whispered something into Pete's ear. Zoe strained to hear, but the older woman's words were too soft. Whatever she said prompted a grin, which he hid by rubbing a hand across his face.

Maddie tapped Zoe on the leg. "We're gonna be neighbors for a while, huh?"

"I guess we are." Rose's house was only two doors away from Sylvia's.

Maddie pointed to Zoe's sling. "I can help you with the barn work until you're all better. Pick me up when you go over to the farm."

The farm. Barn work. Yes, she still had the horses to care for, even though it meant driving past what was left of the house.

Maddie must have read the pain in Zoe's eyes. "It'll be okay. I lost my house, too. But we'll both be fine."

Zoe couldn't help but laugh. The girl was wise well beyond her ten years. "Yes, we will."

Maddie hopped down from her perch. "See you later."

Zoe waved at her and Sylvia as they left, hand in hand. Then she turned her focus to Pete, who was still keeping one hand hidden. "What have you got there?"

"Me?" He was lousy at acting clueless. "Oh. This?" He brought a single peach rose from behind his back and handed it to her. "It's nothing. I stole it from some flowers being delivered to another patient."

"Oh, good. I wouldn't want you going to any trouble on my account." She stuck her nose into the flower and inhaled. Finally. Something that did *not* smell like smoke. "Thank you."

"You're welcome."

"For everything. I'm a little fuzzy on a lot of the details, though. Mind filling in some of the blanks?"

Pete snagged a chair and dragged it next to the bed. "Think you're up to it? Fuzzy might not be such a bad thing."

"I need to know. Dave Evans?" She let the name trail off.

Pete took a seat and crossed an ankle over his knee. "He's dead."

Zoe stiffened. "How?"

Pete told her how the land developer had threatened to blow up himself and little Maddie with a lighter and a gas can. "Baronick and I both fired. We'll have to wait for ballistics to know which was the kill shot. Not that it matters."

"And then she told you Mrs. Kroll and I were still in the basement?"

"Yep."

"How did Maddie get out?"

"She told us she was trying to climb out the basement window. Apparently Evans spotted her and grabbed her."

Zoe shook her head. "I don't understand. Why did he want to kill us?"

"It all started with greed. He wanted to make a lot of money by buying land cheap, selling houses for big bucks and then cutting corners on the construction. Farabee caught on and planned to expose him. Evans wanted to shut him up. I don't believe he intended to kill Lillian, but once he did, everything else was a matter of covering his ass. Except for setting the fire at your barn, which was an attempt to push Mrs. Kroll into selling the farm."

"So he could start his next poorly constructed housing development."

"You got it. I've interviewed a number of local carpenters and word has it he had delusions of grandeur. His dream was to be the biggest land developer in Monongahela County."

"And it all ended in suicide by cop."

"That about sums it up."

There were dozens more questions knocking around inside Zoe's head, but they could wait for another day. Most of them, anyway. "I hear you're moving."

Pete crossed his arms but didn't reply.

"To Hawaii."

He narrowed his eyes, gazing past her, out the hospital window. "I had a pretty incredible job offer from an old friend. Head of security at a luxury resort. Six figure salary. Sweet deal."

Crap. She struggled to swallow the hard lump in her throat. "Beats being chief of police in a small-time township, I guess."

"It was an offer I couldn't refuse."

Zoe twisted the thin fabric of the hospital gown covering her lap. Ever since Sylvia had told her about Pete's resignation, Zoe had been searching for the right words to say to him, to congratulate him and wish him well without going to pieces. At the moment, she couldn't remember one of them.

"Don't go," she whispered.

"What?"

Her eyes felt hotter than yesterday's flames. She looked up, meeting and holding his gaze. "Don't go."

The corner of his mouth twitched. "It's a done deal."

She did not want to cry in front of him. Would not grovel or beg. But the thought of losing him? She couldn't breathe, and smoke inhalation had nothing to do with it.

"I turned it down."

"What?" Her voice squeaked.

"I called Delano last night and told him to find someone else. I couldn't leave the woman I love. Not even for paradise."

"The woman you—?"

"Love. Yeah."

Zoe's cheeks warmed. "You aren't going to say you're sorry now, are you?"

Pete stood. Stepped toward her. Took her face in his hands. And pressed a kiss to her lips. "About loving you? Never. Now get dressed and let's get out of here."

ANNETTE DASHOFY

Annette Dashofy, a Pennsylvania farm gal born and bred, grew up with horses, cattle, and, yes, chickens. After high school, she spent five years as an EMT for the local ambulance service. Since then, she's worked a variety of jobs, giving her plenty of fodder for her lifelong passion for writing. She, her husband, and their two spoiled cats live on property that was once part of her grandfather's dairy. Her short fiction, including a 2007 Derringer nominee, has appeared in *Spinetingler*, *Mysterical-e*, and *Fish Tales: the Guppy Anthology*. Her newest short story appears in the *Lucky Charms Anthology*.

In Case You Missed the 1st Book in the Series

CIRCLE OF INFLUENCE

Annette Dashofy

A Zoe Chambers Mystery (#1)

Zoe Chambers, paramedic and deputy coroner in rural Pennsylvania's tight-knit Vance Township, has been privy to a number of local secrets over the years, some of them her own. But secrets become explosive when a dead body is found in the Township Board President's abandoned car.

As a January blizzard rages, Zoe and Police Chief Pete Adams launch a desperate search for the killer, even if it means uncovering secrets that could not only destroy Zoe and Pete, but also those closest to them.

Available at booksellers nationwide and online

Visit www.henerypress.com for details

In Case You Missed the 2nd Book in the Series

LOST LEGACY
Annette Dashofy

A Zoe Chambers Mystery (#2)

On a sultry summer afternoon, Paramedic Zoe Chambers responds to a
call and finds a farmer's body hanging from the rafters of his hay barn.
What first appears to be a suicide quickly becomes something sinister
when Zoe links the victim to a pair of deaths forty-five years earlier.
Her attempts to wheedle information from her mother and stepfather
hit a brick wall of deception, one that brings into question everything
Zoe knows about her late father, who died in a car crash when she was
eight. Or did he?

Police Chief Pete Adams fears Zoe's inquiries are setting her up for
deeper heartbreak and putting her in danger. As Zoe and Pete inch
closer to the truth, they discover that a missing gun links the crimes
which span more than four decades. But the killer isn't done. Two more
Vance Township residents fall victim to the same gun, and when
tragedy strikes too close to home, Zoe realizes her family is in the
crosshairs.

Available at booksellers nationwide and online

Visit www.henerypress.com for details

Henery Press Mystery Books

And finally, before you go...
Here are a few other mysteries
you might enjoy:

MACDEATH

Cindy Brown

An Ivy Meadows Mystery (#1)

Like every actor, Ivy Meadows knows that *Macbeth* is cursed. But she's finally scored her big break, cast as an acrobatic witch in a circus-themed production of *Macbeth* in Phoenix, Arizona. And though it may not be Broadway, nothing can dampen her enthusiasm—not her flying caldron, too-tight leotard, or carrot-wielding dictator of a director.

But when one of the cast dies on opening night, Ivy is sure the seeming accident is "murder most foul" and that she's the perfect person to solve the crime (after all, she does work part-time in her uncle's detective agency). Undeterred by a poisoned Big Gulp, the threat of being blackballed, and the suddenly too-real curse, Ivy pursues the truth at the risk of her hard-won career—and her life.

Available at booksellers nationwide and online

Visit www.henerypress.com for details

WHEN LIES CRUMBLE
Alan Cupp

A Carter Mays Mystery (#1)

Chicago PI Carter Mays is thrust into a house of lies when local rich girl Cindy Bedford hires him. Turns out her fiancé failed to show up on their wedding day, the same day millions of dollars are stolen from her father's company. While Carter takes the case, Cindy's father tries to find him his own way. With nasty secrets, hidden finances, and a trail of revenge, it's soon apparent no one is who they say they are.

Carter searches for the truth, but the situation grows more volatile as panic collides with vulnerability. Broken relationships and blurred loyalties turn deadly, fueled by past offenses and present vendettas in a quest to reveal the truth behind the lies before no one, including Carter, gets out alive.

Available at booksellers nationwide and online

Visit www.henerypress.com for details

THE RED QUEEN'S RUN

Bourne Morris

A Meredith Solaris Mystery (#1)

A famous journalism dean is found dead at the bottom of a stairwell. Accident or murder? The police suspect members of the faculty who had engaged in fierce quarrels with the dean—distinguished scholars who were known to attack the dean like brutal schoolyard bullies. When Meredith "Red" Solaris is appointed interim dean, the faculty suspects are furious.

Will the beautiful red-haired professor be next? The case detective tries to protect her as he heads the investigation, but incoming threats lead him to believe Red's the next target for death.

Available at booksellers nationwide and online

Visit www.henerypress.com for details

SHADOW OF DOUBT

Nancy Cole Silverman

A Carol Childs Mystery (#1)

When a top Hollywood Agent is found poisoned in the bathtub of her home suspicion quickly turns to one of her two nieces. But Carol Childs, a reporter for a local talk radio station doesn't believe it. The suspect is her neighbor and friend, and also her primary source for insider industry news. When a media frenzy pits one niece against the other—and the body count starts to rise—Carol knows she must save her friend from being tried in courts of public opinion.

But even the most seasoned reporter can be surprised, and when a Hollywood psychic shows up in Carol's studio one night and warns her there will be more deaths, things take an unexpected turn. Suddenly nobody is above suspicion. Carol must challenge both her friendship and the facts, and the only thing she knows for certain is the killer is still out there and the closer she gets to the truth, the more danger she's in.

Available at booksellers nationwide and online

Visit www.henerypress.com for details

CPSIA information can be obtained
at www.ICGtesting.com
Printed in the USA
LVOW04s1255110516
487760LV00025B/345/P